ARCHANGEL

Justin Hart Crary

First Edition January 2022

Cover Design by Jeff Brown

ISBN 978-1-7362210-1-3 (hardcover)
ISBN 978-1-7362210-3-7 (paperback)
ISBN 978-1-7362210-4-4 (ebook)

Published in the United States by Lionhart Publications

Dedicated to my Mom,
who truly believed and inspired others to believe that
"Courage is not the absence of fear but the presence of faith."

ACKNOWLEDGMENTS

For me, it starts by thanking God. Nothing in my life, including my life itself, would even be possible without His infinite love, grace, guidance, and mercy. He's given me everything I don't deserve and spared me from everything I do. I owe a debt of gratitude to my parents for fostering my love for fiction and turning a blind eye when I stayed up way past my bedtime to read under the covers with a flashlight. Because that's what heroes do. I also owe significant thanks to my family and friends, as well as everyone on my editing team—in particular Art Fogartie, Catrina Mehltretter, Nadene Seiters, and Katelyn Cooney—for your tireless diligence and hard work. Special appreciation goes out to every single one of my students as well, for your endless patience and support. I hope the wait was worth it. To my brother Ryan Doss, the first to ever read this book, I don't know if I'd even want to be a writer if it wasn't for you. All the late nights making up our own games and stories because we weren't satisfied with the original endings are some of the best memories I have. And last but certainly never least, I'd like to thank my beautiful and amazing wife Cierra, who faithfully supported, encouraged, and inspired me throughout this entire process. This book and any after it wouldn't even be possible without you. Again, everyone, thank you. You are all just some of the blessings I don't deserve that I mentioned earlier, and I'm beyond grateful to have each and every one of you in my life.

CHAPTER 0

The Nebraskan night hung blacker and eerily quieter than usual. Perhaps it was the passing of the new moon overhead, or the anticipation of something darker to come, but whatever it was hushed the creatures of the night into a perfect silence that made the summer air seem cold.

As shadows drank in the darkness of the devil's hour, six black-robed figures met and stood at a crossroads leading to the outskirts of Kearney, Nebraska. Surrounded by massive stalks of corn, their faces were enshrouded by the hoods of their black cloaks, and they presented themselves with the same evil that masked their features. Five of them bowed to one—the most powerful among them. At least he used to be. But as long as they still believed it, that was enough.

"Have the preparations been made, Legate?" he asked.

A hulking figure responded. "As you requested." Legate's voice echoed like gravel grinding under someone's foot. "We've eliminated many of the guardians in this town and have taken control. We're ready for him."

"Good. I've pinpointed the Seventh Seal here. The King will arrive soon, and when he does, he will discover its exact location for you."

"Does he already possess the Arch Steel?"

The leader of the hooded figures raised his head as if sensing something far away. "He does. Remember to retrieve both it and the Seal."

"Of course." Legate bowed, grinning beneath the darkness of his cloak. "Still, Choshek, I do wonder why you summoned me for this. Wouldn't one of your fallen have been better suited for the task? Or perhaps... yourself?"

Choshek frowned, glad it couldn't be seen. Legate was testing him, and he clutched his chest over the folds of his cloak to show he knew it. "I am still recovering," he said sternly. "These bodies burn faster and faster, and some of my lessers are getting... overly ambitious. But make no mistake. Right now, I'd rather deal with the demon I can beat than the devil I can't." He spoke his words confidently, underplaying the fact that he was actually a shadow of his former self. A shell. "You have four months until the Seal turns of age, Legate. Do not disappoint me."

The demon grinned again. "I never do."

As the six prepared to depart, they heard loud engine noises coming from farther up the highway. A group of two dozen bikers, all riding choppers, appeared in the distance, quickly coming upon the hooded figures standing in the middle of the road. When they refused to move, the gang skidded to an abrupt halt.

"Well, what kind of freak show do we have here?" the lead biker asked, prompting the gang behind him to snicker. "You boys in some kind of cult or something?"

Silence reigned as the group sized up the potential threat in front of them. Not that they were really a threat. More of an annoyance.

"Hello?" the same biker asked again, moving to dismount his motorcycle and confront the cloaked figures. Four of them tilted their heads in uniformity as a response. "That's right!" he said. "I'm talking to you!"

"Well, Legate?" Choshek asked, already bored.

"It's actually a shame. Most of them are pure souls. Killing them won't serve us very much, I'm afraid."

"Do it anyway," the leader replied. "We can't have any witnesses before the appointed time."

Legate bore all of his teeth in a devilish smile. "As you wish."

A deeper chill filled the air as the four robed figures before Legate stepped aside for him to do his work. Darkness—tangible darkness—billowed forth from the arms of his robe like smoke, taking the shape of seemingly humanoid quadrupedal creatures that snarled and licked their sharp teeth with whiplike tongues.

Fear-stricken by the black demons facing them, the bikers had no time to react as Legate sent the manifestations hurtling toward them at the speed of darkness. Each gang member's screams could barely be heard before they were seized by a chilling paralysis that began at their feet and snaked its way up their legs until it engulfed their entire bodies. Though paralyzed, pain was intact. Agonizing pain that lit up their skin until they were slowly disintegrated into ash, most of them before they could even get off their bikes.

However, as twenty-three choppers clattered to the road in a crash, there was still one biker who remained. Not by his own power but by Legate's restraint. He was the largest and fattest of the former gang, but he was still trembling in terror from the supernatural onslaught he just witnessed.

"You missed one," Choshek said before sensing the sickening desire in his underling's heart. "Oh, alright. But make it fast."

The demons that encircled the obese man bared their black teeth, lapped at the air with their blacker tongues, and stared hungrily at their next meal with the blackest eyes the man had ever seen.

And in the pitch darkness of the witching hour, the only sounds that could be heard for miles were his screams.

CHAPTER 1

Each house in the community of Glenwood Park neatly lined up next to its neighbor. The symmetrical layout of the middle-class American dream was one any suburban homeowner would have adored. Trouble rarely found its way across the freshly cut lawns of those who lived in Kearney, but on one particular night, trouble was actively searching for such a suburb to prey upon—trouble in the form of a seventeen-year-old boy named Kael Clark.

He never would have been there if he had the choice. But in the still darkness of the rapidly approaching dawn, he was frantically searching for one of the residents' cars to steal.

The full cover of night made it easy for Kael to hide but difficult to see. The only source of light came from flashing red and blue patrol beacons as they relentlessly searched the neighborhood for their target. The only sound came from the labored breathing of that target—the runaway teenager trying desperately to escape the police car's floodlights.

Kael was a foster kid and had been trying to escape every foster home he'd been thrown into since the age of nine. He was tall with dark brown hair, tan skin, and a muscular physique, but all his good looks were overshadowed by the one distinguishing feature he hated most about himself.

He had heterochromia. His left eye was emerald-green while his right was a royal kind of purple. Shades of violet and indigo were rare when it came to eye color but were even rarer when coupled with heterochromia. Kids growing up didn't need much of a reason to pick on other kids. Standing out as much as Kael did just made him an easy target for the abuse.

However, the young man wasn't running because of bullies, nor was he running just to run. No, every escape always had the same purpose—make it to California and find the only person who could possibly give him the answer to the only question that had been plaguing Kael for the last eight years…

"What am I?"

But every single attempt to make it to the Golden State failed. Every single time stopped by the police or something else completely outside his control. This time he hadn't even made it across Nebraska state lines before running out of gas. Consequently, he knew he wasn't going to make it much farther. He would eventually be forced back into juvie or the loving Gabriel group home he'd run from. Or worse, he'd be shuttled to another optimistic couple whose mercy hadn't quite run out. Yet.

Still, none of that meant he had to make it easy for the ones trying to drag him back. After all, what would be the fun in that?

Acting on instinct, Kael ducked behind the nearest bush just in time for the police car tailing him to pass by for what seemed like the hundredth time.

He cursed under his breath. "When are you going to give it up?" He obviously knew they wouldn't. He had already stolen one vehicle to escape the home in Omaha. They definitely expected him to steal another to escape again. But he needed something faster than a beat-up old Chevy with a broken fuel gauge if he wanted to pull it off a second time.

As he waited for the lights to disappear around the corner and illuminate the street behind him, Kael pushed his sweat-soaked brown hair out of his eyes and began examining the driveways of the houses across the street. It was still pitch-black and hard to be too picky, but he needed to be selective if he wanted to make it back to the interstate without getting caught.

Driveway after driveway, he shook his head. All family cars and minivans, he noted, decorating the parking pads of the ones who owned them like sad symbols of the average nuclear family. However, when his eyes fell upon a driveway closer to the end of the street, he perked up. Finally, he thought.

Bursting from his hiding place like a runaway street cat, Kael darted across the poorly lit street to the only driveway that had a car masked by a cover. From the outline of it, Kael could tell it was some sort of sports car. He couldn't tell what kind, but after whipping the cover off, he realized just how low his expectations had been...

1967 Shelby Mustang GT500—a solid black fastback.

Kael couldn't believe his eyes. Anyone who left a beautiful car like this just sitting in their driveway obviously wanted him to have it, he reasoned. After gripping the large Celtic cross hanging around his neck and tucking it back underneath his shirt, Kael threw open the door and plopped himself down behind the polished wooden wheel. After vainly checking for the keys under the visor and anywhere else they might be hidden, he sighed and roughly pulled the wires from underneath the dashboard in an attempt to give the car life. He had barely started when he noticed the red and blue lights of the police car rounding the corner of the neighborhood.

He cursed again. They'd see the car cover on the ground and put two and two together. With no time left to do things the normal way, Kael finally stopped pretending to be so normal. He closed his eyes and began to concentrate. Ever since Kael could remember, he'd been different. He never knew where that difference came from, but he knew it made him strong. Powerful.

Hotwiring was a useful skill to have. What he had was much more useful.

"*Start.*"

He said the word as a command, not a plea or request, letting it carry power into the car itself. Not another second passed. Sparks flew from the wires and singed his fingertips as the engine roared to life with such ferocity that it shook Kael out of his concentration. Wasting no time, he threw the car into gear and peeled out from its confinement in the driveway.

The teenager howled in excitement. He reasoned with himself that a car like the one he just… borrowed… needed to be opened up every once in a while. Not kept under a sheet to rust.

However, unbeknownst to the seventeen-year-old, his grand theft auto did not go unnoticed. From the bay windows of the house, a pair of sad, aging eyes watched as his stolen car disappeared into the night, chased by the police cruiser that had been alerted to its presence by the thunderous ignition. However, the sadness in the old man's eyes wasn't for himself or his car. It was for the boy driving it.

Drifting around the last corner of houses, Kael gunned the engine onto the main road as fast as his new ride would carry him. He might have been driving one of the most idolized sports cars ever made, but it was still half a century older than the more modernized cruiser on his tail. It would take a miracle to escape it. But Kael never believed much in miracles. He always bet on himself.

With the highway too far away to continue driving straight, Kael cut the wheel hard into the summer cornfields lining the side of the road. Stalks of corn smashed against the windshield, obscuring his vision and forcing him to drive on luck alone. After harvesting what felt like a full season of crops into the bumper, the jet-black car finally exited the fields and spun its wheels back onto the empty early morning highway.

Exchanging dirt for asphalt, the Mustang's squealing tires caught traction and sped off against the rising sun. Eventually, Highway 10 turned into Interstate 80, and Kael felt as if he might have actually lost the cops. As he hit 90 miles per hour under what the residents of Kearney called the Archway, he flipped on the static-filled radio to celebrate his escape.

"Highway to Hell" was playing. Kael grinned at the irony.

The carjacker felt sure he'd lost the cops until the orange and yellow of early morning became engulfed by flashing lights of red and blue. One police cruiser turned into two. Which turned into three. Four. Five. And finally, six. All speeding up from behind him at 120 miles per hour.

Kael smirked and pushed the pedal to the floor, hoping whoever car he'd just stolen didn't want it back. At least not in one piece.

The roar of the car's engine was exhilarating. Kael watched as the red arrow on the speedometer flew past 100, 120, and buried itself into 140. He was still accelerating, he knew, but 140 was the last digit the antique car was designed to display. Kael bent his eyes back on the road.

The cops were still gaining. Their superior models were souped-up to catch almost anything. Kael was lucky to have even made it back to the interstate at all, let alone outrace them on it. However, the young man had two things he was sure none of the officers chasing him had—cooler music and a power none of them could possibly understand…

With the pedal floored, Kael briefly shut his eyes to focus.

"*Accelerate.*"

Willing the Mustang forward, he visualized it moving faster and faster, far more than the engine would normally allow. It obeyed. Reopening his eyes, he looked back at one of the police cruisers in his side mirror.

"*Overheat.*"

As soon as the word left his lips, the hood of the cruiser began blowing smoke from its engine, fishtailing until it had no choice but to slam on its brakes and pull over.

One by one, the same inexplicable curse afflicted three more cruisers as Kael repeated the same word over and over again. He gave an exhausted smile. There were only two left, he mused, though the other two cruisers had mysteriously slowed down so much that they had all but disappeared from Kael's rearview mirror.

It was too late when the young man realized why...

Like four claps of synchronized thunder, the Mustang's tires all exploded simultaneously. Time seemed to slow down as Kael put it all together. Spike strip, he realized. Should've expected it. Stupid.

Once he understood his perilous predicament, time sped back up to prove just how powerless he was to stop it. He completely lost control of the vehicle.

The first flip felt the worst. Although it should've smashed Kael's head against the side window, an unknown force stopped it from happening as the weaker glass in the car exploded against the pavement.

During the second flip, Kael thanked the universe for centrifugal force. It kept him rooted in place as the front windshield caved in, almost gashing into his forehead but somehow being stopped short yet again.

The third and fourth flips seemed like one continuous motion as the car flipped door over door in its losing battle with gravity and concrete.

Sometime during the fifth, sixth, and seventh flips, Kael watched with great interest as the cross necklace he wore danced alongside the glittering glass, all of it like shards of lightning surrounding him, all of it without a single piece cutting into his flesh.

The remaining nine flips tore at the metal frame of the car, systematically ripping it apart until there was almost nothing left but the driver's seat and a pretzeled remnant of what the car used to be.

What remained of the vehicle landed upright on its exploded wheels, the sound of shattered metal still ringing in Kael's ears as it did. He was perfectly fine, but he could feel the faint trickle of something running down the side of his face. Oil, he thought. Or gas. It couldn't have been blood. Kael didn't bleed.

"Step out of the vehicle and put your hands on your head!"

"I doubt the moron's alive enough to even do that, Sarge."

"Well, this should be fun," Kael said, focusing his mind enough to throw his shoulder against the caved in door next to him. It creaked as metal grated against metal.

"Get on the ground now!"

Stepping out of the car, Kael looked back to see the final two police officers rolling up the spikes that caused his wreck. To his front, a barricade of cop cars had each officer standing safely behind their doors with guns and tasers trained keenly on their target's chest.

"On the ground!"

Kael threw his hands into the air, acting as innocently as possible. "What seems to be the problem, officers?"

They were all looking at him like he was some kind of monster. Maybe he was. A wreck like that and not even a scratch? Kael sometimes wondered it himself. Still, he'd never been hurt before. He wasn't even sure he could be. Though as he listened to the conversations of the officers trying to make sense of what they had just seen, he realized that wasn't really true.

"Kid's a freak…"

"No human being could survive a wreck like that…"

"Just what the hell did Omaha send us?"

The door of the Mustang creaked again and fell completely off its hinges to the concrete below, snapping all of them back to full alert. With his arms still raised, Kael looked to the car and then back to the officers. "That's crazy," he said. "I promise it passed inspection when I bought it."

"I'm only going to say this one more time! Get on the ground! Now!"

Kael could feel the tension and fear saturating the air like morning dew, but neither his heart nor his mouth skipped a beat. "Alright, alright," he replied with a shrug. "We can play cops and robbers if you guys want.

I just feel bad I brought you all the way out here. How about a joke to lighten the mood?"

Lowering his right arm, he slowly began reaching his hand inside the front of the black military-style jacket he was wearing.

"Don't do it, kid!" another officer warned, a hint of desperation filling his voice.

But Kael didn't stop. He continued reaching inside the lining of his jacket, provocatively grabbing something unseen.

"This is your last warning!" the sergeant said. "We will open fire!"

Kael knew they weren't lying because he knew what they were thinking. He wanted them to think it. He wasn't worried. Wasn't scared. Everything happening was happening perfectly within his control. Most normal people wouldn't be able to say the same thing. But Kael wasn't normal. Normal was overrated.

Slowly pulling his arm from his jacket, he focused his mind on each and every one of the officers' weapon chambers. He had to concentrate hard for his next move. Not only on the pistols and revolvers, but on the tasers as well. While doing so, he could feel everything intensify for just a moment. He couldn't read minds, but he knew emotions. The officers' fears. Their anxiety. Their concern over possibly having to take a teenager's life. He had to move with sedulous care, suppressing his every movement to avoid setting off any itchy trigger fingers.

Gradually, almost mockingly, Kael kept inching his arm from the inside of his jacket. After seconds that seemed like hours, moments that passed like millennia, he finally finished willing his thoughts into reality. And then he smiled.

"Okay, you got me," he said, his next word coming through only as a whisper.

"*Misfire.*"

With a sudden jerk of his arm, Kael pulled his hand from his jacket and shot it forward provocatively. The triggers of the officers' handguns and tasers all clicked once—once only—as each firearm simultaneously misfired in a chorus of empty clicks, a symphony that filled the dead silence of dawn with an eerily cacophonous echo of wasted effort.

As the officers instinctively inspected their guns, their utter confusion was replaced with the hysterical laughter of their former target. Kael's hands were empty, but the cops couldn't bring themselves to care anymore. They were too preoccupied with what they couldn't explain. How could each and every one of their state-issued weapons misfire simultaneously?

Still chuckling, Kael got down on his knees and interlaced his fingers behind his head. He knew it was over at that point. There was no use running or continuing his little charade. Not that his cooperation earned any sympathy from the aggravated officers. They shoved his face onto the pavement, weaved his arms behind his back, and bound them as tightly as they could with their handcuffs.

Kael thought it was amusing that, even though they couldn't explain what happened to their guns, they still put their faith in something as simple as metal wrist binders. He could bust them with a thought but decided against it for the time being. Escaping again would be more trouble than it was worth. Besides, he was starving. The drawback of using his power so much was that it took a toll on his body. The benefit of being arrested was that they had to feed him.

"I want you guys to remember my safe word," he said while being guided to one of the police cruisers. "It's Chris Pratt. Star-Lord if you're freaky."

To date, none of the officers who ever arrested Kael found any of his jokes amusing. He was determined to change that and make at least one of them laugh in his lifetime.

The ride to the Kearney Police Station was awkward. All of Kael's jabs and jeers were met with obstinate silence by the two officers in the front seat. Therefore, he decided to have a little fun with them.

Unlock.

The handcuffs fell from his wrists, and Kael pointed to the nearest restaurant. "Ah, yes! Can we stop for sliders? I'm starving!"

The driver lurched the cruiser onto the shoulder. His partner re-cuffed Kael, but the teen didn't wait long to use his power a second time. Not only to uncuff himself but also to lower the back seat window and enjoy the wind whipping through his hair. After exclaiming that wasn't even possible, the flummoxed officers grabbed a different pair of cuffs and tried again.

By his third show, Kael had a captive audience. The officer in the passenger seat was eyeing him like a hawk in the rearview mirror when two uncuffed hands raised very slowly, middle fingers extended higher than the others. Several obscenities escaped the lips of the irritated officer as he was forced to cuff him yet again.

Once they arrived at the station, Kael was practically thrown into the nearest holding cell. He must have worn out his welcome, because his two police escorts immediately proclaimed they were taking a break and stalked toward the exit.

"Thanks for the ride!" Kael called out. He received the same obscene gesture he'd shared in the cruiser as a response.

Smiling, he turned to meet the eyes of his cellmates. One was an obese, bald, and angry-looking biker who wouldn't stop staring at him, and the other was a disheveled businessman nursing what looked to be a bad hangover. Neither looked particularly friendly, but that never stopped Kael from trying to make friends.

"So, what are you in for, Tiny?" Kael asked the big one.

Instead of responding, the biker stared at the boy's chest with injected eyes. It took Kael a minute to realize he was glaring at the cross necklace that had fallen out from behind his shirt during the wreck. Once he realized it, he quickly tucked it back underneath his white V-neck and motioned with his fingers to draw the biker's gaze upward. "Hey, buddy, my eyes are up here. I'm not that kind of cellmate."

Finally making eye contact with the young man, the bald behemoth put his left thumb to one end of his sweaty throat and slid it across to the other side, then forcefully pointed to Kael. The teenager rolled his eyes, sat on the bench farthest from the two, and interlaced his fingers around the back of his head. He felt the oil and gasoline that had burst from the car matting his hair down. It reminded him why he wasn't worried about the imposing figure staring daggers at him. If a two-ton car imploding all around him couldn't take him out, a three-hundred-pound beached whale wouldn't get the job done either.

After closing his eyes, Kael realized just how tired he was. He'd been driving all night, and he'd never used his abilities so many times in quick succession. Even for someone like him, there was a limit, and he figured he had a couple hours until his probation officer made it all the way from Omaha to drag him back.

For the first time in a few days, he planned to get some sleep.

CHAPTER 2

Kael awoke to the secretary behind the front desk reaching up to turn on a staticky wall-mounted television. He'd already been woken up once before by a cute twentysomething-year-old nurse who was checking to make sure he didn't have any internal injuries. The officers who arrested him were still baffled as to how anyone could walk away from a wreck like his without a scratch. Much to their amazement, Kael was just fine. Still, that didn't stop him from exaggerating the entire story to the nurse, regaling it to her in a failed attempt to get her phone number. It got a light giggle out of her instead.

At the front of the station, the secretary was standing on a chair, incessantly flipping through the channels until she finally landed on the morning news. Through the static, the hazy anchors were in the middle of a report about a gang of bikers who mysteriously disappeared on Highway 10 just outside Kearney, their motorcycles left abandoned on the side of the road with no trace of the riders anywhere.

Kael looked at Tiny. Then to the news screen. Then back to Tiny. "You didn't... eat them, did you?"

The large man stood for the first time since Kael had met him. He was tall, taller than the young man originally thought. And big, though still about as big as he originally thought. Partially rested, Kael cracked his neck and knuckles. He was ready for a good fight. However, the threat of one was quickly quelled by the sound of a police baton clanking against the cell bars.

"On your feet, Clark! Someone here for you. And sit down, Clarence, the kid isn't worth it."

"Clarence?" Kael asked, stifling a laugh.

The giant glared and plopped to the bench as the arrogant teenager strolled past him. Only when Kael was at the cell door did he bother to turn back.

"Oh, Clarence, I almost forgot to ask! I've always wondered... Just how much mileage does a Harley get with a sexy sea cow such as yourself riding on the back of it?"

The colossus lunged at Kael, deceptively quick for his size, so quick that the young man barely had time to close the door as the giant's round frame bounced against the bars. Kael swore he saw his eyes glaze black for a second as his meaty arm tried to reach through the metal. No doubt to strangle him. Kael chuckled at the attempt.

"Making friends as always, I see," a gruff voice said from behind him. Kael didn't need to turn around to recognize who it belonged to.

"You know me, Graves, always trying to brighten someone's day."

The wrinkled black man standing behind him was Solomon Graves. He was the probation officer assigned to Kael when he was just nine years old, right after his mom died, and he committed his first major theft. Graves had been with him ever since. Every assault. Every larceny. Every burglary, battery, trespassing, vandalism, and grand theft auto. He was the closest thing Kael had to family, much to their mutual chagrin.

"You know, I was having the best dream before I got the call that your stupid butt had broken out of the Gabriel's home again." Graves led Kael to a desk used for out-of-town cops and shoved him down into one of the chairs.

"Here we go," Kael said.

"Do you want to know what the dream was about, Cabbagepatch?"

"Cabbagepatch" had been Graves' nickname for Kael ever since the old man met the little nine-year-old deviant. Kael, pronounced like kale, the cabbage-like vegetable. It was corny and embarrassing, and Kael hated it, which was exactly why Graves kept using it, especially around the other kids in juvenile detention. His mindset was that Kael couldn't fall into the wrong crowd if the wrong crowd was too busy making fun of him. It worked. Every time Graves visited, Kael lost more and more respect with the other delinquents. Faster than he could ever earn it back.

"Let me guess, I was finally eighteen—"

"You were finally eighteen, and I was finally retired. I was on a beach somewhere very warm sipping mojitos as far away from your pasty little white butt as humanly possible."

"Did you take the missus with you?" Kael knew Graves was divorced. It happened about four years ago when he was thirteen. The old man could have retired then, but he told his wife he only would after all his current cases turned of age. His youngest at the time was Kael. The stress of the job and his inability to compromise strained their marriage until she finally reached the breaking point.

Kael always told him he should've just retired.

"Oh, don't you worry about me. I'll meet me a nice little honey while I'm down there and tell her all the stories about this little kid I used to know who couldn't stay out of juvie long enough to get a real girlfriend."

"Well, now you're just being hurtful."

"Truthful."

It was kind of truthful. Kael bounced around from juvie to foster care so much that he barely ever got to know anyone for very long. He only had one real friend. A friend who was a girl. But not a girlfriend. He didn't think so anyway.

"Listen, Graves," Kael said while leaning back on the legs of his chair. "Can we just skip the whole lecture part of this and get me back to Omaha? I need to collect on some bets I made with the others that I couldn't make it out of the city."

"Lord, fix it. Only three more months," Graves said, his eyes rolling to the ceiling in open prayer. "You really think I'm sending you back to the city so you can use that same Houdini crap you've been pulling to escape again?"

"Oh? Another foster home agree to house me then? Or did you finally realize your life is meaningless without me and decide to adopt me yourself, old timer? Fair warning, I've been told I'm quite a handful."

Graves faked a laugh. "Nope, not me," he said. "It appears you made quite the impression on that Mustang's owner. He wants to foster you."

Graves nodded behind Kael, who turned his chair around to face the front of the station. An elderly Asian man was fumbling with a stapler at the secretary's desk. When he dropped it, he knocked over the container of pens arranged neatly on her counter. The secretary, who was still standing on a chair trying to tighten the cords behind the television to fix the static, shot bullets from behind her glasses once she heard the commotion. As the old man tried clumsily to pick up her supplies, the secretary stepped down from her makeshift perch just in time to hear the TV spark violently behind her and short out.

"What the...?" Kael gazed in confusion while the secretary yelled at one of the older officers nearby.

"That's it, Frank, I've had it! Buy a new TV! I'm over trying to fix that death trap!"

As the secretary stalked toward the old Asian man, Kael's eyes followed. He was shorter than average with salt and pepper gray hair and coal black eyes. He wore a beige windbreaker over a white button-up and khakis. He looked like what Kael imagined everyone's grandfather might look like. Assuming everyone's grandfather was Chinese.

Still, something else seemed off about him. Something that made Kael feel uneasy. He didn't know exactly what it was, but he decided then and there that he wasn't going to go with him. After all, it was really weird that the person who just had his very expensive car totaled wanted to foster the kid who totaled it. That meant he was either a saint or a serial killer, neither of which Kael felt like dealing with.

The old man helped to pick everything back up for the aggravated secretary, smiling, bowing, and apologizing repeatedly as he did so.

"You can't put me with him," Kael said, turning back to meet Graves' chuckling grin. In all the time Kael had been a foster kid, he'd only been adopted once, and that didn't work out. Since then, he always sabotaged the interviews when anyone else tried. He became proud of the fact that he was unadoptable.

"And why's that?"

"Look at him! He's ancient!"

"He's sixty-three."

"Probably going to keel over and break a hip. I'll be the one taking care of his ancient a—"

"First of all," Graves interrupted, "I'm fifty-six, so watch the old man jokes, youngblood. And second of all, I really don't care if you are the one taking care of him. Would do you some good to do something selfless for a change. Maybe learn how to act like a real human being."

"Do you even know this guy?" Kael asked. "He could be a murderer or kidnapper or something."

"He could be Hannibal Lecter for all I care," Graves said. "With everything you seem to walk away from, I'd worry more about the guy trying to put you down." The probation officer's eyes drifted back to the old man. "Besides, you have a debt to work off."

"What are you talking about?"

JUSTIN HART CRARY

"You totaled a two-hundred-thousand-dollar car. What did you think was going to happen? You need to learn that your actions have consequences. Mr. Shen over there agreed not to press charges so long as you do some work around his house until you turn eighteen, which is beyond generous. And the state agrees."

Kael was starting to worry.

"Listen, Graves," he said. "I'll make you a deal. I'll fly completely under the radar for the next few months. I turn eighteen. I'm out of your hair forever. Then you get to sip whatever drinks you want whenever you want on whichever beach you want, and you never have to see or hear from me again."

Graves sighed. When faced with something he didn't want to do, Kael only had two modes: sarcasm and more hurtful sarcasm. The boy was really desperate if he resorted to begging. However, the probation officer didn't care. He was even more desperate to save a kid who, for the entire time he had known him, refused to be saved.

"While I would love three months of peace out of you, kid, I would love it even more to see you actually turn your life around. There's something special about you. We both know it. But the road you're walking down leads one of two places—prison or you dead on the streets somewhere. And I'll be damned if my last case is going to be another lost teenager. Too many of those already... I called in every favor I had left with the state to make this deal work. I don't know why on God's green earth anyone would want to foster the kid who stole from them, but he's got no criminal history, he's already in the system as a foster parent, and like it or not, he's your last chance for a normal life."

There was that word again, Kael thought. Normal. He wasn't and never would be. Graves never knew why or how Kael could do the things he could do, but the boy didn't want the life the old man wanted for him. He was wrong about the nine-year-old boy he kept trying to save. And he

— 20 —

was wrong about the seventeen-year-old one sitting in front of him now.

"You know I'm just gonna run again," Kael declared. "If I can break out of juvie, I'm sure I can sneak out of some old Chinese dude's house."

Graves took a deep breath and shook his head. "One thing I've learned about you, kid, is that you're going to do whatever you want to do. Just don't get caught this time. State's been wanting to try you as an adult ever since you were fifteen, and I'm running out of reasons to convince them not to. I can't protect you anymore."

"Never asked you to," Kael muttered, low enough that Graves couldn't hear him.

The visibly annoyed secretary escorted Kael's soon-to-be-ex-guardian over to the desk where Graves had been temporarily stationed and gratefully deposited him there with an exasperated sigh.

"Mr. Shen," Graves said, greeting him with a smile and a handshake. "It's a pleasure to meet you."

"The pleasure is all mine, Captain." The old man bowed with overdone cordiality, his heavy Chinese accent emphasizing every syllable in his speech. Neither Graves nor Kael were sure how he knew about the probation officer's former rank in the military, but both shrugged it off as a weirdly good guess. "Please, call me Gregory," he continued. "This must be Kael. It's very nice to meet you, young man."

Shen bowed and extended his hand. Kael ignored it and stared the old man down instead. He was a walking Chinese stereotype. More than that, though, Kael was still trying to figure out why the guy he stole an irreplaceable car from wanted to foster him. Good Samaritans that forgiving didn't exist, he reasoned. And if they did, they were hiding something.

"You'll have to forgive our juvenile delinquent here," Graves interjected. "He isn't used to interacting with adults who aren't wearing a badge."

"It's okay, Mr. Graves. From what you told me on the phone, I didn't expect a warm welcome."

"Are we done here?" Kael stood. The faster he was released from police custody, the faster he could escape the potential lunatic housing him.

"Of course," Shen said. "I'll pull the car arou—"

But Kael was already moving past the two men on his way out the door. If not for the myriad of police officers standing outside the building, Graves was sure he would've taken off right then and there.

"Are you sure about this, Mr. Shen?" he turned back to ask. "I'm not sure you know what you're getting yourself into. Heck, I'm not even completely sure I understand why you're doing it in the first place. That boy stole and destroyed a car most millionaires pay fortunes for."

"Cars are just things," Shen replied with a smile. "And things can be replaced. That's what insurance is for."

"Hell of a hike in your premium," Graves said.

"Captain, I understand this is a most unusual situation. But I'm in the business of helping people. And that boy needs more help than the government has been able to offer him. Again, possessions can be replaced. People cannot."

Graves stood silent for a moment. He glanced at Kael's back. The boy was leaning against the glass doors of the police station entrance and heckling two officers outside.

"You're right," he finally said. "I just hope you have more luck with him than I ever have. Or anyone has for that matter." The black man stopped, his face contorting into an expression of dead seriousness for a moment. "But let me tell you something, Mr. Shen. If anything happens to that boy while he's under your care, you need to know that I've been able to retire for some time now. Fear of losing my career won't stop me from doing what that boy's mother would want me to do if someone hurt him. Are we clear on that?"

Shen smiled. "Of course, Captain."

After driving away the two officers standing by the door with his witty

banter, Kael thought about making a break for it. And if not for the same
two officers who'd arrested him earlier standing by their cruiser staring
him down, he would have. He smiled and waved until Shen and Graves
pulled on the door he was leaning against.

"I'll be in touch with your next court date, Cabbagepatch."

"Can't wait."

"Mr. Shen." Graves turned to shake the old man's hand. "Let me know
if there are any problems. You have my number."

"Safe travels, Captain."

As Graves made his way across the parking lot to his old Buick, the
diminutive Chinese man led Kael to what passed for his other vehicle—a
red Ford pickup so old that Kael could barely tell the make and model of it.

Kael pulled hard on the passenger side door to force it free from its
rust-encrusted hinges. When it finally creaked open, he found a black cat
with large green eyes and a white mark on its chest sitting presumptuously
on the seat.

"What's this?" Kael asked with a cocked eyebrow, watching as Shen
shuffled his way into the driver's seat on the opposite side.

"Oh, that's just Thackery. He likes going for car rides." Shen petted
the black cat, who meowed in response. "Thackery, this is Kael. He's going to be staying with us for a while."

"You talk to your cat?" Kael asked.

"Oh, Thackery's not a cat. He's a cat-sith."

As if that explained anything, Kael thought. "Whatever," he said
instead.

The cat eyed the young man for a moment before begrudgingly moving to the middle of the truck's bench seat and allowing Kael to enter,
something he was more reluctant to do than ever. To him, the eccentric
Chinese guy who agreed to foster him just turned into the crazy cat man
who introduced his pets as people... to other real people. If Kael hadn't

been planning to run before, he was certainly planning to now.

Kael hesitantly slid into the open seat and closed the door. The sound of mangled metal creaked throughout the cab so loud that the cat shook its head from the noise.

"You know, you should really think about upgrading," Kael said. "Maybe a sports car?"

Ignoring the obvious jab at his Mustang's destruction, Shen inserted the key into the ignition and started up the old truck. It puttered to life with such vibration that it could've registered on the Richter scale. Kael would've worried about the integrity of the vehicle if he planned on riding in it more than once.

Instead, he just noted that it wouldn't be the next car he "borrowed."

CHAPTER 3

On the same street Kael hijacked his joyride that morning, there lived a young blonde-haired girl named Laney Lessenger, who was struggling to get out of bed before her cell phone signaled that it wasn't her choice anymore. Laney was seventeen years old and about to start her senior year of high school. While that may have elated most teenage girls, it made the girl lying in bed groan into her pillow. Her senior year meant only one thing—her eighteenth birthday—and she had grown up dreading that as a very bad thing.

As if signaled by her anguish, the cell phone sounded the noise every teenager grew to hate hearing in the morning. The alarm. Laney had about eight of them set on her phone, each one about five minutes apart from the other, but this one was her final warning. When she was younger, she had made the mistake of making her alarm her favorite song at the time, thinking it would make getting out of bed easier. She couldn't have been more wrong. All it did was make her favorite song her least favorite song. She hadn't listened to it since.

"Laney!" her father called from downstairs. "How many times are you going to hit snooze? Come on!"

"Coming, Dad!" she called back. Luckily, she had already showered and washed her hair the night before. All she needed to do was pick out her outfit. But first, she had to muster the willpower to untuck herself from the comfort of her cozy covers, swing her legs over the side of her warm bed, and force her feet to meet the unforgiving coldness of her hardwood floors. All of which she did. Reluctantly.

After she got dressed, Laney looked herself over in the mirror. She would love to say she didn't care what she looked like, but that just wasn't true. Not on the first day of school anyway. She had decided on a pink skirt and white blouse with a headband to hold back the mane of wavy blonde hair that always threatened to encroach upon her ocean blue eyes. If she was going into her senior year with the dread of knowing it may be her last year of normalcy, she was doing so with style. And she was determined to make the year a good one. Family, friends, things she wanted to do that she never did… She wasn't going to let a single day go to waste.

Skipping down the steps, Laney pranced into the kitchen and gave her dad a hug from behind. He always smelled like aftershave. It even stung her lips as she leaned up to kiss his cheek. He was fixing breakfast at the stove in his full sheriff's uniform but smiled at his daughter's surprise affection.

"I thought you'd be in a much worse mood," he said without turning around. "You know I haven't changed my mind. We still have to leave in a few months. You won't get to finish your senior year."

"I was more upset last night," Laney said, thinking back to their most recent argument. "But I've decided to make the best of a bad situation." She grabbed a piece of toast and started loading her plate with the bacon and eggs her father had prepared for them. Laney was thin, but by the way she ate, she shouldn't be. "Besides, I can sulk for the next few months or make some final memories with my friends. That's a no-brainer."

"Well, I'm glad to hear…" Her father trailed off as he turned around to see his daughter wearing a pink skirt much shorter than he would have liked—though what he would've liked was a burka. "What is that?" he asked with a forced smile that contorted his mustache.

"It's a skirt, Dad," she replied. "Mid-thigh, per the school's dress code."

"It's still a little short, don't you think?"

"For a nun? Yes. What would you like? Something past my ankles?"

"That'd be great. Let's do that," the sheriff replied. "You go up and change. I'll sign you up for the convent next week." Laney's father knew he wasn't going to change his daughter's mind or her attire. The only way to cope with her independence was with sarcasm. It was also the only way he stayed sane through the last few years of puberty and adolescence.

Laney rolled her eyes but grinned as she sat down. For her dad's sake, she turned it into a charming smile before digging into her breakfast.

"So apparently we missed all the action this morning," her dad said. "Some genius kid decided to hijack Old Shen's '67 right out of his driveway. I told the old man to park it in that garage of his, but he never listens to a word I say."

"Did they find it?"

"Kid totaled it on I-80. Crews were picking up pieces of the car for half a mile."

"What about the boy?" Laney asked inquisitively. "Is he okay?"

"That's the weird part…" Her father paused for dramatic effect. He loved how much Laney got into his work. If she wasn't what she was, he would've guided her into becoming a detective. She would've been a natural. "The kid stepped out of the vehicle without a scratch on him. The car must have flipped a couple dozen times. Mangled the frame into a pretzel. Still, literally not a scratch. Boy has the grace of God looking after him."

"Maybe… or maybe he's like me." When her father gave her a skeptical stare, she continued the thought. "What? We both know I could probably walk away from a crash like that."

"You're pretty rare, sweetheart," he replied. "Not many of you just walking around Nebraska."

Laney hesitated before posing a question she'd spent the last few months forming. "But what if there were? What if they're just good at hiding like we are? If we got enough of us together—"

"Laney. Stop."

"We could fight what's coming!"

"You don't even know what's coming."

"Yeah, because you never tell me anything!"

The house went dead silent with her outburst. Her father's stare was all she needed to know she pushed a little too hard too fast. Laney knew everything her father did he did for her. It just didn't stop the feeling of helplessness she had. And the questions.

Why did they have to hide?

Why did they have to run before she turned eighteen?

Why couldn't they be the ones doing the chasing instead of the ones being chased?

She just wanted to be a normal teenage girl with normal teenage girl problems and have a normal teenage girl life. That obviously wasn't going to happen.

"I'm sorry, Dad," she finally said while gathering her stuff together, avoiding eye contact at all costs. "I'm going to be late for school. I'll—"

Sam Lessenger cut his daughter off with a hug. He didn't show his affection often, mainly because Laney never seemed to need it. But in his arms, she just felt so small. He'd been trying to find the right words to say to her for weeks. He knew he still didn't have them.

"I'm sorry I haven't been honest with you about everything," he said, breaking his embrace while still struggling to comfort her. "Before your mother died, she made me promise to give you a normal childhood. And that was easy to do for a while… until…"

"Yeah," Laney said, already knowing what her dad was referring to. The moment she found out she wasn't normal. The moment she had to start living in fear of someone else finding it out too.

"Listen, when you turn eighteen, they're going to know. And once they know, they're going to come looking. You don't understand the whole situation. I know that's my fault, but—" Sam stopped himself after seeing the hurt in his daughter's eyes. All that training in the force and none of it prepared him for those eyes. "I promise I'll explain everything in a few months. I know you've been patient, sweetheart. I just need you to be patient a little while longer. Let me keep my promise to your mother."

Laney didn't want to say what came out of her mouth next. Sometimes her anger was like a volcano. Other times, it was like a sniper shell. This was the latter. "She's gone, Dad. Maybe you shouldn't make promises to the dead and focus on those of us who are still living."

She grabbed her bag and stormed out the door before giving her father a chance to respond. Before letting the feelings of guilt hit her. They did anyway. And they only made her angrier. Not at her dad. But at herself.

CHAPTER 4

Riding along in Shen's truck was even more awkward for Kael than his earlier ride to the police station. The gray-headed old man kept trying to strike up conversation, but Kael remained resolute in his brooding. Shen's cat also kept staring at him the entire time. Suddenly, he understood how he made the officers feel that morning.

Karma sucked, he thought.

The drive revealed exactly what Kael already knew about Kearney. It was small, and there were a lot of cornfields. Dull and boring. Excruciating for someone like him.

Luckily, he wouldn't have to suffer it much longer. By his estimation, it would take less than ten minutes to get from the police station to Shen's neighborhood.

Then he was out of that town forever.

He was snapped out of his daze when Shen took a turn he didn't expect, cutting into the parking lot of the local high school.

"Home of the Bearcats!" a big blue sign read. Kael stared at it with a mixture of wonder and confusion. What's a bearcat? he thought.

"Here we are!" Shen exclaimed.

"High school?" Kael almost laughed. "You've got to be kidding."

Shen replied with a smiling nod to answer the first question and shaking his head no to answer the second.

"I hate to break it to you, Gray, but I'm pretty sure it takes longer than a few minutes to enroll a new student."

"It does. Which is why I already enrolled you."

Kael's amusement quickly turned to disbelief. "What are you talking about? We just met ten minutes ago. When could you have enrolled me?"

Shen smiled again, this time so wide the creases under his eyes furrowed like one of those wrinkly old dogs. "What is that song they sing in Tarzan? 'Be prepared!'"

"I'm pretty sure that's from The Lion King. Or the Boy Scout motto." Kael could tell he wasn't going to get an explanation out of the crazy old Chinese guy. "Whatever, man," he said, stepping out of the parked truck. "I'm just gonna ditch anyway. After that, I'm out of this hick town."

However, when Kael went for the backpack he had thrown in the back of the truck, he found the bed mysteriously empty. Upon checking back through the window of the cab, he found it tucked under Shen's arm.

"When did you—"

"If you want your bag back, you will at least have to get through one entire day of high school and come back to my home first." The old man's accent seemed even thicker through the small crack of the passenger side window. "Oh! And no coming home early. Otherwise, I hide the bag."

Kael frowned, furiously trying to open the door for a few seconds. He wasn't sure if the rust had reclaimed it or if Shen had locked it, but either way, it wasn't budging.

"This is insane, old man. You're crazy!" Kael nearly shouted. The other kids passing by in the parking lot began staring at him. He lowered his voice. "How am I supposed to go to school without a backpack?" he said through clenched teeth. "Or even a pencil?"

Suddenly, an unsharpened number two pencil stuck itself through the crack of the window. Held by the cat. It had the pencil in its mouth and was offering it to Kael as if in direct response to his last question. When Kael refused to take hold of it, it fell to the ground.

"Your reaction time needs work," Shen remarked.

"Your sanity needs work."

"Indeed. I must be crazy to put you in a loony bin like this one!"

"What's with you and the movie quotes?" Kael asked. "Was that supposed to be Jack Nicholson?"

"Is that who said it? Well then, yes! And now I'm going to quote Bruce Willis…" Shen threw his truck into gear. "Hasta la vista… sweetheart!" He sped off before Kael could even try to correct him.

He settled for yelling after him instead.

"That's Arnold Schwarzenegger! And it's baby!"

More looks. More judgment. Kael had barely ever attended public school before, but he'd seen enough movies in foster care to know that making a spectacle of himself wasn't the right way to go about his first day.

As he picked up the pencil and stashed it inside his jacket's interior pocket, he sighed and resigned himself to his new fate.

Reluctantly walking toward the front doors, he noticed the building was more modern than anything he'd seen before. It looked brand new. And much bigger than anything he would've anticipated for the kind of town he was stuck in. It was Nebraska, so while the giant football field next to the school didn't surprise him, the size of the school itself certainly did. The ostentatious blue "K" on the front windows did seem like a bit much though.

On his way into the building, Kael noticed the variety of high school clichés littering the parking lot. Every clique was perfectly situated so as not to overlap with another. That was when he noticed a small circle of football players pushing around a smaller Asian kid, laughing as they tormented him. Kael balled his fists but ultimately decided to ignore it. He hated bullies, but he wasn't going to be around long enough for it to matter.

As Kael entered the school, a group of cheerleaders, all in uniform, were chatting about their summer vacations on the sidewalk. While laughing with the others, one of them had her brown eyes subtly glued to the parking lot, waiting for her best friend to appear from the line of cars obstructing her view.

Her name was Mercury Grant. She was captain of the cheer squad at Kearney High, and she had been Laney Lessenger's best friend since kindergarten.

On any normal day, she wouldn't have been waiting like a lost puppy for her friend to appear. But it was the first day of school, and that meant the two best friends had to step through the front doors together. It had been their tradition ever since their very first day at Glenwood Elementary.

However, before she could spot her, the morning bell rang out, letting everyone know that summer vacation was officially over. As the rest of the squad began to make their way inside, Mercury kept scanning the parking lot.

"Mercury!" one of the cheerleaders yelled. "Come on! We're going to be late!"

The raven-haired beauty never turned. Just waved with the back of her hand. "I'll be there in a minute! Just go in without me."

Finally, Mercury saw what she'd been looking for all morning—the blonde head of her best friend weaving through the rows of parked cars. When Laney finally made it to the sidewalk, Mercury leapt upon her with a hug.

"I was afraid you weren't coming," Mercury said.

Smiling, Laney replied, "You know I wouldn't break tradition."

After releasing her, Mercury looked her friend over from head to toe, finally taking notice of what she was wearing. Or rather... wasn't wearing. "Where's your uniform?" she asked without missing a beat. "Did you forget there's an assembly this morning?"

"Merc, we went over this all summer. I'm not cheering this year."

"What? I thought you were kidding!"

"You thought I was kidding when I sat you down and said, 'Mercury, I don't think I'm going to cheer this year'?"

"Well, yeah…"

Laney arched an eyebrow.

"Well, I at least thought you'd change your mind," Mercury relented. "The squad needs you. You're the only reason we even place anymore."

"No, that's your awesome choreography. Besides, it's our senior year." Laney was half-pleading for her friend to understand. "I'd like to focus on some other stuff before we graduate. My photography, the school paper… You guys will be just fine without me."

"No, we will not," Mercury said, scrunching her eyebrows together. But then she took a deep breath and tried to respect her best friend's wishes. "But you know I want you to do whatever's going to make you happy."

"And that's why we're best friends."

"Still, you know I'll kick Chloe Bennett off the team in a heartbeat if you change your mind."

"So you did let Chloe on the team?" Laney asked, grinning as they began walking toward the school. "Then you were listening to me this summer."

"Hey, I still had to be prepared!" Mercury replied, grasping her friend's hand as they entered the main doors for their final year of high school together.

Minutes earlier, Kael had entered through the same large glass double doors of the main entrance before realizing he had no idea where he was going. For several minutes, he found himself aimlessly lost in a sea of controlled chaos. When the bell finally rang and the chaos intensified, he watched as the students became a maelstrom of purpose, moving around him like he was in the way, which was exactly how he felt. He was a wrench thrown into a very complex piece of machinery, grinding against every gear as they scraped past the foreign object in their path.

It had just started, but for Kael, the day couldn't be over soon enough. As he thought this, he heard an unfamiliar voice call out to him from behind.

"Kael Clark?"

The young man turned to find a curly-headed middle-aged man standing in a suit and tie with his hands in his pockets and an inquisitive look on his face.

Kael tilted his head and raised an eyebrow, surprised at being called by name in a school where no one should know it.

"You are Kael Clark, aren't you?" the older man asked again.

"Nope, afraid not," Kael lied, turning to walk away. "But I'll let you know if I see him."

"Are you sure? I was hoping I wouldn't miss him. Mr. Shen told me to look for a confused and brooding young man wearing a black jacket. Also, heterochromatic green and purple eyes. Sorry to say, but so far you're the only student to fit that very rare description!"

The man's cheerfulness was off-putting. "Yeah…" Kael hesitated. "Who are you exactly?"

"Right, where are my manners? I'm the principal. Mr. Matthews." He extended his hand to shake Kael's. Once he realized that wasn't going to happen, he smiled awkwardly and turned it into a side gesture, motioning to the main office located next to the front entrance. "Please, if you'll come with me, we'll get your classes set up for your senior year at Kearney High!"

The principal was trying to be enthusiastic. Kael cringed at the effort. It was lost on someone who barely planned on staying the rest of the day, let alone the rest of the year.

"Listen, I'm sure you just put the 'pal' right back in principal and all, but if you could just let me make a phone call, we can skip the howdy-dos and cut right to the chase. Which is me leaving."

"Wow, you're a tough one, aren't you?" Mr. Matthews asked, somewhat put off by Kael's defiant attitude.

"I'm soft on the inside, I promise."

"Well," the principal said, recollecting himself, "as your new guardian, Mr. Shen was very clear about not letting you make any phone calls today."

"Are you kidding me? Is that even legal?" Kael asked. "Everyone gets a phone call."

Mr. Matthews arched his brow. "You know you're not in prison, right?" Letting that reality wash over Kael, the principal waited for a moment before taking pity on his new student. "Listen, get through today, and then you can talk with Mr. Shen all you want about what you want to do tomorrow. But just let me get you through today."

The older man gestured to the office once again. Instead of fighting it, Kael decided to follow the man's instruction. After all, what was one day?

The two made their way through the front office and past two secretaries stationed there. One of them was young and cute and caught Kael's eye, even exchanging a brief grin with him as he passed. However, before he could think to say anything flirtatious (inappropriate), Mr. Matthews led him into his private office and sat him down in a chair facing his desk.

"So, I hear you got into a bit of trouble with the police this morning," the principal said while booting up his computer.

"Misunderstanding," Kael replied. "Just a simple traffic stop." He found that sarcasm usually saved him from having to answer a bunch of questions he didn't want to answer.

"Must have been some kind of traffic stop to alert half a dozen police cruisers," Mr. Matthews said. He noticed Kael probing and grabbing at the various paperweights and knickknacks lining his desk. Mr. Matthews stood from his chair and grabbed one out of the boy's hand after witnessing it disappear and reappear to what looked like sleight of hand. He placed it back on his desk and continued. "You're lucky to be alive, my boy."

"Yeah, I'm just the luckiest kid on the planet." Kael slouched and interlaced his fingers behind his head, trying desperately to ignore the principal's penetrating stare.

Mr. Matthews continued regardless. "The luckiest and one of the most gifted. Omaha faxed your transcripts over this morning." He raised a manila folder from his desk and began flipping through the pages. "High test scores, gifted in science and language arts, off the charts IQ..."

Kael shrugged. He had heard it all before, which meant he knew what was coming next.

"If you'd only apply yourself..." Kael mouthed the words that left Mr. Matthews' lips. "For every positive comment you have in here, there's a negative one. Poor work ethic, behavioral disorders, and your grades in the foster care and juvenile detention systems have been abysmal."

"What?" Kael asked with fake shock. "They always told me I was a model student with straight A's and a perfect attitude. Those liars..."

Mr. Matthews ignored the sarcasm and swiveled back to his computer to print more papers. "Either way, I was surprised when Mr. Shen told me yesterday that he would be fostering someone this year. Don't get me wrong; he does a lot for this community. I just never expected foster care to be one of the acts in his charity bag."

"I thought he was a legal foster parent? And wait a minute!" Kael shot up in his seat. "Are you saying he enrolled me... yesterday?"

As the printer's methodical hum came to a halt, Mr. Matthews grabbed the papers from its tray and stood. "Yes? What's wrong?"

Kael's mind started racing. He thought something was odd about the old man having somehow already enrolled him in school, but finding out he had done it a full day before they even met? It set off every red flag Kael's mind could imagine.

"Nothing," he lied. It didn't matter. All he had to do was get back to the old man's house, retrieve his backpack, and leave. Kearney was just an inconvenient pit stop. California was the real destination.

Mr. Matthews led Kael out of a second exit from his office that spilled into another hallway of the school. They were surrounded by blue lockers and full classrooms all leading to an open floor cafeteria. There was barely anyone left in the empty halls, but the principal seemed to be surveying the area regardless, as if he was looking for someone in particular.

"Ah, Laney!" he finally called out. The blonde girl and her friend had just rounded the hallway. When they heard the voice of the principal, their shoulders stiffened. "And Miss Grant," the principal continued. "Perfect. Come here for a moment, will you?"

Not that they had a choice, but both girls turned and made their way over to where they were being summoned. As they drew closer, Kael became conscious of how much he was actively staring at the blonde in front of him. He had to practically force himself to look away.

"Late on the first day, huh?"

"Sorry, Mr. Matthews!" Laney said. "Dad and I got into it this morning, and I was running a little late. Mercury was waiting for me the whole time. It wasn't her fault. And—"

Mr. Matthews shut his eyes and held up his hand.

"It won't happen again, sir," she finished.

Even from far away, Kael noticed just how stunning the girl in front of him really was. Up close, it only became more apparent. She had features that seemed supernatural. Wavy golden hair that seemed to glow. Blue eyes that sparkled like two starry sapphires. She put the girl next to her to shame.

Mr. Matthews smiled. "It's quite alright, Laney, you're not in trouble. Quite the opposite actually. I'd like you to do me a favor."

Laney glanced at Kael, who averted his eyes and acted like he hadn't noticed her. "What kind of favor?" she asked, judgmentally scanning Kael from head to toe. He was good looking, his unique eyes mesmerizing, but she was rarely impressed by looks. Her best friend, on the other hand, couldn't take her eyes off the boy—her instant infatuation with him obvious.

That was fine by Laney. Even if she hadn't sworn off boys for the year, this one seemed arrogant, and that was all she needed to know to know she wasn't going to like him.

"I'd like you to show our newest student around," Mr. Matthews said, turning to introduce him. "His name is Kael Clark."

Without taking her eyes off him, Mercury grinned and leaned over to whisper in Laney's ear, "And I was just thinking we needed new boys in this school…" As soon as she said it, she snapped up with a cheery smile. "I'd be happy to show him around, Mr. Matthews!"

The principal chuckled uncomfortably. "I'm sure you would, Mercury. But I think we'll leave this one to Laney. Especially after the last time…"

Mercury pouted. "Oh, come on, Mr. Matthews, it isn't my fault that other kid became obsessed with me. Doesn't mean I can't be polite to… Kael, right?"

Laney rolled her eyes as Mercury batted hers. The flirtation ended when Mr. Matthews cleared his throat, insinuating it was time for Mercury to get to her first class.

"Fine," Mercury said. She backed up but kept her eyes on Kael with a playful smirk. "See you around."

Kael wanted to say she wouldn't but decided against it.

"Well then," Mr. Matthews said, "Kael Clark, meet Laney Lessenger. Laney here is one of our top students."

The two exchanged glances that were awkward at best. Neither of them was going to argue that the other one wasn't attractive, but both of them could tell they weren't exactly cut from the same cloth. Laney was social and outgoing. Kael was bored and didn't even want to be there. Both began to protest the arrangement simultaneously.

"Sir, if I could, I'm already late for class and—"

"And I don't need a babysitter. This is public school, not NASA. I just follow the schedule and go to the classes, right?"

Mr. Matthews raised his hand again and paused. "And when was the last time you attended a public school, Mr. Clark? Do you know where your classes are? When lunch is? Your free period?" There was the briefest silence as Kael tried to think up one of his usual witty retorts. Mr. Matthews didn't give him the chance. "Just think of Laney here as your personal tour guide for the day. Come tomorrow, I think you'll have a good enough handle on everything to do without a…" The principal cleared his throat again. "…babysitter."

He flashed Laney an amused look until she finally sighed and nodded to Kael. "Fine. Follow me, Fitz."

"Perfect! I'll have the office call your first block and excuse your tardiness, Laney," the principal said as the two students turned to walk away. "Oh, but Laney!" She froze and looked back. "Go easy on your old man, will you? He may have a heart of ice these days, but you're the only one I've ever seen who melts it. If you guys got into it, I'm sure he's got a good reason."

Laney half-smiled. "I'll try, Mr. Matthews. Thank you." But her smile disappeared the second she turned away from the principal, partly because she knew he was right and partly because she knew she was being stared at by her new obligation.

"What?" she asked.

"Nothing. Just noticing your dad's friends with the principal. Must make your life pretty easy around here."

"We're a pretty close-knit community," she replied. "Everyone knows everyone."

"Shocker."

Laney ignored the obvious insult. "Anyway, where are you fro—"

"So where to?"

Laney rolled her eyes and continued past Kael. So much for small talk, she thought. Not that she cared. The sooner she led him to his first class, the sooner she'd get through her day as indentured tour guide. "Do you have your schedule?"

Kael handed over the paper the principal had given to him and watched as Laney scanned the contents of the sheet. She really was striking, Kael thought. Naturally beautiful. It was too bad he'd met a million girls like her. Ones who judged first and never bothered to ask questions later.

"We actually have first block together," she said. "It's—"

"So what was with the nickname earlier?" Kael asked. "Fitz?" It stuck out to him because usually he was the one giving the nicknames.

"Nothing," she replied. "Like I was saying, your first cla—"

"Because my name isn't Fitz. But you already knew that so…"

Laney took a huffy breath as her left eye twitched at the thought of getting cut off for the third time. "Your first class—"

"Is it just a thing you rich girls do?" Kael continued. "A secret bearcat insult?"

"Your—"

"Or maybe it's—"

Laney exploded. "The character! Geez, do you always interrupt people this much? I called you 'Fitz,' like Fitzwilliam Darcy from Pride and Prejudice. You know, the book? Not that you read, but he's a real jerk, and you remind me of him!"

Kael knew the book she was talking about. Foster homes had as many classic novels as they did movies. But even though her use of the reference didn't make any sense to him, he feigned his immense hurt regardless. "Whoa, just a question, princess. Don't get so excited."

"What can I say? I call them like I see them." Laney wasn't planning on holding back. She was directing all the frustration of her morning at Kael like a bazooka. She had to admit, it felt pretty good. "Honestly, you seem like one of those guys who's going to fall into that group that pretends not to be a group but really is a group because they all think they're too cool for groups. The ones who think they're unpopular because no one understands them, but really they're unpopular because they treat everyone else like crap."

Kael had been prepared to deflect a bullet or two for purposefully provoking her, but Laney was emptying an entire clip into him. Where he initially just wanted to annoy the little blonde, now he wanted to prove a point.

"Listen here, your majesty, you don't exactly strike me as the nicest person either. Tell me, how long did it take you to size me up? Give it a whole ten seconds or just shrug after one?"

Laney did shrug. "One's all I needed." She shoved the schedule onto Kael's chest, pinning it to the muscular physique she pretended not to notice. He finally snatched it from her hand.

"Yeah, you're right," he said. "That's all I needed for this hick town too."

Laney narrowed her eyes. She was done. She had let off some steam and just wanted to be done with the conversation. "Your first class is—"

"English. Room 204. Like I said before, it's not rocket science." Kael was already walking toward the stairwell behind him when he turned around to wink. "Later, rich girl."

He disappeared behind the stairwell's double doors before Laney regained enough of her composure to respond. Shooting her arms down by her sides, she groaned loudly enough to echo off the metallic lockers lining the walls. "I'm not rich!"

✝✝✝

The next few hours passed with extraordinary slowness. Kael never went to his first class. Or his second. Or his third. What was the point? He wouldn't be staying the week, let alone the semester. And if it were up to him, he wouldn't have even stayed the whole rest of the day. The only reason he had to was because of the resource officer patrolling the parking lot around the school, and in his wandering the sparsely populated halls, the seventeen-year-old realized there was no way out without getting caught. All exits led to either being seen by a teacher, an administrator, or the officer, and he really didn't feel like dealing with any of them. He was trapped until three o'clock.

The wall clocks positioned around the school felt like they were taunting him. Every time he looked at one, their minute hands refused to move, even though it felt like hours were passing by. Kael was getting bored and wondered if actually going to class would've been less torturous.

He had already made several laps around the school and could tell the whole place was state of the art—large cafeteria, expensive gymnasium, technology labs and library, eight-lane swimming pool, massive auditorium, and basically everything else any young Nebraskan teenager could dream of in their high school. If he were staying, he might have admitted it was a nice facility. If he were staying.

According to his schedule, his lunch was in a few minutes. He had effectively wasted four hours of his life doing nothing.

A true high school experience, he mused.

However, before he could congratulate himself further, he heard the distinct sound of dress shoes tapping against the tile floors. A teacher must have been out of their classroom patrolling the halls. That or the principal again. Kael didn't feel like coming up with an excuse for why he wasn't in class, so he shot to the nearest door that didn't look like a classroom.

Locked.

Adrenaline pumping, Kael concentrated for just a moment to remedy the situation. The word he spoke into action carried forth his desire. And his desire became reality.

"*Open.*"

As it did, Kael realized the door was heavier than the others in the school, padded with what felt like foam on its interior side. Upon closing it, Kael quickly learned why. The sound of a piano fell upon his ears as he found himself in a small hallway. Almost hypnotically, the music lured Kael into a large room that had several instruments hanging along its walls and a massive ebony grand piano in its center. Its virtuoso, a slim, dark-haired man in his thirties, was masterfully darting his fingers along the keys, producing a classical melody that had Kael in a trance.

The man's back was turned as he played, so when Kael finally regained his senses and realized it was probably another teacher, he turned around to leave unnoticed.

"Skipping class?" the man asked, startling Kael as he lowered the volume of the music by striking the keys less forcefully. Eventually, he ceased the music altogether and turned on the piano bench to face him. "Don't worry, I'm not going to tell on you."

The man's voice was smooth as silk. Every syllable uttered accentuated his intelligence. It occurred to Kael that he was probably from out of town. Smiling, the teacher turned back to the large instrument before him and resumed playing, softer this time so their conversation could continue.

"In that case, could I hide out in here for a couple more minutes until lunch?" Kael asked, investigating the rest of the room curiously.

"Be my guest," the man said. "But the first day's normally just the syllabus and a game or two to learn names. If you're feeling the need to skip now, I'd hate to see you by the end of the year."

Kael grinned. "What can I say? School's not really my thing."

"Then what is your thing?" the man asked, aloof but genuinely interested.

Kael had to pause and think for a moment, halting his scan of the room. "Finding answers," he finally said, unsure of why he said it.

"Doesn't school seem like a pretty good place to do that?"

"Not those kinds of answers."

"Ah," the man replied. "I see. You're looking for the kinds of answers only life can provide you. Lessons from experience. A true seeker. That's why you don't plan on staying here much longer, isn't it?"

Kael couldn't hide the shock that streaked across his face, though it quickly turned into one of annoyance. This guy was the second one in this backward town who could seemingly read his mind, and Kael didn't like it.

The man stopped playing. Much to his surprise, the cessation of music filled Kael with an inexplicable disappointment. The teacher stood from his bench and glided over as smoothly as he played "Relax, it's written all over your face," he explained. "My name is Mr. Cade. Tobias to my friends. I'm new here too." He extended a hand.

"Kael Clark," the bewildered teenager replied, guardedly reciprocating the handshake. The man barely looked thirty but gave an impression of being much older.

"Those are some interesting eyes you have there, Kael," Mr. Cade said, his own arctic blue ones staring into Kael's heterochromatic purple and green. "And an even more interesting necklace." Kael grabbed at the Celtic cross that had fallen into plain view from underneath his shirt. "It's not every day you see a teenager in today's world display their faith so proudly."

Kael quickly tucked it back under his shirt, always amazed by how warm the metal was. "Just a gift," he said. He didn't want to go into the fact that it was the last gift his dead mother had ever given him, or that he was bullied incessantly for his heterochromia. He didn't like to talk about either.

Mr. Cade's eyes snapped up to Kael's with a genuine smile. "Never be ashamed of what makes you different. Unique is rare, and rare is good."

For some reason, Kael believed him. Most adults had said something similar to him at one point or another, but none of them ever actually meant it. This man did. Which made him the unique one.

However, instead of continuing the conversation the way it was going, the teacher motioned to the piano. "Do you play?" he asked.

"I did when I was younger," Kael admitted. "But I haven't since I was a kid."

"My colleagues tell me it's like riding a bike. I wouldn't know, of course. I never stop playing. But they say you never lose the gift. Would you like to give it a shot?"

Just then, the bell sounded for lunch to begin. It was a relief for Kael, who didn't want to get caught playing the piano for some strange guy he just met.

"Maybe another time," he lied, making his way back to the door.

"Sure," Mr. Cade replied with a smile. "I hope to see you in your classes tomorrow."

"Sure," Kael said back, knowing he wouldn't. Then he left.

In the hallways, Kael became lost in the sea of students flooding into the cafeteria. A thousand bodies of various shapes and sizes whirled around one another to get to their chosen stations before other groups swooped in and stole them for the year. Just like outside the school, the same cliques remained intact on the inside as well.

Ordered chaos.

While he didn't want to admit it, Kael was famished. He'd barely eaten anything for two days and was running on fumes, struggling to even sustain consciousness. After waiting for the commotion to die down, he got in line and loaded his plate up with everything the hard plastic tray could hold. There was only one thing he hadn't anticipated...

"Student ID number please," the lunch lady at the end of the line said with little enthusiasm.

Kael stared at the woman in a confused daze. He thought public school lunches were supposed to be free. He had no idea he had to pay with a number. He reached for his schedule, hoping to find the number on it, but realized he had thrown it away after skipping his first class.

"Student ID number please," she said again, this time more annoyed than before. "Or you can pay the $21.50 in cash."

That was an even worse option. Kael didn't have any money on him. When he was about to take the food back, he heard a familiar voice call from behind.

"Hi, Gladys!" It was Laney. She glided gracefully around Kael to give the lunch lady one of the biggest hugs he had ever seen, causing the woman to instantly brighten her expression and hug Laney back like a mama bear.

"Hi, sweetheart!" she cried. "Ooh, it's so good to see you again! How was your summer?"

"It was great!" Laney replied. "Got a lot done at the hospital. The externship was amazing!"

"That's so good to hear! How's your pop?"

"Oh, you know, Dad is Dad."

"Mmhmm, I know that's right."

Kael stood there like he was invisible, unsure of what to say or do but even more confused than he was before. Suddenly, all three of them heard someone shout from the back of the line. "Hey! Move it, will ya!"

Laney's and Gladys' heads whipped around Kael's body so fast that the line of students behind him shrank back. The frustrated expression of the boy who yelled at them transformed into one of apologetic terror. When their heads turned back to each other, there was no hint of malice in their eyes; it had been replaced completely by the same warm, endearing smiles they wore before their interruption.

"So, Gladys, this kid here is new, and Mr. Matthews wanted me to lead him around for the day," Laney explained. "Can we put his lunch on my number until he gets his?"

"Well, honey, you know I'm not supposed to do that," Gladys said, hesitating for a moment before cracking a smile. "But since it's you, you know it's not a problem."

Laney smiled back. "You're the best."

"You owe my girl here $21.50," the lunch lady said, directing some of that white-hot metal behind her eyes in Kael's direction. "Don't make me come find you to pay it back."

"No, ma'am," Kael replied. What was wrong with him? He never called anyone "ma'am."

Awkwardly leaving the line, Kael followed Laney to one of the nearby tables. He hadn't planned to sit with her, but it was the only empty table in the entire cafeteria. Again, though, the difference between them was clear. Every other table made sense. There were jocks, preps, nerds, outcasts... even Mercury had her own table of socialites. Sitting next to each other, Kael and Laney didn't make much sense.

"You're really going to eat all that?" Laney asked.

"Why? Worried you overpaid?"

Laney shook her head in permissive response and began politely eating her own meal. In contrast, Kael gobbled away at everything on his tray like he'd never seen food before in his life.

"You know," Laney said, "I didn't see you in first block. And then I asked one of my friends you're supposed to have third with how you seemed to be adjusting. Funny, she didn't know anything about you. Said there wasn't anyone new in her class this year."

"Thad ish weird," Kael replied with an entire mouthful of food.

Ignoring her own disgust, she continued. "You might actually like it here, you know. I get that I wasn't the most welcoming person this morning..."

Kael swallowed hard. "What? You? Unwelcoming?"

"Yeah, I know, I'm sorry about that. Just a lot going on this year. I shouldn't have taken it out on you. But I promise, if you give this place a chance, it really is a good…"

Laney's voice trailed off in Kael's head as he noticed something across the cafeteria. The same Asian kid who was getting picked on by three guys earlier that morning was getting picked on again. By the same three guys. Kael couldn't make out what was being said over the combined noise of the cafeteria, but he put together that it wasn't a friendly conversation.

"…if you really give it a shot, I think you'll—"

"Excuse me," Kael said, picking up his tray and leaving the table abruptly.

Visibly annoyed, Laney gripped her tray so hard her knuckles turned white. She was tired of trying to be nice to someone who was so into himself he couldn't even finish a simple conversation. Or say thank you for the free meal! As she mentally screamed, Laney's grip became so tight that the tray beneath her cracked. When other students at another table noticed, she laughed it off until they turned back around.

"What was that about?" Mercury asked, having come over from their usual table to sit with her friend.

"Nothing," Laney said curtly, standing up to leave the cafeteria. "I'll see you in gym."

"Okay," Mercury replied, confused by her friend's attitude. She turned to watch Kael walk away. "Hopefully, we'll see him too…"

Kael had assessed the situation unfolding before even approaching it. The three seniors weren't stupid. Teachers were stationed just outside the cafeteria to monitor behavior, so two of the boys kept smiling, each with one of their hands on the kid's shoulders to keep him pinned, while the tallest one—the leader—did all the talking. To anyone else, it might seem as if they were just having a normal conversation. But as someone who'd had the same thing done to him when he was a kid, Kael knew better.

"Say it again," the tallest boy said calmly. He had black hair and was dressed in a polo and jeans. "Tell me again what you're going to do for Frankie this year, Lee?"

"I won't have time, Brody," Lee replied. "I've got all AP classes. And right after school, I have to babysit my little sister and then—"

"No excuses!" the fat one shouted, drawing some unwanted attention. Obviously, he was the dumbest of the three, made to look even dumber by wearing his football jersey like some sort of status symbol. Brody patted his shoulder.

"He may be a little overexcited, but Frankie's right. You see, he's my best left tackle. If he doesn't have a 2.0 GPA during the season, he can't play. And if he can't play, I could get really hurt. If I get really hurt, there goes my shot at a scholarship. Do you see where I'm going with this? You do Frankie's homework, or I could lose out on my chance for a real future. Does that sound fair to you, Lee?"

"Why doesn't Reggie Ray there just study and make his own bad grades?" Kael had come within earshot of the conversation just in time to get the gist of what was happening.

Brody looked up and turned to face Kael, unamused at first but quickly transforming his expression into one of fake pleasantry. He was trying to size up his potential challenger. "Sorry, I don't think I know you." He extended a hand while the other two kept theirs on Lee. "I'm Brody Maxwell. This here's Drew and Frankie."

Kael eyed the hand while still holding his tray of mostly uneaten food. When it became obvious that he wasn't going to accept the handshake, Brody put his arm back down.

"Listen, you're obviously new here..." the quarterback trailed off for a name.

"Kael."

"Kael?" Brody repeated in amusement as the other two chuckled.

"Alright then. You're new here, Kael, so you obviously don't understand what's going on. So if you could just—"

"I understand that I'm looking at three douchebags who have nothing better to do than pick on some nerdy little Asian kid." Kael paused for a moment to look at Lee. "No offense."

"None taken," Lee replied, innocently shaking his hands in front of him while simultaneously wondering why anyone was standing up for him at all.

Kael continued. "So why don't you just leave him alone and fail your own assignments for the rest of the year?"

Brody chuckled, clapping his hands together while taking two steps toward Kael to stand directly in front of him. Face to face, Brody finally took notice of Kael's purple eye contrasting his green one. "Nice speech, freak eyes," he said. "Who are you supposed to be anyway? Marilyn Manson?"

Drew and Frankie laughed on cue while Kael kept his eyes focused solely on Brody's. Marilyn Manson. Wow, he'd never heard that one before.

"Seriously, though, tough guy, you have absolutely no idea who you're talking to. So just go sit back down and mind your own business before you go and get yourself hurt."

Brody tapped Kael on the cheek twice with an open palm to get his point across. On the second slap, though, Kael tipped the entire mountainous tray of food forward, emptying its contents down Brody's shirt and pants, cascading it to the floor in a waterfall of mush.

"Whoops," Kael said without remorse. The incident caught the attention of the entire cafeteria, which shifted from roaring loudness to deafening silence in between heartbeats. The other two football players immediately let go of Lee, preparing to attack Kael until they were stopped by the outstretched hands of Brody.

All four teenagers took note of their being watched by the teachers on duty. Even though Kael couldn't have cared less, the football players didn't want a fight that could get them suspended. Especially with the season just about to begin. Too bad, Kael thought. He was craving a fight.

With milk, pudding, and every other assortment of mushy morsel staining and dripping down Brody's expensive-looking clothes, the tall and muscular football player smiled and leaned in closer to Kael. "That was a mistake," he said with an evil grin. "You won't get the chance to make another one."

Begrudgingly, the three left the lunchroom. And with no more free entertainment to hold their attention, the commotion of the cafeteria resumed as if nothing had even happened.

"Thanks," Lee said, his eyes wide with gratitude.

"Don't mention it," Kael replied.

Without giving the boy a second glance, Kael turned and left the cafeteria as well. He was still ravenously hungry, but his financial situation hadn't changed in the last five minutes, and he wasn't about to face Gladys for another free lunch.

CHAPTER 5

The rest of the day passed quicker than it had when Kael first arrived. Skipping his last class after lunch, he used his final period to explore any other parts of the school he hadn't had a chance to see that morning.

When the last bell finally rang at 3:40, Kael breathed an irrepressible sigh of relief. He hurried to the front doors and pushed his way out of his temporary prison, past the line of yellow buses, and onto the sidewalk by the main road. It wasn't as fast as stealing a car, but he began his trek back to Shen's house. He just needed his backpack, and then he could get out of town.

However, though he tried to resist his mind's wandering thoughts, he found himself thinking about Laney. She probably hated him, which was fine, but he still couldn't get the thought of her out of his head. And trying not to think about her just made him think about her all the more. It had been like that all day.

Kael was snapped out of his daydream by the sound of an engine accelerating from behind him followed by the obnoxious honking of a large blue truck with white stripes. He turned just in time to see the three jerks from earlier, two in the front seat and the fat one riding in the bed of the truck. They floored it past him on the main road, blowing a cloud of black smoke from augmented twin exhaust stacks mounted on both sides of the cab.

"Morons," Kael muttered.

However, the truck passed by him so fast he didn't get the chance to react to what it brought with it. The one in the back launched a full smoothie at Kael, splashing the pinkish-purple beverage all over his face and clothes.

Kael's eyes lit ablaze as the truck sped away, the three in it cackling over the engine's roar. He reached out to use his powers to pop one of the truck's tires or send it careening into a ditch, but his stomach growled in protest, quaking the ground beneath his feet and forcing him to realize just how hungry he really was. He lowered his arm in restraint.

As he mopped his face with his hand, another car came speeding up behind him. On guard this time, Kael turned defensively only to find a beat-up red Nissan pulling off the side of the road.

"Need a lift?" the driver asked.

Kael peered into the passenger side window to find the kid from earlier. Lee. His shoulder-length black hair crowded his face, but his big brown eyes shone with nothing but innocence in his offer. Reluctant, Kael hesitated to say anything, trying to think of a reason to refuse. He hated the feeling of owing anyone anything.

"Come on," Lee said. "You saved my butt earlier. Let me at least give you a ride home."

Kael weighed the options. Drenched from head to toe in wild raspberry, taking the offer seemed like a far better choice than walking around looking like he'd been crapped on by Toucan Sam. Eventually, he opened the passenger side door and plopped into the seat.

"You smell pretty," Lee teased.

"Just drive," Kael said, ignoring the sarcasm. Lee threw a small towel to him while trying to contain some of his laughter. The trip wouldn't take long, but Lee wasted no time beginning a conversation Kael had absolutely zero interest in continuing.

"So, you're new around here, huh? I know how that feels. I was the new kid a few years ago when my parents moved us here from California."

"Turn here," Kael said.

As Lee did so, he continued. "They said it would be better for me to grow up in the heart of America, whatever that means. I'm not sure how Nebraska makes me any more American than California did, but whatever. Where are you from?"

"And a right up here."

Lee ignored Kael's blatant disregard for his questions and kept talking. "My family is from Japan, but they have this weird obsession with acting as American as possible. I'm Nisei, I tell them. Second generation. Don't even have the accent. But convincing Japanese parents to listen to their kid is like telling the sun not to set. Pretty sure my pop-pop is the only one who gets me."

"And another right," Kael said. The kid could talk faster than his uninterested passenger could process. Luckily for Kael, he didn't have to try much longer.

Lee didn't take the hint though.

"So hey, your eyes are freaky cool, huh? What's it called again when they're like that? Hetera… Hetero…"

"Heterochromia," Kael finished for him. "A left up here."

"Heterochromia! Nice! And one of yours is purple? I don't think I've ever met anyone with purple eyes before. That's gotta be rare. Almost as rare as someone standing up to Brody."

Kael continued gazing out the window with intention. They were pulling into Shen's neighborhood where Kael had been a fugitive less than twelve hours ago.

"Speaking of Brody, thanks again for the save earlier today. No one's ever done anything like that for me before."

Kael didn't really know how to accept gratitude, so he didn't. He just made brief eye contact and nodded.

"Oh, my name's Lee, by the way. Lee Muramasa. My parents tell me I'm horrible at proper introductions." The seventeen-year-old kept one hand on the wheel while extending the other for an awkward handshake.

Eyeing the hand like it was a snake, the brooding teenager eventually returned the gesture. "Kael Clark," he replied. He didn't know why, but he actually began to feel some pity for the kid sitting next to him. "So how often are you the target for those guys in the lunchroom?"

"Well, it's been a lot worse recently…"

"What do you mean?" Kael figured Lee was the type of kid who had been bullied senseless since kindergarten.

"I don't know," Lee said. "A lot of weird stuff's just been happening around town lately. And people are acting different…"

For some reason, Kael was curious. "Different?"

"Well, take Drew for instance. We used to be friends. Like right-before-summer-hit friends. And he used to be skinnier than me. Now he's completely shredded, joined the football team, and somehow become Brody Maxwell's right-hand stooge next to Frankie."

Kael shrugged. "People change."

"Not like this," Lee replied. "And anyway, he's not the only one. People are committing crimes who've never even gotten a parking ticket before. Others are just disappearing…"

"Maybe there's something in the water."

Lee hummed. "I have my theories. I know this is random, but have you ever heard of—"

"Stop here," Kael said, finally picking Shen's house out from the rows of houses they'd been passing by.

"Stop… where?" Lee asked, confused. "Here? This is old man Shen's house."

"Yeah." Kael didn't feel like explaining. Before the car came to a complete stop, he threw open the door and pulled himself onto Shen's lawn. "Listen," he said, leaning forward against the roof and open window. "Thanks for the ride." He was about to turn and leave but felt compelled to add, "Just watch yourself around those guys. I won't be there next time they decide to start something with you."

Just as he was about to walk away for good, a relatively new Toyota Camry pulled into the driveway across the street from Shen's house. Both boys stared intently as Laney stepped out of the white car and began walking to her porch steps.

"Dude!" Lee half-whispered, half-shouted while gripping the steering wheel excitedly. "You live across the street from Laney Lessenger!?"

"News to me."

Sensing herself being watched, Laney paused and turned toward the street, locking eyes with the two boys staring at her. She noticed Kael, then what house he was parked in front of, and then put it together that he must have been the boy Shen had talked about fostering.

"Oh, you have got to be kidding," she groaned, suddenly wondering if he was the same kid who wrecked Shen's Mustang that morning.

While Kael continued staring, Lee smiled so wide his eyes disappeared. Nervous, he began waving enthusiastically. Laney, too preoccupied with thoughts of the rude boy standing next to Lee's car, shook her head and went inside. If he could ignore her, then she could ignore him too. Even if he intrigued her, there was no way she'd let him know it.

"She must not like you very much," Lee said. "I can't imagine why. You're such a treat."

"Maybe it was your spazzy hand-waving and creepy smile," Kael replied. He wasn't about to be outdone sarcastically by anyone, especially someone he just met.

"Nah." Lee shrugged. "I'm adorable and endearing. Honestly, I'm a delight to be around."

Kael grinned. Or maybe he was. "See you around, Lee."

"See you tomorrow, Kael."

As Lee drove away, Kael looked around. Now that it was daylight, he had a better view of the neighborhood. It was nicer at night, he thought. The houses weren't low income or anything, but they weren't high class mansions either. A few of the lawns had vibrant green grass, but others were brown from neglect. Shen's was full of dandelions. Almost like he'd let them grow on purpose. Some were still yellow, but most were already beginning to turn white, ready to scatter. Kael already had some of the seeds stuck to his jeans.

"Welcome home!"

Shen came from the side of the house wearing a gardening apron. Moving quickly to remove it, the gray-headed old man half-jogged to the garage to manually lift it open. Although the absence of the windbreaker made him look less like a grandpa, he looked just as awkward running as he did doing anything else. Kael was embarrassed for him.

When the double-car garage was fully open, Kael noticed that, except for the old truck Shen had picked him up in, there was nothing inside it. Nothing. He expected it to be full of boxes and other junk that most people kept stuffed inside their unused spaces, but it wasn't. Just pristinely clean and otherwise empty. Thinking back to that morning, he realized he hadn't seen the truck when he stole the Mustang either, so it must have been parked inside the garage then too. Who kept a two-hundred-dollar truck in the safety of their garage and a two-hundred-thousand-dollar sports car under a sheet in their driveway?

"How was school?" Shen asked.

"You mean you don't already know?" Kael asked. "I mean, you apparently know the future since I was already signed up for classes yesterday."

Shen remained silent, neither confirming nor denying the assertion. He maintained his jovial expression until it transformed into one of sincere compassion. "I understand why you're not very happy with this arrangement, Kael, but if you give me a chance to explain, I think you will—"

"No thanks." The teenager had already moved past him into the garage. He wasn't interested in the old man's explanations. Whether he was planning to adopt someone for real, he was one of those weird people who listened to police scanners to know Kael was coming, or he really was just crazy, Kael didn't care. He was out of there as soon as he could find his backpack.

"Listen, I appreciate you apparently letting me steal your car." Kael grabbed his bag from the bench seat of the truck and threw it over his shoulder. "And sorry about totaling it. But I'm not staying here. You're obviously a little unhinged, and I have somewhere else I need to be."

Kael took a few steps toward the open garage door, but just as he was about to cross the threshold, the huge metal door came crashing down in front of his face. He turned to the old man who was smiling sheepishly from the latch that let the garage door fall.

"What are you doing?" Kael asked in a mildly annoyed manner.

No response.

"Listen, Gray, you can't stop me." Kael moved around the old man toward the white interior door that led into the house. As he entered, he paused for a moment to find he had stepped into what looked like a library, just not the kind he would've expected from an elderly Chinese man pushing seventy. Ceiling-high bookshelves lined all four walls with a large, ornate fireplace on the far side of the room. However, not a single book was on any of the shelves. Instead, they were all filled with Blu-rays, DVDs, and VHS tapes. He swore he even saw a couple old film reels.

"Explains the movie quote obsession," Kael muttered, even if it didn't explain why he got them all wrong.

While scanning the room for a way that led to the front door, he spotted Thackery sitting on a large wooden desk several feet in front of the fireplace. He had been watching the boy curiously ever since he entered the room.

"You know the way out of here?" Kael asked. Thackery cocked his head to the side in response. "You know what, never mind." Kael's eye caught a cased opening that looked as if it led to the front door.

Just as he reached it, however, Shen slipped around him to block his progression yet again. He was still smiling with his hands up to arrest the six-foot-tall teenager's progress. Kael was starting to get annoyed.

"You know the more you try and stop me, the creepier this looks, right?"

"Mr. Graves and the state of Nebraska have entrusted me to protect you. I'm afraid you're stuck with me for at least the next three months."

"As your slave?"

"As my responsibility."

Kael smirked and took note of the small elderly man trying to stop him. "Listen, Gray, I'm going through that door, and I don't want to accidentally hurt you when I do. So I'm asking nicely. Move."

Shen took a deep breath. His demeanor became unapologetically calm, much different from his clumsy, bumbling self. "Like the Terminator says, I'm afraid I can't do that, Dave."

"That's not the Terminator," Kael replied. "But whatever. Have it your way."

He put his right hand on Shen's shoulder to gently shove him aside. However, before Kael knew it, his arm was behind his back, and he was facing the opposite direction. After feeling a palm on his shoulder blade, Kael went tripping forward, back into the library of films.

He spun rapidly back around, unable to hide the surprise on his face, though he tried to compose it quickly. This old guy was Chinese after all, he reasoned. It would figure he'd have a couple tricks. But if that's how crouching tiger, hidden dragon wanted it…

"Very racist," Shen remarked as he stepped into the room with his arms folded behind his back. "Great film though."

What the...? Kael thought in utter shock. Was he really reading his mind?

Scanning him carefully, Kael noticed that the collar of the old man's white shirt was unbuttoned several down from the top. He hadn't noticed it before, but hanging between the buttons was a long silver chain with a Chinese cross at the end. The cross was more of an X the way it was shaped, but its structure still reminded Kael of his own necklace.

"What are you? Some kind of Shaolin monk?"

"Why? Are you some kind of Celtic warrior?"

Kael knew the old man was talking about his necklace. As he tucked it back in, he warned, "Seriously, Gray, get out of my way. I really don't want to hurt you."

"What is it they say in the Stallone movies? Make my day."

"That's Clint Eastwood."

"Oh, right..."

Kael tried another break for the door but was sidestepped yet again by the old man's deceptive quickness. This time, he had the loop on his backpack grabbed, yanked back, and spun completely around—with Kael still attached.

Shen's humble attitude had all but evaporated. He was still smiling, but it was the calmest and most confident smile Kael had ever seen. He began wondering if the frail and clumsy old man he met at the police station was just a ruse. It didn't seem possible that he was the same martial arts master now kicking his butt. Which one was the real Gregory Shen?

"Are you ready to listen?" the old man asked, still holding Kael upside down by the loop on his backpack, facing him away from the door.

Bent over backward, the angry teen responded by twisting his body in a full rotation toward the ground. The turn forced Shen to release the strap. Realizing the bag was a liability, Kael decided to use it as a weapon. He threw it at Shen, who simply plucked it out of midair and cradled it to the ground beside him. With one arm still behind his back, the old man smiled and raised an open palm to his younger opponent. He curled his fingers toward himself twice like one of those old kung fu flicks, taunting Kael to attack again.

Kael thought back to one of the foster homes he'd been shipped to as a kid. The dad ran a small group karate class that he and the other boys decided to join in on. It was supposed to teach them discipline and self-control. Instead, it taught them how to better kick the crap out of each other. Like tiny delinquent ninjas.

"Alright, old man, let's see what you've got." Kael threw his hands up and charged Shen, tossing out a series of jabs, crosses, and hooks at full speed. None of them landed. Not even close. Shen moved too much like water, flowing around each punch like a river and crashing against each strike like a tidal wave.

"Too slow," Shen instructed.

Kael's forearms and elbows were starting to hurt from Shen's constant blocking. The old man hadn't thrown a single punch of his own yet. And anytime he wasn't blocking, he was dodging. Which hurt even worse. Kael's fists kept landing painfully against the oak bookshelves and wall panels behind his opponent.

"Too predictable," Shen instructed again, though it sounded more like mocking.

Kael started throwing out snap kicks and side thrust kicks to give his hands a rest, but every time one of his legs raised to leave the ground, Shen's were there to monkey kick them back to their original positions. How was this guy sixty-three years old? Kael wondered.

"Too... pathetic?" Shen finished.

Yep, definitely mocking.

With throbbing fists, sore shins, and a bruised ego, Kael was beginning to get angry. He wanted out of that house. He just needed to get past the geriatric grandmaster to do it. He'd only used his special abilities on other human beings a handful of times before. But he was so tired of getting his butt handed to him that he seriously considered doing it again. And after the fourth palm strike to his chest in a row, his mind was made up.

"Alright, that's it! Don't say I didn't warn you, old man!" Kael yelled, summoning forth all the anger welling up inside himself. Every time he accessed his power, it felt like tapping into an infinite well of perfect energy—whiter than snow but hotter than fire. While he normally used it to alter tiny aspects of reality like he had with the guns that morning, he'd recently learned he could weaponize it as well.

With the house trembling and the air crackling, Kael let out a shout of authority. "Now…"

"Move!"

He pushed out with all the force he'd gathered in an attempt to throw the old man back into the wall. If he was strong enough to fight like Bruce Lee, then he was surely strong enough to take a hit like him too.

The air currents shifted. Movie cases surrounding Kael flew from their shelves. Loose paper was thrown into the air. The cat hissed and ran. And the wave that rippled out from Kael's palms slammed into the unassuming old man with enough force to topple a bear. But still…

Nothing.

Nothing at all. Shen didn't move. He didn't even flinch. The pulse of energy broke against him like a gust of wind breaking against a boulder. It only retained enough power to jostle a few picture frames on the wall behind him.

As Kael stood panting, exhausted from the expenditure of so much energy in a single day, he couldn't help but wonder who the Chinese man standing before him truly was. Unfortunately, that was the last thought he wondered as the lack of food, sleep, and self-restraint finally caught up with him. The world blurred and fell into a myriad of faded colors.

Then.

Black.

†††

Kael awoke several hours later lying on the desk in the middle of the large film library. Shen must have been cleaning the mess his young guest had made because the multitude of movies thrown from their shelves had been pristinely placed back in their original positions on the cases. However, there was a broken antique picture frame on the mantle of the fireplace. It looked as if it had a slightly younger Shen holding a baby in it.

"What happened?" he asked, attempting to sit up while simultaneously being assaulted by a stone-splitting headache.

"You passed out," Shen explained. "My guess is you have never accessed The White that frequently in a single day before."

"The what?" Kael didn't know what he was talking about. Shen didn't respond immediately, just continued organizing his movies on the shelves.

"The White," he finally said. "It's the extra-spiritual energy source that gives you your powers. It comes from… well… something much greater than yourself. Many humans are called to wield it. Few choose to. And the ones who do vary widely in their ability to properly access it through The Word."

"What the hell are you talking about?" Kael asked, rubbing his temples together while slowly rising to a seated position and swinging his legs around the side of the desk.

"Please watch your language."

"Are you serious?"

Shen was. Kael noticed the Chinese man's behavior had completely altered from earlier. The bumbling old fool had completely disappeared.

The man who replaced him was more serious, more solemn, and somehow far more graceful. He moved with feline elegance.

"Tell me," Shen said in a more polite tone. "How long have you been asking yourself where these abilities of yours come from? And yet, you still know nothing about them. You still wield them like a child."

Kael was trying his best to regain his senses. He always assumed his powers were a genetic mutation of some kind. A neurological anomaly that could be explained scientifically if he just knew where to start. He'd read articles on the topic and figured he couldn't be the only person in the world with powers like his. Not with all the reports of ordinary people doing such extraordinary things. Ultimately, that was why he needed to get to California—to track down the one person who might be able to give him answers. Or at least a reason why he had the kind of powers he did in the first place.

Noticing he wasn't going to get anywhere with the conversation as it was, Shen abruptly changed the subject.

"How well do you remember your mother?"

Kael winced at the question, putting himself on guard. He didn't like when people asked about his mom. "I remember her well enough to know it's none of your business."

"Do you remember the dreams she used to tell you?" he continued. "How convinced she was that they were going to happen?"

Up until that point, Kael had been acting uninterested in the conversation, trying to nurse the nightmare of a migraine he was experiencing. Shen bringing up his mom's dreams though... that got his attention. "What did you just say...?"

"Dark winds that lift love to destroy it... Judges who judge kings... And a king—"

"To rule the judges..." Kael finished. "You left out the part with the armor and the dragon."

Despite his bravado, the youth was stunned. Either this old man knew his mom personally, or there was something much scarier happening in that house. He composed his thoughts and jumped down from the desk, making a supreme effort to stand straight up. "She had a brain tumor. Those stories were hallucinations. Her mind playing tricks on her."

"What if they weren't?"

"What are you—"

"What if they were visions?" Shen proposed.

Kael narrowed his eyes, sizing up the being in front of him to decide whether or not he might be dangerous. Deciding he might be made him want to leave the house even more than before. "You're insane."

"Your mother was a Seer, Kael," Shen said. "She could see the future."

"No, she was a cancer patient," Kael retorted. "The tumor in her brain was pressing against her temporal lobe, causing her to see things that weren't there. Trust me, I did my research."

"Because you like things explained, don't you?"

"Factually? Scientifically? Yeah, I do."

"Then how do you explain what you can do?"

Kael couldn't. Not yet anyway. A mutation had been his best guess so far. But that was still just a theory. "Listen, who are you really?" the young man asked.

Shen chuckled, returning for the briefest of moments to the unsuspecting old man Kael had initially met. "Ironic question," he said, "since you don't even know who you are."

The old man locked eyes with Kael, an intense seriousness saturating the air around them like a heavy fog. "You lost your mother, lost your home, lost your family, and lost yourself. Despite all that power you have…" Shen had been circling the teen's unsteady frame, speaking each word like a dagger into Kael's flesh. "…you're still just a scared little boy who does not have the one thing he wants more than anything else."

"Yeah, what's that?" Kael tried to sound confident. "Answers?"

"Purpose," Shen stated. "Answers mean nothing without purpose. A reason to go on living in a world that seems to want nothing more than to destroy you."

Kael froze. For the first time in a long time, he felt like he was in genuine danger. Like this Chinese man could actually succeed in doing what nothing had for the last eight years. Hurt him. And he didn't like it.

"I have been watching you for a long time, Kael Clark," Shen said, finally breaking the silence. "And waiting for you so much longer than that."

Kael felt his chest tighten. It became hard to breathe. It was like the air in the room had been sucked out into the walls… walls that were starting to close in. He only knew one thing. He didn't want to be in the same room as Gregory Shen any longer.

"I'm leaving," he managed to say, taking a few dizzying steps toward the door. He was still exhausted from his previous exertion and paused to lean on the banister of the staircase for momentary support.

"That is your choice. I cannot stop you," Shen replied. "Well, actually, that's a lie. We both know I can stop you. I already did. I just won't. Not this time. I have laid out one path before you. The other one is out that door. Either is yours to walk, Kael. You just have to let me know when you're ready."

Kael inched his way toward the front door, mentally forcing himself to keep from passing out again. He only leaned against it to deliver one final message to the old man, regaining some measure of the confidence he had lost just moments before.

"Don't ever act like you know anything about me or my mom again," he said sharply. "I may not know everything, but I know she never mentioned some sadistic Chinese dude from Kearney. And even if you did know her, then where were you when she was dying, huh?"

Shen's expression became despondent with despair. However, as soon as it appeared, it transformed itself into a smile of such pure happiness that Kael almost couldn't recognize the emotion properly. He realized it was because he had never actually been that happy before in his life. He hated it.

"You're a freak," he said coldly. "And I don't need you freaking me out anymore."

He hefted his heavy backpack over his shoulder and began to open the door. On the way out, he noticed a small table in the foyer with a glass dish filled to the brim with M&M's. It hadn't been there before.

Shen's irises lit aflame like blue fire. "Your blood glucose level is below sixty. You should take that." He nodded to the bowl while his eyes returned to normal. "You must be hungry."

"Don't tell me what to do," Kael replied.

But he did take it. His hands betrayed him as his left grabbed the whole dish from its pedestal and his right began shoveling the multicolored chocolates into his mouth on his way out the door.

When it slammed behind him, he was overcome with the feeling that he'd made some kind of terrible mistake by leaving. However, the feeling wasn't as gnawing as the question he couldn't get out of his mind...

Who was Gregory Shen?

CHAPTER 6

Upon exiting Shen's home, Kael quickly realized he must have been knocked out for more than just a couple of hours. With no streetlights around and clouds obscuring the starlight above, the pitch-black night reminded him of earlier that morning. He couldn't believe how much had happened in just a day. Then he shuddered while sorting through the thoughts of what had just happened in the house behind him.

Whatever, he thought, trying in vain to brush all his apprehension to the back of his mind. After chomping ravenously at the rest of the M&M's in the bowl, his energy returned a little as he took a step off the porch to resume his original journey. However, before he could take another step, he noticed a shadowy figure across the street sneaking out of her second-story window.

She had a backpack slung over her shoulder and was sliding down the ivy-covered trellis attached to the side of her front porch with the ease of someone who'd done it a thousand times before.

"What are you doing?" Kael said under his breath, genuinely curious as to why the supposedly good-natured small-town girl was sneaking out of her house so late in the evening.

Once safely on the ground, Laney carefully glanced back into a window of her house before sprinting off through her side yard into the yards of the houses behind her. Kael hesitated to follow her but decided he had nothing better to do before skipping town, so he took off stealthily behind her. If nothing else, it was impressive to watch the girl vault over fences like a leopard.

Kael actually found it difficult to keep up with her at times. She obviously knew the terrain better than he did, and she was fast—really fast. While he never lost her completely, there were times when he had to rely on instinct to find her again. Finally, though, after what felt like an hour of solid sprinting, he watched her climb and leap over one very large gate.

Kearney Cemetery.

Kael stood dumbfounded. He expected her to be heading to a party or sneaking out to meet friends, not hang with the dead.

Having lost sight of her, Kael decided he had come too far to turn away now. He threw himself onto the large gate and clambered over it, landing oafishly on the burial ground on the other side. Like all cemeteries, it was unnervingly quiet. Even the sound of crickets died away in the distance as he passed into the realm of the dearly departed. As if out of a horror movie, a very light fog permeated the ground surrounding some of the tombstones.

Was it foggy before he stepped foot in this place? He couldn't remember. Not much made the young man feel uneasy, but crazy old men bringing up his past and being surrounded by the dead certainly did the trick. So far, Kearney was two for two.

Kael hunched his shoulders and threw his hands deep into the pockets of his jacket. He wasn't cold, but he still couldn't stop himself from shivering.

After making his way deeper and deeper into the grounds, Kael finally found Laney sitting next to a grave with her bag lying off to the side. Even in absolute darkness, she lit up the area like a living star—radiant light in utter desolation.

Kael hid behind a large tree and peered earnestly through the night until Laney pulled out a small lantern from her bag. It was only then that he could see the name inscribed on the tombstone she was sitting next to.

Laurel Lessenger
January 1, 1980 – June 6, 2015
Beloved Wife and Mother and an Angel to All

It was all Kael needed to understand immediately, suddenly feeling a touch of guilt for trespassing on a girl he had judged so harshly. A girl who had lost her mother. The guilt quickly grew into shame.

Turning to leave, Kael stepped on a small branch, snapping it underfoot with an audible crack that echoed off the concrete slabs surrounding him.

Laney's head shot up. "Who's there?"

Not wanting to make it more awkward than it was already going to be, Kael stepped out from the shadows.

Laney sighed with relief, then turned that relief into obvious frustration. "What are you stalking me now?"

"No!" Kael said. "I was following. I mean… before I knew you were coming here to see your mom. I saw you sneaking out of your house and got curious."

"Curious about what? Where did you think I was going at midnight?"

Midnight!? Kael was shocked. He really was passed out for longer than he thought. "I don't know," he said. "Maybe a party?"

"On a Wednesday?"

"Yeah, you're right, definitely not in this town," he said. "Listen, I didn't know you were coming to a graveyard. If I did, I wouldn't have—"

"Cemetery."

"What?"

"It's a cemetery," Laney explained. "Graveyards are attached to churches. Cemeteries aren't."

"Okay…" Kael was annoyed by the correction. He didn't like feeling stupid. But Laney was annoyed by being followed, so they were even. "Cemetery. Whatever. Listen, I'll let you get back to whatever you were doing. I really didn't mean to interrupt."

Laney hesitated for a moment while Kael was turning to leave but then said, "You know, I heard about what you did for Lee Muramasa in the cafeteria today. That was pretty nice of you."

Kael turned back. "I thought I was a jerk?"

"Oh no, you're still a jerk," she said quickly. Then grinned. "A real Fitzwilliam Darcy. But unlike him, you might be a jerk with a heart."

Kael still didn't understand her use of the reference. He knew the book she was referring to was Pride and Prejudice, and he knew who she was talking about, but her use of the character didn't make sense to him. He decided to ignore it though. "It was nothing. I just don't like people who punch down."

"Well, it obviously meant something to Lee, since he gave you a ride home and all."

"Yeah, I guess," Kael said, wanting to change the subject. "Anyway, your football friends got me back after leaving the school."

"Is that why I smell strawberries?" she asked, nodding to the faded stain on Kael's shirt.

"Raspberries, actually. I think anyway. Hard to tell."

Laney smirked but then shook her head. "Those guys can be idiots. They think they run the school. Don't let them get to you."

"I wasn't planning on it." Even in absolute darkness, Kael was mesmerized by how attractive Laney made sitting next to a grave look. Even surrounded by death, Laney somehow made a cemetery feel alive.

Kael turned to leave again, this time without warning, until he was stopped by Laney's voice once more. "You know, not a lot of people would understand why I come out here in the middle of the night." She didn't bother to look up as she replaced the older flower arrangement on her mother's tomb with new ones. "You don't seem to think it's that weird. Why?"

Kael arched an eyebrow. "Oh no, I think it's weird," he said, watching as Laney pinned each flower perfectly into place. "But everyone's got their weird. What you do with yours isn't anyone's business. Especially not mine."

Through the darkness, Kael thought he saw Laney smile. He smiled too until his curiosity finally got the better of him. "Can I ask you a question, though?" When she nodded, he continued. "What's with the backpack?"

She smiled wider as she reached for the light pink satchel and unzipped it. As Kael made his way closer to Laney's seated position on the ground, he noticed the backpack was filled with various books of all different genres. One of them was Pride and Prejudice.

His confused expression prompted Laney to explain. "When I was little, my mom used to read to me every single night. It didn't matter how big the book was or what the story was about; she'd just start reading. And after I fell asleep, she'd keep going. I think most moms quit after their kids knock out but not mine. She'd always keep reading. She loved books, so I think she did it for both of us. Sometimes my dreams would become the endings to those stories."

Kael wanted to smile but couldn't. "That sounds nice," he said instead, somewhat bittersweetly.

"Anyway, now that she's the one who's sleeping," Laney said, "it's my turn to read to her."

Kael didn't know how much he liked or believed that Laney's mom was just "sleeping," but he didn't want to correct her. If Laney wanted to believe it, and it helped her in some way, fine. But it just made him think of his own mother and how he didn't believe she was sleeping at all. She was dead. And no amount of happy thoughts was going to wake her up.

"Well, I better get going," Kael said uncomfortably. "It was nice talking with y—"

"You're the kid who totaled Mr. Shen's car this morning, aren't you?" the blonde girl asked, glancing back up to catch Kael's reaction. He hadn't been prepared for the accusation, but before he could ask how she even knew about it, Laney explained, "My dad's the police chief. I don't get names out of him, but I usually get everything else. After Lee dropped you off right outside Mr. Shen's door, it wasn't that hard to put together."

Kael still didn't say anything. He just stared back with the answer obvious behind his purple and green eyes.

"You don't have a scratch on you," Laney said, eyeing the boy up and down. "How is that even possible? I saw pictures of the car on the news when I got home. It was barely a car anymore…"

"Just lucky, I guess," Kael replied nonchalantly, hoping the vague excuse would be enough of an explanation to let the conversation die. It wasn't.

"Or maybe you have an angel watching over you," Laney offered, eyeing him with a scrutinizing gaze, as if trying to peel back the very layers of his mind.

"An angel?" Kael almost laughed.

"You don't believe in them?" she asked, noticing the condescending smile around his lips. "That's strange for somebody who wears a cross around his neck."

Kael tucked the cross back into his shirt once again. "It was my mom's. She believed. I don't. But it's the last gift she ever gave me, so…"

"I'm sorry," she said. They were the same two words everyone said after learning his mom died, but somehow, they seemed more real with her. More genuine. Honest.

Kael felt obligated to say something. "It's fine." It wasn't. But she knew that. Sitting in front of her mom's own grave, she knew better than anyone. "Anyway..." Kael shrugged. "Let's just say I've never seen any proof of angels. And if they did exist, I doubt they'd be racing to protect some delinquent orphan boy who doesn't believe in them anyway."

"So you only believe in the things you can see?"

"I only believe in the things that make sense," Kael shot back quicker than he intended. "And angels don't make sense in a world like ours."

"Why not?"

"Because a world like ours wouldn't exist if they did."

Laney dropped her stare. She was disappointed in Kael's response, but the young man couldn't tell why. Finally, she muttered under her breath, "Maybe you are just a stupid lucky kid after all."

"What?" he asked.

"Nothing," she said, shaking her head. "I was just thinking you're probably right. If I were an angel, I wouldn't want to save someone who didn't believe in me either..."

The silence between them was uncomfortable for a second, but then became lighthearted. With a side-eyed smirk punctuating her final words, Laney made sure Kael knew she was just joking with him. Kael realized he'd let himself become too serious. He smiled back and shook his head. The air filled with a light laughter from each of them.

"Well, you won't have to worry about dealing with me much longer," Kael said. "I'm not sticking around. I was already on my way out of town when I saw you pulling A Walk to Remember."

"First of all, great reference," Laney said while unpacking some of the books from her backpack. "Second of all, that's too bad. I was just getting used to your obnoxious attitude."

Kael chuckled again. He had never met a girl who could give back as much as he could dish out. It was refreshing.

"So where are you going?" Laney asked, laying out each book neatly on the ground in front of her mother's tombstone. Kael got the impression this was not something she did in front of just anyone.

"To find my dad," he replied without thinking, mesmerized by the girl's meticulous organization of the novels. Being so open and honest about his intentions was unusual for him. Before he could stop, his lips continued. "He left me and my mom around the time she got sick. I don't really remember him, but I have some questions."

Laney looked up, surprised. "So you knew your parents before you were fostered?"

Kael took a moment before nodding. He couldn't believe he was telling a girl he just met so much about his past. Not even the kids he was raised with in the foster homes heard him speak this much about his parents. One died, and the other didn't want him. Who wanted to share that? He began to wonder what this power was she had over him...

Laney turned back to arranging the books in front of her. "You know, I know we don't know each other that well, so take this for what it's worth, but... if my dad left me and my mom when she got sick... I don't know... I just think I might stop focusing on somebody from my past who might not care about me and start focusing on the people in my present who actually do."

Kael could tell she was being sincere. He just couldn't tell why. She hated him, didn't she?

"No one knows a lot about Mr. Shen," she continued. "And I know he can be a little... odd... but for some reason he decided to foster a kid who stole from him. To try and give him a better life. If it were me, I think I'd at least give it more than a few hours to find out why."

Of course, Laney didn't know about what happened right before Kael left Shen's house, but that didn't change her point. Shen knew something about Kael that Kael didn't know about himself. How was he going to walk away from potential answers about his own life? No matter who they came from, answers were still answers.

Laney must have sensed a desire to change the subject, so she quickly did. "Anyway, I hope you stick around. Don't get me wrong. You're still a jerk, but you're an interesting jerk. And Kearney could use some more interesting."

Kael grinned. He'd definitely misjudged the girl in front of him. He wanted to continue their conversation but sensed that she was ready to get on with her midnight ritual. He turned to leave until curiosity got the better of him one last time, and he turned back.

"You called me Fitz from Pride and Prejudice earlier today," he said. "You obviously read a lot. Why haven't you read the end of that book yet?"

"How do you know I haven't read the end of it yet?"

"Because if you had, you wouldn't have called me that."

Laney looked away, a sad smile forming on her lips. "I haven't finished it because it was the last book Mom was reading to me before her cancer. She never finished it. And I've never had the heart to finish it either. No matter how many times I start it, I never read past her bookmark."

Kael understood immediately. There were still things he couldn't look at after losing his mom either. Things he kept tucked away in a backpack. Still, he couldn't help but think that avoiding old wounds just kept them fresh.

"Well, maybe one day you will," he said with a smile.

"Yeah," she replied. "Maybe one day."

"So what book are you reading her tonight?"

Laney's sad expression turned hopeful. "I was actually just deciding. We're starting a new one this week, and I was thinking one of her favorites…"

She held up Mansfield Park.

"Big Jane Austen fan, huh? I've never read that one. What's it about?"

The young girl started to respond but then caught herself after thinking better of it. "Will I see you tomorrow?" she asked instead. "I can explain it then."

Kael didn't respond immediately. He wanted to, but he knew what Laney was trying to do. He smiled instead. "We'll see."

Nodding her goodnight, he shoved his hands into the pockets of his jacket and made his way back toward the gate of the cemetery.

Maybe he could stay for a little longer, he reasoned with himself, already subconsciously walking back toward Shen's house.

California wasn't going anywhere.

CHAPTER 7

On his way out of the cemetery, Kael noticed the wind begin to pick up around him, howling as leaden-hued clouds quickly covered the night sky. Even though a storm was rolling in, the young man felt strangely at peace. He breathed in the crisp, clean air with a calm he hadn't felt for a long time. Maybe it was his conversation with Laney, or maybe it was his decision to return to Shen's. Either way, Kael always loved storms. He always felt at home in them.

As the trees rustled and bathed him with their falling leaves, Kael saw the fence that would lead him out of the cemetery. However, before he could reach it, he felt himself being watched. And knew he wasn't alone.

"Who's there!?" an old but loud voice cried out from a couple tombstones away. When Kael looked, he noticed an elderly man wearing overalls wielding a bright yellow flashlight. The shaky beam locked directly onto Kael's eyes before the old man continued. "Who are ya?"

"Nobody," Kael replied, shielding his eyes from the intense light.

"Well, Mr. Nobody, what are you doing out here?" The old man's voice rumbled with a thick Scottish accent. He was obviously the groundskeeper of the cemetery, one who was relentless with a flashlight.

"Leaving," Kael said. He turned back for the fence when the old man suddenly sprang in front of him.

"Oh, no ye don't, lad!" he yelled. "I still have me questions."

The groundskeeper's light fell from Kael's eyes to his chest—where it remained for a little too long. At first, Kael thought it was a reprieve until he noticed that the large and luminous eyes of the old man were intensely fixated on the cross hanging around the teen's neck.

Becoming uncomfortable, Kael tried getting out of the conversation entirely. "Listen, I was just passing through. Won't happen again. Promise."

However, the eyes of the old man would not be swayed. Instead of replying, the groundskeeper maintained his laser focus on the necklace, becoming so entranced by it that his bony hand began to rise in front of him.

With lightning splitting the sky behind him, Kael finally saw the old man's face clearly. His eyes—the entirety of his eyes—were as black as charcoal. And before Kael could utter another word, the seemingly harmless old man lunged forward with a snarl and gripped the cross of the necklace in his hand.

But something happened that Kael had never seen before...

The silver of the cross began to glow white, shining through the closed fingers of the grave keeper and sizzling against his skin. The man unleashed a hellish cry as the stench of scorched flesh filled the air. Releasing the necklace, he recoiled a few paces and grabbed at his burnt hand. For a moment, Kael swore he saw more than just darkness in the old man's eyes... He saw a creature...

Kael didn't hesitate. He seized the moment to flee around the groundskeeper and sprint for the fence, scrambling over it with extraordinary quickness.

What was that light? he thought. And the darkness he saw?

Like his powers, they were just something else he couldn't explain.

As thunder rolled in the distance and the winds picked up with even more fury than before, his mind was made up. His decision to return to Shen's was cemented by the fact that he truly did need answers. Now more than ever.

CHAPTER 8

Kael stood shivering on Shen's wooden porch. It had begun to rain just before he reached the house, so his clothes were just damp enough to send a chill through his entire body. The sporadic gusts of wind didn't help either. As he stood trembling, he desperately contemplated his decision to return to a place that almost scared him more than being assaulted in a cemetery by a creepy old Scotsman. But still, there he was.

With his right arm raised and fist clenched, Kael made a strained effort to knock on Shen's front door. He had been standing there for what felt like hours trying to swallow his pride. Having stormed out with such vehemence earlier, he was somewhat ashamed to be crawling back. It reminded him of the time he tried to run away from home when he was six, and his mom just let him go. He got to the bottom of the driveway with a suitcase full of action figures and stuffed animals before turning around and heading back inside.

It was embarrassing then. It was more embarrassing now.

"The door is unlocked!" a heavy Chinese accent cried from inside the house. Startled from his thoughts, Kael opened the door to find Shen sitting at the bottom of the steps petting Thackery. He was wearing a white Chinese tunic and looked as if he had been sitting there for a while.

"How'd you know I was coming back?" Kael asked, closing the door gently behind him.

"The same reason you did," Shen responded. "I really am quite fascinating."

"Yeah, well, I need answers, and I need them right now." Kael wasn't trying to get wrapped up in the old man's semantic wordplay again. "Starting with who you are and…" Kael linked his fingers under the chain of his necklace. "…what the hell this actually is?"

"Language," Shen said. "So, they came for it."

"Came for what?" Kael asked. "And who's they? Up until I met you, this was just a keepsake from my mom, and I never had any freakshows in a cemetery trying to steal it from me."

"You're upset."

"Wow, you're like the Chinese Sherlock Holmes, you know that?"

"That's Detective Dee," Shen replied. "Three movies about him. Quite good. You should watch sometime."

Kael rubbed his fingers against his eyes. He was falling for the old man's tricks again. He needed to refocus and ask exactly what he meant to ask.

"Who are you?"

"Don't you already know?"

"Gregory Shen… right." Kael should've expected that one. "What I mean is what are you? Why weren't you affected by that power blast earlier?"

"Power blast?" Shen asked, obviously amused. "Is that what you call it? Kind of nerdy."

"Coming from the guy who misquotes movies all day? And sorry, I didn't have time to read the instruction manual for The White or The Word or whatever you called this," Kael said.

"The White is the source of your power," Shen explained. "The Word is the manifestation of the power itself."

"So, what? You're saying it's like magic or something?" Not that Kael believed in that either.

Shen shook his head. "Not quite. Sorcery and magic are something else entirely."

"Whatever," Kael said, perturbed by Shen's mocking tone. "Now just answer the question. Why weren't you affected?"

Shen smiled and stood up with his arms folded tightly behind his back. He walked down the hallway next to the staircase and into the kitchen at the back of the house, barely swiveling his head to give his response. "If an infant tried to push you, would you move?"

Kael stood momentarily puzzled by the response. Was this old man calling him a child? By the time he regained his senses, Shen was in the kitchen pouring himself some herbal tea that had been heating on the stove since before Kael arrived. The seventeen-year-old followed him hotly into the kitchen and continued. "What the hell is that supposed to mean?"

"Language…"

"Sorry." He wasn't sorry. "What the heck is that supposed to mean?"

"Is that another one of your questions?" Shen asked, turning to face Kael while offering him the cup of tea he had just poured. The young man took it begrudgingly. "Because I think it would be wise for us to limit our questions for tonight. It's quite late and waiting on you has cut into my movie time. Besides, I have my own questions."

"Yeah, like what?" Kael asked.

Shen grinned at his guest. "How about this," he said. "You get three questions tonight. I get three questions for the entirety of your stay here. If you answer my first question tonight honestly, you can ask as many as you want for the next few months until I ask my final one."

"How generous. Does the limit start now? Because you never answered my first question," Kael said.

"Yes, I did," Shen said. "I answered a silly question with a silly answer. You just do not wish to take the time to understand my silly answer. So…" Shen lifted one hand higher than the other. "…learn to ask better questions…" And then switched them. "…receive better answers."

"This is ridiculous."

"Only a fool takes no pleasure in understanding while still expressing his own opinions."

Now he was calling him a fool? Kael felt himself getting heated again. He could feel his blood begin to boil at the thought of being made to look like an idiot over and over again in one night.

The Chinese man shook his head. "You are ruled by your emotions, Kael," he explained. "Easily distracted. More easily manipulated. Emotions can be a powerful tool, but only when you control them instead of letting them control you."

Kael listened closely, concentrating on his own anger. Instead of letting it consume him, he finally took a deep breath.

"Fine," he said through gritted teeth. "Then I'll reiterate… My first question is what are we?"

Shen sighed. "First of all, we are not the same. You assume we are because we appear to possess similar abilities, but I was only unaffected by your attack because your attack was ineffective. Think back to it. Don't you feel like it lacked something? Conviction, maybe? Willpower? Despite your frustrations at the time, do you feel like you truly wanted to harm a defenseless old man?"

Far from defenseless, Kael almost said aloud. But he refrained. "So you're saying my heart wasn't in it…" He was careful not to phrase it as a question.

"No. I'm saying it was."

Another few moments of silence passed as Shen poured himself a cup of tea, and Kael sipped on his own. It was bittersweet. Something natural with honey in it to mask the medicinal taste.

"Okay, but you still didn't answer the question," Kael stated. "If we're not the same, then tell me what you are."

Shen smiled mischievously. "According to your conversation with Miss Lessenger, you don't believe in what I am."

Shen led the way into the living room, which was a small room to the side of the library of films. Inside, there was a couch, a flat-screen television, and movie posters lining the walls. The perfect room for a film obsession to be enjoyed.

Kael thought back to his conversation with Laney. Surely this old Chinese man wasn't trying to insinuate that he was… "What? An angel?" Kael asked dubiously.

"Yes," Shen replied while turning on the DVD player. Thackery had already jumped onto the couch and positioned himself in the indentation that marked his usual spot.

"Like an angel from God kind of angel?"

Shen kept nodding with his back turned. "And the one who attacked you in the cemetery was a demon. That's why your necklace burned him. It's special."

"Yeah, right," Kael said, both amused and concerned over the sanity of his new caretaker. "And I'm the King of England."

"The King part is correct," Shen said, fidgeting with the disc of the movie he wanted to watch. "Just not of anything… and yet of everything. Many are called. Few are chosen. But you were chosen, Kael Clark, to find and protect one of the most important things in this world… one of the Seven Seals."

"Seven Seals?"

As Shen nodded in response, Kael questioned his decision to come back to such an obviously demented old man. He clearly had the power to read minds and know things about Kael's past, but illusionists and fortune-tellers seemed to have the same powers to those who didn't know any better. For Shen to declare himself an angel, though, was the most absurd thing Kael had ever heard.

"If you're an angel, why can I see you? Aren't angels supposed to be invisible spiritual beings?"

"We are," Shen replied. "But we have the power to make ourselves known. You can see me because I allow it."

Kael narrowed his eyes. He realized he'd have to use science to dispel delusion. "And how does an immaterial spirit have any effect on a material world?"

"Aren't emotions immaterial?" Shen asked. Kael didn't respond. "Don't they have an effect on you?"

He didn't have a response. "Alright then, angel man, where are your wings?"

"Hidden at the moment."

"How convenient."

As if in direct response to his sardonicism, Shen pushed the disc into the DVD player and then stood slowly, his back still turned away from Kael. There was another uncomfortable silence as Shen refused to turn around for many seconds.

"I could show you what you want," the old man said ominously. "But you're not ready to see it. So what if I show you something else instead?"

"Yeah, whatever," the skeptical youth replied. "Bring it on."

Silence filled the air as Shen, still turned away from Kael, began to concentrate. Without warning, all the lights in the house began to flicker, crackling loudly before going completely black. The fireplace in the library behind them extinguished itself, and the entire home began shaking, slowly at first and then with quaking strength.

As Shen turned to face the now nervous teen, his narrow eyes narrowed further, becoming thin enough to slice Kael in half. When they snapped back open, they were glowing bright blue as he manifested what looked to be a small golden sun in his right hand that flashed with all the radiance of an actual star.

Because it was one. A miniature version of their own yellow sun.

It even had its own gravity—a vortex of invisible energy that seemed to be pulling Kael toward it. The tempestuous power emanating from the old man was unlike anything Kael had ever seen or felt before. He wasn't nervous anymore. He was terrified. With every reason in the world to be so.

However, just as suddenly as the phenomenon appeared, Shen twisted the hand that held the star and made it disappear in an instant, plunging the house back into darkness. After another moment, the lights sparked back on while the fireplace in the other room roared back to life.

Kael stared at Shen in mute astonishment.

"You question everything you are, Kael Clark, but why?" he asked. "You know you have powers, yet you cannot explain where they come from. You say you want the truth, but you disregard it when it knocks." Shen paused, waiting for the boy to regain his senses. "I understand people are afraid of truth. It makes them see what they don't want to see. But you're just going to have to decide whether it's really the truth you want… or to keep living your own version of the lie."

Kael wasn't sure what he wanted anymore. It was all fun and games when he was using his powers to jumpstart a car or escape juvie, but what the old man in front of him was offering was outside the scope of what he was willing to believe in. He only knew one thing…

He couldn't do what Shen just did. Not even close.

"I'm not saying I believe you…" Kael's voice wasn't as confident as it was before. "But let's just pretend for a second that I did. If this Seal or whatever is so important, then why would God choose someone who doesn't even believe in him to protect it? That doesn't make any sense."

"For someone who does a lot of reading, you really do need to read the whole Bible and not just the verses you think prove your points. God often chooses the unexpected to do His most important tasks. He chooses the foolish to confound the wise. He chooses the weak to confound the strong. Perhaps He chose you to confound you... knowing one day you would understand."

Kael didn't. And he certainly didn't want to believe. His mind reverted to all the scientific explanations for his and Shen's individual powers. Evolution... mutation... even theories science couldn't yet prove were more comforting to him than the idea of angels, demons, seals, and God. Those were fairy tales to him, and he wanted them to stay that way.

"Can I ask my other two questions?" Kael requested, a little humbler than before.

Shen simply nodded.

He already knew the two he wanted to ask. Even though there were a million racing through his head, only two of them were important enough to know at that very moment. He'd never admit it, but he was scared. And if he planned on staying in that house for more than one night, he needed to alleviate some of that fear.

"Are you dangerous?"

Shen's eyes became like lasers, more serious than Kael had seen them all day. "Extremely," he replied. Then smiled as soon as he finished the word. "But not to you."

The first response coupled with the previous display of raw power sent a shiver down Kael's spine so cold he couldn't help but tremble. Shen noticed the tension and sought to alleviate it.

"Go ahead with your final question," he said kindly.

Kael had been wanting to ask about his mother ever since he reentered the house. At that moment, though, he was scared of the answer he might receive.

"You said you knew my mom," Kael said. "Did she trust you?"

Shen smiled wider than he had previously, as if recalling some pleasant memory while also feeling a swelling sense of pride for the young man standing before him. "Finally," he said with approval. "A good question."

Kael had never used his powers to read minds before. Even if he could, he didn't know if he wanted to. The world was a dark place and the minds of humans even darker. But if this man had the power to read his mind, then maybe Kael had the power to read his too. If he could make sure Shen was telling the truth, this next question would answer everything he needed to know about staying in that house. Good or bad, he'd know where to go from there.

Kael waited patiently for Shen's response. Maybe he really didn't want to hurt the old man before, which could've been why his power had no effect on him, but at that moment, he really did want to know the truth. He willed it as hard as he possibly could to manifest itself in his mind. Tapping into his power and picturing the word that would get him what he wanted…

Reveal

"Your mother was a dear friend," Shen stated. "We trusted each other."

Kael sensed for his thoughts to relinquish more of the story than his words were willing to, but they didn't. He couldn't make them no matter how hard he tried. The old man's mind was a fortress.

"You did well trying to read my mind," Shen said. Kael wasn't surprised he could sense the attempt. Shen had already proven he could read minds, so it made sense he'd be able to detect when his own was being invaded. "However, you're still a long way from being able to do what you just tried. With training however…"

"You're saying I'll be able to read minds like you?" Kael asked, leaning against the couch for support. He was exhausted.

Shen grinned. "No, I'm saying that when you're ready, you won't have to."

There was a pause in the conversation as Kael realized Shen had done it again. "The Matrix?" he asked. "Seriously?"

"Was it? I thought it was Blade Runner! Either way, would you like to watch them sometime? They're both around here somewhere."

As Shen looked around for the movies, Kael began to ponder the response he'd gotten. Up until then, he'd been assuming Shen spoke in enigmas to annoy or confuse him. He was starting to realize there was more to it than that.

"Alright," Kael said. "My three are done. Are you going to ask me yours?"

"Just one for tonight," Shen replied. "What do you love?"

Kael couldn't hide the confusion on his face. He didn't know what question he expected the old man to ask, but he didn't expect that. "What do I love?"

"Yes."

Kael creased his brow. "What do you mean? What kind of weird question is that?"

"A very important one," Shen replied. "By answering what you love, you learn what is important to you. That is the first step to something greater."

After pointlessly glancing around the room, the seventeen-year-old finally sighed in frustration. "Nothing, I guess," he replied. "I don't love anything." Everything he ever loved had been taken from him. And he found it hard to love the past. As Shen nodded ruefully, Kael continued. "Is that what you wanted?"

"I wanted you to be honest, and you were honest," Shen replied.

"Right..." Kael said. "Well, as fun as these word games are, I think I'm going to bed."

"Make sure you get a good night's sleep. Your training begins tomorrow."

"Training?"

"Yes," Shen said with finality. "The training of a King. You didn't think I agreed to foster you for nothing, did you?" He took a sip of his tea and made his way around the couch, picked up the remote, and sank into the cushions. "We start tomorrow," he added with a thumbs-up in the air.

"Are you really not going to sleep?" Kael asked.

"Angels don't sleep," the old man replied. "So I'm going to enjoy one of my favorite films with Thackery here. Unless of course you'd like to joi—"

"No thanks," Kael said, yawning halfway through his words. "It's been a long day."

"I understand." He sounded disappointed. "Well then, your room is the first door on the right at the top of the staircase."

Shen briefly smiled at the teen before using the remote to turn on the television. He was talking to and petting Thackery as he got his movie ready for the same nightly ritual he'd been performing for decades. Kael grabbed the backpack he had dropped on the floor next to the door and made his way up the stairs in search of his new room.

Once upstairs, Kael found two hallways that met in a T-formation. Skipping past the room that was supposed to be his, the young man briefly investigated the other rooms on the second story, curious as to what he could uncover about the man he'd be living with for the next few months.

Upon entering each room, Kael was floored by the sheer amount of movie posters lining the walls. In fact, the walls couldn't even be seen, just one poster on top of another covering every inch of every room. The movies varied, ranging from romantic comedies to science fiction. Gangster films to epic fantasies. If Kael hadn't already suspected obsession before, this new discovery would have confirmed it.

However, there was one door that was locked. Only one. It was a large six-panel wooden door made of a different kind of wood than the rest of the oak doors upstairs. The door itself had markings and symbols etched into every square inch. The mystery of it piqued Kael's curiosity...

Open.

He willed it, but nothing happened.

"*Open.*"

He said aloud, but again, nothing. Instead of forcing it, however, Kael merely shrugged and walked back toward the room designated for him. He was tired and had already used his abilities more in one day than he had since they first manifested. They must have needed a break, he reasoned, and so did he.

Kael entered what was to be his bedroom and found it completely barren of anything the other rooms contained. No movie posters or paraphernalia. Just a dresser, a bed, and a small desk. It was plain and modest, but Kael actually appreciated the simplicity of it.

Throwing his bag onto the desk, he hesitated to open it. Struggling for the necessary courage, he remembered his conversation with Laney and unzipped the front pocket to pull out a small picture frame of him and his mother. She was beautiful with long brown hair and a smile that could change the seasons. Kael wasn't older than three or four in the picture, but he looked happier than he had in a long while.

Can't love the dead, he thought, stashing the frame back into the bag before plopping down onto the twin bed with a roaring sigh. Listening to the silence that followed, he realized that for the first time in a long time, he had his own bedroom. He didn't have to share it with other foster kids or bunk with other delinquents. It was just... his.

Staring at the ceiling, he noticed something out of the corner of his eye just as he was beginning to drift off. Moving to the window, the young man had a perfect view of the Lessengers' house across the street, as well as the petite young blonde climbing her way back up the side of her front porch to sneak back into her house the same way she'd snuck out.

She must have sensed someone watching her, though, because once she made the climb, she looked directly back at Kael staring at her.

Laney smiled and waved.

Kael waved back awkwardly.

She didn't want to admit it to herself, but she was actually happy he stayed.

He would never admit it to anyone but himself, but she was the biggest reason he decided to.

When Laney finally climbed in through her window, Kael fell back onto his new bed, once again relishing in how different it felt from other beds he'd slept in. Where they felt hard and temporary, this one felt warm and comfortable. Kael felt himself drifting off to sleep in seconds when it usually took him hours.

That was until…

A thunderous musical score began blasting loudly from downstairs. It was so loud it jolted Kael out of his slumber, wide-eyed and ready to defend himself from any more would-be attackers. But that was before he understood the music that was playing.

"Star Wars?" he realized.

Shen was watching Star Wars. The orchestra for the opening crawl could be identified anywhere, but the eccentric Chinese man had it blasting at maximum volume. It was a wonder he didn't receive complaints from his neighbors.

Kael threw his head back into his pillow and folded it over his ears. He couldn't drown the noise out completely, but it did help to muffle it. It was already three in the morning. Kael wasn't going to get much sleep, but he was too exhausted to let the sounds of lightsabers and blaster fire keep his eyes open for very long.

With his eyelids falling like iron gates, he slowly transitioned from the waking world to the unconscious one, trading the insanity of the last day for the hopeful rejuvenation of his dreams.

Little did he realize just how misplaced that hope was…

CHAPTER 9

On one side, an infinite expanse of white light.

On the other, a contrasting plane of black darkness.

In between them a line of gray where a nine-year-old boy stands crying. Alone. Scared.

"Hello…" he whimpered, listening to his own voice echo back to him through the vast nothingness. No other answer. Nothing to answer but nothingness.

However, suddenly the boy became aware of two figures—one standing on one side of him in the light and the other sitting on a chair on the other side of him in the darkness. Both were several steps away in their respective realms, but the boy could see each of them clearly.

They were him.

He was they.

And all of them knew it.

The boy standing in the light was barefoot wearing a white t-shirt with faded blue jeans.

The boy sitting in the dark wore a black shirt, dark jeans, and expensive-looking tennis shoes.

Neither said anything for several moments as the young boy standing in the gray looked back and forth between them, trying to wipe the tears from his eyes out of embarrassment.

When the boy's vision finally cleared, he saw the boy in white with his arms wide open in invitation for a hug. Comfort. Something the young boy wanted more than anything in that moment.

However, just as he was about to take a step into the white, he heard a voice call out to him from behind… from the black.

"Hi!" It was the boy in the dark plane, looking and sounding friendlier than anyone the teary-eyed boy had ever seen. "Why are you so sad?" he asked compassionately.

The boy in black's voice sounded so innocent, so inviting. The young boy turned completely around to face him and saw the concern of a true friend in his eyes. Stepping away from the white, the young boy took a step toward the black, giving one last look to the boy in the white plane behind him…

He was shaking his head not to go. He was sad. Trying to give him a message.

A warning.

"Do you want to be my friend?" the boy in black asked, trying to regather the young boy's attention. "Whatever it is you're going through, I promise I can make it better!" The boy in black's voice was so heartfelt and sympathetic. To the young boy standing between them, the promise of a friend was more enticing than any hug.

He got enough hugs at the funeral. Now he needed something more.

Another step and he was in the darkness. The light and the gray path were still behind him, but now he was immersed in the black plane. He took several more steps until he was standing in front of the boy sitting in the black chair.

"Why are you so sad?" the boy asked.

"My… my mom… she…"

"Died?"

The young boy shook his head. It couldn't be true. It couldn't be. He was fighting back the tears again. He didn't know how long he'd be able to win against them. So far, he never had.

"I'm so sorry," the boy in black replied. Somehow, the apology made him feel better. Even though he'd heard it a hundred times from a hundred different people, it somehow sounded different this time. More genuine. "It's not fair, is it?"

The nine-year-old shook his head in agreement.

"You know, I lost something once. Something so important to me it hurt. You know what I did to make the feeling go away?"

The young boy shook his head again, this time in wonder while still trying to stifle his tears.

"I fought back. The world takes something from you. You should take something from the world. That's how it's fair. That's what makes it right."

Now instead of being sad, the young boy was confused. "Take something like what?"

"Oh, it doesn't have to be big," he assured him. "It can be anything. Just something you want. I can help you if you want to be my friend."

"Okay…"

"So does that mean we're friends?"

The young boy nodded.

"Best friends?"

He nodded again.

"Great!" the boy in black responded gleefully, finally standing to eagerly shake his new friend's hand. "It's been so long since I had a best friend." He looked past the boy standing in front of him to the boy in white who seemed forever away. "The last one betrayed me."

"So… what should I take?" the young boy asked, having been temporarily distracted from the loss of his mother. "I've never stolen anything before. I don't know if I cou—"

"Don't be silly! I'll help you. I can give you the courage to take whatever you want. And the power to beat up whoever tries to stop you." The boy sat back down in his plastic chair and leaned his fist against his chin. "But as my new best friend, can I ask you to do me a favor first?"

"What is it?" the young boy asked.

With the snap of his fingers, the boy in black made a gray brick appear in his left hand. However, it wasn't a normal brick. It was ethereal and translucent, radiating with an invisible energy that seemed to morph and phase it in and out of existence.

"Will you place this brick at the edge of the gray line on my side?"

The young boy took the brick in his hand. Although it emitted a strange energy, it felt cold. He was confused by both it and the request. "Sure, but why?"

"I don't like the boy on the other side. We used to be friends, but he thinks he's better than me. He judges me. He'll end up judging you too, just wait. I want to build a wall between us so he can't judge us anymore. Will you help me?"

The request seemed innocent enough. "Okay..." the young boy replied.

As he took the brick to the edge of the black and placed it down in front of the gray, his head rose to meet the eyes of the boy in white once again. He didn't look judgmental at all, the young boy thought. Just sad.

The young boy decided that he'd get the boy in white's side of the story one day as well. Later. When he wasn't hurting so bad. He could cross sides whenever he wanted to.

After all...

It was just one brick.

CHAPTER 10

Kael's eyes crept slowly open with the end of his dream. It didn't feel much like a dream though. Something more, he thought. Something real. As his eyes adjusted to the morning light piercing through the window, he suddenly felt the odd sensation of a weight on his chest as well as the chilling effect of eyes watching him closely.

When his vision finally cleared, he found Thackery seated on his sternum, staring at him intently with emerald eyes.

"Morning, cat," Kael said, awkwardly waiting for the feline to jump down.

"Good morning!" a voice replied in a cheerful tone.

"Gah!" Kael jumped, causing the cat to leap from the bed to a desk chair. When Kael's eyes followed its trajectory, he found Shen sitting on the chair petting Thackery and smiling.

"What are you doing!?" Kael asked.

"Waiting for you to wake up" was the plain response.

"Yeah, I got that." Kael brushed the brown hair out of his eyes. "Why?"

"Because your training begins today," Shen answered. "I attempted to wait patiently for you downstairs by watching another film, but Thackery thought it was time to wake you."

"You're blaming the cat for you being weird?"

"I'm not blaming anyone," Shen replied.

Kael shook his head. "Well, thanks for the privacy."

"You are quite welcome."

"No, that was sarcasm…" Kael tried to explain. But after realizing the type of person he'd be explaining it to, he decided against it. "You know what? Never mind."

Shen stood from the chair and walked over to the window. "So," he said without looking at him, "how did you sleep?"

"Well, I would've slept a lot better without 'The Imperial March' blasting at maximum volume."

"Yes, isn't John Williams magnificent?" Shen turned his head toward Kael with an innocent smile.

"Not so much at three in the morning, no," the young man replied while yawning and stretching. "Seriously, what's with the movie obsession?"

"We angels are fascinated by different aspects of human creativity," he replied. "My kind may have been given power, but yours was gifted with everything else."

"Still with the angel thing, huh?" Kael said. "You'd think you could remember the lines better then…" He trailed off, recalling something from his short-lived slumber. Not images really. But feelings.

"Yes?" Shen asked calmly, already knowing the answer.

"I had this crazy dream," Kael started, unsure if he wanted to finish. He felt like he could trust the old man… just not entirely sure he wanted to. "I think I was a kid again. I don't know. I've never had a dream like that before. It felt real."

"That's because it wasn't a dream," Shen said. "It was a memory—from what we angels call the Soulscape."

"Soulscape?" Kael asked, ignoring the fact that Shen refused to stop calling himself an angel.

"Humans like to believe that memories are only stored in their minds. But just as a scar is a reminder of the past on your body, your actions are written as reminders of the past on your soul."

"Souls now?" Yet another thing he was supposed to take on faith.

"Yes, Kael, even you have a soul," Shen replied, gently petting the black cat lying on his lap. Suddenly, he turned an ear down to it. "No, you're right, Thackery. His is very depressing."

"So the cat can see my soul too?" Kael asked, almost laughing at the absurdity. "Funny how everyone can but me."

"You still don't believe me?"

"You know what they say… seeing is believing."

"You believe in macroevolution, right? When did you see it happen?" Shen paused for a response that wasn't going to come. "Everything in this world takes a modicum of faith, Kael. Even science. They just don't like to call it that."

Shen's deadpan responses always made Kael angry. He didn't know why. He only knew that when it came to the esoteric, he wanted to steer clear. To him, souls made about as much sense as angels. They didn't.

Shen closed his eyes for a moment and took a deep breath. When he opened them again, his irises were circles of blue fire. "Your soul wars with itself," he said. "Chaotic. As if what it wants to do it does not do. And what it does not want to do, it does."

Kael remained motionless as Shen's eyes returned to their usual shade of brown. He hated it, but he was scared again. Scared of the powerful being before him who could seemingly do anything he wanted.

Read his mind.

Read his soul.

If Shen really was an angel, he was a lot more terrifying than Kael would've imagined angels to be.

"For every action we take, we make a conscious decision to either stay in the gray center of our lukewarm complacency or take a step… either into the light…" Shen raised one hand as he said the word. "…or into the darkness." Now the other hand replaced it in elevation. It didn't take a genius to figure out where Kael had been tipping the scales.

"But if the dream was a memory, why don't I remember it?"

"Because you chose not to acknowledge it in the first place. Human beings enjoy pretending their actions do not have consequences. And I have found they are the best pretenders in the whole world."

Kael could tell that was the extent of the answer he was going to receive that morning. Shen gave his usual smile, grabbed the towel he had draped over the desk chair, and tossed it to Kael.

"Now, you better shower and get ready for school."

"What?" Kael asked, genuinely surprised. "We're still doing the whole school thing? I thought you said I was starting a King's training today."

"Education is a part of any King's training!" Shen exclaimed. "Consider school to be one battlefield—the mental. When you come home, I will train you in the second—the physical. And when you sleep, Thackery will show you the third—the spiritual. Only a true King has mastery over all three—mind, body, and spirit."

"Seriously, the cat's going to train me too?"

"I told you," Shen replied. "Thackery's not a normal cat. He is a cat-sith."

Kael took a tired breath. "Alright, I'm in it this far. I might as well bite," he said. "What's a cat-sith?"

Shen didn't hesitate. "A sorcerer who practiced the wrong kind of magic one too many times. Thackery will be a cat-sith forever, I'm afraid, stripped of his powers. But I've shared with him some of my own." He pointed to the white spot on Thackery's chest. "He's more connected to the spiritual plane now than he ever was as a human. He can manipulate your spiritual energy, which makes him a valuable asset to you."

"Aren't you an angel?" Kael said sarcastically. "Are you even supposed to believe in magic?"

"Believing or not believing in something doesn't make it any less real, Kael. Magic is forbidden to humans for good reason. It tricks them... corrupts them. So who do you think taught it to them in the first place?"

Kael paused to detect even the faintest hint of a joke. Or a lie. There was neither. Shen was completely serious, almost sorrowfully so.

"Whatever," he finally said, leaving for the bathroom he saw last night. On his way out the door, he gave an inconspicuous sniff to his armpits.

Whether Shen was right about angels and magic, Kael didn't know. The only thing he knew he was right about was him needing a shower.

After scrubbing down and drying off, Kael returned to his bedroom to find that the very few clothes in his backpack had somehow been washed and folded and were lying on his bed ready to be worn. The old man must have snuck into his room last night and went through his bag, he thought. He tried to be angry but found he couldn't bring himself to be. They did stink.

In the house across the street, Laney was getting ready for school as well. However, while she was already fully dressed, she noticed from across the street that Kael wasn't. With only a towel around his waist and cross-shaped necklace around his neck, the half-naked boy made his way in front of the window, where Laney couldn't help but notice the muscular features of his chest and abs.

When Kael felt someone staring at him from afar, he looked up to make eye contact with an embarrassed Laney. He waved with a knowing smile until the small red-faced girl quickly dropped the blinds on her window, turned, and stomped away mortified. She hated that it looked like she'd been staring on purpose.

Kael chuckled to himself, got dressed in a plain white V-neck and jeans, and made his way downstairs to find his jacket hanging on the coat hanger by the door. He noticed Shen in the library sorting his movies with a cup of tea in hand.

"There's breakfast in the kitchen if you're interested," he said.

"No, thanks," Kael replied. He was interested. Starving really. But he needed to be serious. "Hey, Gray, listen, if I'm going to be staying here, don't go through my stuff, okay?"

"My apologies. I was just under the impression you didn't want to smell like a Wookiee for Miss Lessenger."

Star Wars references all day, Kael thought. Great.

"What does she have to do with…?" He stopped at Shen's telling smile behind his teacup. Of course he knew about their rendezvous in the cemetery. So far, he knew about everything. It was steadily becoming less surprising and more annoying. "Just hands off, okay."

Shen threw up both hands innocently, his pinky finger perfectly holding his teacup without spilling a drop. He smiled and went back to sorting his movies. "You better hurry," he said. "You don't want to miss the bus."

"Bus?"

"School bus," he said. "A bus that takes you to school."

"Yeah, Gray, I know what it is. Why am I taking it? Why can't you just drop me off like yesterday?"

"I simply do not have the time," Shen answered, deciding carefully whether to put one movie in alphabetical order or in the order of its series. "I'm afraid my schedule is booked up for the day."

"Yeah," Kael said. "You look swamped."

While Shen pondered where to place the film case, he used an otherworldly hearing to detect the bus already making its rounds through the neighborhood. "Here comes the bus," he said. "Have a great day!"

Kael stared at Shen for several moments, still wondering if he was serious. Waiting on a punchline that never came, he finally realized he was…

"Whatever," Kael said, rolling his eyes. He moved toward the door and grabbed his backpack. "I guess I'm riding the bus home too?"

Shen gave a thumbs-up around the cased opening of the library. Kael sighed. He may have been a foster kid, but he knew that only underclassmen and social pariahs rode the bus. Definitely not seniors and definitely not kids like him. Whatever image he was going for was about to be shattered.

Outside, the bus came to a screeching stop as the air from the brakes was released in a high-pitched wheeze. Kael left the house and made his way around the front of the bus with his head down. The driver didn't bother greeting him, just nodded for him to get on. When he did, he was greeted by the faces of several surprised middle schoolers and freshmen who hadn't yet earned enough social currency to receive a ride to school from an upperclassman.

However, just as Kael was about to sit in an open seat toward the front of the bus to avoid anyone seeing his face, he noticed a familiar one staring at him.

It was Laney.

She motioned for him to sit next to her, and he obliged, more out of a shock than anything else.

"Stuck riding the bus too, huh?" she asked, watching as Kael slung his backpack into his lap and sat down next to her. She noticed he smelled a lot better than yesterday. Must have been the shower earlier that morning...

"What's wrong with your car?" he asked, noticing it still sitting in her driveway as the bus lurched forward with a screech.

"My dad caught me sneaking in last night," Laney said. "I lost track of time and missed his nightly check-in to make sure I was still in bed. That on top of the fight we had yesterday morning..."

"Wait, your dad checks to make sure you're in bed every night?"

"Yeah. He's a little... overprotective."

"A little?" Kael replied under his breath without thinking.

"Anyway," Laney continued, "I got grounded for a month, so I'm bus bound until then. Or at least until I talk to Mercury later. Oh, and only day visits to the cemetery for a while, so it'll be harder to stalk me," she teased with a shrug. "Sorry."

"Not sure I'd even try again," Kael joked back. "Your dad probably has a gun trained on anyone who comes near you."

"Oh, he does." Laney half-smiled, watching house after house pass by outside the bus windows. "Seriously, though, he really is a good dad," she added. "Just worries too much. Wants to take care of me and everything else in this town."

Kael glanced over at his bus partner. As her eyes locked onto the rising sun, his eyes locked onto her. Her words weren't spoken like a typical teenager upset at her parent for some unjust punishment. It was the exact opposite. She exuded maturity.

"Hmm," Kael said. He closed his eyes and interlaced his fingers behind his head to lean back against the uncomfortable blue bus seat. "Well, you seem like someone who can take care of herself."

Laney turned back toward Kael and smiled before staring out the window again. "I want to be," she replied. "It's just ever since Mom died…"

Kael already understood. "Yeah," he said. "I get it."

And unlike everyone else in the town, Laney knew he really did. All her friends always told her the same thing. The same apology. And nice as it was to hear, that's all it ever was. They couldn't understand. They'd never lost a parent. Never lost their mom…

Now she had someone next to her who hadn't just lost his mom, but everything. Someone who had it much worse than her. The only thing she didn't know is if that made her want to smile because she wasn't alone. Or cry because he was.

"But hey, if your dad's really bent on protecting this town, then tell him to take care of that creepy old groundskeeper in the cemetery," Kael said. "Guy's insane."

Laney looked genuinely confused. "Are you talking about Mr. Dampé?" she asked. "He's just a kind old man who takes care of the graves. He even takes especially good care of Mom's as a favor to us. He's harmless."

"Well, he could've fooled me," Kael said with his eyes still closed. Shen's warning was still in the back of his mind. "Just be careful the next time you go there alone."

"That shouldn't be a problem for a while."

"Right, grounded," Kael said, smiling. "Well then, with all that time alone in your room, don't let me catch you peeping over at me getting out of the shower anymore." He opened one eye to peek at Laney. "And definitely don't let your dad catch you. I think he'd agree I'm not just some piece of meat for you to ogle over."

Laney glared at Kael. "Yeah right, Omaha. Please tell Mr. Shen to invest in some curtains for your room. My eyes are still burning."

"That's what happens when you don't blink," Kael replied with a smug grin.

The young man's arrogant response earned a surprisingly powerful punch on the shoulder from the little blonde. He laughed, even though it actually stung. She smiled, even though she wasn't sure she wanted to.

CHAPTER 11

The trip to school took far longer than Laney expected and ended up being much shorter than Kael wanted. Laney hadn't ridden a bus for three years and forgot all the stops they had to make. What should have been a ten-minute drive turned into a thirty-minute sojourn. However, as anxious as Laney was to get to school, Kael could not have been more opposed to it. He just wanted ten more minutes to rest his eyes and fit in as many micro naps as he possibly could before going to classes.

It could've been worse though. He could've been riding the bus with less enjoyable company.

Upon reaching Kearney High, the bus came to its final screeching stop. Laney nudged Kael awake for the third time—the first was to stop his snoring, and the second was to get his unconscious hand off her leg. As they stood, Kael slid back to let Laney pass in front of him while pulling his backpack over his shoulder. She scooted past him until she was halted by the impatient underclassmen trying to push their way off the bus. Shoved face-to-face, the two seniors tried to avoid eye contact. When they were free, Laney noticed her opportunity to break the awkward silence.

"Better tuck that necklace back underneath your shirt," she said. "Wouldn't want anyone thinking Kael Clark actually believed in anything."

As the last freshman cleared the bus, Laney slid out into the aisle and disappeared down the steps. Kael tucked the necklace back into his shirt and followed after her but lost her in the crowd of students flooding toward the school.

Unlike the day before, Kael actually decided to attend his classes. He figured it took less effort to sit through a teacher's lecture than try to dodge administration in the hallways all day. Still, his thoughts were preoccupied. They kept drifting to Shen flexing his power on him last night and whether all his talk about Kings and Seals was the real deal...

Could he really be what he said he was? Kael wondered. An angel? Or was he just nuts? There had to be a reasonable explanation for everything. The things they could do and why Kael ended up stealing from the one person who could explain it to him. Still, he couldn't help but wonder if the kind of power Shen possessed would be the kind he could have as well.

The questions were too much for Kael's sleep-deprived brain to process, so he decided to focus on more pleasant thoughts instead.

Laney.

However short it was, his time with her in the cemetery had been the first time in a long time he hadn't felt so... lost. He'd spent half of his life trying to escape his life, and just the few moments he'd spent with her somehow seemed to slow everything down. Kael had always looked to the future, to the next step in getting what he wanted. Laney made him focus on the present. Like it was the only thing that mattered.

Before Kael knew it, the bell was ringing and sending students off to their first class. English for him, a subject he actually tended to enjoy.

When he entered the classroom, Kael was surprised to find Lee sitting in the middle row a few seats back. When the slender teen saw him, he immediately perked up and began waving overenthusiastically. Kael sighed and shook his head, then walked over and took the seat right in front of him.

"Dude, I didn't know you were in this class!" Lee said while leaning forward. "Where were you yesterday?"

"I got arrested after wrecking a car at a hundred and twenty miles per hour and didn't really feel like coming to class."

Lee leaned back into his chair, and Kael could almost feel him roll his eyes. "Whatever, man. You could've just said you were sick or something. No need to get sarcastic. Not at eight in the morning."

Kael smirked.

As students began pouring into the class and taking their seats, Kael noticed the three football players from yesterday saunter in as well. Brody and his thinner friend were dressed in a couple of Abercrombie polos and jeans while the big dumb one was still wearing his football jersey. It didn't take long for Brody to notice Kael and Lee. When he did, he motioned for his two cronies to follow him.

"Well," Brody said. "If it isn't Lee and his freaky-eyed bodyguard. Hey, I was meaning to ask… how'd that smoothie taste yesterday?"

"Why don't you ask me again after class?" Kael replied. He was going to try ignoring them, but his ego wouldn't let him. Instead, he turned sideways in his seat and leaned back on the bar with his arms on his and Lee's desks in open invitation for a fight. "Or we can just settle this right here. Your choice."

As Kael maintained direct eye contact with Brody, Lee slowly leaned back in his chair as far as he could, watching the potential brawl unfold with trepidation.

"You know," Brody said, "I did a little digging on you last night…"

"Creepy," Kael remarked.

Brody chose to ignore him. "You're an orphan, right?"

"Actually, I prefer the term un-parentally encumbered."

"From Omaha—"

"Lincoln," he corrected. "Moved to Omaha when I was nine."

"Pretty long criminal record…"

Kael shrugged. Couldn't correct that one.

"And you were adopted by that weirdo Shen after stealing and wrecking his ride yesterday morning, am I right?"

"Wait!" Lee exclaimed, leaning forward in his chair. "That was true!?"

Kael didn't respond, only kept his eyes on Brody. "See, now this is just embarrassing," he said, shaking his head. "All I know about you is that you're a douchebag with a superiority complex."

Brody grimaced, then chuckled. His parrots followed suit behind him. When they stopped, the quarterback leaned down on the two desks, trapping Kael in his seat. "You know, if I didn't already have colleges scouting me, I'd gladly wipe that smug grin off your face. A nobody like you might not care about his future, but somebodies like us? Well, we've got more to look forward to than jail time and food stamps."

Kael sat up and came face-to-face with Brody. "Right, like being washed up has-beens who peaked in high school."

The tension between the two teenagers tightened. Both considered how easy it would be to land a punch on the other one's chin. Their fists even clenched. That is until a small but powerful voice shattered the staredown.

"If you two are finished acting like testosterone-filled idiots, would you mind if I sat down?"

The two looked in the direction of the voice. Laney was holding her books against her stomach and waiting to sit in the seat in front of Kael.

"Hey, babe!" Brody said cheerfully.

Babe? Kael thought. Surely Laney wouldn't date this guy.

"Don't call me that, Brody," she said sharply, her eyes like daggers. "We went on one date. One. And it was the last one, you got it?"

Brody's demeanor shifted almost instantly. "Come on, Laney, don't be like that…"

So far, in two days, Kael had seen three versions of Brody Maxwell.

The bully. The "testosterone-filled idiot." And now, the lovestruck moron. Needless to say, he didn't like a single one of them.

"Good morning, ladies and gentlemen," a familiar voice called from the door. Kael noticed it was the same man who'd been playing the piano in the music room yesterday. He barely remembered his name... Tobias Cade? he thought. Did he teach music and English?

Visibly annoyed, Brody looked back to Laney. "This isn't over," he said, trying to be as charming as he could manage. As he turned to make for his seat somewhere in the back of the room, he leaned down on Kael's shoulder and whispered far more menacingly into his ear. "For you either..."

Kael smiled and leaned forward just as Laney took the seat in front of him. "So, you and Brody, huh?"

Laney was glad she was turned forward to hide the repulsion on her face. "He wishes," she said while arranging the materials on her desk. "Our dads work together, so I've known him my whole life." But then she smiled, thinking she'd have some fun. "Though he does have his moments... And he is pretty cute... Why? Jealous?"

Kael plopped back against his seat. Whether she was messing with him or not, he decided his best response was no response at all.

"I trust everyone had a good first day yesterday," Mr. Cade said, placing his satchel on his desk and facing the students, who were still groaning their responses. The English teacher was dressed better than most public school educators were paid to dress, wearing a navy blue sportscoat and black button-up shirt with a Victoria-knotted tie and meticulously ironed slacks.

Kael couldn't tell if the teacher recognized him, but he slumped lower into his seat to avoid finding out.

As the groaning subsided, Mr. Cade smiled and said, "Well, let's see if we can make today a better one then, shall we? Who purchased the novella I told everyone to buy yesterday?"

An array of books suddenly raised into the air around Kael, who quickly understood he was in an advanced placement course for English, one that apparently required the students to buy their own books.

"Good," Mr. Cade responded, pacing the aisles before subtly dropping his own novella on Kael's desk without a word.

Guess that answered whether he recognized him or not, Kael thought. He looked down at the book he was apparently supposed to be reading.

Heart of Darkness by Joseph Conrad.

It was a story about two Englishmen who travel deep into the Congo, each having to wrestle with the savagery of the natives living there and each using them for their own ends.

It was a book Kael had read before.

As Mr. Cade continued pacing the classroom, he added, "And who actually read the first Chapter?"

Hands holding paperbacks plummeted back to their desks like planes being shot out of the sky. Most of the hands. Though there were a few that survived the teacher's question.

Laney's being one of them.

"Alright, Miss Lessenger, please entice the rest of the class into actually completing their homework assignments by regaling us with what you thought of the first Chapter."

"It was... interesting," Laney said, obviously holding back what she really wanted to say.

"You didn't like it?" Mr. Cade probed.

"I didn't hate it?" Laney replied politely. Some of the students in the room began to chuckle.

While Mr. Cade smiled with them, he hushed their laughter with a wave of his hand and said, "Please continue."

"Well, I just felt like we could've seen more from the natives' perspective. We spend so much time detailing the degrading effect the Congo is having on the Europeans stationed there, but the novella doesn't spend nearly as much time detailing what effects the Europeans' presence is having on the natives…"

Mr. Cade grinned. "So, you read ahead."

"The whole thing's only seventy-four pages long, sir."

"Fair enough," the teacher replied. "Don't you think that was the point though? The irony? Those thinking they could civilize the savages becoming savages themselves?"

"Yeah, but what makes the natives savages in the first place? Isn't it all relative?"

Mr. Cade was practically beaming. "Go on," he said proudly.

"Well, I mean, Marlow spends a good deal of time talking about the barbarism of the natives and in the same breath tells how brutal and dehumanizing the Europeans are to the natives. But Marlow himself is no better. Even if he agrees the natives are human beings just like him, he still thinks of them as lesser human beings. He treats them like animals or pieces of machinery. Like possessions."

"What about Kurtz?" Mr. Cade questioned. "Isn't he still worse?"

"I know Kurtz is supposed to be the villain and Marlow the hero, but the only difference I see between them is that Kurtz is at least honest about his prejudice. Kurtz thinks he's doing the right thing, Marlow pretends to know better, but neither one of them is a good person."

Kael noticed Laney's passion. Her voice had sped up since she began and was louder and more confident than before. She almost seemed mad.

"I just feel like if you're going to have all your characters objectify an entire group of people in a story, at least give them the dignity of having one character that tells the situation from their point of view."

The classroom was mostly silent with heads swiveling around to see if others in the room were as confused and uncomfortable as they were.

Kael, however, wasn't uncomfortable. He was intrigued. "I think you're forgetting the time it was written in," he said under his breath. The room was so quiet, though, that even if he had whispered, it would've been as loud as a snare drum.

"Mr. Clark?" the young English teacher asked. "You have something to add?"

Kael sat up while Laney turned around in her seat, her eyes daring him to disagree with her.

"I just feel like you're forgetting that this was written in the nineteenth century," Kael said. "Racial equality was a relatively new concept then."

"I know the time it was written in," Laney retorted. "I'm not saying the story is or isn't racist. I'm saying I wanted more insight into the native perspective."

"But it's not their story to tell. It's about the duality between Marlow and Kurtz—a man appalled by the brutality of the Europeans against the natives and a man who embraces it."

"Something that would've been made better with another native character to challenge both of their flawed perspectives."

"Yeah, but the natives aren't the point of the story."

"And I'm saying they should be."

The tension in the air was thicker than anyone was prepared for on their second day. Kael's and Laney's eyes were deadlocked, neither one backing down from their position. Finally, it was up to Mr. Cade to break the silence.

"Both of your points are well-founded," he said. "But the novella isn't so simple as to be boiled down to meaning one thing or another." Mr. Cade was speaking to the entire class once again. "Conrad wrote this story eight and a half years after his own expedition in the Congo. What he realized then was that power without restriction corrupts. The Europeans were corrupted by their power over the natives. Kurtz was corrupted by his elevation of power among the natives themselves. And Marlow could have been corrupted had he stuck around long enough to taste the influence of power without society's laws to hold him back. You see, ladies and gentlemen… power is the true heart of darkness. Not Marlow and Kurtz. Not the Congo. Not its people. Power."

With Mr. Cade's final explanation looming over the entire class to ponder, he surveyed the room and finally added, "But most of you would have had to actually read the text to comprehend any of what I just said."

There was a light, nervous chuckle from the entire room until the bell suddenly sounded for second block.

"I suppose that's my cue," Mr. Cade said. His grin turned into a sadistic smile as his students tried to gather their things and flee for the door before he could give them any homework. "Your assignment tonight is to read the entirety of the novella and be prepared for a quiz regarding the hypocrisy of imperialism tomorrow."

A series of groans overlaid the sound of students packing up and shuffling toward the door. Mr. Cade playfully laughed at their bemoaning as he made his way back to his desk.

"This conversation isn't over," Laney said, grabbing her things and pointing at Kael, who remained seated while waiting for everyone else to leave. At least she didn't seem mad at him this time, he thought. He hoped.

"Dude, thanks a lot," Lee said. "Because of you and Miss Genius, now we all have to read the entire thing in one night."

"Pretty sure you would've had to anyway," Kael said, nodding to Mr. Cade who was sitting at his desk preparing for his next class. "Guy doesn't strike me as someone who takes it easy just because it's the second day."

Lee groaned. "I knew I shouldn't have let my parents talk me into taking AP my senior year. Senior year is supposed to be fun."

"At least you got a choice," Kael muttered.

"What do you mean?"

"Nothing. Listen, I'll catch up with you later." Kael stood up from his desk and threw his backpack over his shoulder, tucking the book the teacher lent him under his arm.

As Lee exited the room with the last remaining students, Kael approached Mr. Cade's big oak desk and laid the novella down in front of him. "Thanks anyway," he said.

Mr. Cade smiled. "Right, I suppose you won't be needing it since it seems you've read it already. I must say, I'm impressed."

Kael shook his head. "Don't be. One of my foster homes just had a good library."

"I'm surprised you found the time for literature with all your... extracurricular activities over the years."

"You been looking into me too?" Kael asked, suddenly on guard. "You and Brody should start a fan club."

"I look into all my students," Mr. Cade replied, earning a questionable look from the seventeen-year-old in front of him. "Not in a creepy way," he assured him. "No, you've just had an interesting life, Kael. A lot more so than most of these kids have ever seen."

"You say interesting; the judge says troubling."

"And what do you say?"

Kael thought about it for a moment, unsure of why he wasn't just giving another quippy remark. "I'll tell you once I figure it out." However, just as Kael uttered the words, the tardy bell for second period rang. "Well, at least I made it to one class on time today."

"Don't worry about it," Mr. Cade replied. "It's primarily my fault. I'll write you a note, and we can finish this conversation third block."

Kael's eyebrow raised. "Third block? I have driver's ed third block."

"Not anymore," the teacher said without looking up from the cursive note he was signing. When he finally did, he was met with Kael's confused expression. "You skipped driver's ed yesterday and ended up in the music room, remember? I spoke with Mr. Matthews this morning, and he agreed that, rather than putting you behind the wheel of another car, my class would be less dangerous for everyone. Personally, I just think the school budget won't allow for another driver's ed car, but either way, your new third block is Piano I."

Mr. Cade slid the tardy slip, a copy of Kael's new schedule, and his English syllabus across his desk to the dumbfounded teen. As Kael glanced at both the schedule and syllabus, he searched for an excuse not to take his piano class. He just met this guy. He taught two subjects and changed his class schedule without even asking. Kael wasn't so sure how to feel about that.

"Come on," Mr. Cade urged with an encouraging smile. "You'd be doing me a favor. You saw my enrollment yesterday. Zero. I'm a music teacher who can't teach music. Do you know how frustrating that is? Mr. Matthews agreed to make it an independent study, and Coach Winters couldn't care less about losing one more kid out of his class of forty."

Kael didn't know why, but he actually felt sorry for the thirtysomething-year-old man pleading with him to take his piano class. Maybe it was the fact that he seemed like a genuinely good teacher... or maybe it was just that Kael didn't feel like driving around the parking lot at fifteen miles per hour in whatever granny mobile the school owned. Either way, playing the piano again couldn't be the worst thing he did if he was going to stay in Kearney.

"Fine. Whatever."

"Great! Then I'll see you around elev—"

"One condition, though," Kael stated.

"Yes?"

"I saw Pride and Prejudice on the syllabus for next month. Change it to something else, and I'll take your little class."

"But Pride and Prejudice is a classic... Pretty sure the Board has it as required reading in the curriculum."

Kael shrugged. "That's the deal. Take it or leave it."

Mr. Cade took a moment to stare into the unique eyes of his new student. He was the kind of kid who grew up learning how to be resourceful. Something the teacher took note of before grinning back at the brazen proposal. "Deal."

Kael shook the teacher's hand before exiting the classroom. For the first time in a long time, he was beginning to feel like an actual student in an actual public school.

Though he was pretty sure students didn't get to strike deals with their teachers over the books they'd be reading that semester. Worth it though.

CHAPTER 12

Kael's second block was as boring as he expected it to be. It was an advanced environmental science class, and his teacher, plain as she was, didn't make it any more interesting than it sounded. He also didn't have Lee or Laney to distract him from the tedious lecture. At one point, he would've even taken Brody's company to keep from falling asleep.

By the time eleven o'clock rolled around, he was actually glad to attend a different class, which was now Piano I thanks to his English teacher. Still, even if he was the only student in it, it had to be better than learning about the composition of literal dirt.

Kael entered the small hallway between the two soundproof doors that led to the music room, where he could already hear someone masterfully playing the piano. The strength of the music seemed to pulsate into his very soul, getting louder and more powerful with each step he took.

Upon entering the large inner room, Kael was careful to be as quiet as possible. Despite crashing chords and impressive arpeggios, Mr. Cade had somehow heard him yesterday, and Kael didn't want to interrupt again today.

"Are you going to try and enter unnoticed every time you walk through those doors?" the teacher asked, softening the blows against the keys so that the volume of his playing lessened. He tilted his head to listen for Kael's response.

"Yesterday I didn't want to be noticed," Kael said. "Today I just didn't want to interrupt."

"Ah, I see," Mr. Cade responded. He played one last note and turned on the piano bench to face his new student. "Well, now that you're here, are you ready to begin?"

Kael took some uncertain steps toward the piano. "I'm not sure what you're expecting," he warned. "It's been a while since I've played, and no, I don't think it's like riding a bike."

"Let's just see," Mr. Cade replied kindly.

Sitting down, the teenager stared at the keys in consternation. What was he doing here? he thought. He hadn't played the piano since his mom got cancer. And he only ever played with her. Why did he agree to do it now? And who was this guy who even convinced him to pick it up again in the first place?

Kael was just about to get up and head to the office to change his classes when...

"Play." Mr. Cade said the word so softly that Kael barely heard it. "Anything you remember."

Kael's hands positioned themselves over the keys automatically. There was only one song he truly remembered. Before he knew it, two of his fingers pressed down, producing a note that instantly took him back to his childhood. The notes that followed produced a chord, which soon transformed into a song—a melody so advanced that even the music teacher standing behind him was surprised by the complexity of it.

The notes poured from Kael's fingertips and memories poured with them. His hands seemed to move on their own as Kael was thrust into the past, sitting on a piano bench next to his mom, who played the exact same song he was playing now, humming along with it to teach her son.

However, almost as soon as it began, the song ended. Kael couldn't remember any more of it, and so he finished on a subtle note that sounded like it had finality. Nevertheless, Mr. Cade clapped slowly from behind him.

"I think I'm going to have to go ahead and retitle this class Piano IV," he said. "What was that song? I don't think I've ever heard it before."

"'Requiem for a Prince,'" Kael answered without turning, surprised at how deeply affected he'd become just by playing it. "My mom wrote it before she died. I don't remember the rest of it. I'm not even sure there is a rest."

Kael turned around on the bench to find Mr. Cade's warm smile.

"Then we just found the purpose of this class," the teacher said. "We have eighteen weeks. I'm pretty sure we can work together to complete that song just in time for finals. You do that, you get an A."

"One assignment? For the entire semester?" Kael almost laughed at the absurdity of it, though he wasn't about to complain.

"It's an independent study." Mr. Cade shrugged. "And I'm the teacher. I can do whatever I want. Besides, I think doing this would benefit you a lot more than Beethoven and Chopin ever could. But if you really want me to write up an entire curriculum—"

"No, no, it's fine." Kael threw up his hands in surrender. "I'm good with that."

"Then get to work," Mr. Cade said as he turned for the door.

"Where are you going?" Kael asked, somewhat confused that he was leaving.

"To my office," the teacher replied without stopping. "Work on mastering what you remember first. Then we'll work on finishing what you don't."

Once he was out of sight, Kael smiled to himself and spun back toward the piano keys. He wasn't expecting the day he'd had so far. But even he had to admit, as his hands traced back over the white and black bars, he'd had far worse ones.

After class, Kael nodded to Mr. Cade on his way out the door and headed for his locker. He couldn't remember any more of the song, but he still found the practice of playing again soothing.

After lunch and his free period, Kael realized he only had one class left. Gym. But even as easy as it was going to be, he desperately didn't want to attend it. With most of the day behind him, he was far too anxious to get back to Shen's house and get some real answers about his powers. Still, his mood perked up a bit when he realized he was in the same class as Lee and Laney. Then turned sour again when Brody made his appearance as well.

Outfitted in the school-provided shirt and shorts, the entire class was led out to the football field to run laps around the track. The teacher, a shredded sculpture of a man named Coach Winters, used the class time as an excuse to have his football players practice in full gear. Kael was sure that Winters, who looked more like an Olympic bodybuilder than a high school football coach, took his job too seriously. But just like everywhere else in the Midwest, football overshadowed everything. It didn't surprise him that Kearney was no exception.

While the football players ran drills on the field, the rest of the class was expected to occupy themselves with the various track and field equipment the coach had set up behind the goalposts. Most of the students just jogged the track, but a few of them participated in the more challenging events. Laney being one of them. Meanwhile, Mercury and her cheerleaders were stretching and tumbling on the sidelines.

Every time Kael jogged by them, he could feel Mercury's eyes following his every move. It was uncomfortably obvious, but he still pretended not to notice. Besides, his eyes were locked on Laney.

Kael watched as she performed flawlessly on everything from the high jump to the shot put, though her favorite seemed to be the pole vault, which she excelled at.

As everyone else struggled to hit eleven feet, Laney consistently hit at least fourteen over and over again, close to the collegiate record. Her performance astounded everyone, including Kael, who was more amazed by the fact that she never seemed impressed with her own talent. Almost like she was holding back.

After another Olympic leap, she grabbed some water and started jogging. No... Kael was jogging. Laney was sprinting. Sprinting and making it look as effortless as jogging. He'd never catch up with her.

Though someone else managed to catch up with him.

"Hey, man, what's up?" Lee asked, coming up on Kael's side.

Kael could tell he was already out of breath. They'd only been running for ten minutes. "Hey," he replied. "You okay?"

"Asthma," Lee explained, pulling out and shaking his inhaler to take a puff. "But I'd rather drop dead than listen to Coach Winters explain how it's a made-up disease to get out of gym. But yeah, I'm fine. Running's just not really my thing."

"Yeah? What is your thing?"

"Hmm, I'd say people watching. Kind of like you... you know... watching Laney."

Kael kept his eyes forward. "I don't know what you're talking about."

"Mhmm, yeah, I'm sure. Maybe it was the other blonde bombshell running the track. Oh wait..."

As they jogged and Kael ignored Lee's sarcasm, they passed by Mercury, who kept her eyes intensely focused on her attractive new target. Noticing her attention, Lee beamed and began waving at her. Not getting the reaction she wanted from the person she wanted it from, Mercury rolled her eyes and turned back to her squad.

Lee's head dropped.

"So is that why you're running with me?" Kael asked in an amused tone. "To get the head cheerleader to notice you?"

"What? No! Of course not! And I'm offended you would even think that!" Lee gasped. "Can't a skinny, asthmatic Japanese kid run with his much better looking, much more athletic best friend without being accused of having ulterior motives?"

"Best friend?" Kael asked, ignoring the rest of Lee's response.

"Do you have any other friends?"

Kael grinned. "I'm sure Mercury would be my friend..."

"Hey! Not funny!" he practically yelled. "Seriously, though, you think you could put a good word in for me? She plays hard to get, but I'm pretty sure she's into me."

Just as Kael was about to let his sarcasm take over, both boys felt a gust of wind on their backs as Laney blew past them on the track. "You two are so slow," she casually remarked while running backwards. "Try to keep up."

As she took off again, Kael smiled. "Sorry, bestie," he said to Lee before accelerating. "Gotta keep up."

Lee finally came to a dead stop, hands on his knees in utter exhaustion. "I hate gym," he panted. When he finally regained his composure, he stood back up to steal another glimpse of Mercury on the sidelines.

Laney made running at top speed look effortless. Kael had to practically sprint to catch up with her. Not that he was surprised. Chasing her to the cemetery had already made him realize how fast she was. Lightning moved slower.

"Finally catch up?" Laney teased as Kael pulled alongside her.

"Just thought I'd give you the chance to finish our conversation from earlier," Kael replied. "Something tells me you're not used to people disagreeing with you in class."

She grinned. "No, I'm used to people disagreeing with me. Just not used to them being so wrong about it when they do. Look, to avoid future embarrassment, all you need to know is that I'm always right."

Now Kael grinned. "That's crazy... so am I."

As they rounded the track laughing, Laney slowed her pace to give her struggling companion a break. On their next pass, Mercury made her usual flirtatious glances toward Kael from the field. Although he continued to ignore them, Laney couldn't help but comment.

"I think you have a not-so-secret admirer in my best friend."

"Oh really? Didn't notice," Kael replied sarcastically. "Mercury, right? That's an interesting name. Not that I'm one to talk."

"Well, her middle name's Mercury. Her real name's Freddie," Laney explained.

"Freddie Mercury?"

"Her parents are huge Queen fans."

"Cool parents."

Having already run several miles on her own, Laney veered off the track to the water cooler Coach Winters had set up on a folding table by the benches. Thankful for the reprieve, Kael followed. As they filled up two cups, Laney looked at Kael, then at Mercury. She didn't want to ask the question she knew she was about to ask. She didn't want to be that girl. But her mouth made the words before her brain could stop them. "So... what do you think?"

"Of what?" Kael asked, noticing her gaze. "Your friend? Nah, she doesn't look a thing like Freddie Mercury."

Laney laughed. "Seriously," she said, looking back to Kael. "I'm sure she'll ask me what we talked about after school, and she'll get mad at me if I don't ask eventually..."

"She's not really my type."

"What? Tall, tan, and beautiful isn't your type?" Laney asked.

"Beautiful is, sure." Kael turned to meet Laney's gaze. "I just have this thing for blondes."

Laney blushed and looked away, unable to hide her smile. "Subtle."

Out on the field, Brody became distracted by the two laughing by the water cooler and got sacked hard after snapping the ball. Aaron Kobba, one of his receivers, ran over to help him up.

"Come on, man, I was wide open! Where's your head at?"

"Yeah, yeah, my bad," Brody replied, removing his helmet for a breath of fresh air. "Just hard to concentrate with some new kid macking all over my girl."

Aaron looked over in the direction of Laney and Kael. "You sure Laney Lessenger's actually your girl?" he asked, smacking Brody's chest plate with a smile. "She always looks happier when you're not around."

"Yeah, well, I'd be a lot closer to making her my girl without the competition," Brody replied, an idea forming slowly in his head. "Hey, how do you feel about helping a brother out?"

The dark-skinned teenager looked back to see Brody's devious smile and immediately understood. After strapping his helmet back on, he sighed and shook his head. "I'll get open."

Kael and Laney were too engaged in their conversation to notice what was happening. As Brody got back into formation and snapped the ball, he waited for Aaron to charge diagonally for the sidelines. Once he was in position, he chucked the ball as hard as he could at Kael's head.

Time slowed down for Laney, who just barely noticed the football spiraling to beam Kael in his left ear. She tried to reach out and warn him, but it was too late. The football was inches away. However, before it made contact, the ball was redirected—as if pushed by some invisible force. It altered from a perfect spiral to a haphazard spin that passed between Laney and Kael and fell harmlessly to the ground behind them.

But that didn't make any sense, Laney thought. The ball was about to hit him.

"What just happened?" she asked, but Kael was already glaring at a confused Aaron and Brody. It was obvious who their intended target was.

Kael leaned down to pick up the football and then pumped it in his hands. "You missed," he said, bringing it close to the side of his face to concentrate and whisper something over the leather binding.

"*Hurt.*"

When he threw the football back to Brody, it took on a mind of its own and became a rocket aimed directly for his solar plexus. It struck just under his shoulder pads like a missile, causing Brody to keel over in pain the moment he caught it.

Silence consumed the track. Everyone was stunned. And Kael realized he might have overdone it.

"Whoa…" Laney even said beside him.

Coach Winters finally took note of the situation unfolding and quickly yelled to disperse the gathering crowd. "Alright, that's enough gawking! Get back to work!" But just as Kael thought he was in the clear, he heard his name called just as loudly from the goliath of a man. "Clark! Get over here!"

Yep, definitely overdid it.

After nodding to Laney, Kael jogged over to where Brody and the coach were standing. As the quarterback stood passive, Winters lowered his usual screaming tone to a more tolerable holler. "That was quite the throw," he said, staring first at Kael and then at Brody. "Both of you. You two have a problem I should know about?"

The two glared at each other with more malice than usual. "No, no problem," Kael replied. "Your team might, though, if your quarterback doesn't learn how to throw the ball better this season."

"What'd you just say?" Brody demanded, hot-tempered and ready for a fight after essentially what amounted to a punch in the gut from Kael's throw. Winters stopped him with a hand against his chest.

"You know, in my day, if we had a problem with another kid, we settled it on the field. We didn't bicker about it like a couple of little pansies. What do you say, Clark? You man enough to see what you're made of out here?"

Kael smirked. He knew he was being baited, but he also knew his gym teacher had no idea what he was capable of. Neither did Brody.

"You know, why not?" Kael replied. "Your boys could use the exercise."

"Alright then," Winters said. "You know how to play?"

"I may be from the city, but it's still Nebraska," Kael said. "Yeah, I know how to play."

"Then you'll be quarterback for the blue team and Brody for the gold." Coach looked up to call over some other players. "Get Clark here some pads and a helmet, will ya?"

"Don't bother," Kael said. "They won't touch me."

Coach Winters eyed the youth suspiciously as Brody scoffed at the notion of playing full contact without gear. The coach, however, gave a sickening smile as he came up with a terrible idea. "Then how about we make it more interesting… You play chess, Clark?"

The question seemed odd coming from a gym teacher. "I've played it before…"

"Ever heard of cursed chess?" Winters took the boy's silence as a no. "In cursed chess, no piece can occupy the squares surrounding the kings, leaving them more exposed. How about we apply this idea to your little game? No gear for either you or Maxwell. Shirt versus skin. First one of you to bleed loses. Deal?"

Both boys looked at each other with uncertainty before Kael shrugged. Brody, on the other hand, wasn't as content with the agreement. "But Coach," he complained, "our first game's next weekend. What if I actually get hurt?"

"Then you'll learn not to start a match you can't win, won't ya?" Winters replied seriously. "Besides, a little fear on the field does the mind good." He turned to Kael. "You don't mind being skins, do ya, Clark?"

"I mean, usually I wait for a second date first, but…" Kael took off the school gym shirt and tossed it away, revealing his muscular build underneath. "Sure."

The gym teacher's eyes became transfixed on the cross dangling from Kael's neck. "Lose the jewelry too," he said. "Wouldn't want you getting choked on it."

The look Coach Winters gave Kael as he eyed his necklace made him feel uneasy. He'd gotten a lot of looks from a lot of different types of people, but they didn't usually scare him. He wasn't sure why, but for some reason, the gym teacher did.

"It stays on," Kael finally replied.

The coach scowled. "Then show us what you've got." As Kael and Brody jogged out to the middle of the field, Winters stopped Drew and Frankie by raising his hand. "You know what to do," he said, waiting for the two to acknowledge his order before allowing them to chase their target onto the field.

Kael waited as his team took off their shirts from underneath their pads and tossed them to the sidelines. Meanwhile, the entire gym class stopped their running and stood on the track to watch. All but two of them were waiting for a massacre to occur. And as Lee came to stand beside Laney, they waited for the two teams to get into position.

"Geez, no wonder you're crushing on him," Lee said to Laney. "You see those abs? I think even I'm crushing on him now."

The accusation snapped Laney out of her concentration. "I am not crushing on him, Lee."

"Uh huh, okay," Lee replied before watching the players set up their formations.

But Laney became fixated on Kael's right shoulder blade. She hadn't seen it earlier that morning, but he had a black tribal lion tattoo that took up most of his right side. She didn't know why it surprised her that he had a tattoo.

"I hope he knows what he's doing..." Lee said.

"Yeah." Laney kept her scrutinizing gaze on Kael. "Me too."

"It's your ball, Clark!" Brody yelled as his part of the team formed up the defensive line. "Try not to end up in a wheelchair when I come for it!"

"Do you wake up extra early to sound like a Degrassi villain or is it just natural for you?"

Setting up for the hike, Kael watched as Brody nodded to each of his own offensive linemen. The teen grinned, fully realizing his "team" wouldn't be providing much coverage for him at all. Something they didn't realize he was completely fine with.

As he snapped the ball, Kael immediately drew back several paces. His offensive line slammed half-heartedly against the defensive one, letting more than half the opposition through to sack him. Kael did a pump fake to cause one to jump while dodging around the rest to find an opening.

Realizing that none of his receivers had even bothered to get open, the temporary quarterback instead concentrated deeply on the power within him. If they weren't going to play fair, then neither was he...

With Brody and the entire defensive line charging him, Kael raced back toward them at full speed, his eyes full of fierce light. As they tried to tackle him, he began whispering words too low for anyone but him to hear.

"*Trip.*"

"*Miss.*"

"*Fall.*"

And they did. Everyone who came near him.

Once he had created a sufficient opening, he dodged around the rest like a ghost. And to the players, that's exactly what it felt like they were trying to grab. Every time they even got close, something invisible seemed to stop them.

Some of them tripped over their own feet, others crashed into one another, but not a single one of them succeeded in laying a hand on Kael.

Drew and Frankie came the closest—Kael's powers failing to trip them up for some reason—but even they fell short of touching him.

After dodging the entire defensive line single-handedly, Kael sprinted to the end zone on the other side of the field, leaving his unhelpful and uncooperative teammates speechless as he did so. Lee, on the other hand, was anything but. He couldn't contain himself. He raced down the field on the sidelines, cheering Kael on.

However, Laney continued watching every one of Kael's movements even more carefully than before. No human being could move like that, she thought. She doubted even she could dodge the entire football team and make it look so effortless. She began reevaluating her original assessment of Kael's normalcy. There was just no way.

"Please tell me you got his number for me," Mercury said, appearing beside Laney in her overly revealing crop top and cheer shorts.

"I don't think he has one," Laney replied, maintaining her laser focus on the field. "Hey, have you noticed anything weird about him?"

"You mean beside the fact that he's kicking our entire football team's butt and he's superhot?" Mercury replied, biting her lower lip. "Nope, just those things mostly."

Realizing she wasn't going to get anywhere with her smitten friend, Laney decided to abandon the conversation until Mercury was a bit less entranced. Reluctantly, she joined in with the now enthusiastic applause the rest of the class was giving Kael.

For the next half hour, every play turned out remarkably similar to the first. Kael would snap the ball, his offensive line would all but abandon him, he would do an entire run solo, and he'd score a touchdown. This happened over and over until, eventually, he was more embarrassed for the team than they were for themselves.

"So," he said, tossing the ball to a furious Brody, "how'd that taste?"

Kael made sure to pass by Laney on his way to the locker room. She was still standing next to Mercury.

"You gonna try out for the team?" Mercury asked with a flirtatious smile. He looked back toward the fuming football players.

"Something tells me I'm not wanted," Kael replied with a grin of his own before flashing his green and purple eyes to Laney with a wink.

She rolled hers in response.

After instantly becoming one of the most popular people in school, the last thing Kael needed was an even bigger head.

CHAPTER 13

After class, the students were dismissed to the locker rooms to change back into their normal clothes and wait for the bell. Once it sounded their freedom, the front of the school flooded with escaping bodies.

Lee offered Kael another ride home in his beat-up old Nissan, which he was about to decline until he saw Laney walking with Mercury right past the row of buses. He guessed she wasn't bound to public school transport anymore.

"Where's your car?" Mercury asked Laney as they entered the parking lot.

"Grounded," she replied.

"Seriously? Why didn't you tell me this morning? I would've come and picked you up."

"I didn't want to make you drive all the way over to Glenwood, Merc. Besides..." Laney drifted off, noticing Kael and Lee making their own way through the parking lot. This was her chance to get some answers.

"Hey, where are you going?" Mercury asked, watching as her friend bounded away from her.

Laney turned but kept walking backwards. "I'll text you later, okay?" she said, waving.

But Mercury could see where she was heading. Directly for Kael and Lee Muramasa. She didn't want to admit it, but she began to feel the familiar touches of jealousy. She hated that part of herself, but it wasn't the first time she'd been jealous of her best friend. And judging from Laney's sudden interest in her new crush, it wouldn't be the last.

Laney appeared next to Kael as he opened Lee's passenger side door. They were surprised to see her, but Lee recovered fast enough to say, "Oh hey, Laney."

"Hey, Lee," she replied with a warm smile. "Do you mind if I grab a ride home?"

The young Japanese kid blinked, obviously taken aback by her request. Not that he wasn't willing to grant it, just that he wasn't expecting her to ask. "Sure…" he said, still confused.

Laney took it as reluctance and wanted to make sure she wasn't imposing. "You are taking Kael to Mr. Shen's, right?"

"Yeah! I mean, it's no problem at all to take you! I just thought you'd ride with Mercury."

"She can't today," she lied. "And I lost my car for a month. So I really appreciate this!"

Still holding the passenger door open, Kael remained silent through the exchange until motioning for Laney to take the front seat. Closing the door for her, he climbed into the back.

Lee plopped into the driver's seat and turned the key. The car made several guttural utterances that told everyone it wouldn't be starting. Embarrassed, the young man smiled awkwardly at his two passengers. "This happens sometimes," he explained. "No worries, though! I know how to fix it."

He didn't. But as he popped the hood and went to investigate, he tried to make it look as convincing as possible that he did.

"What do you think the chances are that he actually knows anything about this car?" Laney asked.

"Zero," Kael replied, leaning back with his hands behind his head. "But I'll give him a minute before I go help him."

Laney casually eyed the boy behind her, as if trying to peel back the layers of the mystery surrounding him. "So," she finally said. "That was some show you put on earlier…"

Kael didn't like how skeptical she sounded. "Yeah," he replied, opening his eyes. "Just got lucky, I guess."

"Between that and the wreck that obliterated Mr. Shen's car, you must be the luckiest guy alive." Laney analyzed him, desperate to find some hint of a lie behind his multicolored eyes.

"What can I say? Adrenaline does weird things." Kael was uneasy with how close to accusatory their conversation was becoming. He should've known not to let his ego get the better of him in that football match, but was she actually onto him? Deciding not to find out, he tried to turn the conversation around.

"What about you, huh?" he asked with a smile. "You didn't even break a sweat out there. I like to think I'm in pretty good shape, and I could barely keep up with you. Not to mention you jumping that cemetery fence last night like a gazelle."

"What can I say?" she repeated mockingly. "Adrenaline does weird things."

Kael remained quiet. If Laney was suspicious of him, it was obvious she wasn't going to come right out and say it. And it was just as obvious to Laney that Kael wasn't either.

Kael decided to end the tension quickly by squeezing through the space between the two front seats and turning the key one more time—this time with supernatural assistance.

Start.

Lee, who was randomly tapping on things underneath the hood with no idea what he was actually doing, was shocked when the engine suddenly sputtered to life. He joyously slammed the hood and returned to the driver's seat just as Kael was leaning back.

"Guess it just needed one more crank," Kael said.

The quiet drive back to Shen and Laney's neighborhood was deafening. None of the three knew what to say to the other, and even Lee's usual chattiness had been silenced by the awkwardness.

When they finally pulled up on the street in front of Shen's house, Laney thanked Lee before walking across the street to disappear behind the red door of her house.

"Man, that was weird, huh? I mean, why would Laney Lessenger ask me for a ride home? Do you think Mercury asked her to?"

"Thanks for the ride," Kael said, ignoring Lee's attempt for conversation and stepping out of the car.

"Hey, you want one in the morning?" Lee yelled while manually rolling down the passenger side window. No response. "Oh my gosh, Lee, that would be great, how generous," he imitated in a mocking tone before shifting back to his normal voice. "Oh, no trouble, Kael. What are best friends for?"

While the teen put his car into gear and drove away, Kael mentally prepared himself for whatever waited for him behind Shen's front door. He'd been trying to distract himself all day by playing the part of a typical high school student, but it was time for the weird part of his life to take over. The real part. Convince the man or angel or whatever lived in the house looming before him to give up all his secrets.

He turned the knob to do just that.

What Kael heard when he entered the foyer surprised him. Laughter? From the kitchen?

But it wasn't Shen's laughter he heard. The accent underneath it wasn't so distinct, even though the laughter itself was. Low, hardy, and boisterous, as if right from the belly…

"Graves?" Kael asked, entering the kitchen to find both Shen and his probation officer sitting and chuckling at the kitchen table over two cups of tea.

"Well, hey there, Cabbagepatch!" Graves said while raising the cup of tea to his lips. "How's my favorite fostered delinquent?"

"Wondering why you're still in Kearney," Kael replied. "Couldn't trust me for one day?"

"Couldn't trust you for one second," Graves said. "Especially the second you were out of my sight. But that's not the only reason I'm here."

Graves placed the empty cup back on the table where Shen began to refill it from the pot between them. Graves nodded to his host with a smile and continued. "No, I wanted to get to know the man who would be fostering you for the next few months. I gotta tell you, kid, I think you hit the jackpot with this one. Mr. Shen here is a hoot."

"A hoot?" Kael raised an eyebrow. "Be older, Graves."

"You see how he treats me? I don't know how you're gonna deal with it, Mr. Shen, but God bless you for trying."

Shen smiled. "Would you like to stay for dinner, Captain? I must warn you, though, I've heard the Chinese food here is terrible."

Without warning, Graves burst out laughing again, and Kael could immediately tell it wasn't the first time that phrase had been uttered that day. Inside jokes? the young man thought. The two already had inside jokes? Because there was no way Graves knew that line was from a movie.

When he finally got his laughter under control, Graves wiped a tear from his eye and exhaled with a whistle. "No, no, I better get going back to Omaha," he said, staring down at the mostly full cup of tea. "But I wouldn't mind taking some of this delicious tea for the road. Only if it's not too much trouble."

"Certainly," Shen replied. He retrieved a travel mug from a cupboard and set it down in front of his guest. After the probation officer emptied his cup of tea into the mug, Shen began pouring from the pot to fill it the rest of the way. However, halfway through his pouring, Shen slipped and spilled some of the herbal mixture on Graves' shirt and blazer, causing him to shoot back from his seat.

"Oh! I'm so sorry!" Shen grabbed a kitchen towel and patted the taller man down to dry him off. The whole scene looked suspicious to Kael.

"No, it's alright," Graves said politely, sweeping his hands over the wet spots to finish Shen's attempts at drying. "It's just tea." Graves reached back to the table to put the lid on the travel mug, which still had most of its contents inside. "Really good tea, I might add. Thank you, Mr. Shen, for the hospitality. Cabbagepatch, you stay out of trouble."

Kael rolled his eyes while Shen bowed his head in response. "Safe travels, Captain," he said as the trio made their way from the kitchen to the hallway to the front door where Shen opened it for Graves.

"Actually, Mr. Shen, may I speak with Kael alone for a minute?"

"Of course," the Chinese man replied. He departed with another bow and strolled back into the kitchen to start cleaning the dishes.

When Shen was out of earshot, Graves turned back toward Kael. "So, seriously, how's it going so far?"

"Oh, are you asking me now? I seem to remember not having a choice in the matter."

"You really don't," Graves replied. "Still, that doesn't mean I don't care. You know how this relationship works, kid. You act like a jerk. I act like a jerk. I try doing what's best for you. You complain about it. We wake up the next day and do it all over again."

"Wait," Kael replied with his hand over his heart. "You think I'm a jerk?" When Graves gave no response except for his serious stare, Kael understood the time for jokes had passed. "Fine," he relented. "It's actually been better than I thought it'd be." Kael's eyes drifted toward the kitchen.

"More interesting anyway…"

Graves was shocked. In the eight years he'd been assigned to Kael Clark, not once had he heard him describe anything as "interesting." The smile that parted his lips was telling of someone who'd finally obtained some small victory over one of his life's greatest challenges.

As Graves stepped out onto the front porch, he and Kael caught Laney walking a full trash bag down to one of the two bins at the bottom of her driveway. When her eyes met theirs, she tried to give a polite smile to the stranger she'd never met while still studying Kael. After realizing she was staring for too long, she turned back and disappeared around the side of her house.

Graves turned back to the boy standing next to him. "Oh, now I get it! I should've known. Does that interest of yours have anything to do with a pretty blonde?"

"What?" Kael snapped out of his stare. "Of course not."

"Really?" Graves asked with a grin. "Well, that's good to hear because I know another girl from Omaha who wouldn't be too happy about it. You may be special, kid, but trust me, one girlfriend's enough for any man."

"Laney isn't my girlfriend," Kael stated. "And neither is Renae. We're just friends."

"So, Laney's her name?"

Kael quickly realized he needed to end the conversation. "Alright," he said, leaning inward on the doorframe to usher his probation officer toward his car.

Graves raised his nose and sniffed the air ostentatiously. "No, yep, there's no doubt about it. That's definitely love in the air."

"Shut up and focus on getting back to Omaha before midnight, old-timer."

Graves' smile became all teeth. "Do you guys have pet names yet? She can't use Cabbagepatch. That one's mi—"

Kael swung the door shut on his probation officer whose boisterous laughter could be heard throughout the entire neighborhood. Kael winced in embarrassment before making his way back into the kitchen to find Shen finishing the last dish in the sink.

"I see you didn't tell Captain Graves about the hostilities you're experiencing at school," Shen said without turning. Kael tried not to show his surprise.

"Did Mr. Matthews call?"

"No, you were just thinking about it the entire time he was here."

Which he had been. Kael was worried the only reason Graves paid a visit at all was to drag him back to juvie. The officer had made it pretty clear that this was the state's last chance for Kael. Any kind of altercation would be enough to revoke it.

"Fortunately, that's not the case," Shen said, divining his thoughts once more.

"Can you not do that?"

"Do what?" Shen asked innocently.

"Read my mind without my permission. It's kind of annoying."

"As you wish." Shen's eyes dropped to the floor, seemingly staring at something unseen until he raised them back to meet Kael's. "Just one more thing. You should invite Miss Lessenger and Mister Muramasa over for dinner sometime. It's nice you are making friends."

"Dude..."

"Okay, okay," Shen chuckled, waving his arms in front of his chest.

Kael stared at him incredulously. Not because of the apparent humor his caretaker found in invading mental privacy but because of another question that came to mind.

"So why'd you spill tea on Graves? We both know you're not really that clumsy. Actually, the last time I saw you act like that was at the police station with that secretary. So what gives with the dumb and dumber act?"

Shen was mildly surprised Kael had caught on to his police station stunt at all. He would've thought him too inwardly focused at the time. He was happy to be mistaken.

"Spilling tea on Captain Graves caused him to leave four seconds later than he would have otherwise."

Kael furrowed his brow. "So what?"

"He left four seconds later. Which means he had his conversation with you four seconds later, got into his car four seconds later, and will now miss a deer crossing the highway just outside of Lincoln four seconds later than when he would have collided with it head on."

Kael's expression changed from confusion to skepticism. "Are you saying you just saved his life?"

Shen shrugged in response. "Or from a mild concussion and several lacerations to his face and forearm. Either way, he will make it back home without incident now."

"So you just saved him from some car trouble and a couple scrapes and bruises?"

"You do not need a life-or-death reason to help someone, Kael. No reason at all is enough. Learn to apply in the right place... at the right time... the power to change something for the better. Even something small. Doing so you can change the world."

Shen let Kael ruminate on his words while he put away the last of the dishes. Kael knew he didn't want Graves to get into any kind of wreck on his way home, not even a mildly inconveniencing one like what Shen had described, but still... He thought about all the times he had the power to help someone and didn't. Yeah, he helped Lee, but that was still out of personal interest and a desire to hit something. If the theory of evolution was correct, it dictated that the superior members of the species—namely Kael and Shen with their powers—should adapt and survive while disregarding the others to die off. What Shen proposed was the exact opposite.

It recreated a gnawing question in Kael's mind that he'd been wrestling with for years...

What was the purpose of his power?

"So," Shen said, breaking into Kael's thoughts. "Are you ready to begin your training?"

"Sure," Kael replied, acting uninterested on purpose. In truth, he'd been thinking about it all day. "Where do we start?"

"Upstairs," Shen said. He motioned for Kael to exit the kitchen and head for the staircase. When both were at its top step, Shen pointed to the strange-looking wooden door at the end of the hallway. The one Kael couldn't open last night.

"Now what?" Kael asked.

"Open it."

Kael tried the handle and found that it was still locked. He was hesitant to admit what he was about to say but figured Shen already knew about it anyway. "I tried my powers on it last night," he said. "It won't budge."

"I know." Shen smiled. "It will now."

Shen made another hand gesture for Kael to continue, so the young man closed his eyes and began to concentrate.

Open.

His thought became reality. He heard several clicks and turns of locking mechanisms unlocking themselves on a door that appeared to only have one lock. When he turned the handle, a blinding white light shot through the cracks of the door and illuminated the entire hallway behind him. Brazenly, he swung the door open and stepped through until he was entirely engulfed in the warming sensation of the light. When he was on the other side, he found that he was standing in an endless void of blank white space.

"What... is this?" Kael asked, looking everywhere at the nothingness that surrounded him. He turned back to make sure Shen had followed him through.

"This is your training arena," the old man replied, closing the door behind him. Kael watched as it evaporated into mist as if it were never there.

"What happened to the door?" he asked frantically.

"Oh, don't worry about that. It disappears so it won't get in the way."

"Get in the way of what?" Looking around, Kael realized there was nothing to get in the way of. It was him and Shen standing in an infinitely vast white dimension of nothing. It was jarring. His eyes couldn't adjust to looking everywhere and nowhere all at once. And every word he spoke seemed to be smothered under an unseen blanket of fog. The entire atmosphere was oppressive. Even the gravity felt heavier.

"Where the hell did you bring me?"

"Language," Shen scolded.

"Sorry," Kael said sarcastically. "Where the h-e-double-hockey-sticks did you bring me?"

Shen ignored the sarcasm in favor of a lesson. "You appreciate science. You know what three-dimensional space is, correct?"

"Length, width, height, yeah," Kael replied, annoyed that he couldn't ever just get a straight answer.

"What about four-dimensional?"

"You mean like a tesseract?" Kael asked, proud of himself for not getting tripped up. "Or the theory that the fourth dimension is time?"

"Why does it have to be one or the other?" Shen asked. "For your universe, time, space, and matter form a continuum. They are linked."

"What do you mean by your universe? What else is there?"

"Everything else," Shen said matter-of-factly. "For someone who says the word 'hell' a lot, if you think the real Heaven and Hell exist inside your universe, you're vastly mistaken. Even in this place, we're outside the laws of reality. In a higher dimensional space of my own design. A pocket dimension if you will. Bound only by my imagination. Research

Euclid's five postulates and Gödel's incompleteness theorems for a deeper explanation."

Kael was shocked by how casually Shen explained advanced physics like he was explaining how to make tea. "So, what? God's a scientist now?"

"Science is just man's explanation for God's creation."

Kael hated that. "Yeah, who created God then?" he asked while peering around the empty space.

"Asking who created God begs the question who created the thing that created the thing that created God. It keeps retreating backward with no answer. Therefore, logic dictates there must be an uncaused cause. An infinite God."

"Or nothing at all," Kael replied. "What if the universe is a closed system where nothing outside of it exists?"

"If that were true, the universe itself would be illogical and science invalid. All that love you have for it would be pointless. If the universe was always an infinite singularity of time, space, and matter prior to the big bang, then why would it change? What could possibly cause infinity to change? Unless it wasn't infinite in the first place and something truly infinite outside of it caused it to change." Shen eyed the struggling youth with sympathetic eyes. "True infinity is a difficult thing for human beings to understand. You think of everything in beginnings and endings because that's all you've ever known. Therefore, the concept eludes you. But if you think the Creator of the universe is bound by the laws of the universe He created, then you're thinking of the wrong kind of creator. God is no more bound by time, space, and matter than the moviemaker is bound by what he creates on screen. They both exist outside their own creation."

Kael hesitated, letting it all sink in. "It's a good argument."

"I'm not trying to argue, Kael. Or belittle you. You asked a question. I answered."

All of Shen's knowledge and power combined with the fact that he could seemingly create entire dimensions started to make Kael wonder if he could actually be an angel. And wonder what other massive stunts of otherworldly power the old man was capable of…

"Yeah, well," the teenager remarked, trying his best to change the subject. "For a complex higher dimensional space, this place is a little bland, don't you think?"

"Right," Shen replied. "Which is why I think I'll call it the Canvas… a room built for creation."

"How far does it go?" Kael asked while trying to find a point in the distance to focus on. There wasn't one.

"How far can you imagine?" Shen grinned. Kael half-expected him to say, "to infinity and beyond." He was glad he didn't.

"Why's it feel like I'm drinking the air in here?"

"Perfect training conditions. I made the gravity slightly harsher too. It will minimally affect the time dilation, but if you can master exerting yourself in this atmosphere, imagine what you will be able to accomplish outside of it."

"So, we're working on my physique now? And here I thought I was in pretty good shape already."

"For a human, sure," Shen said. "But not for a King. And not for what you will be fighting."

"And what exactly will I be fighting?" Kael asked before Shen's silent stare gave him his answer. "Demons. Right…" Kael had to stop himself from rolling his eyes. "Well, I've never been hurt before so…"

Shen knew Kael's next question before he even asked it. "You've never been hurt before because you have a guardian watching over you."

"A guardian?" Kael asked. "Like a guardian angel? Just how many of you are there? I don't suppose he wants to show himself either."

"In time, he won't have to," Shen explained. "You'll see him with your own power. Right now, he'll remain invisible and continue protecting you."

"Of course."

Shen grinned. "Have a little faith."

Kael didn't know why, but Shen's confidence always seemed to win him over. Every word he ever said was spoken with absolute certainty. Like the old man couldn't lie even if he wanted to. That was reassuring to Kael. All people ever did was lie to him.

"Alright, well let's get this glorified gym class started then," Kael said, stretching his arms across both sides. "What's first?"

"First, your necklace." Shen pointed.

Kael didn't respond, just looked down and gripped the bulk of the cross hanging over his shirt. "What about it?"

Disappearing from his position with pure speed, Shen reappeared in front of his student and grabbed the chain hanging around his neck. "We are going to begin with it."

Too shocked to counter at first, a lagging Kael swiped at Shen, but the old man disappeared back to his original position faster than he had initially moved. He let the Celtic cross dangle from his fingertips next to the Chinese cross he wore around his own neck.

"Give that back, Gray!"

"Do you know what this is?"

"Yeah, the last thing my mom ever gave to me. Now give it back."

"And why did she give it to you? You've made it quite clear you do not believe in anything you cannot see for yourself. Why would she entrust a symbol of her faith to a son who has none?"

"Maybe she believed enough for the both of us, alright? Now give it back!"

"Or maybe it's because this is something far more valuable than just a keepsake…"

Without warning, the cross in Shen's hand extended and became a four-foot-long, silver-white broadsword composed entirely of a metal that shined with an otherworldly brilliance.

"What… what did you just do?" Kael asked.

"This was never a necklace, Kael. It goes by many names… adamantine, orichalcum, the prime compound, element x, the all-forge, omnimetal. But it is what we angels call Arch Steel. The chief steel. Our metal."

Shen began slicing the sword in front of him in grand sweeping gestures, as if to demonstrate its power. "It is composed of every element. And none of them. All at the same time. Elements that do and do not exist in this universe."

The broadsword suddenly became a solid gold bo staff that Shen began whipping masterfully around his body. "It can become anything," he said, transforming the staff into a katana blade made of jasper that he used to practice several sword techniques with. "It can cut through everything." Becoming its original silver-white form once again, the katana sliced through the air in front of Shen, splitting open the very fabric of space between him and Kael, allowing the shocked teen to see back into the wood-paneled interior of Shen's home. The tear in space closed in on itself almost as quickly as it opened.

Shen stood straight with the sword still in his hand. "Here," he said while tossing the katana underhanded to him.

Frightened, Kael closed his eyes and reached out. What he caught was the necklace transformed back into its original form.

"Now, you do it," Shen said, as if he was asking Kael to hit a tee-ball off the tee rather than wield one of the most powerful weapons in the universe. "Concentrate and form it into a weapon."

"Wait, is your necklace the same thing? Arch Steel or whatever?"

"Yes. All angels possess their own." Shen nodded. "Now concentrate."

"I'll try…" He regretted the words immediately.

"No! Do or do not—"

"Please do not quote Yoda to me right now," Kael begged. He switched his gaze from Shen to the pendant in his hand. To him, it had always just been a memento of his mom. He couldn't believe it was a metal wielded by angels. Assuming he was starting to believe that's what Shen really was.

It begged the question though... Why did his mother have it?

As Shen finished Yoda's line under his breath, Kael closed his eyes and concentrated on what he wanted the necklace to become. He imagined it was just like using any of his other powers. Think it. Will it. Make it a reality.

And then it was.

In his hand, he suddenly felt the metal change in shape as his necklace transformed into what his mind had pictured. A sword. Similar in shape to the one Shen first made but still different. It had a slightly smaller handguard and didn't possess the same silver-white glow, instead taking on a dullish gray hue.

"Hey, I did it!" Kael marveled at his creation while struggling with its weight.

"Very good," Shen said, stepping forward to examine it more carefully. "And interesting... You transformed it into lead. Why lead?"

"I don't know," Kael replied defensively. "I just pictured a sword, and it became a sword. It's my first time, Gray, give me a break."

A deeply thoughtful "hmm" was Shen's reply. "Well, even if it isn't true Arch Steel just yet, the shape of the weapon itself is not bad at all for your first try."

"So how do I turn it into true Arch Steel?"

"With time and training."

Kael could tell that was the only answer he was going to receive at the moment, so he let the lead sword return to its original state and stared at the cross in the palm of his hand. He still couldn't believe everything that had changed in his life since yesterday morning.

It all still felt like a dream.

"Last night, you said my mom was a Seer," he said, gingerly winding the chain through his fingers. "So then how did she come across something like angel steel?"

"A good question," Shen replied with a smile, "for another time."

Again, Kael knew that was all he was going to get out of Shen for the time being. Still… "Then just tell me this… I'm not like some half-angel or something, am I?"

"Why? Are you starting to believe me now?"

"No," Kael stated. "It's just…"

Knowing his thoughts without reading his mind, Shen smiled but shook his head. "Your mother was an angel to everyone who knew her, Kael. But she was human." Then, as if seeing the boy's actual question behind his eyes… "And so are you."

Kael didn't want to admit it, but he was disappointed in Shen's answer. If he had been half-angel or whatever, it would explain so much. More importantly, if his mom had been one, that would mean she wasn't really gone. After all, angels couldn't die… could they?

"So are you finally ready to learn more about what you really are?"

"You already went over this," Kael said. "A King, right? And I'm supposed to find and protect some Seal using the power of The Word, which comes from some spiritual energy source called The White. Oh, and something about demons. Did I miss anything?"

Shen sighed.

"Nothing personal, Gray, but I'm just barely starting to believe in the supernatural," Kael said. "Throw in all this other stuff I've never even heard of, and you've lost me."

"Hmm." Shen nodded. "Then perhaps this will help…"

The old man raised his left hand in a closed fist. When he opened it palm forward, he cast a never-ending shadow from his position that stretched into the infinite white landscape, painting the whole of it pitch-black. In the darkness, Shen closed his fist again and ignited a single flame of white fire on the ground that snaked its way into a large white symbol—a crown with seven points and heraldic flourishes on the edges that surrounded the base. Somehow the symbol felt familiar to Kael. He studied it, losing his train of thought until Shen snapped his fingers, prompting a disembodied voice to begin speaking.

"The Crown of Kings is an organization that has existed for nearly two millennia…" The voice came from the void itself and was not Shen's. It had a much deeper and more authoritative tone.

"Did you seriously create your own narrator to explain this to me?"

"My dimension." Shen shrugged. "My rules."

"I'm shocked it's not Morgan Freeman."

"Ooh, that would be better…"

Suddenly, the projection changed, as did the voice. The fiery white symbol extinguished itself and was replaced with a group of seven multicolored rune-like symbols, each with a different pattern and color associated with them. Red, orange, yellow, green, blue, indigo, violet… They began rapidly encircling Kael and Shen. While the young man was analyzing them, the voice, now Morgan Freeman, continued.

"Two thousand years ago, Seven Seals forbidden to be unsealed were hidden on Earth. However, there were mortals who became obsessed with finding and breaking the Seals under the false belief that they could forcibly cause Eschaton to occur. The end of the world. Believing their actions to be the will of God, these fanatical men grouped together and became known as the Court of Judges."

The image of the Seven Seals smeared into a painted pastel of assorted colors and reformed as seven infants drawn in the style of serigraphy. An army of black-robed warriors then appeared to slay the infants—the Seals—in order from the first to the seventh. However, seven swordsmen with glowing purple eyes and crowns adorning their heads stepped forward to protect each child, fighting back with shining silver-white swords like the one Shen had wielded earlier.

"Eschaton would only occur if all Seven Seals were undone by an Arch Steel weapon in the proper sequence. Therefore, seven warriors were chosen to protect them. These men were imbued with The White, gifted with the power of The Word, and called Kings. Their power would spread to others, an organization that came to be known as the Crown. Every generation, Seven Kings would be chosen above the others, sworn to protect the Seven Seals until the advent of the King of Kings."

As the swordsmen in the luminous painting fought off the infants' attackers, all fourteen figures aged and faded to dust. Then seven new Kings and seven new Seals were born to take their place. As the painting continued, it illustrated this process on loop until a Seal was eventually slain by one of the Judges. After the host died, a disaster in the world took place. Famine, storms, war... However, the Seals were never destroyed in the proper order, so the sequence always reset, sparing the world time and time again.

It was a lot for Kael to take in. A lot more than he wanted to believe.

"You never told me the Seals were people..." he said as Shen waved away the dark visions and returned them to the blank landscape.

"Yes," he replied. "And you are one of the Seven Kings chosen to protect them."

Kael held his hand just under his right eye. He thought of its purple hue, how he had never seen anyone else with any color like it. But they each had two. Why did he only have one?

"What happens when the host of a Seal dies naturally?"

"Then the Seal moves on to a new host without being unsealed."

"This can't be real..."

"It is real, Kael," Shen replied. "You must find the Seventh Seal. Your Seal. Protect them. And fulfill your destiny."

Kael winced at the word "destiny." He hated it. Hated everything that this was turning into. Give him an enemy to fight. Give him monsters even. But don't give him responsibility. Not over someone else's life. He could handle anything. He couldn't handle that...

"You know, I never asked for any of this!" he shouted. "And I don't want it. You chose the wrong guy."

"I did not choose you."

"Right, it was God or destiny or whatever." The disdain in Kael's voice was evident.

"And that's hard for you to believe?"

"I just don't like the thought of not being in control of my own life."

"You are in control, Kael," Shen said seriously. "Walk away now if that's what you want. Like I said last night, I won't stop you. But your understanding is flawed. You think fate and free will are mutually exclusive."

"They are," Kael replied. "Just another problem I have with God. If he's real and knows everything like everyone claims, then he knows what I'm going to do before I do it. I don't have free will."

"Ironically, the only way you don't have free will is if God doesn't exist," Shen said. "If you're just a collection of atoms projected randomly forth at the onset of the universe, then everything you do is predestined fatalism. The atoms that make up your brain would give you the illusion of free will, but wouldn't they still just be moving forward in the direction they started from? No choice should mean no consequences, so why care? But no one truly lives that way."

Shen remained silent, staring deeply into Kael's eyes. Deciding show was better than tell, he raised his hand to change the vast landscape around them once again, this time to a park where kids were running around a playground. One little girl whose mother wasn't watching her was climbing on top of the monkey bars, trying to balance herself on the slick steel beams.

"Hey!" Kael called out until Shen held a hand on his chest.

"They can't see or hear you," he said.

"She's gonna fall, Gray! Let me go!"

Before Kael could do anything, the little girl did fall, and slammed to the hard ground below. She clutched her wrist and wailed. Her mom ran to her in worry. Shen waved away the scene just as she reached her.

"You knew she'd fall," Shen said.

Kael shook his head, realizing the lesson. "It's different. I suspected. I didn't know."

"Want me to replay it so you know?"

"That'd be different too. It'd be like going back in time."

"And God exists outside of time. He sees everything all at once, beginning to end. Just like when you know someone is making a mistake before they make it, you know the outcome they refuse to believe is going to happen. But your knowing doesn't mean they don't have a choice."

Kael remained silent, unhappy he didn't have a rebuttal.

Shen continued. "Just because God knows everything does not mean He forces you to do anything. My Father does not take slaves. We all make our own choices. And live with our own consequences."

"All the while he allows evil and horrible things to happen in the world," Kael retorted. "If God created everything and he's all-powerful, then he can't be all good. Nothing all good would create evil."

"He didn't create evil. He permitted choice. For a being of pure goodness, there are only four options when making creation. Not to make it at all. Make it obey Him. Make it amoral without good or evil. Or make it with the possibility of choice. Only the last one allows for free will. And only free will allows for love." Shen studied the young man before him with compassion. "You can't have it both ways, Kael. Either free will with the possibility of choosing evil or no free will at all."

Kael contemplated his response. "There are still a lot of things that don't require choice to create suffering. Disease. Disasters. Death. He allows those to occur. That's all I need to know about your father."

Shen's reply was quiet and calm. "And all I need to know," he said, "is that I do not know all. Do you?"

Kael's eyes narrowed. He was arrogant, but he wasn't arrogant enough to start declaring he knew everything. Especially since he barely knew where he was at the moment. But when it came to living with the consequences of his actions, he knew who was to blame...

Still, it was so much easier to blame God.

"For argument's sake, let's say I buy into all this," Kael said. "God, angels, demons, all of it. You're never going to convince me to follow him. Believing he exists and believing in him are two completely different things. If we're going to move forward with this training, you need to respect that."

Shen stared with the compassionate eyes that perplexed and infuriated Kael, ones that combatted his own sharp gaze. "And that is also your choice."

The old man's answer didn't satisfy the conflict Kael craved. So he committed himself to making one more decision of his own free will. "I'm also not searching for or becoming the protector of someone I've never even met. I'm no King. I'm here for myself and that's it. To see what I can do." At this point, Kael was venting, speaking emotionally just to speak. "You said there are others like me out there, right? Let one of them do it."

Shen raised his hand and made a massive ghostly globe appear above it, expanding its size until he could zoom in on Nebraska and illuminate the roads between Omaha and Kearney. "All Kings are drawn to the Seals closest to them," he explained. "But the Seven are drawn to their chosen Seven. That's why you ended up here in Kearney."

"Doesn't mean I have to do a thing about it."

"True," the angel replied. "As I said, it's your choice."

Kael hated how patronizing Shen sounded. Still, his mind was made up. He wasn't protecting anyone. He couldn't. "Alright then. As long as we're clear. Now, what am I supposed to do in here?"

Shen grinned. Raising his right hand, he snapped his fingers and waited for his young ward to be mesmerized by his power once again.

The Canvas began to quake as countless columns of wood, metal, and stone appeared from the floor of nothingness and soared high into the air of oblivion. With cracking and twisting sounds, the earthy elements began fashioning themselves into enormously complicated structures.

One was a large heptagonal sparring platform made from the wood and metal that descended back to the floor and seemed to display an archaic form of the yin-yang symbol at its center.

Another was an even larger area where most of the massive boulders fell like meteors into a haphazard pattern Kael couldn't understand.

However, farther away, and much more to the teenager's amazement, an array of supernatural blocks appeared out of thin air and began fashioning themselves into a massively complex cylindrical tower that appeared to be thousands of feet tall. Even though it was gray in color and monstrously larger, it somehow reminded him of a straightened-out version of the Leaning Tower of Pisa. Or even the mythical Tower of Babel. The only difference was that the entire structure was rotating, spinning in a slow-moving vortex on the outside while the inside shifted its own moving parts around like some insane Rubik's Cube.

To finish off his display, Shen spun his finger one more time in the air to make a golden crown appear slanted atop Kael's head. "You're supposed to train like a King."

Kael took the crown off and dropped it to the floor. "Cute. But I told you I'm not a King." He gripped the necklace in his hand and transformed it into a lead broadsword once again. "I do see a sparring ring though. Does that mean you're ready for a rematch?"

Shen had to force himself not to laugh at the confident youth's over-estimation of his power. "You would die." Tucking his own Chinese cross of Arch Steel back under his shirt, he added, "No, first you will start with that."

Shen pointed at the spiraling tower of mystical blocks, its seemingly infinite number of shifting parts levitating just above the white ground and disappearing high into the white sky.

"And what exactly am I supposed to do?"

"Climb it" was the overly simplistic reply. "Until you find the piece that looks like a bull's head. Then plunge your blade into it. Hopefully by then, it will be true Arch Steel. If so, you will have passed the Tower and will be ready for the next challenge."

Kael stared at the circling spire with injected eyes. His heart skipped several beats as he tried to fathom what Shen was asking of him.

"Surely you can't be serious…"

"I am serious," Shen replied, pausing too long afterward and giving away the movie he was about to quote.

"And don't call me Shirley."

"And don't call me Shirley."

Kael said it in unison with the old man, temporarily distracting himself from the daunting task placed before him.

"No human being can climb that," he said, not even sure where he would begin even if he wanted to try. Which he didn't.

"Center yourself in The White," Shen said. "You've used it to manifest the power of The Word before, but its power can also flow through your body as well, lending it strength and speed beyond anything you can imagine."

Kael's eyes were still fixated on the Tower. It wasn't so much how he was going to climb it as the act itself that really bothered him.

Shen noticed the apprehension. "Do you remember I had three

questions I wanted to ask you over the course of your stay here?" he said. "Time for my second one. What are you afraid of?"

Still staring and starting to tremble at the thought of climbing the monstrosity before him, Kael hesitated but didn't lie. "I'm not that great with heights."

"I know," Shen replied sympathetically. "And I know why…"

Kael's eyes widened, realizing this man knew the worst thing he'd ever done in his life. The thing Kael had let define him for half of it.

It didn't seem to bother Shen though. "Use whatever you can to overcome your fear and reach the top."

"I'll…" He was about to say "try" but remembered. "Fine," he said instead.

"Well then, I will leave you to it." Shen waved, already on his way toward the door, which had rematerialized while Kael wasn't looking.

"Wait, where are you going?"

"To watch my films, of course!" the angel replied. "Just come get me when you make it to the top." Shen turned the knob on the door and was about to step through when he thought of something else. "Oh! One more thing. I have created this entire space as a place your guardian cannot enter. He will not be able to protect you while you're in here. I know you've never truly been hurt before. You can be in here."

"What? Why?"

"It would not be very good conditioning if there were no repercussions to your physical form. Just don't be reckless, and you'll be fine."

Shen turned to leave again when Kael thought of one last thing. "Hey, wait! How do I get out of here?"

"Just think about the door when you're ready to leave," Shen called back without turning around. "It will appear to you wherever you are."

With that, the door slammed shut and evaporated into thin air once again, leaving Kael alone with a lead broadsword in his hand and a cyclonic tower of supernatural blocks facing him.

He turned the sword back into its original form, clasped it around his neck, and walked forward until he was at the foot of the spinning mass. There was a small opening that would allow him to enter. He stepped inside and gaped at the enormity of the challenge before him.

Tens of thousands of moving parts made up the outer layer of the Tower, but the inside was even worse. Shifting platforms and footholds danced around each other above him like they were waltzing in no particular direction or order.

Staring up from the white ground of the Canvas, Kael was almost hypnotized by the impossibility of it all. He became lost in how the outer layers moved in a uniform spiral around the interior layers, while the interior layers all shifted as individual floors on top of one another like tiers of some hellish labyrinth.

Kael had to shake off his mesmeric state to do what Shen had instructed him to do. He concentrated on his power, not to affect the outside world like he had always done, but to affect himself. When he felt the power of The White surging through his legs, he waited for a large and low enough beam of brick to circle above him. When it did, Kael timed his jump and grabbed ahold of it as it continued to make its way around the other pieces.

After pulling himself up, Kael steadied his balance and analyzed the various makeshift platforms moving at different speeds all around him. Standing within the Tower, everything seemed to move much faster than it appeared from the outside. It was chaos.

However, there was one block that looked like a girder that kept circling in the opposite direction just above his head. If he could jump and grab it just as it was passing by, he'd be one step closer to the top.

Again, Kael waited for the piece to make its way around the spinning structure before timing his jump. Leaping straight up, he grabbed the new beam around its bottom flange and held himself steady.

Even though he was only a tier and a half up the structure, he made his first big mistake. He looked down. Twenty feet off the ground might as well have been twenty thousand as his vision betrayed and paralyzed him.

Just as he was about to drop and recollect himself, a small block came soaring just underneath the girder and crashed into his chest with enough force to knock his grip loose. As the block exploded into dust against him, he fell and hit another lower piece before landing painfully on his back on the ground where he began.

Kael groaned, actually feeling the pain of the fall. He couldn't remember the last time he felt pain. Real pain. He didn't even know how to respond to it.

Suddenly, he felt another tinge of the same sensation—this time something sharp beating in his arm. As he began to stand, he glanced down to find a small gash on his forearm. After wiping it clear with his hand, what Kael saw next was something he knew he'd never seen before... blood.

His blood.

Juts a couple drops, but it was enough.

Shen was right, he thought. He really could be hurt in this place. And if he could be hurt, he could be killed. He could die.

With every action now having dire consequences, all Kael could think about was how lucky he was he hadn't been higher up for his first fall. And that the higher he went, the more careful he was going to have to be.

The whole ordeal seemed impossible. But as fear gripped him for a moment, as well as the possibility of quitting, he fought through them both and resolved to climb even higher on his second try.

He refused to be a King, and he didn't want to be called one. But he was still determined to conquer anything Shen threw at him.

He needed to know more about what he was capable of...

CHAPTER 14

In the solitude of the Soulscape, an eleven-year-old Kael sat with his face buried into his knees. Unlike the last time he was there, he began deeper in the black plane instead of the gray path between it and the white. He wasn't just crying like last time either.

He was bawling.

The pulsating ethereal brick he had laid at the edge of the black during his first visit was now a small knee-high wall that stretched farther than sight could see. However, the wall was not perfect. Though it still separated the opposing sides, individual bricks were haphazardly missing from its structure, creating small gaps every ten or twenty pieces.

The young Kael swore there were always more bricks in place the next time he showed up than the last time he left, but he knew he could still jump the wall easily enough if he wanted to. He just never did. The boy in white standing on the other side never gave him a reason to. Never offered him anything he wanted.

"Hello, Kael!"

The voice that called his name was the same voice that had done so every time he'd been there. It called from the darkness, and Kael immediately recognized it as the boy in black. However, this time, it sounded older. More mature. He only knew it because it was his own voice. Their voice. One and the same.

"Leave me alone!" the young Kael yelled back through his tears, refusing to turn to meet the boy's gaze.

"What's wrong with you today?" the boy in black asked. Just as Kael had aged, so had he. "I'm your friend, remember? Friends don't yell at each other."

"You said I couldn't be hurt!" Kael yelled anyway. "No matter what I did that I couldn't be hurt! That it was one of my powers!"

"And were you?" the boy asked. "Hurt, I mean?"

"Not me…"

"So did I lie?" As always, the boy in black wasn't malicious in his questioning. He was kind. Sympathetic. He felt like a friend. Though Kael started to suspect things weren't as they appeared…

"Did you know?"

"Did I know what, Kael?"

"Did you know she was going to die too!?"

When Kael finally turned around in his anger, he saw the boy in black sitting in an upholstered black dining chair rather than the simple plastic foldout from before. He was dressed in much nicer clothes than he wore previously. In the darkness that surrounded him, a considerable number of random objects lay scattered about. But they weren't random. They were all items Kael recognized. Items he knew well. Items he had stolen ever since meeting the boy in black, both insignificant and expensive.

"I promise you, Kael," the boy said genuinely, "I did not know she was going to die. If I did, I would've helped you stop it."

Kael's head fell back into his knees in defeat. "I was supposed to protect her," he cried. "She trusted me…" He began repeating that over and over again. "She trusted me…"

While Kael wasn't looking, the boy in black locked eyes with the boy in white from across the planes. Unlike his dark counterpart, the boy in white hadn't aged a day since the first time Kael set foot in the Soulscape. Still nine years old, he stared back at the boy in black, who grinned devilishly while licking his lips.

"You know whose fault this is?" the boy asked, returning his expression to one of empathetic understanding for Kael.

"Mine," the eleven-year-old replied through clenched teeth, his fists balled in anger.

"No, Kael," he said. "It's his."

Kael looked up to see the boy in black pointing to the boy in white. He sat up to peer over the knee-high wall and saw the boy standing on his side the same as he always did. Unchanged. Even in the face of hurled accusations, the youngest of the three made no effort to defend himself.

"You know how I have the power to give you what you want?" the boy in black continued. "Well, he has the power to see and change the future. And yet he didn't lift a single finger to stop your mom or your sister from dying. He just let both happen."

The boy in white's eyes never faltered. They locked onto Kael's the same as they always did, the same as they always had since the first day Kael saw him. But where his eyes were filled with nothing but sorrow for Kael, Kael's were filled with nothing but contempt for him.

"All that anger you feel? Use it. Direct it toward the one you really hate. The one who had the power to save the ones you love and chose not to. He's your real enemy."

Deep down, Kael knew something wasn't right about what the boy in black was saying. But the anger felt too good to deny. It numbed the pain and allowed him to cover his agony. It didn't matter with what.

"You're right," he finally said, wiping away his tears. "This does feel better." As he stood, he hid his sadness behind a veil of anger. Without thinking, he walked over to the boy in black and took another ethereal brick from his hand. His life was in pieces. Anger was all he had left to hold it together.

"Good," the boy in black said, watching as Kael laid it on the wall. "Stick with me, Kael, and I promise you'll never have to hurt again."

And as Kael walked back to the boy who looked and sounded just like him, the brick he laid multiplied to become another broken tier upon the dark masonry.

And then another.

And another.

And…

CHAPTER 15

More than three weeks had passed since Kael began his training inside the Canvas. Nearly a month that had been filled with hundreds of failed attempts at climbing the Tower. A month of blood, sweat, tears, and cursing, which Shen somehow always managed to hear and chastise him for later.

Despite Kael's begging, Shen refused to train him in anything else until he completed the first challenge. He said it was to build patience and stamina. Kael thought it was so he could watch his movie collection in peace. Both of them knew which one was true.

As he groggily awoke from one of the deepest sleeps he had ever fallen into, Kael groaned as he tried to move. Painfully sore from the hundreds of falls he'd taken, his whole body screamed at him in protest whenever he tried to perform even the most mundane movements.

For the last few weeks, his time had consisted of school for seven hours, training for another seven hours, a hot shower, sleep, and seven hours of the Soulscape—courtesy of the black cat-sith who was always on his chest when he awoke. Graves visited to check in on Kael once a week as well, but his comments were always the same.

Was he treating Mr. Shen right?

Was Laney his girlfriend yet?

And Kael's personal favorite…

"Dang, Cabbagepatch, you're finally getting some real meat on those bones!"

Which he was. So far, the only benefit of Shen's arduous "training" was that Kael's already chiseled physique was now as hard as steel. His chest was bigger, his muscles more defined, and his abs could cut diamonds. Still, it took all his strength just to lift his arms, which he needed to do to shield his eyes from the piercing morning light streaming directly through his window.

"Gray put me in this room on purpose," Kael said, realizing he'd never sleep in again. Every morning, the sun would rise, and Kael with it. His window faced due east, and Shen refused to provide him with blinds to cover it.

"Kings don't have the luxury of sleeping in," he would say, as if that was supposed to make Kael feel any better. Though even if the sun's intense rays weren't there to wake him, the additional weight on his chest every morning would certainly do the trick.

"Thack, you have to stop doing this, man," Kael said, his eyes having just barely adjusted to waking from his subterranean slumber. He couldn't understand how the black cat kept getting into his room. He shut the door, he locked the door, he even put his desk chair against the door one time. None of it kept the sable feline from invading his soul every single night and sitting on his sternum every single morning.

Kael rose and shooed the black cat off his bare chest. As it jumped to the floor, he threw his own legs off the side of the bed and stretched. Thackery stared at him with a tilted head. "Well, at least it's just you this morning and not—"

"Good morning!" Shen burst through the door with maximum enthusiasm. "How'd you sleep?"

Kael cupped his palms to his face and ran his fingers through his messy hair. "You know how."

"And how far up did you make it yesterday?"

"I don't want to talk about it."

"Still that bad, huh?" Shen looked amused instead of disappointed. Kael was disappointed by his amusement.

"Maybe I need a break from it." Kael had tried to postpone the task before. No success. "Maybe if we focused on a different part of my training... say... this." Kael laced his fingers through the chain in his necklace to emphasize his point. He was desperate to learn more about the mysterious metal that Shen had explained once and then abandoned in favor of making him climb his angelic tree house.

"I've already told you—"

"Yeah, yeah, to the top, I know." Kael was getting tired of the same speeches by his caretaker. "Even school isn't this repetitive."

"Speaking of," Shen said while Kael stood up to put on a shirt. "How are classes going?"

"Fine."

"Enjoying public school?"

"Sure."

"What about your friends? Mr. Muramasa and Miss Lessenger. How are they?"

"Fine."

Kael knew accepting rides home from Lee every day would eventually lead to him meeting Shen. Both of them constantly pestered Kael to make it happen. However, having the two most annoying people in his life in the same room at the same time was too much to think about.

"If you want me to respect your wishes and not read your mind, you're going to have to give me more than one-word responses."

"I might let you read my mind to avoid these conversations," Kael replied.

Clothed in his usual dark jeans and white V-neck, he left the room. Thackery darted between his feet just as Shen moved quickly around him to stop him at the staircase. The serious look in the old Chinese man's eyes demanded an actual response. Kael sighed. "Everything's good, Gray. I promise."

Everything at school actually was good. Brody had backed off. Classes were cake. He'd made friends with Laney, Lee, and Mercury. And under Mr. Cade's tutelage, he was getting further into recomposing the song his mom had written for him. It was only when he got to Shen's house that his troubles began.

Stupid tower, he thought.

"Well," Shen said, turning to march down the steps. "What about the Seventh Seal? Any idea who it might be yet?"

"I told you I'm not looking." Kael followed the old man to the foyer. "I'm doing this training of yours to master these powers, and then I'm gone. No Seals. No King stuff. This is it. Besides, even if I wanted to look, and I don't, I'd have no idea what to look for."

Shen shrugged. "You don't need to. Remember, angels are drawn to Kings. Kings are drawn to Seals. As the Seventh King, you will be drawn to the Seventh Seal closer than anyone else."

"Not the angel stuff again, Gray. Come on. Unless, of course, you're ready to show me some wing and make me a true believer?"

Truth was Kael already believed Gregory Shen was something more than human. And the groundskeeper in the cemetery already had him believing in creatures of darkness. Still, he figured the best way to get Shen to show him what he wanted to see was to fake disbelief.

Shen shrugged again. "Your overreliance on your sight may be the reason you keep failing to climb the Tower."

Cryptic as always, Kael thought, but Shen refused to be anything else. At this point, Kael was taking whatever hints he could get. He needed to finish Shen's sadistic merry-go-round of death so he could move on to bigger and better things.

"Whoops! I've said too much!" Shen said, laughing heartily all the way to the kitchen. Kael wanted to follow and press the conversation to see if he could get more out of him, but he could already see Lee and Laney in the car waiting for him.

"Whatever," he grumbled. He grabbed his backpack from the coatrack and opened the door. "Try not to overdo it watching movies all day, Gray!" he shouted back down the hall. "Wouldn't want you actually doing anything!"

Kael slammed the door shut before Shen could reply and jogged toward Lee's rusted Nissan. The same offer to give Kael a ride to school every day had extended to Laney as well. And once Lee realized he'd be giving Mercury's best friend rides until she was ungrounded, he started parking in front of her house instead of Shen's.

As he climbed into the front seat, Kael could actually feel the heat emanating from the blonde behind him, like tiny laser holes being burned into the back of his head.

"Guess you win, Lee," Laney said with her arms crossed. "He only made us wait fifteen minutes instead of his usual twenty-five."

Kael's lateness wasn't a one- or two-time occurrence to provoke this kind of reaction from her. It was every single day.

Lee chuckled until he noticed his friend's exhausted purple and green eyes. "Wow, man, you look rough."

"You would be too after taking several dozen two-story falls a day" is what Kael wanted to say. "I'm fine" is what he said instead. "Just need some more sleep."

"Well, maybe if you went to bed at a decent hour," Laney scoffed.

"Here we go…" Lee whispered while trying to start his car.

"How do you even know when I go to bed, Laney? Unless you're stalking my window again?"

"So we're doing this again?" Lee tried the ignition for a second time.

"Oh, get over yourself, Kael. Your window faces mine."

"Guess we're doing this again…" Lee tried a third time. Nothing.

"I mean, is it physically impossible for you to wake up on time?" she asked.

"Innocent bystander here…"

"I don't know," Kael replied, whirling around to meet Laney's white-hot stare with his own. "Is it physically impossible for you not to be so crazy about it every morning?"

"Oh, no…" Lee sighed.

"You think I'm crazy?"

"No one thinks you're crazy, Laney," Lee tried to mediate.

"I think you're acting crazy!" Kael followed up.

"Keep talking, Omaha, and I'll show you crazy!"

"Can I just say something here?" Lee asked, finally speaking above a whisper.

"No!" was the unified reply. The only thing they both agreed on.

Kael sighed and turned back in his seat, resting the side of his head against his fist on the window. "Can we just drop it?"

"Best idea I've heard all morning," Lee replied, still desperately flipping the ignition over and over. "Come on, you piece of junk, start!"

"You're going to flood the engine," Kael said, annoyed by the car's continued grinding.

Laney reassured Lee with a pat on the shoulder. "One more week and I'll start giving us the rides." Then she glanced at the napping Kael. "And we'll leave at exactly 7:30 every morning."

Lee smiled back but was too determined to quit. He cranked the key one last time, holding it just a second too long as the injectors pumped too much fuel into the car's cylinders and did exactly what Kael warned him they would do. The high-pitched turnover noise was the dead giveaway that they were going to be there for a while.

"Maybe I can call Mercury?" Laney offered.

"No!" Lee practically shouted. He wasn't willing to undergo the humiliation of being the guy whose car wouldn't start in front of his crush. "I just need to check under the hood for a minute."

Kael wasn't willing to wait that long. Before Lee popped the door handle, Kael formed a thought and then projected it into the real world with a stare.

Start.

His power came to life and so did the engine. Sputtering back from the dead, the car shook, then stabilized into a healthier hum than usual. It usually sounded like two chainsaws rubbing together. After Kael's jump-start, it almost sounded new.

While Lee and Laney were dumbfounded by the car's miraculous recovery, Kael was shocked at how much quicker and more easily his power came to him. It wasn't just The Word either. When he tapped into The White, he was physically faster and stronger as well. All that training in the Canvas was paying off.

"Well, that was weird..." Lee said, plopping back down into the seat he barely left.

"Yeah, crazy," Kael replied and resumed his napping position. "Can we go now?"

The two eyed their friend for several seconds before Lee threw the old car into gear and pulled off down the street.

He assumed it was just dumb luck.

But Laney thought maybe it was something else...

†††

The only two classes Kael cared about in the mornings were English and Piano IV, and it wasn't any coincidence they were taught by the same person. Mr. Cade was unlike any teacher Kael had ever known. Whereas a lot of teachers offered their lessons like programmed robots, he actually seemed to care about the material he was teaching. More importantly, he actually seemed to care about his students, even if half of them couldn't care less about him.

That half being the boys. The girls all had crushes on the handsome thirtysomething-year-old.

In the weeks following Heart of Darkness, Mr. Cade expected the class to read Hamlet and The Great Gatsby on their own and come prepared to contribute insightful discussion daily. Kael made the mistake of telling Shen what they had been reading one time, only for the old man to pull out seventeen theatrical versions of Shakespeare's tragedy and three of F. Scott Fitzgerald's masterpiece on decadence and idealism.

"Why read it when you can watch it?" he said, something Kael thought he'd never hear from an adult. Though it didn't surprise him from the old cinephile.

After the first half of the day passed, Kael sat down at what had become his usual table to eat a meal that was way too large for him. Ever since his training started, the ravenous teen loaded his plate up until it nearly cracked.

By this point, he knew the routine. Lee would sit down next and complain about something in his last class. Laney after him. And then possibly Mercury if she felt she could stomach Lee that day.

True to form, Lee slid into the seat next to Kael.

"Aw, man!" he groaned. "You got the last piece of pumpkin pie?"

Kael continued chomping away at the burger in his hands, eyeing the pie next to his plate and weighing its caloric value against Lee's friendship.

The disappointment in the youth's eyes was enough to make Kael relent. Sighing through bites, he slid the plastic plate toward Lee. He wasn't going to eat it anyway, he lied to himself.

"Dude! You're the best!"

However, while Lee's timing in Kael's routine had been spot on, Laney was nowhere to be seen. Surveying the cafeteria, Kael found her talking to Mercury by the hallways. The raven-haired girl looked upset. Laney just looked angry.

Without warning, she stormed away from her best friend in a beeline for Brody's table. As she confronted him in front of his friends, Mercury came to sit with Kael and Lee, looking conflicted.

"What's wrong?" Kael asked.

"It's Brody," she replied. "He's telling everyone he slept with Laney over the summer."

Kael's eyes narrowed. He was so incensed by Mercury's sentence that he couldn't even form a coherent response.

"It's obviously not true," she continued. "But the rumor's gotten around. I don't know. Maybe I shouldn't have told her?"

"She knows this is high school, right?" Lee managed to say while chomping away at his pumpkin pie. "This place is like a snake pit of rumors. Do you know how many get spread about me every day? Contrary to popular belief, I do not, in fact, still wet the bed, and I don't have a grandfather responsible for Pearl Harbor either. My Pop-Pop wouldn't do that. I don't even think he was alive during World War II."

With Mercury giving him a strange look, Lee realized he was being awkward and turned to Kael for support. "Back me up, man—"

But Kael was gone. Already on his way to Brody's table.

"Come on, Laney," Brody said, stabbing his fork into his baked steak. "I'm eating here."

Laney didn't hesitate. In one fluid motion, she flipped Brody's tray off the table, causing the freshman cheerleader beside him to shrink back and shriek. "And now you're not."

"Whoa!" Brody said, laughing and looking around at the others at his table. "Where was all this fire that night we spent together?"

Laney's eyes became white-hot metal. "What night?" she shot back. "That fantasy in your head? I'm sure you have a lot of them."

"Come on, Laney," the quarterback said with a shrug. "It's okay to admit it now."

"Admit what?" she asked. "That you're a liar? A jerk who needs people to think I slept with him to make him relevant?"

"I don't need people to think it," Brody said. "They know it's true. Everyone knows you've had a crush on me since freshman year."

The other football players, even some of the cheerleaders at the table— her former friends—began laughing at her expense.

"Just tell the truth," she said, her voice seething with anger.

Brody grinned. "But I already have."

With her fists balled up, Laney thought about how easy it would be to knock Brody out. With how powerful she was compared to him—what she was compared to him—it would be child's play. But she'd hurt him. Really hurt him. And she knew she couldn't do that.

So she did the next best thing.

The purple slushie in front of Brody was almost topped to the brim with grape-flavored ice. She grabbed it and splashed it into his face, painting him purple and watching as the colored ice chunks fell into his lap.

"That's for lying," she said, turning to walk away until a hand grabbed her by the wrist and pulled her back. Brody was standing and towering over her. She could still take him down in one move. But...

"Let her go."

It was Kael. He was standing in front of Brody and Laney, waiting for Brody to release her wrist. When he didn't, Kael punctuated his command with more authority. "I said... let her go."

After Brody realized the whole cafeteria had been made aware of how tightly he was holding Laney's wrist, he gave the same cocky smile he always gave and released her. "It figures you'd show up, Clark," he said, wiping some of the slushie clear from his face. "You're practically obsessed with getting in my business. What's your problem with me anyway?"

"You are my problem," Kael replied. "Touch her again, and we're going to have a much bigger one, you understand?"

"What? Are you two dating now? Makes sense, I guess. An ace degenerate like yourself needs a girlfriend like Laney..." Brody paused for a moment before adding, "...just another whore."

That was it. Kael's mind went dark. All that was left was instinct. People think anger makes a person see red. It doesn't. It makes them see black. Because at the height of any true anger, the only thing anyone sees is always exactly the same...

Nothing.

Kael's fist curved into a hook around his body so fast that even he couldn't track it. And it landed against Brody's eye socket so hard that it sent the muscle-bound quarterback spiraling like a corkscrew into the wall behind him.

As the other football players leapt up from their seats, Kael prepared himself for a fight. Brody rallied against the wall, reared his fist, and came back at Kael with all the speed of someone who knew how to throw a punch. Unprepared to block in time, Kael turned his head to absorb some of the blow. But the blow never came. Altered by the same invisible force that always protected him, Brody's punch missed Kael's cheek completely and turned down toward the ground.

Kael should've been surprised, but he wasn't. He wasn't inside the Canvas. He couldn't be hit. Couldn't be hurt. Not out here. And after Shen's explanation that he had a guardian looking after him, he finally had a pretty good reason why.

Though it felt like cheating, Kael didn't care. The fight was about to be six on one. If they weren't going to play fair, why should he?

Brody's sidekick Drew was the first to lunge at Kael. He was also the first to get kneed in the gut and thrown to the ground. Then came another. Kael threw a front kick to his chest and sent him careening backward. One of the smaller players tried to rush Kael from the side, but a well-placed back fist to the cheek sent him to the ground as well.

Kael's body was moving on instinct, but he could tell it was different from any other fight he'd ever been in. His training inside the Canvas was paying off. His whole body felt lighter and more fluid. It wasn't just muscle memory controlling him. It was The White. Flowing through him to make every movement faster. Every strike hit harder. He was stronger than he'd ever been before. And he liked it.

But just as Kael was about to land another hit, Frankie grabbed him from behind in a bear hug. Momentarily bound, Kael was in a prone position to be attacked by one of the recovering players. Thinking quickly, Kael jumped back on Frankie's large chest and kicked out against the attacking player, sending him into another one who was still picking himself up off the tile floor.

As he landed, Kael realized he needed to break Frankie's indestructible grip. However, before he could make a move, he heard a sizzling sound that reminded him of something... and a smell that solidified the memory as something he could never forget.

In the scuffle, Kael's necklace had fallen outside his shirt and was lying against Frankie's meaty arm, burning against it like hot iron. It was just like the groundskeeper who tried grabbing it before, only this time the one being burned refused to let go.

Feeling a sharp pain in his right eye, Kael suddenly became aware of black smoke and cinders emanating from where his necklace was making contact with Frankie's arm. Eventually, the fat football player released him in a cry of agony, and the smoke disappeared back into his body. Free from his embrace, Kael just barely sidestepped another football player who accidentally tackled the reeling Frankie to the ground.

Kael couldn't believe what just happened. What did it mean? Why was his necklace burning random citizens in a town like Kearney? Could they really be...?

Luckily for him, in the chaos of the fight, no one seemed to notice what just happened. No one except for Laney, who was staring at Kael in mute astonishment and disbelief. But before she could say anything, Brody slipped past her and charged Kael with another punch. However, before he could make contact, a lightning thin frame slipped between him and Kael like a ghost and put his hands on both of the boys' chests.

It was Mr. Cade.

"That's enough!" he shouted with authority, instantly silencing the pandemonium in the lunchroom. The hoots and hollers of every student fell perfectly quiet, replaced by fearful stillness.

However, Brody's anger could not be quelled, and he was too humiliated to stop. His arm twitched, just a little.

"Try it," Mr. Cade said. "I dare you."

That was enough to bring Brody back to his senses but not enough to lessen his fury. The quarterback yelled and swiped a tray to the floor before storming out of the cafeteria with the rest of the players limping behind him.

Mr. Cade looked back at Kael. "You come with me."

With the situation diffused and the cafeteria silent, Lee shot up from his seat and began to clap slowly for Kael, who'd just done what he always wished he could do. But when everyone turned to stare at him awkwardly, the teen's applause died off.

"Oh, this isn't one of those... Okay... Yeah... Right." He quickly sat back down next to Mercury, who hid her face in embarrassment.

While being led out of the cafeteria past Laney, Kael noticed her confusion. He couldn't blame her. He was confused by what just happened himself. Why would demons want to possess a useless waste of space like Frankie Fredericks?

Mr. Cade led Kael into one of the many adjoining hallways that connected the cafeteria to the rest of the school. Kael was positive he was heading to the principal's office. But when the two finally reached an area of the hallway that was devoid of other students, Mr. Cade stopped and turned around to face him.

"You alright?" he asked.

"Yeah, I guess" was the only response Kael could think to give. He wasn't sure if he was in for a tongue-lashing or a lecture, but he wasn't in the mood for either. To his surprise, however, Mr. Cade was smiling.

"Was it worth it?" he asked. When Kael looked at him, confused and unable to answer, the teacher changed the question. "Did they at least deserve it?"

The young man couldn't believe it. A teacher was siding with him over the star quarterback after it was obvious that he instigated the fight... Why? He didn't know what to say so he just nodded.

"I'm new here too, you know," Mr. Cade said. "Only started at the end of last year. But I've seen enough to know that everyone here thinks Brody walks on water because he can score touchdowns. That kind of admiration usually leads to arrogance. And arrogance always leads to justice. This time, it just so happened to come in the shape of your fist."

If Kael was shocked before, he was dumbfounded now. The only adult who ever stood up for him before was Graves, but even Graves wouldn't take his side in a situation like this one. Kael had become so used to defending himself. It was nice to have someone else defending him for a change.

"Go ahead and get to your free period," the teacher continued. "I'll talk to Mr. Matthews and take care of this. You made your point with Brody. But try and stay out of trouble from now on. I can't always be there."

Kael nodded again without thinking. He stared at the relatively young teacher and wondered what he could've done to deserve such a big get-out-of-jail free card.

Maybe he just really liked the fact that he took his piano class?

"Kael... Go." The word snapped Kael out of his thoughts so abruptly that he turned and began walking to the library without thinking.

CHAPTER 16

Kael waited impatiently for the rest of the day to crawl along. After lunch, he spent his free period replaying the fight with the football players over and over again in his head. But there was one detail he couldn't get over... Frankie.

Why did the Arch Steel burn him? Shen said it only burned creatures of darkness—demons. But why would a demon want to possess some idiot high school linebacker? It just didn't make sense.

Kael tried to put the questions out of his mind. All he wanted was to get back to Shen's and ask him about them, but that would have to wait. The end of the day offered his last class, the one he'd despised since the second day of school. Gym. Ever since Kael outclassed his entire football team, the ire of Coach Winters had been difficult to avoid. And he was sure it was about to be even more difficult now that he'd pummeled half his offensive line.

Like every other day, the middle-aged bodybuilder took them outside on the football field to have his players run drills while the rest of the class ran track. Kael was always too tired from his training in the Canvas to run, so he jogged slowly.

"Dude, how are you not suspended?" Lee asked, coming up from behind him.

Kael turned to see the look of disbelief on his friend's face. "Our favorite English teacher just let me go," he replied. "Said he'd take care of it." Noticing the explanation wasn't nearly good enough for Lee, he added, "I know, I thought it was weird too. Don't you think there's something off about that guy?"

"What do you mean?"

"I mean, what kind of teacher breaks up a fight and then covers for the kid who started it?"

Lee shook off his disbelief. "Man, if I were you, I wouldn't be asking questions. You ever heard not to punch a gift horse in the teeth?"

"No, because that's not the saying," Kael said.

"What? Nah, I'm pretty sure that's it."

Noticing the pair jogging half-heartedly, Winters made his wrath known from the sidelines. "Clark! Muramasa! You two ladies plan on picking up the pace anytime soon!?"

Kael was too tired for his usual quippy comeback and jogged just a little faster. Lee followed suit until both upgraded from being lapped by absolutely everyone on the track to being lapped by everyone except Willy Mason, the only kid in class lazier than both of them combined.

"Come on, you two, this is embarrassing," Mercury said, passing in front of the two boys before turning around to jog backwards. "You especially, Kael. First, you show up the entire football team at lunch, and now you can barely run a mile? How many times have you guys been lapped anyway?"

"Just catching our breath, beautiful," Lee said, trying his best to sound flirtatious.

Mercury ignored him. As always, her eyes stayed on Kael. Even though she had eased up on her advances in the last few weeks, Kael's demonstration in the lunchroom flipped her interest dial back to eleven. And since the cheerleaders weren't practicing that day, she bit her lip and focused all her energy on getting him to notice her.

"Hey, where's Laney?" Kael asked, glancing around the track. "I didn't see her come out."

Mercury looked disappointed. "She got signed out after lunch," she replied. "Her dad picked her up. Actually, I'm surprised you're still here after what happened…"

"That's what I said," Lee muttered.

"Just lucky, I guess…" Kael wanted to ask more about Laney, like if she was alright after everything that happened, but figured he'd just ask her later.

The three stopped at the water cooler for a quick break—one that only Mercury really deserved. "So, you guys got any plans this afternoon?" Lee asked.

"Same as always," Kael responded, telling the half-truth he always did. Lee had been desperate for all of them to hang out ever since the first day he'd given Laney a ride home in his car. Laney and Mercury always declined for various reasons, but Kael had to come up with an excuse solid enough to last a while for Lee. He told him that Shen made him do chores around the house every evening. That was the lying half of his half-truth. Unless he counted torturesome training as a chore. Which he did.

"Man, you should really call CPS or something," Lee said. "It can't be legal to foster a kid just to make him your own personal slave."

The idea of Kael calling Child Protective Services on Shen almost made him laugh since he was positive the old man would just Jedi mind trick whatever poor sap they sent out. It wasn't worth giving him the satisfaction. "It's not that bad," he said instead.

"What's he like anyway?" Mercury asked after downing her cup of water. "Old Man Shen… No one really knows anything about him."

"He thinks he's a lot funnier than he is, never gives you a straight answer, and he has an unhealthy movie obsession that keeps both of us up half the night." Kael was ranting before he realized it. But as he vented his frustrations, he realized that no one had really asked him to describe his caretaker before. Thinking back to what Shen did for Graves, Kael didn't want to paint too bad a picture. "But he does care about people. And he's given me a pretty decent place to sleep, so I guess I can't complain too much."

Mercury was about to respond when the clash of helmets snapped the trio out of their conversation and turned their attention to the field. The football players were tearing each other apart more ferociously than ever in a scrimmage between the team's best players. Coach Winters was watching from the other side of the field with keen eyes.

As the hulking bodies of each high schooler crashed into one another during a play, Brody faded back from the twenty-yard line and launched the ball in a perfect spiral seventy yards downfield. It feathered into the outstretched arms of Aaron Kobba as he raced into the end zone.

Kael was impressed.

Having played against them less than a month ago, he never expected them to actually be good. He began to question whether they had improved that much or whether his powers were the only reason he ever stood a chance in the first place.

"Is it just me or were they not this good three weeks ago?" he asked.

"Yeah," Lee said. "That's the thing. They're a little too good this year."

"Oh, not you too..." Mercury said, rolling her eyes.

"What do you mean?" Lee asked.

"Laney said the same thing a couple weeks ago. She's always got a conspiracy theory for everything in this town. You two should write a book, I swear. Can't you just be happy we're winning games for once?"

"What are you guys talking about?" Kael asked.

"Well," Lee said, slightly offended by Mercury's comments. "Last year, the team sucked. They couldn't win one game. So far this year, they're undefeated. It doesn't make any sense. I mean, Brody's always had a pretty magical arm, but now it's like beyond godly. And the other players are all bigger, stronger, and faster too."

"I didn't take you for a football fan," Kael said.

"I like to bet on the games," Lee explained with a shrug. "Which is another reason I'm so ticked off. I made a killing last year betting on the other teams."

Kael and Mercury exchanged looks.

"Hey, don't hate!" Lee said. "Guy's gotta make money somehow!"

Ignoring Lee's gambling addiction, Kael returned to the original subject. "So what are you trying to say? That they're all juicing now or something?"

Lee stared at the field, watching as the behemoths on it performed another perfect play with such ferocity and viciousness that it sent a shiver down his spine.

"I don't know, maybe…" he said. "Is it just me, or have you guys ever noticed anything weird around town? Like in people's eyes?"

The question confirmed it for Kael. He hadn't imagined it. The flash of black in Frankie's eyes, like his pupils had suddenly become too large for his irises to contain. Then he thought of the biker in his jail cell the first morning he had arrived in Kearney. And the caretaker in the cemetery. Their eyes had done the same thing.

"It's like they're possessed or something," Lee finished, finally revealing his true thoughts.

Mercury raised an eyebrow. "Isn't your family like Buddhist or something? Do you guys even believe in possession?"

"We're Shinto traditionalists actually," Lee said before realizing he was getting snippy with his crush. "But besides, there's possession in Shinto. Almost every religion really. What's that old saying? The rival farmers who tell different stories still sell the same crop."

"Who says that?"

Lee shrugged. "I don't know. I swear my dad makes this stuff up. I just know I've seen too much strange stuff in this town not to think there's something weirder going on around here."

Kael was curious about that statement. What else had he seen? Had Shen slipped up and shown too much of himself sometime before Kael got there? Or was something else really going on?

Having revealed his true thoughts, Lee had the courage to continue. "Have you guys ever heard of yōkai?" he asked, earning a confused look from both of them. "In Japan, they're usually evil spirits that possess people and make them do their bidding. Sometimes they even manifest elements of themselves on the victim's body. Like black eyes..."

"Come on, Muramasa," Mercury said. "Sure, our team's never exactly been good, but demonic possession? That's a stretch, even for you."

"I'm just saying it would explain a few things," Lee replied. "A couple weeks ago, I was at Sozo's picking up dinner for my family, and some of the players were there. Anyway, they got so upset with the waitress for messing up their order they picked up the whole table and threw it into the wall hard enough that it went through the plaster!"

"Yeah, you know what else explains all that?" Mercury replied. "Steroids."

Lee started sulking. "If Laney were here, she'd believe me..."

"Yeah, because she's the only person in the whole school with a weirder imagination than you. I love her, but she'd probably want it to be true just so she'd have something better to write about in the school paper."

"Yeah, because that'd be one awesome headline!" Lee said. He waved one hand through the air while staring off into space. "'Hellish High School Football Team Resorts to Demonic Power to Win Games.' Catchy, right?"

"You're so weird."

"Mercury!" a voice called from the track. It was one of her cheerleaders.

"Come on! Coach Winters said we could leave early to get ready for the game tonight!"

"Well, gotta run," she said. "Listen, do me a favor and don't tell anyone we had this conversation. I've worked hard to make it through all of high school with my reputation intact. I'd like to keep it that way."

As Mercury took off with her friends toward the locker room, Lee gulped down the rest of his water and turned to Kael.

"You were suspiciously quiet during all of that," Lee said. "What do you think about my little theory?"

"I think I don't know what to think," Kael replied. He had to deal with enough supernatural weirdness at Shen's. If he had to start dealing with it at school too, he was going to lose his mind. "Yōkai or demons or whatever you call them… it's a lot to take in."

"I know how weird it sounds," Lee said. "But if you knew all the weird stuff that happens in this town… I don't know, just seems like this would be the least crazy explanation. Or maybe I'm just the one going crazy."

Lee had no idea just how much Kael empathized with his last statement. While keeping his eyes laser-focused on the football team running yet another pro-level drill, Kael thought about the possibility of every member being possessed by a demon.

The thought made him shudder. And the fact that he was actually afraid made him angry.

CHAPTER 17

Once Lee pulled up to Shen's house, Kael hopped out of the car before his friend could say much to him. He had to use his powers to start Lee's car for him again before leaving school and really didn't want him pressing him on it. Lee was already suspicious of weird things happening around town, and Kael didn't want to be another thing on his list.

Stepping onto Shen's driveway, Kael looked up to see the old man's truck parked outside instead of its usual place in the garage. And with the garage door open, he quickly realized why.

Sitting inside was a mangled heap of black and silver metal that used to be the '67 Mustang Kael had wrecked his first night in Kearney. Had he not seen it immediately following the accident, Kael didn't think he would've been able to recognize it. Other than the frame, the vehicle was utterly obliterated. Thousands of glass shards and shredded fragments of metal lay strewn around it like pieces to an impossible jigsaw puzzle. The crushed rims and blown out tires were leaning against the fenders, unable to fit in their original spaces. The driver side door was detached and leaning against the garage wall. It wasn't even right to call it a car anymore, Kael thought. It was scrap metal.

"Well, what do you think?" Shen appeared from behind Kael, having rounded the house in an attempt to sneak up on him. After the first dozen or so times, Kael had become used to it.

"Tell you what I think of what?" he asked. "Your memory of a car? Yeah, Gray, it's really something."

Kael couldn't tell if Shen was trying to make him feel bad or not, but he wasn't about to let it work. When they stepped inside, Shen pulled the drawstring for the garage door to shut behind them. The fluorescent lighting made the corpse of a car look even worse.

"Why'd you close the door?"

"Because I want you to do something before your training in the Canvas today," he replied. "I want you to fix my car."

There was a moment of silence… confusion… and then more silence as Kael tried to figure out what Shen was up to. It took him a second, but he finally understood. This wasn't a guilt trip. It was a prank.

"Nice one, Gray," he said, smirking.

"I'm completely serious," Shen said. "I want you to put this car back together again."

"Yeah, okay," Kael mocked. "Do I get all the king's horses and all the king's men to help me?"

"Nope, the King is going to have to do this one all by himself."

"Come on, you've got to be…" But staring into Shen's eyes, Kael couldn't detect even the faintest hint of sarcasm or joviality. "You're serious, aren't you? Gray, it's not possible. Even if all the parts were here and in brand new condition, it would take weeks… months doing it alone."

"You're never alone."

"Oh? You gonna help me then?"

"No."

"Then that's literally the definition of me doing it alone," Kael said. "Seriously, how am I supposed to do this?"

Shen sighed, disappointment filling the breath of his exhale. "Since you were nine, you've been using your abilities to perform parlor tricks. Starting cars and unlocking doors. You have no idea how much power actually resides within The Word. It's time you learned."

Kael winced at Shen's admonishment but knew he was right. Still, he gave his own sigh and shook his head to show he didn't care what Shen thought. Even though he did. He didn't know why, but for some reason, he always did.

"Fine, whatever," he said. "I'll try it, but it's not going to work. It never works on anything this big."

"The Word works on everything," Shen replied. "Big, small, doesn't matter. The problem is not in the power. It is in the one using it. Now..." The old man stretched out his arm and gestured to the car. "Make it happen."

"You're so serious today," Kael said, stepping up to the destroyed car. "I never thought I'd say this, but I think I prefer you misquoting movies and being annoyingly jolly all the time."

Shen didn't respond, just gave a look as if to proceed. Kael did.

Closing his eyes and reaching out his hand, Kael concentrated and tapped back into the part of himself that was connected to The White— the energy source his abilities came from. Even though he felt the power coming more easily to him in the last three weeks, what he was attempting wasn't like starting an old car. He was basically rebuilding one from the ground up. Which took a lot more focus and willpower.

Kael had to understand absolutely everything about a car for this to work. He had to know where every part went, how it was supposed to look, how it was supposed to operate. Luckily, he'd stolen enough of them to have a pretty good idea, but he'd never attempted anything on this scale before. However, when he finally pictured in his mind what he wanted to occur, he let himself fall into the infinite energy of The White and then channeled it into the amazing power of The Word...

"Repair."

Saying the word aloud, Kael had to force himself to keep his eyes closed as he heard the parts scraping against the floor in accordance with his will. He kept concentrating as they lifted from the ground and floated to their intended positions. Kael could hear the various metal pieces twisting and grinding back into their original forms as everything began reassembling itself at the points of their original destruction.

Even Shen, standing behind Kael, was impressed by the display. He wondered if the young man could really do the task before him on his first try.

However, as every single piece of the car hung suspended in midair around the spaces they were supposed to fit into, Kael ran into a problem in his mind. While he could imagine crushed metal being twisted and dented back out to become its original design... and he could imagine where every single one of the thousand components was supposed to fit into... he couldn't fathom how the fragments that were broken and torn apart were supposed to magically mend themselves back together into one solid piece.

The metal shrapnel...?

The glass shards...?

How was he supposed to bond them into a full hood or windshield? With his will becoming doubt, Kael's concentration was broken, and the almost-reassembled car fell loudly back into a mangled heap on the concrete garage floor. Kael put his hands on his knees, panting heavily.

"It's too much," he said between breaths. "I can't do it."

Shen stepped forward to stand beside the hunched over boy. "Yes, you can," he said. "There are three stages to using your power. The first is that you have to want it to work. That one's mandatory. Without it, you'll fail like your push in the foyer failed against me. The second and third are branch options, though. One is fully understanding what you're manipulating. This is how you've used the power in the past. You know the mechanics of a lock, so you can unlock doors. You understand how a car starts, so you can jumpstart cars. However, there's an alternative option to knowing..."

"Yeah, what?"

"Believing. After wanting it, if you truly believe the power will work, it just will."

"Think I'll stick with the way I've been doing it," Kael replied coarsely.

Shen shrugged. "Your choice."

"But I already know how to build a car from the ground up with my bare hands. Knowing that didn't help me do it just now."

The old man stared at the boy. "You enjoy science, right? Science gets a lot wrong at first, but I've always been astounded by mankind's ability to admit their mistakes in search of greater truth. Take the atom. Up until recently, man thought it was the smallest particle in the universe. When they discovered it wasn't, it pushed them one step closer to understanding a much grander design. You, Kael, may already know how the pieces of this car fit together. But tell me, how does matter itself fit together?"

Kael stood straight to meet his stare. "You want me to fix something on an atomic level? Are you serious?"

Shen nodded.

Pondering it, Kael guessed the idea wasn't completely out of the realm of possibility. Even everyday scientists could manipulate atoms for different purposes, though they had nanoscopic machines to do so. All Kael had was his mind.

"How am I supposed to fit atoms back together when I can't even see them to know what I'm working with? That's impossible."

Shen sighed and stretched out his hand toward the car without ever taking his eyes from Kael.

"*Repair.*"

The confident way Shen said the word contrasted sharply in Kael's mind with how unsurely he said it before. That confidence made all the difference and was instantly made manifest in its result. The parts of Shen's destroyed Mustang rose into the air once again and began fitting themselves into the same places Kael had them before. However, there was one big difference. With Kael, the smaller fragments of the car only hung in suspended levitation. With Shen, a bright white light shone in between the thousand tiny cracks of their being fitted together. In astonishment, Kael watched as each shard of glass, each piece of metal, and each shred of rubber fused perfectly back together into their original shapes and colors.

In seconds, the entirety of the '67 Shelby was restored to the same pristine condition Kael had found it in the night he stole it. Stepping forward in amazement, the young man ran his hand along the polished black paint job just to make sure it was real. When he realized it was, he was speechless.

"You don't need to see something to know it's there," Shen said. "Do you see the wind? No, you feel it. Stop relying on your eyes to tell you everything. Once you learn to do that, you'll be amazed at what you can do and how well you can do it."

Kael still couldn't believe it. Shen had done in seconds what should've been impossible to do ever. He knew he was an angel, or at least something out of this world, but seeing him perform these miraculous feats of power was so much different than just knowing he was capable of them. Almost inspiring.

"What else can I do with this power?" Kael asked while circling the car in utter astonishment.

"I told you. Anything."

Kael was hesitant to ask what he really wanted to know. "Could I control someone? Like mentally. Could I control their minds?"

The question garnered a very serious look from Shen—more serious than he'd ever seen him make before.

"It's not for anything bad," Kael said defensively. "Something weird just happened at school today…"

"Go on," Shen said.

"Well, there was a fight…"

"Always."

"And one of the football players was burned by my necklace," Kael finished, ignoring Shen's sarcastic interjection. "Just like the groundskeeper in the cemetery. I think he was possessed. Lee thinks the whole football team is. He calls them yōkai."

"Yōkai, jinn, wendigos, demons…" Shen rattled off a long list. "Different cultures' names for the same thing. They're here because of the Seal."

"Okay, but you still didn't answer the question. If they're possessed, can I use my powers to take back control of their minds?"

"Even if you could, it wouldn't matter," Shen replied. "For possession, demons inhabit the body. Not the mind."

"What's the difference inhabiting one and not the other?

"Think of the mind, body, and spirit as three interconnected entities working toward the same goal." Shen looked at the Mustang. "Like a vehicle. If your body is the car, your soul is the driver. What you take with you, your possessions, are your thoughts. Your mind. Evil spirits hijack the body and throw the soul helpless into the trunk. Meanwhile, they have access to all the luggage in the car. Your memories. So that they know everything you know."

"If it's that easy, why don't demons just possess everyone?"

"They try to," Shen replied simply. "They want a physical form more than anything. But that's where guardian angels come in. They protect humans from most supernatural attack."

"Most?"

"Guardian angels are the lowest rank of angel. Their power to defend comes from the soul of the human they're defending. People with weak, fractured, or evil souls are easy for evil supernatural creatures to latch onto and inhabit. Stronger, more righteous souls are harder."

Kael thought back to Frankie. "So how do you free someone who's already… inhabited?"

"Currently, you only have one weapon in your arsenal that can defeat a demon." Shen pointed to the Arch Steel dangling from Kael's neck. "When you learn to use its true form, it will destroy them. Though as a weapon, it should be used with caution. What is done to the body of the possessed is done permanently."

"You mean I could accidentally kill the ones being possessed?"

Shen nodded. "Just because you have the power to do something doesn't mean you should. Always remember this. Knowledge is having the ability. Wisdom is knowing when to use it."

As he continued rounding the repaired car, Kael pondered on that for a moment. It was certainly not a mantra he'd ever applied before. He had power, so he did use it. Often. Restraint was never one of his strong suits.

"And demons don't care what happens to their vessel," Shen continued. "They have no morality. Every limb, organ, and faculty become possessions to them. The souls trapped within can only watch what their body does without permission."

"Sounds like puberty," Kael remarked, earning another serious glare from Shen.

"Do not be so flippant in the matters of spiritual warfare, Kael. Human beings, even ones who believe, never like to think of demons constantly prowling around their souls waiting for the perfect moment of weakness to strike. But they should. For the most important battles we fight are not against flesh and blood, but against the rulers, the authorities, and the powers of this dark world. Those who believe in nothing understand nothing."

"Alright, alright, chill, okay?" Kael replied with his hands up in surrender. His goal hadn't been to upset Shen, but that was all he seemed to be doing. "Just trying to lighten the mood. So, what are they anyway? Demons, I mean."

Shen paused. "You have enough to think about. Let that be a question for another day."

Kael shrugged. He opened the driver side door and fell into the perfectly reupholstered leather seat. Gripping the wooden steering wheel, he inhaled the car's vintage smell in pure bliss. For a car lover like him, it was heaven. He was fine with dropping the dreary subject. He had another question he wanted to ask anyway.

"So…" he started. "Since you repaired her, you think you'd be okay letting me drive this beauty to school? I promise to bring her back in one piece this time."

"Sure," Shen replied, turning and heading for the house door. Kael was shocked, almost elated, until he heard the rest of Shen's response. "Once you repair it yourself."

"What do you mean?"

Shen held up a hand while passing through the door.

"*Destruct.*"

As he disappeared behind the open threshold, the car began shaking violently around Kael. The steering wheel came off in his hands, the tires exploded and sent the car sinking to the ground, glass shattered, metal twisted, and the car was soon back in its original state of annihilation.

Kael sat horrified in the driver's seat, putting the wheel slowly back into its hole on the dash where it wouldn't stay. As it fell and rolled across his knees to the passenger side floorboard, he sat back against the shredded leather seat and sighed.

CHAPTER 18

Once he got over the initial shock of having Shen's car self-destruct all around him, Kael tried his best to imitate exactly what the old man had done to restore the Mustang to its former glory. He thought about the atoms that made up the car. He thought about them interlocking together in perfectly synchronized formations. He thought about the number of protons, neutrons, and electrons necessary for each element of the vehicle. However, when he gave the word for all of them to bend to his will, they refused. Like obstinate children, they wouldn't obey, leaving Kael angry and exhausted.

After several hours of attempting the same feat over and over, Kael eventually gave up for the evening and retired to his room. Before entering, he peered down the hallway to the door that would lead him to the Canvas, tempted to try his luck with that...

He shook his head. One failure was enough for one evening. Maybe sleep would give him a new perspective on how to accomplish both impossible challenges the next day.

Entering his bedroom, he noticed Thackery sitting regally on his desk. When the two made eye contact, the cat-sith tilted his head slightly to the right and meowed loudly, as if to ask what was wrong. Kael sighed and flopped onto his bed, waiting only seconds for the cat to follow his lead and leap onto his chest. When he did, Kael started petting behind his ear while staring into the feline's emerald eyes.

"I don't suppose you have any advice on this crazy training?" he asked, deciding to believe for just a moment that Thackery really was a thousand-year-old wizard trapped in a cat's body. Receiving only heavy purring as his response, Kael replied to himself, "Yeah, I didn't think so."

As the sun began to set, Kael was drifting off to sleep when he happened to turn his head toward the bedroom window and see Laney sneaking out of hers. Being grounded, she hadn't gone to visit her mom in the cemetery for weeks, so Kael was surprised she was taking the chance just a few days before her sentence was lifted.

Turning back to the black cat who was now lying full spread on his chest and stomach, Kael asked, "What do you think, Thack? Should we follow her?"

Instead of responding vocally, the cat leapt down and waited patiently by the door. Taking that as his answer, Kael jumped out of bed, opened the door, and ran down the stairs with Thackery racing ahead of him. He grabbed his jacket from the rack by the front door and called out to Shen, who was already in the middle of watching his films.

"I'm heading out for a bit!" Kael paused to look down. "And I'm taking Thack with me!"

If Shen was listening, he didn't respond, which Kael took to mean consent. Opening the door while simultaneously throwing on his jacket, the young man raced into the cool night air, hoping to catch Laney before she disappeared. But she was already gone.

"How is she so fast?" he asked, watching as Thackery ran ahead of him into the lamplit street and turned his head back to wait for Kael. "Alright, let's see if we can catch her."

They didn't. But after several minutes in a dead sprint through the neighborhoods of Kearney, the two finally arrived at the large iron gates of the town's cemetery. Nightfall had arrived as well. Kael lost sight of Thackery but found him poised on the other side of the metal bars, waiting for his human companion to catch up. When Kael hopped the gate, he and Thackery continued at a much slower pace into the cemetery.

Unlike the last time he was there, the sky was calm and lit only by a crescent moon. If there were clouds, Kael couldn't see any, which only made the waning lunar cycle all the more prevalent and beautiful.

They found Laney sitting where Kael knew she would be—right beside her mother's grave. However, while the young man wanted to wait a couple of minutes to give Laney the chance to settle in, Thackery had no such intentions and ran over to her almost immediately.

"Well, hey there, little guy," Laney said as Thackery nuzzled himself underneath her arm. He circled back and forth so she could pet him from head to tail. "Where'd you come from?"

"Sorry about him," Kael said, glaring at the cat but deciding it was pointless to remain unnoticed any longer. "Thackery has privacy issues. So are you ungrounded?"

"Nope," Laney replied, now scratching Thackery behind his ears to earn a very audible purr. "Still a few more days. Just a little time off for good behavior."

"So your dad knows you're here?"

Laney nodded.

"Then why the whole Mission Impossible act out your window?"

She smirked. "Maybe I didn't want the sheriff watching from the front door as a certain juvenile delinquent followed his daughter all the way to the cemetery at night."

Kael grinned and looked away. "Hmm, so I've become predictable?"

Laney held her thumb and index finger an inch apart, then smiled. "But I mean, it's not like you have anything better to do in this boring town, right?"

He definitely didn't think so anymore. Things weren't always what they seemed...

As Laney put her hand back onto the grass, Thackery slammed his furry head against her arm to insist that she resume her petting. "Oh, I'm so sorry, kitty cat," she replied sarcastically, using her free hand to rub his face and chin once more.

There was an awkward silence as Kael tried to form the right words he'd been wanting to say since lunch. He didn't know whether to apologize for the fight or to ask Laney if she was okay. He just knew he wanted to make sure she was.

"Listen," he said. "About earlier toda—"

"Thank you," Laney said, sparing him the chance to stumble through what surely would've been a terrible apology.

"Thank you?" Kael asked, perplexed. "That's... not what I expected. You're supposed to tell me how stupid it was. Brash... reckless..."

"Impulsive..." she continued for him. "Unnecessary... macho..."

"Yeah, those things," he said.

"But sweet," Laney finished with a smile. "It was really sweet. Seriously, besides Mercury, no one's ever stood up for me like that before. Especially not against the entire football team."

"Something tells me you didn't need me to," Kael said, not knowing just how true the statement really was. "Anyway, they had it coming."

"Yeah..." Laney's eyes focused on Kael's chest, where the outline of his necklace was imprinted under the V of his thin black shirt. Her stare told him she was thinking about exactly what he'd been worried she saw.

"Who's there?" an old but loud Scottish voice cried out from a couple tombstones away. It was the same groundskeeper who'd attacked Kael a few weeks ago. He was in overalls and wielding the same bright yellow flashlight, focusing it into the two teens' eyes.

"It's just me, Mr. Dampé," Laney said, shielding herself with one hand from the blinding light.

"Oh, Laney!" The old man lowered the beam but drew ever closer. "I haven't seen you all month. Where have you been? I see you brought along a friend…"

The way the old man hissed through his final sentence made Kael's hair stand up on the back of his neck. Watching the caretaker's eyes drift down to Kael's chest where his necklace was, the young man immediately stood and put himself on guard.

"Laney, get behind me."

"What are you talking about?" she asked, pulling herself up from the ground. "Kael, this is Mr. Dampé. He's the groundskeeper here. Mr. Dampé, this is Kael Clark. He's—"

Before Laney could finish, Thackery had stealthily crept atop a tall tombstone next to Mr. Dampé. Without warning, he began hissing and growling with such feline ferocity that his eyes flashed like green fire. As he arched his back and bared his teeth, a well-placed paw swipe left three distinguishable red lines across the old man's face.

Laney sprang forward. "Mr. Dampé! Are you…?" But as she neared the Scotsman, she saw his face turn back to the cat with glazed-over black eyes and a row of sharp teeth. It was unlike anything she had ever seen before. Like he wasn't even human.

Snarling, Mr. Dampé swiped back at the black cat, forcing him to leap down from his perch. He then slowly turned his shadowy eyes to Kael and Laney. The extraordinarily nimble old man pushed the girl aside and lunged for Kael, tackling him to the ground in a heap that should've hurt but didn't.

As Kael struggled to hold back the wrinkled wrists of his surprisingly strong attacker, he noticed his onyx eyes were still fixated on the cross around the teenager's neck. However, before he could get to it, Laney smacked him off Kael with a heavy fallen tree branch she found on the ground—one she shouldn't have been able to lift, let alone swing around like Babe Ruth.

"Thanks," Kael said, springing to his feet.

"No problem," Laney replied, suddenly becoming aware of Kael staring in disbelief at the heavy object in her hands. She dropped it immediately and changed the subject. "What's wrong with him?"

Climbing on all fours like a spider, the possessed caretaker quickly rallied himself and rose unnaturally back onto two legs. Snapping his neck back into place, he flashed a sinister grin at the two teenagers. Only now he wasn't alone. From the trees in the distance, Kael and Laney could make out at least four more dark figures, each one shrouded in a black hoodie and wearing what looked like the skulls of dead animals over their faces. They were drawing closer...

Kael gripped the Arch Steel around his neck as Laney clenched her fists. Both of them wanted to fight, but both of them also had secrets they wanted to keep. Secrets they didn't want to explain. Not to mention Kael still couldn't transform his necklace into a weapon of true Arch Steel, so he couldn't truly defend them. And he doubted whipping demons with a one-ounce metal necklace would do that much good.

"We should run," he said.

"Yeah."

As the two took off in the opposite direction of their attackers, Mr. Dampé and the four masked villains gave chase. Kael made sure Laney and Thackery stayed far enough ahead of him that they wouldn't be caught while Laney made sure not to run too fast to leave Kael behind. Both decisions meant they weren't running fast enough...

The first to catch up to them was the one wearing a wolf skull, who grabbed Kael by the back of the shoulder and tried to drag him down. However, Kael's training kicked in fast enough that he was able to flip his attacker over onto his back.

But the brief lapse in running meant Kael was open to being attacked again. The two running behind the wolf—one wearing a fox skull and the other a bear—subdued Kael's arms and pinned him to a nearby tree. As he briefly struggled to free himself, the fourth figure sauntered up to him without saying a word.

He was easily the largest and most menacing of them all, wearing the cracked skeletal remains of a deer skull that looked like something out of a nightmare. While most of his other features were all but obscured by the dead of night, it didn't take long for Kael to guess who was behind the mask...

"Brody?" he asked, earning a head tilt from the deer skull. Without responding, the figure grabbed the cross around Kael's neck. However, just like with the grave keeper and Frankie, there was an immediate sizzling sound between the clenched fingers of the demon before him.

Before Kael could respond, a fist flew from around the tree so fast that he barely registered the petite frame of the girl it belonged to. Laney's knuckles landed against the snout of the deer skull, cracking the mask under the weight of her attack and sending its owner flying backward to the dirt. Unfortunately, he took Kael's necklace with him.

With Laney now in front of him, Kael spun in one fluid motion to knee the fox on his left in the stomach then turn the same move into a side thrust kick into the bear's chest on his right. Both techniques made the masked figures release him and crumple backward in pain, though Kael was still mesmerized by Laney's attack.

"Where did you learn to punch like that?" he asked.

"My dad's the sheriff," she replied. "You think he wouldn't teach his little girl how to throw a decent punch?"

A little more than just decent, Kael thought.

As the deer stood back up with necklace in hand, half of his bone mask split apart and fell to the ground, revealing dark skin and the same pitch-black eye of the possessed underneath. It wasn't Brody, Kael noticed, suddenly aware that his right eye was beginning to sting again, just like in the cafeteria.

"Aaron?" Laney asked, recognizing the visible half of his face as that of her childhood friend.

Before the wide receiver could respond, the silver of the Arch Steel in his hand began to glow white, shining through the closed fingers of the possessed teenager. The disgusting odor of burning flesh accompanied the sizzle of skin until the cross suddenly let out a burst of white light that earned a cry of agony from the one holding it. Refusing to let go, Aaron continued gripping the cross tightly as two arms suddenly appeared from his writhing frame. One was still the flesh and bone of the high school football player. But the other was the pure darkness of something else...

Something else that was somehow being separated and destroyed by the intense white light emanating from the Arch Steel that it tried desperately to hold on to. The light disintegrated the shadow arm into ash all the way up to the elbow before Aaron finally released the necklace and recoiled a few paces in a demonic cry of excruciating pain.

As the cross fell to the ground and ceased its unearthly glow, the upper portion of the amputated dark arm faded back into the fleshy counterpart of its host. The entire supernatural event took only a few moments, but it took several more for Kael and Laney to regain their senses. When they did, Kael leapt forward to grab his necklace.

"Come on!" he yelled, turning back to Laney. The two of them took off with Thackery in the direction of the cemetery's fence, leaving their attackers behind while they were still too distracted by their fallen comrade.

Wanting to retaliate, the injured teenager in the shattered deer mask snarled and tried to stand but fell back to his knees. He gripped the now lifeless arm at its elbow, too injured to continue. The other three masked figures surrounded him and lifted him to his feet. They nodded to Mr. Dampé in the distance before disappearing behind the cemetery's many trees. The glazed black eyes of the groundskeeper returned to their usual green as he picked up a nearby rake and began gathering leaves—whistling as the old man often would, like nothing had even happened.

† † †

After escaping the cemetery and running all the way back to their neighborhood at full speed, Kael slowed his pace to catch his breath while Laney spun around in the street in a mix of shock and triumph.

"I knew it!" she exclaimed, more out of breath from her own excitement than from having run several miles. "I knew there was something weird going on this year."

Kael finally caught his breath. "What? You mean being attacked by four masked figures and a geriatric Braveheart in a cemetery isn't your average Thursday?"

"I'm serious," the blonde replied. "Kearney's always had its fair share of strange, but ever since this summer, things have really gotten out of hand."

"What do you mean?"

"I mean people I've known my whole life suddenly acting totally different," Laney explained. "Good people gone bad for no reason… unexplained disappearances… our football team suddenly being good for once… and then there's the stuff that has no explanation… I know you don't really believe in the supernatural, Kael, but…"

That certainly wasn't true anymore. "You saw it too, didn't you?" he asked.

Laney nodded. "Frankie was burned by your necklace at lunch. And I know that was Aaron in the cemetery just now. There was this darkness that appeared from his arm. It was like…"

Kael finished for her. "It was like he was possessed." She looked surprised when he said it. He didn't want to give himself away, but he needed to talk to someone other than Shen about this whole thing. Someone a little more human. "Lee thinks the entire football team is. That's why they're suddenly winning their games."

She regained her composure quickly. "And what do you think?"

"I don't know," Kael answered. "Ask me a month ago about all this demon stuff and I would've said you were crazy. But after today… after that…" It was impossible for him to deny the fact that the things he always thought of as fairy tales were real. He would've preferred they weren't.

"I guess seeing is believing, even for Kael Clark, huh?" Laney asked, starting a slow walk down the street to her house. "Still, what is it with your necklace?"

Kael followed beside her, choosing to ignore the gloating remark. "I don't know," he lied. "It's a cross, right? Aren't crosses supposed to hurt demons?"

"Maybe…" Laney replied suspiciously, still not sure Kael wasn't hiding something from her. "I've just never seen one do that. Either way, we need to figure out a way to save the ones who are affected. Like Aaron and poor Mr. Dampé."

"Yeah…" Kael responded absentmindedly, not sure he could save anyone. He wasn't even past the first stage of his training and couldn't make true Arch Steel out of anything beyond his necklace. He wasn't good enough with The Word to put a car back together, let alone use it to fight an army of demons. The only thing he was good at was not getting hurt. And that wasn't even his doing.

As the pair reached the front of Laney's house, the blonde turned to Kael. "Let's see if Lee has any ideas tomorrow. All mythologies come from somewhere. Maybe he'll have some insight into how to fight possession."

"I'm not looking forward to telling him we think he's right."

"Yeah." Laney grinned. "Me neither. But I want to save this town before I…"

Kael leaned in curiously. "Before you what?"

"Nothing." She smiled wide to hold back her obvious sadness. She quickly leaned down to hide her expression and to pet Thackery one last time, who purred against her hand.

When she stood back up, she realized she was closer to Kael than the two had ever been before. Laney's blue eyes locked with Kael's hypnotic purple and green until both became lost in the other's. However, just before Laney let her body lean in and do what she would've regretted the next day, she snapped back to her senses and instead asked the same question she asked Kael his first night in Kearney.

"So will I see you tomorrow?"

After shaking off the moment they had, Kael smiled back at her. "We'll see."

Kael didn't want her to go. Laney didn't want to either, but she still forced herself to turn and walk away. Kael was about to say something, anything that would stop her. But then he didn't need to…

Laney rushed back faster than Kael could react and kissed him on the cheek. She didn't know why she aimed for the cheek other than it felt right at the time. At seventeen years old, Laney had never kissed a boy before. The cheek felt like a good place to start.

She didn't pull away immediately like she could've if she wanted to claim it was just a friendly kiss. Instead, with her arms wrapped around his neck in a hug, she raised to the highest point of her tiptoes and let her lips rest softly against his skin for what felt like an eternity. Kael was confused, but he certainly didn't make any move to stop her.

As she backed away slowly, their eyes interlocked once more as she moved just inches away from where she actually wanted to kiss…

"What was that for?" Kael asked.

"For earlier," she replied. "And for believing me about this whole thing. And for not leaving."

Kael smiled. "I'm not going anywhere."

Laney smiled too before backing away and walking up the driveway to her house. As she entered the front door, she couldn't believe what she just did. And as Kael tried to process the moment, he couldn't believe it either.

Though it put the first genuine smile on his face that he'd had in over eight years.

CHAPTER 19

In the blackened stillness of the night, the four possessed figures made their way onto Kearney High School's football field. Still wearing their animal skulls, the bear and the fox had the deer's arms draped over their shoulders, limping him across the track to the center of the field, where three more figures awaited.

It was Coach Winters. And on his sides, Frankie and Drew.

"I take it that didn't go well," Winters said, disappointment filling every ounce of his deep voice.

The four removed their masks to reveal four teenagers of different ages. Perfectly normal except for their carbon-colored eyes. All of them were on the football team. And the one who was injured was indeed Aaron Kobba, the team's senior wide receiver.

"There was a problem, Master Legate," one of them said, releasing Aaron so that all four could kneel. "Optio was injured by the Arch Steel. He couldn't continue."

"Couldn't?" the demon inside Coach Winters asked—the one called Legate. "Or didn't want to?"

The other three looked to one another in fear, then lowered their heads even further. When the one called Optio noticed this, he spoke from his prone position.

"I tried, sire! I tried holding on to it for as long as I could like you said to, but the light! It took my arm! It—"

"How long?"

"What?"

"How long were you holding on to it before it took your arm?"

The terrified expression painting Aaron Kobba's face told of the confusion afflicting the dark creature inside him. Through the intense pain of holding angel steel, he hadn't counted the time it took to maim him.

"Do I need to repeat myself?" Legate asked.

"A-a-a few seconds, maybe!" Optio stuttered out. "Ten at the most!"

"Hmm," he pondered. "Not enough time to get anywhere with it."

"My apologies, sire."

"Oh, no, you completed your task," Legate said, offering a hand to his still kneeling lesser. After pulling him to his feet, Legate smirked and placed his free hand on the teenager's forehead. "But you know what happens to a piece that fulfills its purpose. Yes?"

"No, sire! Please! Don't—"

But before his last word could be uttered, a shockwave went from Legate's hand into the forehead of the possessed Aaron Kobba. Instantly, black ash expelled itself from his every pore, burning up in the night air around the others like embers.

"It gets sacrificed."

With nothing now inhabiting the wide receiver's body, his soul took back control. He stumbled backward until he was caught by the three still behind him.

"What's happening?" Aaron asked, utterly confused by his whereabouts. "Coach? Frankie? What's going on? What's wrong with your eyes?"

Legate noticed Aaron had full use of both arms and that only the burn from the Arch Steel remained on his palm. Realizing he could still be used as a vessel, Legate stepped toward the terrified teen and put his hands back on his face.

"Shhh…"

And before Aaron could say another word, darkness flowed from the man who used to be Coach Winters into the boy who was about to be Aaron Kobba no more. Replaced by yet another dark presence subservient to Legate. The malevolent creature licked the lips of his new vessel and smiled as shadows engulfed his eyes.

"Go," Legate commanded the four in front of him. "And wait for further instructions."

As the four walked away, Frankie and Drew stepped forward to be at their master's side. "So what's the plan now?" the demon inside Drew asked.

"Hmm, I've never tried to steal an angel's Arch Steel before," Legate replied. "Choshek should've warned us about its properties. We'll need a new pawn. Someone easy enough to control but not of our stock. Luckily, I've been saving one for this very purpose…"

CHAPTER 20

As Kael reentered Shen's house, he heard the musical score of some '80s movie blaring from the old man's film room. He sighed as Thackery rushed between his feet to go greet his master. Kael followed behind him to inform Shen of the attack he just survived.

By the time Kael reached the room, Shen had lowered the volume of his movie and was petting the black cat from head to tail. "Thackery already told me," he said without turning. "You handled yourself well. Miss Lessenger handled herself better."

Eyeing the cat, who was too busy getting love to notice his glare, Kael replied, "This is getting serious, Gray."

"It's always been serious, Kael."

Kael should've expected that. "Well then, you got any tips on how to fight these things?"

"Master your powers," Shen replied simply.

"Anything more helpful...?" Nothing but silence. It looked like they were going to have to rely on Lee's knowledge of evil supernatural beings after all, which was almost scarier than the evil supernatural beings themselves. "If this really is that serious, why don't you just take care of it yourself?" he asked. "You're an angel, right? Isn't it like your job to vanquish demons or whatever?"

"You want me to do it all for you?" Shen asked.

"Yeah, that'd be nice," Kael replied.

"What about the Tower?" the old man continued. "Want me to fly you to the top? The Mustang? Repair it, so you can drive it around whenever?"

"Well, now that you mention it…"

"What about your grades? I've lived a long time. I could do your homework. And Mr. Maxwell? How about I use my powers to put him in his place. Oh, and Miss Lessenger… I'm sure I could—"

"Alright, alright," Kael pleaded with his hands up. "Some things I can do myself, thank you."

"All of it you can do yourself." Shen turned back around to continue his movie. "Stop living like you can't."

Despite the lateness of the hour, Kael wasn't tired. He didn't know if it was because he was getting stronger or because of Shen's sudden admonishment, but he liked to think it was because he'd been reinvigorated by the kiss Laney had given him outside. For whatever reason, though, he felt inspired and decided not to let the energy go to waste.

The young King threw himself into the two tasks Shen had set before him. Still, no matter how many times he tried, he couldn't scale the tower of terror, and he couldn't piece back together the mutilated Mustang. He attempted one for an hour and then left to attempt the other. Neither with any success. Both with infuriating disappointment.

"Any luck?" Shen's voice barely carried over Ray Parker asking, "Who ya gonna call?"

Kael groaned in response.

"Want to watch Clue with me next?" he asked genuinely, a little disappointed when he heard Kael groan again and head upstairs for bed. "Guess it's just you and me again, Thackery…"

✝✝✝

As he got dressed the following morning, Kael noticed his usual clothes were riddled with holes and tears from his training inside the Canvas. After glancing over at his dresser, he finally broke down and decided to at least look at the new clothes Shen had bought for him the first week he was in the house.

Much to his surprise, they were clothes he would've picked out for himself anyway—a lot of jeans and t-shirts with either simple designs or plain colors. Even more surprising was that they all fit him perfectly. He put on a new pair of dark jeans, a black and gray shirt, leather boots, and he was out the door before Shen could see him or make any remarks.

The teen was relieved it was Friday. Not because he could relax or anything but because he could devote an entire two days to training. What little progress Kael had made in his challenges so far took place over the weekends, and he was hoping to continue that trend.

The second Kael and Laney were in Lee's car, they told him they had something to tell him, but they wanted to do it at school in the Echo—both the name of the school paper and the room where Laney wrote and edited it. Luckily for them, their first period was cancelled since Kearney High School's science teachers were taking their students on a field trip to Cottonmill Park for a scavenger hunt to find different rocks and geodes.

"Okay," Lee said, gently closing the door to the Echo behind him. "Seriously, what's the big secret? And why are you two acting so awkward around each other all of a sudden? Did you guys make out or something?"

The comment was a joke, but the way Kael and Laney avoided eye contact told Lee everything he needed to know. "Oh my gosh, you two made out!?"

"We didn't make out," Kael said harshly, wanting desperately to change the subject before it became even more awkward. "Why would we want to tell you that?"

Laney watched as Kael moved around the room to lean against her desk with his hands gripping the underside. She knew she was going to have to say it. "We think you're right, Lee," she admitted. "About the football team. We think they're possessed."

The skeptical teenager narrowed his eyes and looked back and forth between his friends. "Are you two messing with me?"

"We were attacked in the cemetery last night by four of them," Laney explained. "I saw Aaron Kobba with my own eyes."

"How do you know they weren't just messing with you?" Lee asked, suddenly in disbelief of his own theory. "I mean, they hate Kael, so…"

Kael actually nodded in agreement. It was true.

"The last few months," Laney said, hesitating for just a moment. "You've seen the same weird stuff I have, right? People changing overnight… strength they shouldn't have… their eyes…"

"Black…" Lee finished, remembering all the times he'd seen what Laney was referring to. "Like an abyss." He shuddered for just a moment, then put the thought out of his mind. "Alright, you guys believe me. So what? I joked with Kael about you publishing a story on it, but I wasn't serious. It's not like anyone would buy it."

"I don't want to publish a story, Lee," she replied. "I want to save the ones who are being affected. We were hoping you knew something about possession that could help us do that."

Lee hesitated. Suddenly, he was confused by how scared he was. How real this was becoming. He had conspiracy theories about everything, but even he wasn't sure he believed them all.

"You called them yōkai," Kael said, interrupting his friend's thoughts. "Evil spirits, right? Do you know how to get rid of them?"

"Well, first of all, not all yōkai are considered evil," Lee corrected. "Some are thought to be benevolent spirits that only do good and help people."

Kael immediately thought of angels and wondered if it really was true that different cultures had all seen the same things and just called them different names.

"But yeah," Lee continued, "I know how to get rid of them. Just like any movie ever, you need an exorcist. Someone who knows how to drive away spirits in general."

"I don't take it you know anyone like that?" Laney asked.

Lee shook his head. "I mean, my Pop-Pop might, but I really don't want to get him involved in any of this. He's seventy-three."

"So basically, we have nothing," Kael said, pushing himself off the desk to pace around the room.

"Well, I don't know if it'll help," Lee said. "But there are myths about certain relics that can burn spirits out of a person's body. Only downside is that it actually burns the body at the relic's point of contact. Monks used to set people on fire to try and do the same thing when they didn't have the relics available. It... didn't work..."

Laney looked to Kael. "Your necklace," she said, nodding for him to take it out. "It burned Frankie and Aaron when they touched it. Do you think it could be one of these relics?" Laney moved closer to Kael to get a better look. "Do you know where your mom got it from?"

"No," Kael said, only half-lying. He knew how special it was, but he really didn't know where his mom got an angel's steel from before she died. Still... "How's it going to help, anyway? You want me to slap them with the cross?"

"Legend says you just have to hold it over the possessed person's head or heart," Lee chimed in. "The spirit should come out on its own from there. You know... after excruciating pain and torment."

"So if it works," Laney said, "we just need to find a player to test it on..."

Kael and Lee exchanged worried glances. "How are we going to do that?" Lee asked.

"The field trip today," she replied. "Brody, Frankie, and Drew are in my class. And I'm pretty sure Aaron's in yours, Lee…"

They both turned to Kael. "I haven't paid any attention to which jocks are in my science class," he replied. "I'm too enthralled by Ms. Gilbert's riveting lectures about rock formations."

Laney rolled her eyes. "Whatever, there's four potential targets right there. We'll be alone out in the woods. It'll be the perfect spot."

"Yeah, as long as I don't leave you two alone together…" Lee muttered under his breath with a grin.

"Shut up, Lee," they both replied in unison.

† † †

On the bus, Lee and Laney sat together while Kael sat in the seat behind them staring absentmindedly out the window. Cottonmill Park was only a nine-minute drive from the school, but the trio was shocked by just how many instructions the usually monotone Ms. Gilbert could get out before they got there.

The scavenger hunt was designed to be a race for a list of minerals between a few dozen teams of three, with the winning team not having to take finals at the end of the semester. Luckily, the science teachers had all agreed to allow the students to pick their own partners since, even if they had different classes, their final exams would all be the same test.

After some complaining from Lee that he wouldn't be on a team with Mercury if he joined Kael and Laney, and then a gentle reality check that she wouldn't be caught dead on a team with him anyway, Lee was finally convinced to put his name next to his friends on the list.

Growing up in the city, Kael had never truly been in the woods before. He almost remembered camping with his parents when he was little, but the memory was more of a blur than a solid image. As they turned down a gravel road, he got his first real glimpse of their destination.

The scenery of the park was gorgeous. It had a small lake surrounded by trees and several long trails that led off into either dense forests or grassy plains. It was a large, beautiful area, but all Kael could think about was the potential danger he was putting Lee and Laney in by going along with this plan.

What if something went wrong? What if he couldn't protect them? The thoughts consumed him so much that he didn't even feel the bus come to a complete stop.

"Earth to Kael," Lee said, waving his hand in front of his friend's face. "You with us, dude? We're here."

As everyone began shuffling off the bus, Kael filed in last behind his friends. When he stepped off, he was surprised to find Mr. Cade leaning against the side of the vehicle with his arms crossed.

"Do you teach science now too?" Kael asked as Lee and Laney continued with the group.

"Ms. Gilbert and the others needed a few extra chaperones with the number of kids they had," the teacher explained. "We drove separately." He nodded to one of the few cars in the parking lot across from theirs.

When Kael looked behind him, he was shocked to see a car he'd never actually seen in person—a brand-new Lexus LFA Nürburgring, one of the fastest and most expensive sports cars on the planet. With its lapis lazuli blue paint job, it practically shimmered among the row of dull teacher sedans surrounding it. It was an extraordinary sight and looked completely out of place in a small town like Kearney.

"You can afford that on a teacher's salary?" Kael asked. "Guess I know what kids should be going to school for..."

"It's a little ostentatious, I know," Mr. Cade replied. "But it's just a car."

"Why haven't I seen it at school?"

"I keep it parked out back to avoid the sophomores who just got their licenses."

"Why do you care if it's just a car?" Kael asked with a sly grin.

The teacher grinned back. "Well," he said, "it is still a very expensive car."

Kael almost laughed but stopped himself. He didn't know what it was about this particular teacher that always made him feel at ease, but it was a welcome change to the stressful life he'd made for himself the last few weeks. Plus, he owed him one.

"So, anyway, I'm not really good at thank-yous or whatever, but thanks for yesterday."

"Don't mention it," Mr. Cade said before lightening his tone with a smile. "Seriously, don't. Pretty sure I almost lost my job over it and don't want to remind Mr. Matthews it even happened."

"Ahem!"

In her dark skirt, white blouse, and thick-rimmed glasses, Ms. Gilbert looked more like a young librarian than a science teacher. "Mr. Cade!" she called from the group. "If you wouldn't mind joining us so we can get started…"

"Whoops." The English teacher shrugged. "Guess I'm in trouble." As he stepped past Kael, he stopped to say one last thing before joining the group. "Just try to keep your distance from Brody and his goons out here, alright? They may be dumb, but in my experience, dumb usually means dangerous."

You have no idea, Kael thought, following behind him until he rejoined Laney and Lee.

"Each of your teams has a list of the minerals you need to find," Ms. Gilbert explained. "You'll have three hours to find as many as you can and report back here. The team that finds the most the fastest will be exempt from their final exams. Any questions?"

Lee shot up his hand. "Are these woods really safe? There aren't like any bears or anything in there, right?"

Brody scoffed. "Want me to hold your hand, Muramasa?"

Ms. Gilbert shot a stern look to the quarterback before turning a kind eye back to Lee. "There are no bears in Kearney, Mr. Muramasa. Besides, your chaperones will be patrolling the woods should you need any help. Are there any other questions?" When silence followed, she finished. "Then good luck."

The second the science teacher finished her instructions, most of the groups with barely passing grades took off running past the trees and into the woods. The ones who knew they couldn't legitimately pass the final exams were determined to win.

Laney turned to her teammates to come up with a plan. "Okay, so I think we should follow Aaron. He wasn't grouped with any of the other football players, and I think I saw him separating from his team before he got to the woods. He'll be easy to test this on."

"What about the checklist?" Lee asked.

"What about it?" Laney asked back. "It's just extra credit. Who cares?"

"I barely have an A in this class, Laney," Lee explained. "And the final's worth thirty percent of our grade. Do you know what it's like to have Japanese parents? If I drop to a B, I might as well have gotten an F."

Laney sighed. "Alright, we'll split the list up into thirds, look for the minerals while also looking for Aaron, and then meet back up when one of us—"

"I don't want to be in the woods alone!" Lee said, terrified that Laney would even suggest it.

"Oh my gosh, Lee," she replied, obviously exasperated. "Fine, you go with Kael then. You guys take half the list, and I'll take the other half. When one of us finds Aaron, we'll call the other one. Sound good?"

Kael didn't have a phone, so Lee pulled out his and waved it happily in the air, relieved he wouldn't be alone.

"Just be careful," Kael said to Laney, who smiled and slung her backpack over her shoulder before trekking into the woods alone.

Lee looked back to Kael with an arched brow. "She's kind of bossy, huh?" he said. "Kind of hot. Not that I need to tell you."

Kael sighed. "Come on."

Within the first hour of searching, the relatively nice day had turned overcast and cooled down considerably. Lee mentioned that a storm was probably on its way and that they'd never find anything if it hit. Feeling an unusual amount of sympathy for his friend, Kael began using his powers to speed up their search. Visualizing the same pictures on the pages of their mineral list, he commanded each of them one by one to...

Surface.

And they did, so much so that Lee and Kael barely had to use their trowels to dig anymore. Everything they came across was either partially visible or completely sticking out of the ground. Lee couldn't believe their luck.

In another half hour, they had everything on their list except for one final geode. It was called an amethyst geode, and it was the same color as Kael's right eye. However, when Kael visualized it to make it appear, nothing happened, which either meant that it was too far away or wasn't there at all. Either way, if they wanted it, they'd have to find it the old-fashioned way.

"So..." Lee had finally mustered up the courage to say something. "You and Laney, huh?"

"There is no me and Laney," Kael replied, searching for his next place to dig.

"She kissed you, right? Seems to me like she wants there to be a her and you."

"It was a heat of the moment kind of thing," Kael reasoned. "We had just been attacked by four possessed football players."

"Speaking of which," Lee replied, "what's your plan if we actually do find Aaron? You gonna hold him down and try to exorcize him in the middle of the woods?"

"Nah," Kael said. "I figured you could hold him down."

Lee knew his friend was joking, but that didn't stop him from waving his hands and trowel defensively in the air. "Whoa, whoa, we both know I'm not the muscle here. My skillset is very clearly defined. Brains and trying to make you seem less broody. Which, if Laney Lessenger's going for you, means I'm doing my job right."

Kael ignored him and started digging next to a small creek. Meanwhile, Lee climbed on top of a large rock above the creek bed and held up his cell phone. "There's like no service out here. Even if Laney did call, I doubt she'd get through. You think we should look for her?"

"I'm sure she's alright."

The voice was one both Lee and Kael instantly recognized. And belonged to someone they'd been hoping to avoid. Brody appeared from behind a tree that was growing on the back side of the rock Lee was standing on. Frankie and Drew appeared behind him, and together they encircled the slim teen.

Kael stopped what he was doing and stood, readying himself for the trouble that was sure to come. Lee stood motionless with his trowel in hand and the unzipped backpack of rocks and geodes at his feet.

"Well, would you look at that!" Brody said, reaching down to investigate the bag. "Looks like our boys here have just about found everything on Gilbert's list for us. How convenient."

"What do you want, Brody?" Kael asked calmly, eyeing Frankie and Drew as they paced behind the petrified Lee. He knew at least one of them was possessed.

"Oh, not much. I was just thinking of a trade. You see, Lee here still owes Frankie some overdue homework assignments. And you owe me for this..." Brody turned the side of his face to reveal a dark bruise. "Not having to take these finals would really help us for the playoffs. How about you guys give us what you've found, and we don't tear your heads off?"

"Fine, take it," Kael replied, which wasn't the answer Lee expected.

"Dude! I told you! I don't want to take the final either!" he complained, which earned him a death grip around his deltoids from the large linemen behind him.

"Well, that was easier than I thought," Brody said. "But since you're so eager to agree with me, how about you also give me that piece of silver hanging around your neck?"

Kael peered down to look at his necklace, suddenly becoming suspicious that it wasn't just Frankie who was possessed. "What do you want with a piece of jewelry?"

"Looks valuable," Brody replied. "Plus, Laney's a good Christian girl. I want to show her I can be a good Christian guy. You know, just like you, Kael."

Frankie and Drew started laughing, almost like a low cackling that sounded more sinister than it should have. The quarterback joined in with a snicker of his own.

"So, what do you say, freak eyes?" he asked. "Or am I gonna get my rematch where no teachers can save you this time?"

Before Kael could respond, the group heard a rustling in the bushes next to the creek and became acutely aware that they weren't alone in their little shade of forest. After several more seconds of leaves swishing back and forth, their stillness was rewarded with low grunts and chortling sounds.

The bushes didn't part but exploded apart as a gargantuan grizzly bear burst through them, roaring like a dark brown freight train. Dropping their bags and everything in their hands, the boys took off at what seemed like subsonic speed, hurtling over fallen branches and rocks in an attempt to escape the bear's fury.

However, with Brody, Drew, and even Frankie somehow blowing past him, Kael looked back to realize Lee wasn't anywhere behind them. He wasn't even in his line of sight. A million images of the teen being eaten alive by an angry grizzly bear filled Kael's mind. He wheeled around and started running even faster back toward his friend.

Returning to the spot he'd fled from, Kael saw Lee paralyzed in fear against the tree hyperventilating on his inhaler. His eyes were shut tight as the grizzly roared like thunder once again. It went from all fours to standing on its hind legs, becoming all of eight feet tall and weighing at least eight hundred pounds. Kael had seen a man hold a star in his hands, and this was somehow scarier. More primal.

"Lee," Kael whispered loudly, trying to get his attention without attracting the bear's.

When the young man cracked open a single eyelid to see his friend, he said, "She lied to me, Kael..." He quivered in abject terror. "Gilbert said there were no bears in Kearney. Tell her this is all her fault when I'm gone..."

"You're not going to die," Kael whispered again through clenched teeth. "Just move slowly off the rock towards me."

The behemoth had momentarily stopped to analyze the cowering teen it had pinned. However, as Lee began to inch his way away from the tree, the bear's eyes filled with fire as it let out another roar far more powerful than before. It wasn't curious anymore. It was angry. And that was its last warning.

As the colossal beast took two steps forward to strike Lee down with its massive claws, Kael's legs moved faster than they ever had before. He pulled the Arch Steel pendant from his neck and leapt in front of Lee with one arm extended toward the bear and the other holding an iron sword he didn't want to have to use.

But then, none of it mattered. In his fear, something opened up inside Kael that hadn't been there before. A realization.

"Stop."

He said the word, and the bear obeyed it. Not out of physical force but out of mental—like its mind was being controlled. And then Kael knew. He was controlling the bear because he knew what the bear was feeling. What they were both feeling... Fear.

It was every animal's primary emotion, and the only one that drove them to do anything they ever did. Fear of starvation, so they'd hunt. Fear of loss, so they'd attack. Fear of death, so they'd kill. Every animal's instinct was to suppress fear at any cost.

But as the grizzly bear halted dead in its tracks, Kael took the time to feel the animal's fear. Suddenly, he knew the only reason it wanted to kill Lee was because it was afraid of him. Comparing the two, it seemed ridiculous, but he didn't have to agree with the creature's reasoning to know that was how it felt. So, with another word, he relieved the feeling.

"Leave."

The eight-foot animal shrank to a far less terrifying height on four legs and turned away from the boys to disappear back into the foliage. With the bear gone, Kael finally took the breath he wasn't aware he'd been holding and turned around to face Lee.

The teen's eyes reflected a mixture of amazement and triumph. "I knew it!" he yelled and pushed himself up against the tree so he could stand. "I knew there was something different about you! Surviving that wreck on the news, all the times my car magically started with you in it, living with old man Shen, and just now with that bear! And that sword! What is that thing?"

Kael remembered he'd activated his necklace into a sword of iron. Better than lead, he thought. But now wasn't the time. Once Lee brought it to his attention, he willed it back down to its original form and looped it around his neck.

"Whoa..." Lee said in stunned astonishment.

"Okay," Kael said. "Don't freak out."

"A little late for that," Lee replied, completely freaking out. "Wait until Laney hears about this. She was right about you the whole time."

"What do you mean?" Kael asked. "Laney thinks there's something off about me?"

"Uh, yeah, dude, you've been on her radar ever since the first day you got here. She doesn't know what or anything, but she's gonna freak when she finds out."

"Lee," Kael said seriously. "You can't tell her about any of this."

"Why not? You're like a freaking superhero or something. Do you know what I'd do if I was a superhero? Tell everyone. Besides, if she wasn't into you before, she's certainly going to be now."

"Kael…!? Lee…!?" Multiple voices rang through the forest. They were still far off but heading in the right direction. Brody must have told the teachers what happened, Kael reasoned. He didn't have much time.

"I'm serious, Lee, you can't tell her." He was too flustered to come up with a better reason. "Or anyone else."

"Does this have anything to do with the yōkai?" Lee asked. "Wait, you're not one, right? Man, that'd be so messed up. Double agent…"

"No," Kael replied. "I'm not possessed. I'll explain everything after school. I'll even let you meet Shen. Just promise me you won't tell anyone about this."

Lee thought hard about Kael's sincerity. He'd never heard him sound so desperate before. "Does old man Shen know about you?" he asked.

"Kael!? Lee!?" The voices were getting closer. Too close.

Kael was panicking. What was he supposed to do? Lying would only take longer. He opted for the truth. "Yes, he knows. That's why he's fostering me. He's helping me train." If watching movies all day counted as helping, he thought.

"So, he's like your Yoda? Dude, that's so boss!"

"Kael!? Lee!?"

Time was up. "Lee!" he practically yelled. "Promise me, please." Kael Clark hadn't genuinely said the word "please" in a long time. It felt unnatural leaving his lips.

"Alright, alright," Lee said defensively. "I guess I do owe you like a hundred now after all."

Kael grabbed his backpack, as well as Lee's with all the rocks in it, and walked quickly toward the voices. "Keep this between us, and we'll call it even."

Lee would, but his imagination was already running wild. "You're going to have to show me that sword trick again."

"Fine."

"And tell me all the powers you have."

"Whatever."

"And... Oh! Can I be your sidekick?"

"No."

"Assistant?"

"No."

"Tech guy?"

"I'm not a superhero, Lee."

After meeting up with the small search party, they made their way out of the forest and back to the buses. A large group of teachers and students had been waiting for them just in case they came back on their own.

"There they are!" one of the girls yelled.

While the group ran to them, Kael tried his best to spot Laney in the crowd. He couldn't. And that made him worry.

"What happened to you guys? Are you okay? How'd you get away?"

Kael ignored them all. "Where's Laney?" he asked.

"She went looking for you guys after Brody told us you got attacked by a bear. Why? Is she not with you?"

Kael's head snapped back to the forest he'd just exited. Laney was still in there with a massive grizzly bear. He was about to break into a sprint to find her when she suddenly appeared from behind some trees. When she made eye contact with Kael and Lee, she broke into her own sprint toward them.

Laney threw her arms around Kael in the tightest hug he'd ever experienced. She then grabbed Lee too and pulled him into her embrace.

"Where were you guys?" she asked, tears all but welling up in her eyes. "When Brody said you'd been attacked by a bear, I..."

Kael didn't know how to respond. He'd been so preoccupied convincing Lee to keep his secret that he hadn't given any thought to the excuses he'd need to explain how they escaped the clutches of a grizzly.

Luckily, Lee had no such trouble. "Brody told you what?" he asked with an arched eyebrow and convincing smile. The rest of the group caught up just in time to see Lee patting himself down, not a scratch on him. "Does it look like we got attacked by a bear?"

Everyone turned to Brody, who was astounded to see his two peers alive and unharmed. After collecting his thoughts, he said, "But there was a bear!" With doubtful faces staring him down, he continued. "I'm not the only one who saw it! Drew and Frankie were there too!"

Now everyone turned to Drew and Frankie for confirmation. "Actually, man, we only saw you running. You took off so fast we just ran after you thinking there was something wrong."

Everyone's heads swiveled back to Brody. The group of students began murmuring their own insults as Lee formulated the perfect response. "Looks like you were the one who needed someone to hold your hand, Brody..."

The quarterback's eyes lit ablaze with anger while the teachers discussed the best course of action to take. "Well, in any case," Ms. Gilbert said, adjusting the rim of her glasses, "I think it's time we call it for today.

I just checked the weather, and we have a severe thunderstorm warning. We can count your findings on the bus to see who collected the most—"

"Um, ma'am," Lee spoke up once again. "Actually, I think we collected everything on the list."

Kael leaned over and whispered, "What are you talking about? We still had that one to find."

"Just trust me," he replied. "Laney, did you get everything on your half of the list?"

"Oh," she said. "Yeah, actually."

She set her bag down next to Lee's. Ms. Gilbert and the other science teachers searched through both to find every single item on the list accounted for, including the one Kael only recognized from its picture—the amethyst geode. Somehow, it was in their bag.

Ms. Gilbert held it up, displaying it proudly to the crowd of students. "If any of you were actually listening to my lectures, you'll remember that this is one of the rarest and most expensive geodes that can be found. It contains purple amethyst crystals and black calcite, which is why it's sometimes called the queen's throne. I always put it on the scavenger hunt but never expect anyone to actually find it."

Brody's face contorted in anger. "Yeah, because that one's ours!" he shouted. "We bou... I mean, we found it!"

Kael glanced at Lee, who made a hand gesture implying he stole it from Brody's bag after he dropped it in the woods running from the bear. Kael was too preoccupied to notice, but Lee had slipped it into his pack on their way back.

"Was that before or after you saw a grizzly bear!?" a random student asked, prompting a chuckle from the crowd.

"Alright, alright," Ms. Gilbert said, calming the group down. "Mr. Muramasa, Miss Lessenger, Mr. Clark, you three are exempt from the final. Well done. Now, everyone get back on the bus."

As the group dispersed, the three friends smiled at their victory before realizing it wasn't really the one they were hoping to achieve.

"Well, I guess that was a bust," Laney said. "I never even saw Aaron out there."

"Yeah," Lee replied before smiling wide. "But hey, no finals!"

"Maybe it's for the best," Kael added. "Too many people around. If we try this, we need to be more discreet about it."

"Yeah," Laney said. "You're probably right." But as the three headed toward the bus, she added, "But seriously, tell me… what happened out there?"

Kael glanced at Lee with a worried expression. This was the moment of truth. Would he keep his promise to Kael or his loyalty to Laney?

Lee shrugged. "I think Brody was just mad I stole the queen's whatever from his bag," he said. "I saw him buying it in town last week. One of last year's seniors must have told him it was on the checklist."

"Brody's an idiot," she said, reaching the bus stairs and climbing up.

Lee turned to Kael. "Pretty slick, huh? One might even say… sidekick material?"

"Yeah…" Kael replied without thinking. "I mean no. No sidekick."

"What's wrong?"

"Nothing," Kael said, waiting for Brody, Frankie, and Drew to barge past them onto the bus. "It's just… I know Frankie and Drew saw that bear. Even if they are possessed, what reason would they have to lie about it?"

CHAPTER 21

Once the science classes arrived back at the school, every student trudged slowly off the bus. Having expected to basically have a free day at Cottonmill, they were all visibly upset that they had to return to their usual Friday schedules. Teachers included.

As Laney redistributed all the rocks and minerals they'd collected to her backpack, Lee pulled Kael off to the rear of the bus and started firing questions at him.

"So when do you want to talk about this? Now or after school? Don't you have a free period soon? Mine's right now. Wait, you probably don't want to talk about it here, huh? After school then? You said I can finally meet old man Shen too, right? Do you—"

"Lee," Kael cut in, encouraging his friend to take a breath. "Chill. I'll explain everything after we drop Laney off."

Both boys looked to find her stepping down from the bus, zipping up her now oversized bag of rocks and slinging it over her shoulder.

"Understood," Lee replied with a wink and finger guns.

"So weird, dude."

Lee shrugged. "I'll see you after school th—" He stopped and smacked his palm against his forehead. "Crap!"

"What?" Kael asked.

"I can't give you guys a ride home today," he explained. "I have to take my little sister to cheer after school and stay with her until her practice is over. Mom got a new job, and Dad wants me to take on more responsibility and—"

"Lee," Kael interrupted again. He was getting a headache from how fast his friend was talking. "It's fine. Just come over tomorrow sometime. I'll tell you everything then."

Lee still looked disappointed but knew he didn't have a choice but to wait. "Okay," he sighed. He started backing away as Laney approached them. "You promise, though? Tomorrow morning?"

"Yeah," Kael replied. "Promise."

Lee kept backing away until he finally turned and disappeared behind the large glass double doors of the front of the school. Kael waited for Laney.

"What was that about?" she asked, handing the empty backpack to him as the bus pulled away with a screech.

"Nothing," he replied. "Lee stuff."

"Ah." Laney nodded in understanding. "Well, I'll take these to Ms. Gilbert for us."

"I'll walk you," Kael said, offering to take the bag from her shoulder. When she let him, it dropped to the ground like a ton of bricks. Or at least a hundred pounds of solid rock. It had to weigh almost as much as Laney herself, who was staring at him with a smirk.

He stared back in confusion. How did she always make things look so effortless?

Shrugging off his initial failure, Kael hefted the cumbersome load over his shoulder and led the way around the outside of the school.

"So what's our next move?" he asked, desperate to avoid any awkward silences.

"I don't know," Laney said. "We have to get one of them alone to see if Lee's theory about your necklace really works, but it's not like we can just break into one of their houses while they're sleeping. And they're all typical jocks. They like to run in a pack."

"Trust me, I've noticed." Kael adjusted the backpack strap that was digging into his shoulder, still wondering how Laney could have carried it with such ease. "Still, I'm sure you'll think of something."

Laney pointed to the bag. "Want me to take that back for you?" she teased.

"Actually, could you?" he joked back. "Girl power and all."

She laughed and rolled her eyes. The two rounded nearly half the school, eventually arriving at the exterior side door that led into the stairwell by Ms. Gilbert's classroom. "Well," Laney said, "here we are…"

Kael let the heavy bag slip from his shoulder into Laney's hands, who took it back from him with no issue. When she realized how that looked, she feigned weakness to pretend like it was actually heavy.

"So are we going to talk about last night?" Kael asked. "Or were you secretly hoping I would get eaten by a bear in the woods so we wouldn't have to?"

"That's not even funny," Laney replied. "I came after you guys, didn't I?"

"Yeah, speaking of, what was your plan if you found us? Beat the bear off with your bag of rocks?"

"At least I can lift it," she jabbed back. Kael laughed before he realized just how embarrassing that really was. "Seriously, though," Laney continued, "I was really worried about you."

"Just me?" he asked before he could think to stop himself. Then he was glad he didn't. He wanted to know the truth. "Lee thinks you like me."

Laney's long blonde waves had fallen to cover half her face. One crystal blue eye looked up to meet Kael's stare. "And what if I do?" she asked, immediately regretting the words as they left her lips. Not because they weren't true. But because they weren't fair when she'd be leaving in a couple months.

"Then..." Kael thought about just how much he liked her too. How he hadn't liked anyone like he liked her in a long time. Then he thought about what his life was going to be like if he really bought into all this supernatural stuff with Shen. And just how unfair it'd be to anyone who chose to be with him.

He couldn't do that to her.

"Then I'd tell you what you already know," he restarted, this time with his signature cocky grin. "I'm bad for you, Laney. I break the law. I get into fights. I've stolen from people. Hurt them... Not to mention your dad would absolutely hate me. All in all, I'm just not good for you or anyone else. But you already know that."

Laney would've agreed if that were true. But it wasn't. She didn't know why, because everything Kael was saying technically was true, but that wasn't how she felt about him... Still, he was giving her an out. She thought maybe she should take it.

"Yeah, I mean..." She shook her head with a smile to hide her true feelings. "...you're still the Fitzwilliam Darcy of the story, right?"

Kael forced a grin back at her. "Right."

Laney smiled sadly and opened the door behind her to disappear for the rest of the day. But as it began to close, they each thought about how her kiss on the cheek meant more than either one was willing to admit. That scared both of them. And neither had the courage to do anything about it.

"You wimp," Laney said to herself while walking to Ms. Gilbert's.

"Coward," Kael said, walking away wondering if he'd made the right decision.

†††

Elsewhere, after the buses had pulled away and the rest of the students reentered the school, Brody had ducked away and walked over to the football field. After waiting under the bleachers for several minutes, Coach Winters suddenly appeared behind him like a phantom from the shadows.

"You have something for me, Mr. Maxwell?" he asked.

The young quarterback flipped around, startled. "No, Coach, I mean, I didn't get the chance," he replied. "There was this grizzly bear in the forest. I tried telling the other teachers, but everyone thought I was lying and—"

The coach growled the young man into silence. "I didn't ask for excuses."

Brody was already irritated by how he'd been treated that day. He wasn't about to take it from anyone else. "Hey, it's not my fault! Drew and Frankie wouldn't back me! What's so important about a stupid necklace anyway? Looks like a worthless piece of junk."

"Worth is not the point!" Winters replied angrily. "I asked you to do something, and I expect you to do it."

"Yeah, but why?" Brody shot back. "What's a necklace have to do with anything?"

"It's not about the necklace, you imbecile," Coach Winters said. "It's about proof. Proof you're willing to do whatever it takes to get what you want. To get what's important to you. And what is that again, Mr. Maxwell?"

Brody was silent for a moment. "A scholarship out of this town."

"And who's the only one who can provide that for you?"

"You, Coach."

"Then do what I say and take something that's important to Clark."

Brody was still conflicted. "I just—"

"Have you forgotten how he embarrassed you and this entire team his first week here? Or that he's practically stolen your little girlfriend right out from under your nose?" Winters saw Brody's nostrils flare. "You asked me what you could do to win Miss Lessenger back. Well, this is the first step. In chess, you must plan ten moves ahead to win. Are you a winner, Mr. Maxwell?"

Brody nodded.

"Are you the king on this board or just some useless pawn?"

"The king," he replied.

"And are you going to let the opposing side take your pieces without taking some of theirs in return?"

"No, Coach."

"I can't hear you, Mr. Maxwell!"

"No, Coach!"

"Good," Winters said, crossing his arms. "Now prove it. If you want that scholarship recommendation from me, then go out and earn it. And don't bother coming to practice next week unless you're willing to do whatever it takes."

As Brody left the bleachers, two more figures appeared from the shadows behind Coach Winters, standing on either side of him like sentries. He could sense without turning that it was Frankie and Drew. Though he didn't know them by their shell names anymore…

He knew them as Primus and Pilus.

Likewise, they didn't know him as Coach Winters anymore…

He was Legate.

As the three watched Brody stomp angrily back toward the school, their eyes blackened from the pupils and became sockets of pure darkness.

"Do you actually think he'll be able to get the Arch Steel away from Clark?" Pilus asked, his voice deeper and more menacing than ever.

"We will see," Legate replied. "He's a moron, but even pawns have their usefulness."

"If he fails again, can we just possess him already and add him to our ranks?"

"Yes," Primus added, adjusting the fat head of his fleshy vestige. "I grow weary of playing the fool around him."

Legate turned to meet the pitch-black eyes of his compatriots. "All in due time." He smiled, then turned back to watch Brody enter the school. "Let's allow the game play out first, shall we?"

The demons inhabiting Drew and Frankie glanced at each other with contemplative expressions. They didn't know what their leader was up to, but they knew better than to ask.

"Speaking of failure," Legate continued, "why did you two turn against Mr. Maxwell today?"

"Because field trips give the quarterback the best chance to take the Arch Steel," Pilus explained. "The school has too many witnesses, and Clark's residence is too well guarded by the angel. And if the teachers learned that there was an actual bear attack—"

"Then the school board would likely cancel any other trips," Legate finished, silently proud of his subordinate's foresight.

"And there's another one coming up in November for the championship game. With a ski trip to Iowa afterward if I'm not mistaken."

Legate smiled behind the fleshy exterior of his human puppet. "Perfect."

"Sire, there's one more thing," Pilus continued. "The bear attack was too much of a coincidence. We had the King right where we wanted him. The quarterback would surely have the Arch Steel right now if someone hadn't interfered…"

"You let me deal with him," Legate said. "You two focus on discovering who the Seal is. We cannot utilize the Arch Steel until we do anyway. Keep an eye on the King and make sure he's doing his job in seeking them out for us."

Pilus and Primus bowed in unison with their fists over their chests before disappearing into the darkness from which they appeared. The moment they were out of earshot, Legate smiled and even began to laugh.

Everything was going according to plan.

CHAPTER 22

With Lee having to take his little sister to cheerleading practice, Kael was forced to ride the bus to Shen's for the first time in a month. Sitting alone, he beat himself up for everything he'd said to Laney during their last conversation. He knew it was for the best, but that didn't mean he had to like it. In the thirty minutes it took to get home, he probably muttered the word "idiot" to himself a few hundred times.

As he walked through the front door, Kael was met with something he hadn't heard in the old man's house for a long time. Silence. Nothing cooking in the kitchen. No movie playing in the background. It was almost eerie.

"Gray!" he called out. The only response was a meow from Thackery in another room, who came trotting into the foyer with a note in his mouth.

Had to run to Omaha for business. Be back soon.

Kael wondered what kind of business Shen could possibly have in Omaha but decided not to think about it. He had his own problems after all. And he decided to deal with them through the extreme physical torture of trying to climb an impossible rotating spire of death...

After changing into the clothes he'd already torn up during his previous training exercises, Kael entered the Canvas and began his ascent on the ever-changing labyrinth Shen called the Tower. The first few floors had become easy for him. There was a pattern to the madness, and all Kael had to do was jump from one block to the next, pulling himself up out of the way in time to avoid the ones that circled below.

The next few floors were trickier since the blocks were constantly turning upside down as he tried to step on them. Painful experience taught that speed was the key here. Empowering himself with the energy of The White, he moved across them before they had the chance to invert. The spiraling nature of the spire increased in speed the higher Kael climbed. Still, floor after floor he conquered until…

The tenth story. It was the point he'd been stuck on for the last two weeks, the point he always reached before falling and crashing painfully back down against the shifting pieces of the ninth, the eighth, and sometimes the seventh tier. When he slipped, the power of The White and grabbing on to random pieces on his way down were the only things that kept him from breaking bones. Or worse.

He didn't know which he hated more—falling or having to climb back up after every fall.

The tenth tier was the most difficult because there was only one rectangular block on the entire level, it rotated in place at nauseating speeds, and the only way to get to the eleventh floor was through a series of smaller blocks that only shifted into a single path of steppingstones once every few rotations. If Kael didn't time it perfectly, he would fall. Which he'd done a lot.

Through all this, though, there was also the fact that Kael was still petrified of heights. He mitigated this somewhat by never looking down or even thinking about it, but the paralyzing terror of being so high up was always present in the back of his mind.

Kael closed his eyes to steady the nausea building in his throat. The rapidly spinning beam he was kneeling on felt unsteady in every sense of the word. Kael had to calm himself to time his jump if he wanted even a chance of reaching the next tier.

Opening his eyes to count the rotations, he jumped once he counted three, landing on the first block with his right foot and using it to springboard him to the second... and then the third... then the fourth. But this was as far as Kael ever made it. He was halfway there but needed to possess even more inhuman agility than The White provided him to leap for the next piece—a small misshapen block that was just too far away.

Summoning all of his strength, Kael leapt for the piece that always eluded him.

And missed it completely.

His only saving grace was that during his fall, the beam of the tenth tier was coming around again for another pass. He grabbed ahold of it and pulled himself up before he could be knocked off by another rotating piece below.

At least he avoided a bad fall, he thought, trying desperately to make himself feel better.

Back on the spinning piece, he yelled into the nothingness, hoping Shen could hear him wherever he was. No response. There never was. It just made Kael feel better to yell sometimes.

As he closed his eyes to concentrate on not vomiting yet again, he started thinking about all the little lessons Shen had given him over the last few weeks. Out of all of them, the most recurrent was not relying so much on his eyes. It seemed crazy. He needed his eyes, especially in a potentially lethal training exercise that involved him leaping across certain death. But so far, using them was getting him nowhere.

"Alright, Gray," he said to himself. "Let's try it your way just once."

With his eyes still closed, Kael let himself tap into the infinite energy of The White to bolster his physicality once more. If he wasn't going to use his sight, he was at least going to max out every single one of his other powers—including The Word. While he had never actually used it on himself before, he figured it was worth a try.

No, he thought. Not try. He had to believe it.

"Succeed."

As the word left his lips, Kael leapt forward from the supernatural beam and let his instincts take over. He glided across the first four blocks like water, moving as gracefully as a jungle cat. But when it came time to leap for the last piece, he stopped and waited. He had the right timing to reach it, but something told him not to jump yet.

With his eyes still closed, Kael waited until he knew the piece had passed, and waited some more until he knew it had passed again. On the third rotation, though, his instincts took hold and told him to jump. When he did, his foot landed on something flat and smooth that shouldn't have been there but somehow was…

Kael hadn't seen anything there before, but he knew not to waste time questioning it. From the invisible platform, he leapt again and reached the misshapen block that finally allowed him to ascend to the eleventh tier.

Now standing on a large slab of block as long as a bus, Kael opened his eyes and looked down to where he'd just leapt from. There was nothing between the blocks he could've landed on. Nothing visible anyway. Not that he cared. All he cared about was that he made it. He even cheered and pumped his fists into the air to prove it.

Looking up through the rapidly shifting pieces still above him, he could finally see the bull's head Shen had mentioned the first day they'd entered the Canvas. He wasn't close to the top yet, but he wasn't about to let that spoil his mood.

However, before he could analyze the next path further, Kael heard a door open and shut at the bottom of the Tower. Not daring to look down, Kael inched over to the edge of his new platform as it made its way around the perimeter of the Tower.

"Hey, Gray, I did it! I used your trick! I finally made it!" He was beaming from ear to ear, overjoyed by his success. "Oh, man, you should've seen me!"

However, when silence was his response, Kael became confused. Summoning some courage, he hesitantly peered over the edge, but all he could see was the door that led into the Canvas evaporating back into the nothingness from which it appeared. He couldn't see Shen anywhere...

"Gray?" he asked, wondering if this was another test.

Suddenly, Kael felt a blow against his chest so hard that it knocked the wind out of him and sent him sliding across the block beneath his feet. Standing back up, he felt another blow against his face and then several more against his body, all from alternating directions.

Bleeding from his mouth, Kael wiped the blood onto his hand before feeling the unmistakable sensation of fingers clutching around his throat.

Only there wasn't anything in front of him.

The invisible force lifted the seventeen-year-old into the air and carried him over to the edge of the slab, dangling him precariously over the outer side of the spinning tower.

Kael couldn't breathe. The grip around his neck was so tight that it felt like a vise against his windpipe. But as his vision began to fade to black and he desperately gasped for air, his invisible attacker pulled him in close, breathing on his face in a low, dark growl.

"False King..." it said, before throwing Kael off the Tower and down toward his imminent demise.

Kael sucked in a breath and tried to think of what to do. He was hundreds of feet in the air and falling quickly. The Tower was too far away, and there was nothing else to grab on to that would slow his fall. And no guardian to save him this time. Fear gripped him.

He was going to die.

Then he thought of the door. The door to the Canvas would appear wherever he wanted it to. He just hoped it would appear horizontally the same as it did vertically.

Closing his eyes to imagine it, the door materialized fifty feet below where Kael was falling. But it was closed. Readjusting himself into a downward skydive, Kael reached out his palm…

"Open."

The door obeyed Kael's command and shot wide open, revealing the interior of Shen's hallway. As he fell through the opening, what he hoped would happen happened. Gravity instantly shifted, righting itself and causing Kael's subsonic dive to turn into a substandard belly flop on Shen's hallway rug. It didn't feel great, but it was far from lethal.

However, his attackers weren't through with him. As Kael tried to stand, he felt a tight grip around his ankle pulling him back through the doorway. He felt something else try to grab his wrist to keep him there, but it slipped, allowing Kael to be dragged back through the frame. Once more in the Canvas, he was slung and thrown several feet onto his back. The door, floating just above the ground horizontally, slammed shut and faded into mist once more.

Painfully, Kael managed to stand and steady himself with sheer will-power. He was done being a punching bag. Throwing his fists up to attack whatever was attacking him, he sunk into a defensive stance while trying to catch his breath. When he finally managed to, he yelled, "What are you!?"

Instead of a verbal response, Kael received several more blows against his body from every conceivable direction. They weren't just punches anymore though… They felt like claw marks. They tore through his clothes and into his skin so many times that Kael collapsed back to his knees from the pain.

Panting and kneeling with his hands on the floor, the young King saw the scarlet stains of his own blood pooling around him on the white landscape. Suddenly, the same realization overcame him again. He really was going to die. His attackers could've done it at any moment, but they were toying with him, torturing him for their own amusement. Kael didn't know who or what they were, but he knew they weren't going to let up until he was dead. And he was powerless to stop them. He couldn't even see them.

However, as blood dripped from every gash and wound, Kael felt a searing pain in his right eye. He clamped over it with one hand as the agony intensified and the royal purple iris surrounding his pupil began to glow. And after several more excruciating moments, Kael could see everything...

There were two beings standing several yards ahead of him, staring at their victim's plight with grinning faces. One was a tall muscular man with chest-length black hair and fire red eyes. The other was a lanky hooded figure with bony arms and legs, who was crouching next to the larger one. However, their appearances and even their invisibility weren't the things that struck Kael as being unbelievable.

It was the fact that they both had wings protruding from their backs.

The things that were trying to kill him... were angels.

The larger one's wings were gigantic, double his size, with dark black feathers covering every inch of them. They easily could've encompassed both him and his partner if he wanted them to. But as impressive as the sable-winged angel was, Kael took even more notice of the more animalistic one crouching beside him.

His wings were skeletal—pure bone—with no skin or feathers to speak of. Unlike his partner, who was proudly displaying his angelic staple, the bony protrusions from the smaller one's back were folded in and tucked behind him, almost like he was ashamed of them.

Kael finally put together that his attackers weren't just angels... they were fallen angels. Evil.

With his left eye stung shut from blood pouring into it and his right eye now glowing a deep indigo, Kael managed to force himself back up on one knee. Pulling the Arch Steel pendant from his neck, he transformed it into the strongest metal he could think of in that moment—a carbon steel broadsword that he wearily readied in front of himself.

The smaller one took down his hood, revealing sharp teeth, ashen skin, and glowing yellow irises in the center of black sclera. "Andriel..." he hissed. "Is that...?"

"Yes, Parael, it is," the other replied. "Let's kill him now and take it."

The two didn't hesitate. They charged their target faster than he could react. Time slowed down only enough for Kael to realize his end had come. He wasn't fast or strong enough to stop them. He was fighting angels after all.

As he closed his eyes to accept his fate, he realized he was waiting several seconds for something that shouldn't have even taken one. When he opened them back up, he realized why...

With the door to the Canvas reopened in the distance, Kael looked up to see Shen standing in front of him. Having somehow stopped both angels' attacks by merely grabbing their arms, he was holding them firmly in place. He glanced back to the bruised and bloody body of Kael kneeling behind him and nodded reassuringly.

"You're safe now," he said. "I'll take it from here."

Turning his head back to his opponents, a single but massive gray wing shot out from Shen's right shoulder blade. Kael waited for another to appear, but it never did. Shen's face had changed. His brown irises were now a brilliant blue, and he looked younger somehow. Stronger. As Kael struggled to understand why, he was left with the only answer he'd never fully allowed himself to believe. Shen was telling the truth the entire time. He really was an angel.

A gray-winged angel.

With his hidden appendage now fully extended, a shower of gray feathers fell around Kael. As they landed on him, they glowed with intense silver light before disappearing completely—and with them all of Kael's injuries. He was completely healed.

Suddenly, Shen exploded with power, a shockwave that sent both fallen angels soaring back to their original positions, leaving them gritting their teeth in anger.

"Shenriel…" Parael hissed.

"Parael," Shen replied calmly. "You're looking… unwell. Does Choshek still have you doing his bidding?"

The monstrous-looking angel folded his skeletal wings behind him and turned his head. Andriel spoke in his place. "We came here with an offer from him, Shenriel."

"Oh?" Shen replied. "And were you going to give it to me before or after you killed the boy behind me?"

"It concerns the boy behind you," the dark-winged angel replied. "Choshek wants him."

"You mean he wants his Arch Steel."

"Or yours…" Parael interjected, seething with anger. "If you want to save him, you could relinquish it to us. It's not like you're using it anyway."

Shen clasped the Chinese cross hanging from his neck in contemplation while Andriel waved his partner down, forcing him to show restraint.

"You've always been reasonable, Shenriel," he said with an extended hand. "Surely we can come to a compromise that will be mutually beneficial. After all, you were one of us once…"

The accusation surprised Kael and struck a chord within Shen. "I was never one of you," he replied with authority. "Look how far you've fallen, Andriel. Your wings are as black as night. Soon, you will look like Parael there. And after that…"

"Silence!" the skeleton-winged one shouted. "I've had enough of this! Andriel, let's just kill the boy and take his Arch Steel!"

The dark titan smiled at his friend's eagerness, albeit with pity. "Are you sure you won't reconsider, Shenriel?" he asked. "Archangel or not, you can't defeat us both. We're archangels too after all."

"You were…" Shen shook his head in sadness. "I don't know what you are now."

Andriel grinned. "Then let me show you."

The time for talking was over. The time for fighting was about to begin.

As Shen readied himself for battle, the young man behind him stood back up and gripped the sword in his hands firmly.

"Kael," Shen said, sensing his intentions. "Leave."

"But I can help!"

"No," he replied seriously. "You cannot."

Shen didn't wait for a rebuttal and charged his two opponents like a savage ray of silver light. Clashing with Andriel, he used the force of his momentum to skid him along the ground and take the battle away from Kael. He knew Parael's hatred for him would compel him to follow.

Kael thought about summoning the door but knew he couldn't leave Shen alone. How could he run when Shen just saved his life? However, as the battle between the three angels took to the air, he wasn't entirely sure what he could do to help either.

Shen attacked Andriel with all his might, struggling with him as they each tried to gain an advantage over the other. Meanwhile, Parael soared behind them, trying to catch up. Kael didn't know how he was flying with wings of bone but also knew he was dealing with angels. Science didn't apply anymore.

From the ground, the young King watched as the entire white sky lit up into flames. The three were throwing holy fire at each other between every punch, kick, and claw swipe. Each blast looked like the same golden star Shen had dazzled him with his first night in Kearney, and each one stayed permanently ablaze wherever it landed.

Kael had no idea how powerful these three were until the blank firmament of the Canvas began visibly cracking overhead due to the magnitude of their battle. Each punch was a shockwave. Each kick a quake in the sky that reverberated to the ground below. When parts of the sky finally broke away like shards of glass, Kael could see stars, nebulae, and galaxies in the far-off distance behind it. He was mesmerized until the angelic battle tore across the rest of the Canvas air above him, ripping it open as easily as ripping apart paper.

The three crashed through one end of the Tower only to reappear through the other side. The entire structure halted and then fell, but its destroyers barely noticed. They disappeared behind the broken Canvas sky, then came hurtling back down. When they hit the ground, the entirety of it began fracturing around Kael's feet.

"Look at yourself, Shenriel," Andriel said, holding him down by his neck on what still remained of the cracking Canvas floor. "You are half of what you used to be."

"Yes, the Gray-Winged Angel?" Parael taunted, searing into his opponent's arms with flame-lit claws. "Pathetic!"

"Believe me…" Shen replied through the pain, seeing Kael in trouble in the distance. "Half of me is still more than enough for both of you!"

With a bellow, he blasted the two off him with a burst of his own angel fire, disintegrating the white Canvas around them into oblivion. Outside it was everything that existed beyond dimensional space. Time, matter, even the concepts of identity were meaningless there. Shen used it as a way of finding himself. If Kael fell into its deepest abyss, he would lose everything that made him himself.

Staring into the void beneath his feet, the teenager couldn't tell if he was being pulled up, down, sideways, or some other direction he didn't have a name for yet. It wasn't like the universe of stars he saw above the

Canvas. This was nothingness. Blackness below it. He didn't even know how long he'd been looking down into it. Time became meaningless as he struggled to remember what time even was.

However, Shen flew at top speed and grabbed him just as the ground beneath them shattered. They soared deeper into and landed on a less-destroyed part of the Canvas before Kael even realized what happened.

Before he could say anything, Andriel and Parael came bursting through the white ground in the distance, having escaped the outer dimension beneath the Canvas that Shen had blasted them into.

"Cute trap, Shenriel," the black-winged angel said. "But you should know processing higher dimensional space is nothing for creatures like us."

Shen remained silent. It wasn't a trap. It was a delay to give him time to save Kael. Not that it mattered if he couldn't defeat the two soon.

"Let's end this, Andriel!" the smaller one shrieked. "I want the Arch Steel!"

Andriel grinned sadistically. "My thoughts exactly, Parael."

The two fallen angels lit ablaze with angel fire once more and extended their hands, directing all of it into their palms. Together, they fired twin streams of golden flame that combined into a concentrated inferno of unholy heat. The blaze sought to overtake the entire dimension.

Normally, Shen would just dodge and counter. But Kael was behind him. He couldn't move. With the attack encroaching upon them faster than light, he knew he had to meet their power with his own, erecting an invisible shield of pure willpower.

The explosive blast crashed against Shen's barrier with all the might the two fallen archangels could muster. Gold and white flames licked Shen's and Kael's heels as the attack was deflected around them on all sides. However, as Shen was being inched back by the force of it, he quickly realized he was going to be overtaken. And if that happened, Kael would cease to exist.

Before that could occur, Shen dropped the shield and turned to enwrap both him and Kael under his gray wing. The flames scorched and atomized many of the feathers on the outside, but Shen and Kael remained untouched within. When the attack was over, Shen slowly lifted his charred wing and cringed as the encrusted black exterior cracked painfully apart. When he finally managed to stand and turn, Kael noticed the interior gray feathers of his wing were unscathed, but the exterior resembled that of a burn victim.

He was weakened. Kael could tell. And it was his fault.

Knowing he had to take the fight away from the boy, Shen leapt and flew straight at his opponents, though with much less speed than before. Andriel and Parael didn't hesitate. They pummeled him out of the air and began viciously beating on him while he fell helpless to the ground.

Kael couldn't stand around any longer. He couldn't watch Shen die for him. He wouldn't.

With that resolution, something new happened without him realizing it. The carbon steel of his blade changed. Brightened. Intensified. It wasn't just normal steel anymore. It had ascended.

True Arch Steel.

Gripping the new sword in his hands, Kael charged the two fallen angels who had their backs turned to him. They were trying to rip the Chinese cross from Shenriel's neck but were being repelled by some powerful invisible force.

Kael didn't have time to think. With one powerful sweeping motion, he slashed down across the larger one's back, drawing a diagonal line of blood from the top of one wing to the bottom of the other.

Andriel cried out in pain and turned with furious crimson eyes to grab the young King by his throat, stopping another attempted sword swipe with his free hand.

"No!" Shen yelled but was immediately cast into the void beneath the

Canvas by Parael.

"Insolent little fool," Andriel said, ready to crush the boy's throat. "Now you die."

Floating in the beyond beneath the Canvas floor, Shen was bound by higher dimensions no human could ever fathom. There, the abstract became concrete. His memories, his desires, his fears all became living tangible weapons to be used against him. Knowing he had less than a yoctosecond to save Kael, he had to fight through them all faster than he ever had before.

Angel fire sparked from Andriel's hand as his grip tightened at the speed of light. He didn't want to just kill the boy; he wanted to utterly obliterate him from existence. Revenge for the wound Kael had inflicted upon him. However, as his hand turned into a clenched fist, Kael was instantly gone from his grasp, appearing in the distance next to a freed Shen.

"Tha... that's not possible!" Parael said. "He was in the beyond! No one can move that fast!"

Andriel stared at Shen who stood to face them with a fire in his eyes he didn't possess before. He was dangerous now. Deadly.

"Enough!" Shen shouted, ripping the Chinese cross from his neck and transforming it into the perfect Arch Steel version of a long-bladed jian sword. He'd refrained from using his most powerful weapon against his former brethren, but he wasn't holding back anymore. "Leave. Or you know what happens next."

With the very fabric of the Canvas crumbling all around them, Kael realized he had never heard Shen sound so frightening before. He also realized he'd never seen terror like in the faces of his two enemies before either. They hesitated to move, even to speak, eyeing the Arch Steel blade in Shen's hand with the utmost panic.

"Choshek will come for you himself," Andriel finally said. "Remember that."

"Frankly, Andriel, I don't give a damn." The curse word leaving Shen's lips surprised Kael until he realized it was from a movie. Still, he thought. Language. "You just remember," Shen continued, "that I know his real name."

Scoffing, Andriel turned and summoned the door behind him. "Perhaps Parael and I will just have to visit the house across the street instead…"

Kael's eyes narrowed.

Shen's became ice. "You so much as look in the direction of that girl when you leave here…" His tone punctuated every syllable with percussive focus. "…and this Arch Steel in my hand will be the last thing you ever see."

The dark angel scowled. "Come, Parael," he said. "We're done here."

The skull-winged one bared his teeth once more before turning on all fours and lurching after his partner. When the door closed behind them and disappeared, Shen took a deep breath and transformed his Arch Steel into its original form to slip back around his neck. Kael did the same with his, noticing beforehand that his weapon had become a normal carbon steel sword again.

"Well," he said, his throat still a little raspy, "guess I have no choice but to believe you now. Seeing is believing after all."

Shen shook his head, looking around to assess the damage of his dimension. "Which is why I never showed you. I wanted you to believe before seeing. Faith by sight isn't faith at all."

Shen reached out his arms and began repairing the fractured Canvas that was still falling apart all around them. Within seconds, most of it was pieced back together into its original state—the blank white void of a dimension Kael had grown to hate.

Shen then turned. He placed his hand on Kael's burned throat where the finger indentations of Andriel's angel fire remained.

"Heal."

Kael's burn marks and sore throat instantly disappeared, though Shen still didn't look happy.

"You should've left when I told you to."

"They were going to kill you!" Kael retorted. "I saved you, remember?"

"Angels don't die so easily," Shen replied. "And they weren't after me. They were after this." He poked the Celtic cross hanging around Kael's neck.

"Why would two angels be after Arch Steel?" Kael asked. "Didn't you say it's the weapon of an angel? Shouldn't they have their own?"

"They used to," Shen replied. "But Arch Steel is made from life itself. Use it to take the life of an innocent, and it disappears." He paused to let his words sink in. "You weren't dealing with angels of heaven, Kael. You were dealing with the fallen ones of this world."

With his suspicions about his two attackers confirmed, he gripped the cross around his neck and studied it with renewed interest.

"Alright, but still," he said, "why'd they want mine? And why couldn't they take yours?"

"No one can forcibly take an angel's Arch Steel. It has to be willingly relinquished to them. Think of it as being as much a part of us as your soul is a part of you. But as for why they want it... They want to destroy the Seal. And it's the only material in the universe that can do so."

Kael was confused again. "But I thought the Judges were the ones who wanted to destroy the Seals? To start Eschaton or whatever. Why would angels want to do it?"

"Angels do not. Fallen angels do. They destroy the Seals out of their intended order to reset the sequence and stop Eschaton from ever happening. They fear the day when the King of Kings will return. They know what happens when he does—their time in this world is over."

Shen bent his solitary wing to check the damage of its wounded exterior. The charred burns cracked as he did so, making Kael wince. He averted his eyes, knowing he was to blame for not leaving when Shen told him to.

"Will you be alright?" he asked.

"As I said, angels do not die easily," Shen replied, taking notice of Kael's rueful demeanor. "And we heal quickly."

As Shen turned away to seal the rest of the Canvas back up, Kael noticed that he was right. The charred flesh was already beginning to repair itself, and tufts of gray feathers were already breaching their way back through the slowly regenerating skin.

However, as Shen's injured wing disappeared back into his shoulder blade, Kael instantly felt another sharp tinge in his right eye. As he lightly probed the corners of it, his glowing purple eye settled back to its usual violet state.

"What's going on with my right eye?"

"You're maturing as a King," Shen replied. "The color of your right eye has always been a mark of your chosen status. But it seems the threat of two angels was enough to push you to the next level."

"The next level?"

"King Sight. The power to see an unseen world."

Kael thought on that for a moment and realized he still had a million more questions to ask. "Alright, so those two... They were fallen angels?"

Shen nodded.

"Why'd they look like that?" Kael asked. "So... different from each other? I mean, one looked kind of normal, I guess, but the other one looked like a..."

"Like a monster?" Shen finished for him. When Kael nodded, the old man took a deep breath. "Angels are not like human beings," he said. "Whereas your kind has a body that hides the sin etched onto your spirit, angels are spirits. Our sin is forever etched onto our celestial being. Every sin an angel commits darkens their wings until they become someone like Andriel."

Kael thought about the muscular black-winged angel who had almost killed him. He could still feel the vise grip around his neck from where he almost succeeded.

"However," Shen continued, becoming gravely more serious, "if an angel keeps sinning beyond black, they undergo an even more horrible transformation. Like Parael, they're stripped to the bone of everything they once were until they become something else entirely..."

Kael was surprised by how entranced he'd become in Shen's explanation. "What?" he asked curiously. "A demon?"

Shen shook his head in consternation. "A devil."

"I thought there was only one devil?" In his naivety of biblical language, Kael realized he didn't really know much of anything concerning the subject.

"The terms 'devil' and 'satan' are just words that mean accuser and enemy. The fallen angel Lucifer capitalized on both titles after his rebellion when he led a third of the angels in Heaven to turn against God. He was their leader, but he is only one of many devils."

"So what's the difference between a demon and a devil then?"

"A devil used to be an angel," Shen explained. "A demon used to be... something else."

Kael wanted to ask what but decided it was a question for another time. "Alright, then who's Choshek?" Kael remembered the name from Andriel and Parael.

Shen realized he needed a visual component to give his explanations the weight they deserved. He snapped his fingers, and the entire empty white landscape of the Canvas suddenly turned black with a golden-white flame ignited between them. From the flame appeared a massively muscular angel with red eyes and six fiery white wings, two covering his eyes, two covering his feet, and two that raised him into the air.

"There are nine choirs of the angelic hierarchy," Shen said. "Think of them like ranks. The being now known as Choshek used to be a seraph, an angel in the highest triad of the absolute highest order. Until he fell to darkness chasing his own selfish desires."

The angelic figure descended to the ground with his flames extinguished. His entire body rapidly degraded until his wings were bone, his skin was ash, and he was hunched over in shame. When he looked up, his sclera turned black, horns protruded from his head, and black scales overtook him until the reptilian skin covered his entire body—his six wings resembling that of a dragon's rather than an angel's.

"With his transformation into a devil complete, his old self died, and Choshek was born."

"You told the other two that you knew his real name," Kael said. "Do all angels change their names after becoming devils?"

"Yes," Shen answered. "Even an angel's name is meant to worship the Father. When they become a devil, they stop doing that. Knowing who they used to be means you have some power over what they have become. Even the devil had a name before Lucifer."

Kael didn't quite understand, but he was trying his best to… "So, why did Choshek fall then?" he asked. "Did he follow Lucifer in his rebellion? What's he want now?"

"No, all the angels that fell with Lucifer are locked away in Hell. Choshek fell later around the same time as the Watchers, a subgroup of archangels whose job it was to watch over human beings. Some of them became enamored by the way of humans and fell to the allure of this world." Shen stared into the distance for a moment. "As to this sudden interest in your Arch Steel, I do not know. He's never concerned himself with the Seals before."

"Archangel," Kael said slowly. "The big one called you that. What is it?"

"Another order of angel that I… used to belong to…"

Watchers, angels, archangels, seraphs… it was a lot for Kael to comprehend all at once. He realized he was better off not trying to. At least not the terminology. Not at the moment.

"Used to belong to?" he asked. "And your gray wing…" By Shen's own explanation, it hinted at a dark past. "Does that mean…?"

"Yes." In that moment, Shen decided to be completely honest with the boy in front of him. He deserved the truth. The entire truth. "I'm a fallen angel as well, Kael."

Shen saw the confusion in Kael's eyes.

Kael saw the pain in Shen's.

He wanted to ask him how, but he realized he had never seen Shen so fazed by anything. Let alone hurt by it. But he was hurting now. And it was something Kael didn't want to see again.

As the elderly-looking angel prepared to continue his explanation, Kael threw up a hand to stop him. "You don't owe me anything, Gray." Shen had always been gracious with him. Always. It was his turn to return the favor. "You didn't have to take me in. You didn't have to teach me what I was. And you definitely didn't have to save me just now. I don't need to know what you did a lifetime ago. I know everything I need to right now."

For the first time, Shen stared at Kael with something more than a teacher's gaze. He stared at him with gratitude.

To whom much is forgiven, the same will they love, Shen thought with a smile.

After several moments of silence, Kael began to feel uncomfortable and immediately moved to change the subject.

"So, anyway," he said, turning and strolling into the blank white void, "before He-Man and Skeletor showed up, I used your trick. I made it to the eleventh floor without using my sight. I've almost got this thing down. You going to remake the Tower so I can show you?"

Shen smiled and concentrated, summoning all the wood, stone, and supernatural building blocks to remake the three training arenas Kael had grown accustomed to seeing every time he entered the Canvas. Within seconds, the several-hundred-foot-tall rotating tower was perfectly reconstructed, along with the boulder garden and the large heptagonal sparring platform.

Kael took a deep breath, ready to show how far he'd come. However, as he began to walk over to the Tower, Shen leapt onto the sparring platform and pulled the Arch Steel from his neck. After transforming it into the same jian longsword he'd used to intimidate the two fallen angels, he waved his free hand low for Kael to join him.

"Are you serious?" the young man asked, trying and failing to keep the eagerness out of his voice. "You mean we're actually moving on?"

As he hopped onto the arena to face Shen, the angel replied, "You're ready. From now on, you'll split your free time reconstructing the Mustang with The Word, climbing the Tower with The White, and training with me using this…" Shen gestured to the weapon in his hand.

Kael pulled his own cross from his neck and transformed it into a broadsword. However, it was carbon steel again. Not Arch Steel. Which wasn't going to be good enough to battle against Shen's true weapon.

Closing his eyes, he tried to concentrate, remembering what it felt like when he transformed it before. It was life or death then. It had to be life or death again. At least in his head. But no matter how hard he tried, the blade wouldn't become what it was supposed to be. It stayed its earthly metal form.

Instead of chastising him, Shen simply transformed his own sword into carbon steel as well. "We'll get there," he said, dropping into a low stance with his blade held up by his face and pointed at Kael.

Nodding, Kael held his own two-handed sword in front of him, ready to charge, but he hesitated. There was still one last question plaguing his mind.

"One more thing…" He wasn't even sure he wanted to ask it. "The big one said something about going for the girl across the street… Laney." He'd been trying to ignore it. Even though he knew the answer. "She's the Seventh Seal, isn't she?"

Shen didn't answer. Only nodded.

Kael sighed. "That's not fair, Gray."

"Life isn't fair, Kael," Shen replied. "And it isn't promised to be."

For the first time since Kael Clark arrived in Kearney, he felt like his true training was about to begin. And he didn't mean with a sword.

CHAPTER 23

With labored breath, Kael narrowly ducked another horizontal sword slash from Shen. He wanted to counterattack, but he could barely feel his arms anymore. Both combatants had dulled their blades to be no sharper than butter knives for training purposes, but while that meant their strikes weren't lethal, it also meant nasty bruises for whoever got hit. Which was always Kael. Shen never got hit.

Rolling away on a single hand and knee, the young King quickly brought his blade back to his side in a defensive stance. He had to catch his breath after the close call and wasn't quite ready to engage his opponent again.

"Running away isn't going to defeat me," Shen instructed, gracefully readjusting his own one-handed stance. "You need to attack if you want to win."

The angelic critiques were beginning to irritate Kael and were more patronizing than helpful. They had been training for hours, and Kael passed his tolerance for annoyance a long time ago.

Regardless, he took the advice and lunged forward in a flurry of wide arcing attacks aimed for every blind spot he could see. Only there were none. Shen had no blind spots. He would just block and counter with his own series of diagonal slashes every time. Kael might as well have been trying to cut through a mountain.

Parried to the side, Kael quickly spun low in an attempt to connect his blade with Shen's ankles. However, his opponent knew better and backstepped to avoid the blow. Kael wasn't finished though. In another display of offense, he pursued his teacher off the sparring platform and around the open Canvas like a prowling lion chasing its next meal. But Shen made elegantly complicated footwork look simple, falling backward like a dancer.

Beads of sweat poured from Kael's brow, soaking his dark hair and telegraphing his exhaustion. Still, he persevered, though it only took a second to break his concentration. With another attack, his sweat-soaked hair whipped around his face into his eyes, leaving a trail of perspiration that stung his vision and momentarily blinded him. That moment was all Shen needed.

Relentless and unforgiving, his one-handed style came crashing down against Kael's frail defenses as he tried desperately to see through the blur that afflicted him. Just as Kael's sight returned, Shen pushed his back against one of the massive boulders littering the third training area of the Canvas.

Based on his previous bouts, his back against the wall was the one place Kael knew he didn't want to be. With Shen's final attack closing in, he had to decide between intercepting or evading. He chose the latter.

Using the acrobatic ability he had gained from climbing the Tower, as well as using The White to empower his legs, Kael kicked off the boulder behind him in a somersault over Shen. He landed behind his mentor and attacked with his broadsword in one swift stroke. With no other choice left to him, Shen spun and locked blades with Kael in a temporary stalemate.

Kael pushed against Shen with all his might but knew he wasn't getting anywhere. He was wrestling with an angel after all. Even if Shen was only using a fraction of a fraction of his true strength, that still meant he had an abundance of it to spare. Kael's ego never wanted to know how much.

He had seen the man move faster than light, shoot holy fire from his bare hands, and rip apart a dimension. If Shen wasn't holding back his true strength and speed while sparring, Kael knew he'd be dead.

Their steel swords slid against each other in a grueling lock as Kael's face contorted into one of supreme struggle while Shen's remained one of simple serenity. Kael knew that a prolonged contest of brute strength would eventually end in his opponent's favor. But since power wasn't a contest he was going to win, he decided to use his wits instead.

"So," Kael said, breathing heavily, "you said I have a guardian angel protecting me, right?"

Shen nodded, slowly starting to push Kael back. "Correct."

"Why didn't he protect me against Andriel and Parael then? I know he can't enter this place or whatever, but I assume he's still guarding the door outside, right?"

"He did try to stop them," Shen replied. "But guardians are the lowest order of angel. Against human threats, they do just fine. But against two fallen archangels... too much ask anyone."

"Except you apparently," Kael said, not realizing Shen had quoted another movie. But his plan was almost ready to put into action. He just needed to know one thing. "So that barrier you made that keeps him out of here... it's still up?"

"If it weren't, he'd be right behind you. Guardians like to watch over their humans."

Kael grinned. "Good to know." Tapping into The White, he used his enhanced speed to spin out of the deadlock, feinting back in a blur before Shen could move to pursue him. When the archangel tried, he was stopped dead in his tracks by Kael summoning and opening the door to the Canvas directly between them.

Shen's irises changed from brown to an otherworldly blue. Pure blue. The kind that couldn't have actually existed anywhere except in the eyes of an angel. From his side of the open door, he could see back into his hallway. From Kael's side, all he could see was Shen.

The young King leapt through the doorway to attack his tutor, shortening the blade on his sword to fit through the frame before elongating it once again to strike downward with a massive vertical swing. From his side, it just looked like he was leaping through an open doorway. From Shen's perspective, however, it looked like Kael had materialized from the hallway, passing right through the angel standing in it like a sentry.

"I have you!" the teenager yelled, pleased with the success of his distraction.

"Do you?" The old man smiled confidently.

With a flick of his wrist, Shen deflected Kael's sword to the side while gravity and momentum took it to the ground. As a last resort, Kael went for a spinning horizontal counterattack but didn't compensate for how close he was to the giant boulder behind Shen. If they had been fighting with true Arch Steel, Kael's blade would have cut right through the stone. But they weren't fighting with true Arch Steel...

Instead of cutting right through, the carbon steel collided loudly with the rock and sent a shockwave reverberating up Kael's arms. Before he could recover, Shen's dull blade fell on his hands, making him release his sword, before moving provocatively to his throat. The first move disarmed him; the second would have been a killing blow.

"Alright, fine, you got me!" Kael yelled through clenched teeth as Shen's steel blade held firm against his Adam's apple.

Smiling, Shen took the sword away and transformed it back into the Chinese cross that usually adorned his neck. "At least you're getting more creative."

"You say that like it's supposed to make me feel better," Kael replied, putting his own cross back around his neck. "What style are you using anyway? You fight like you're dancing."

"It's called Rishon," Shen replied. "Angels use one of seven different fighting styles, each based on one of the Seven Archangels we are born under. Mine is Michael's."

"Yeah, well," Kael said, mentally noting the first hint of pride Shen had ever displayed, "I'm not sure how losing these fights over and over again is supposed to teach me anything."

"Failure teaches you everything. But losing is a choice you make. And you make it when you stop trying to learn."

"Still," Kael said, "I feel like I would learn a lot faster if this stupid necklace would actually turn into what it's supposed to. I'm up against demons and now fallen angels. It'd be nice to even the playing field with the strongest weapon in the universe."

"I never said Arch Steel was the strongest weapon in the universe."

"Yeah right." Kael rolled his eyes. "What's more powerful than a sword that cuts through everything?"

"One that doesn't." Shen's shadowy and enigmatic statements always left Kael wanting more of an explanation. But he had learned better than to ask for one. Still, sometimes Shen took pity on his pupil. "Arch Steel is the sword of an angel, Kael. When you learn to wield the Sword of the Spirit, you will understand what true power is."

Kael let Shen's lessons sink in for a moment. His body may have been wrecked from the pain of their matches, but his mind was still sharp enough to etch the wisdom of them into his heart. "So I guess we're done for the day?"

Shen had turned away from him and placed a hand on one of the monolithic boulders protruding from the white Canvas floor. "Not just yet," he finally replied. "Go stand over there." Shen pointed to the massive open space between the Heptagon and the Tower.

"Why?" Kael asked.

"Just do it."

Knowing better than to waste time arguing, Kael sighed and walked several hundred feet away from Shen until he was alone in the open plane. "Now what!?" he yelled, being far enough away he had to.

Shen didn't respond, only turned and raised his arm. With it, the enormous column of rock behind him raised as well. And with another arm movement, it was suddenly hurled in a parabolic arc directly at Kael.

Eyes wide with shock, the teen narrowly leapt out of the way just as the massive monolith came crashing down where he'd just been standing. As it exploded into thousands of smaller rocks, Kael tucked into the fetal position to avoid being pelted.

Realizing he wasn't dead, he turned back toward Shen with injected eyes.

"Good dodge!" the old man called out from afar, having already lifted the other boulders from the ground. He was holding them suspended in midair with his power. "Now, try and stop these ones this time!"

Stop them...!? Kael thought. "Gray! Hold on a second! Let me—"

He didn't hold on a second. He chucked the second boulder just like the first. As Kael stood back up, he was forced to leap out of the way again, just in time to avoid getting squashed by yet another giant pillar of rock that shattered as soon as it impacted the ground.

And then there was a third. And a fourth. And it continued until Shen was out of rocks to throw. When he was, he made his way over to the hunched over young King who was sucking in every breath like it was his last.

"What are you doing?" Shen asked. "I said stop them. Not dodge them all."

"Have you lost your mind!?"

"A long time ago," the old man replied. "Had to lose it to find it."

"You could've killed me!"

"You could've stopped me."

Having finally caught his breath, Kael stood straight up to meet Shen's tranquil expression. The stark contrast between them was always so evident. Kael was emotional with his anger. Shen was calm with his emotion. The young King took a deep breath to be less like himself.

"Just… a little warning next time, okay?"

"Yes, because that's what life always gives us for the stones thrown our way…" Shen replied. "A warning."

As they summoned the door, Kael meditated on his failures. Both his body and his mind needed a lot more training. And if he didn't get it soon, what almost happened to him against Andriel and Parael could happen for real.

Once they were back in the upstairs hallway of Shen's home, both were immediately alerted to the rapid repetition of the doorbell downstairs. Thackery was crouched in the corner of one of the doorframes, holding his paws over his ears, visibly annoyed by the repeated chimes.

"Who's that?" Kael asked.

Shen's irises lit up blue for a moment. "Seems to be Mr. Muramasa at the front door," he replied. "Did you invite him over?"

"Not until tomorrow morning. I meant to tell you. Lee knows about—"

Shen's eyes lit up blue again, as if concentrating on something else. "Oh…" he said ominously. "Whoops."

"Whoops?"

"It seems we were in the Canvas for longer than I realized."

"What do you mean? I thought you said that time in there operates the same as time out here?"

"The battle with Andriel and Parael must have disrupted my control over the fourth dimension. To us, the Canvas moved in real time. But out here…"

Kael was almost too afraid to ask. "Just how long have we been in there, Gray?"

Shen's eyes became gravely serious. "It's been eighty-four years..."

"What!?"

"No, just kidding." Shen chuckled. "It's only seven days. But a joke about worse news in front of good news makes bad news seem less bad, doesn't it?"

Kael took a deep breath. "You're not allowed to tell jokes anymore." He tried to comprehend losing a week's worth of time through the continuous buzzer of the doorbell. Seven days was certainly better than losing an entire lifetime, but he still wondered what he missed after losing an entire week of his life. But then he thought of something else...

When Kael snapped back to reality, he noticed that Shen had already disappeared down the stairs and answered the door. Lee was sitting against the exterior frame, pressing the button above his head while reading a book. It was obvious he'd been there for a while.

"Hello," Shen said, rousing Lee out of his mindless repetition.

"Oh! Hello!" Lee snapped his book shut and sprang to his feet. Having not expected anyone to actually answer the door, he turned around for an awkward handshake. "Mr. Shen, sir, it's an honor to finally meet you. I was wondering if Kael was home..."

"Yes, he's right here," Shen replied as Kael ran down the steps. He stepped aside so that Lee could enter the house.

"Dude! Where have you been!?" he practically yelled. "You said you'd explain everything last Friday and then you disappear for a week? Not cool. What happened?"

Kael didn't stop to answer his friend and slipped past both him and Shen faster than either could question where he was going. There was only one place he wanted to be. And only one person he wanted to check on.

Lee stood dumbfounded as Thackery sprinted down the steps behind him. Without warning, the cat-sith quickly bit down on the back of the teen's ankle, causing him to turn and collapse painfully to one knee. There, he came face-to-face with the animal he'd been inadvertently tormenting. In feline retribution for a week of marathon doorbell ringing sessions, the black cat swatted Lee on the forehead as hard as he could without using his claws.

"It seems Thackery did not appreciate your serenading," Shen said, to which the feline nodded.

"Wait, the cat can understand you?" Lee asked, rubbing his forehead.

"Among other things," Shen replied in an amused tone, stepping aside to close the front door Kael had just bolted through.

"Sorry, kitty," Lee replied, earning a regal nod from his attacker.

Shen smiled. "Would you like a cup of tea, Mr. Muramasa?"

"I would love one, sir, thank you. But you can just call me Lee."

Shen half-nodded, half-bowed, leading the way back to the kitchen.

As Kael sprinted across the street, he started thinking of all the horrible things that could've happened during his lost week. What if Andriel hadn't listened to Shen? What if demons had attacked again? What if Laney was… But as he landed on her front porch and knocked, he watched his fears fly away when Laney swung open the door.

She was still dressed in what she wore to school that day and looked as beautiful as ever, but her face was commingled with contrasting looks of shock and relief.

"Kael…" she said, obviously unsure of what to say. So she didn't say anything else and threw herself forward to hug him as tight as she possibly could. "No one knew where you were," she finally stuttered out. "I thought you left or had been attacked or…"

"I'm okay," Kael said, reassuring her while enjoying the embrace. "I'm okay…"

But he wasn't. Something clicked while holding her in his arms. He was overcome with the realization that fractions of a second meant the difference between him standing there and him not. He could've died. Really died. Laney could've already been dead. And if it wasn't for Shen, both of those outcomes would've come true. That seizing revelation overwhelmed him.

Suddenly, nothing else mattered. He didn't care about his destiny as a King or if Laney really was the Seventh Seal or not. He just cared about Laney, period. And he'd be crazy to let another second of that feeling go to waste.

"What happe—"

"Go out with me."

The sentence leapt from Kael's throat before he could word it with more tact. He didn't care. Laney had put herself out there with a kiss on the cheek. It was his turn to do the same. He released her from the hug, so she could see in his eyes that he was serious.

"But I thought you said—"

"I know what I said. It was crap. Go out with me." The right words floated around Kael's head until he was dizzy trying to sort them out. He realized he didn't have them, and he didn't need them. He needed her.

Still, Laney was processing. Something had obviously changed for Kael, but had anything changed for her? She was still leaving in December. Was it really fair for her to go on dates and have fun when she couldn't even tell him she was leaving? Or why…

Seeing her struggle, Kael continued. "Listen, I was wrong before. But I'm tired of being scared to do the things I want to do. We have one life, and I like you, Laney. I think you like me too…"

She did. She really did. She'd watched him be cocky, arrogant, rude, and sarcastic, but she'd also seen him be selfless, thoughtful, kind, and funny. He'd somehow snuck his way into her heart without her realizing it. "But…"

"Just one date," Kael tried again. "If you hate it, then I promise we can just hunt demon-possessed football players together and pretend our lives are normal. Just one date."

Laney was starting to regain her senses. Why not? she asked herself. Why shouldn't she go on a date with a boy she liked? She deserved to have a life too. At least before it was over.

"Well, there is this carnival in town this weekend," she said, averting her eyes downward. "They do it every year. We all just call it Kearneyval. I know it sounds dumb, but… would you want to go?"

Kael was distracted by the name of the event. But how could the residents of a town called Kearney have a carnival and not call it that? "Sounds perfect," he replied genuinely.

"It's a date then," Laney said with a smile. "I'll pick you up tomorrow at six?"

"Hopefully I'll be able to pick you up," Kael said, thinking of the Mustang.

"Oh?" she asked. "Then don't be late."

"Don't get grounded."

Laney grinned. "See you tomorrow," she said, disappearing slowly back into her house.

Kael turned away from the porch, beaming from ear to ear all the way back across the street. For a kid who used to think he couldn't die, for once in his life, he felt like he was truly alive.

He just hoped Shen would fix and let him borrow his car.

CHAPTER 24

"So you're saying all the different mythologies in the world each have some element of truth in them?"

As Kael reentered the house, he could hear the conversation between Shen and Lee playing out in the library next to him.

"I wouldn't call them truth," Shen answered. "Myths and legends come from a lack of understanding by man of how the world works. Long ago, fallen angels, demons, and the Nephilim took advantage of this, some posing as gods to lead human beings astray and others doing whatever they liked for their own personal gain."

"Nephilim?" Lee asked.

Shen sipped his tea and looked up at Kael. "How was Miss Lessenger?"

"Good." Kael wasn't surprised Shen knew where he was. "And I see you two are hitting it off."

"Yeah, actually!" Lee said. "I told Mr. Shen I was interested in mythology and religion, and he started explaining everything he knew about both. I've been sitting here for five minutes and feel like I already know more than I've studied in the last five years! Why didn't you tell me your foster dad knew so much?"

"Easy," Kael replied. "To avoid the two most annoying people in my life teaming up to annoy me together."

"Psh," Lee scoffed. "Don't be rude. You're the one who promised to tell me everything and bailed." He leaned back in his chair with his fingers interlaced behind his head. "But I've got all night, buddy... or you know, at least until nine when my mom calls."

Kael hadn't been looking forward to this. Still, a deal was a deal. "You didn't tell anyone anything about what you saw, right?" he asked.

"Not a soul," Lee replied. "Which wasn't easy since Laney and I thought you got eaten by a yōkai or something."

Kael was grateful his friend didn't break his promise. He didn't want to imagine how much harder his life could become if he did. "Fine. What first?"

"First, where have you been all week, really?" Lee asked. "I came over every day after school, but it was like no one was ever home."

"I was fighting evil angels in a pocket dimension. Almost died. Then I started training with Gray to try and learn how to use this," Kael replied candidly, flicking the cross of his necklace with his fingers. "Next?"

Lee eyed him with uncertainty. "I hate it when you do that," he said. "I can't tell if you're being serious or making fun of me."

Taking another sip of his tea, Shen stood up to join the conversation. "It was my fault. I lost control over time in the dimension I created to train Kael. A week passed out here, but it was only a few hours for us in there."

"That's trippy..." Lee said, simultaneously interested and confused by every word. "So, wait, you said you created a dimension. What does that make you? Some sort of god?"

"Absolutely not," Shen replied seriously until Kael took back control of the conversation.

"He's an angel, Lee."

Lee had been dabbling in researching other religions for the better part of his teenage years. He wanted to find his own truth, not just rely on his family's. Still, what he knew about angels was pretty limited. He just knew he wanted to know more.

"So you're a real angel?" There was not a hint of skepticism in Lee's voice. Just curiosity. Seeing Kael use powers he couldn't explain meant anything was on the table. "Then, Mr. Shen, sir, I was wondering if I could maybe see your wings?"

Kael laughed at his friend's naivety. "Don't bother, man," he said. "He's pretty private about that. He only showed me recently, and even then—"

Before Kael could finish the sentence, Shen threw out his arm, and instantly his massive gray wing manifested in the middle of the library. In the confined space, it was so large that it almost touched wall to wall.

"Whoa…" was all Lee could say in response. Gray feathers fell around him and Kael as both young men were stunned into silence, though for completely different reasons.

"Are you kidding me?" Kael asked in utter disbelief. "You give me this whole speech on faith and make me wait a whole month to see that, but Lee asks once and what? Suddenly, you're Mr. Show-and-Tell?"

"Lee was already open to believing in what he could not see. You were not. He was asking out of respect. You were demanding out of pride."

"Whatever," Kael said sullenly.

Lee was already circling Shen, inspecting his single wing with a mixed expression of awe and wonder. "Why only one?" he asked. "I thought angels had two wings?"

Kael hadn't asked the question before, but he would've been lying if he said he wasn't curious as well. Based on the way his Arch Steel cut through Andriel's angel body, he just assumed Shen had lost it in battle at some point. However, instead of answering, Shen withdrew the wing back into his shoulder blade and smiled. "A good question for another time."

Lee was disappointed by the disappearance but collected himself quickly. He'd just seen something most people never would.

"Dude, you're being fostered by a real-life angel…" he said, turning his attention back to Kael. "But then what does that make you?"

Shen sensed the hesitation in Kael's mind to call himself what he was.

The teen was still unwilling to accept such a grandiose title for himself, even though it wasn't meant to be grandiose at all. Much to Kael's relief, Shen replied for him.

"He's a King," the old man said. "Empowered by The White. Gifted with the power of The Word. Able to manipulate the realities of this world to hopefully create a better one."

Lee was confused but tried to understand. "So that's how you controlled that bear?" he asked. "You said two words and made it do exactly what you wanted it to do?"

"Yeah," Kael replied. "It was afraid. Once I understood that, I could undo it."

Kael realized he hadn't told Shen about the encounter with the grizzly. Not that the angel looked surprised. Even if he wasn't reading his mind, the old man always seemed to know everything ahead of time.

"Well, as fun as this conversation is," Kael said, hesitating for a moment. "Real quick, Gray, I have a favor to ask." The moment of truth. "Can I borrow the Mustang tomorrow evening?"

"Oh, did you fix it?" Shen asked.

"You know I didn't," Kael replied. "I was hoping you would Fairy Godmother it back together again. You can even turn it back into a scrap heap if I don't have it back by the stroke of midnight." Kael was hoping the movie reference would sway Shen to his favor.

"Hmm... no."

Yeah, Kael didn't think so. "Well then can I at least borrow the truck?"

"And let you wreck my only way to get new movies? Definitely no."

"Why do you need a car tomorrow night anyway?" Lee asked. "You know I'll give you a ride wherever." It took him a second to understand. "Unless... wait..."

Kael didn't respond.

"Holy crap! You're taking Laney on a date, aren't you!?" Kael's continued silence confirmed it. Lee clapped his hands once in excitement. "I told you, man. Now, it's only a matter of time for me and Mercury. I am in full support of this."

"Great," Kael replied. "Then can I borrow your car tomorrow night?"

Lee's face morphed from one of excitement to uncertainty. "Oh… no… thing is my parents would kill me if I let anyone take my car. I'd be more than happy to chauffer you guys around, though!"

That wasn't happening. Kael couldn't imagine anything worse for a first date than sitting in the back of Lee's car while he cracked jokes all evening. "No thanks."

Kael had already given up trying to argue. He was sore, he was tired, and he knew getting Shen to agree to anything was a longer shot than getting Mercury to go out with Lee. Laney would just have to drive, which was embarrassing, but not nearly as embarrassing as being chauffeured around by his best friend.

"Whatever," he said, turning to head for the stairs. "I'm going to bed."

"But it's only six," Lee replied.

"Not for me," Kael yawned with a wave over his shoulder. "I've been up for a week."

"But I have more questions!"

"That's what Gray's for."

Once upstairs, he heard Lee resume his conversation with Shen, trying to absorb all the angel's knowledge of the supernatural world he had stepped into. Kael didn't think he'd ever heard his friend sound happier. Not that he was awake long enough to hear most of it.

CHAPTER 25

In the darkness of his dreams, a fourteen-year-old Kael felt his fists finding their marks against the faces of two bullies in his group home. Their names were Gary Lawrence and Eugene Fordman. Kael's bloodied knuckles had already done the work of knocking the teeth out of one, but in another second, they crashed against the cheekbone of the other. Before he knew it, both boys were knocked out cold on the black plane beneath his feet.

As the heavily breathing Kael stood straight from his last punch, he heard the clapping laughter from the boy in black before him. As always, he was sitting in the dark armchair of his domain, but this time, he was wearing a black dress shirt, pants, and a red tie.

"Very good, Kael!" he cheered, looking just like Kael at fourteen. "That was your best fight yet! So brutal!"

The four teeth that had been knocked out of Eugene suddenly rose from the ground and levitated over to the ebony arm of the boy's chair. As he tapped at them playfully, they danced between his fingertips while he smiled.

"Yeah," Kael said solemnly, turning away to avoid looking at what lay littered around the chair of the boy in black. Some were items he'd stolen. Others were things he'd destroyed. But lately, it was just a countless number of unconscious kids he'd beaten up for any reason he could find. They looked like lifeless mannequins at his feet. "Just leave me alone."

"Why would I leave you alone?" the boy in black asked, feigning immense hurt by Kael's request. "We're friends. I'm trying to help you."

"I don't have any friends."

"What about Renae?" The boy snapped his fingers. Suddenly, a young girl of fourteen appeared behind the chair and wrapped her arms around it to embrace the boy in black. "You two seem to have gotten pretty close."

Kael eyed the two without emotion. "What do you want?"

"To give you everything you want, of course!" the boy replied gleefully. "So, what'll it be next? More money? More girls? Maybe a little more respect?"

Kael had already stolen, flirted with, and fought for all of those. And he'd gotten all of them. Even if they were only temporary. He wanted something more... "Answers."

"Hmm... interesting. What kind of answers?"

"Answers for why I have these powers."

The boy in black smiled and held out his hands. "You're a higher evolved being, Kael. That's why you deserve to take all this and more. It's survival of the fittest. You're the fittest. Everything in this world belongs to you."

"Yeah, but why?"

"I just told you why."

"Then when, where, how?" Kael asked. "Evolution doesn't happen overnight. Where did these powers come from? How do I have them?"

The boy in black sat back in his chair, pensively interlacing his fingers over his lips. He acted deeply contemplative, but Kael had seen the fake stare before. Still, it always came with anything he ever wanted. "You want to know where your father is? If he has the same powers you do?"

Kael thought about it before nodding. His father left him and his mom before he ever really got to know him. Still, with her gone, he was the only family he had left. And he might be the only one who could explain what was happening to him...

"What do you want for it?" Kael asked.

"The same thing I always want..." The boy in black snapped and made another spectral brick appear in his right hand. "We're halfway there after all."

Without hesitating, the fourteen-year-old stepped farther into the darkness to, once again, take another brick from the boy in black. Every footfall closer to him felt ice cold and the brick itself even colder. But Kael managed to grab ahold of it and take it all the way back to the wall he'd been building, quickly locating what he thought was the spot he'd left off.

The wall was chest high but full of small gaps where bricks had unintentionally skipped their intended destinations. An imperfect wall for an imperfect life, Kael thought.

However, just as he was about to put the brick in place, he looked up over the wall to see the boy in white still standing confidently in his empty plane. Unlike the young man sitting on his ebony throne, the boy in white still hadn't aged at all since the first time Kael laid eyes upon him. He was still the same nine-year-old child staring at him with somber eyes and a thoughtful expression. For some inexplicable reason, it angered Kael.

"Give me a reason I shouldn't put this here," he said, holding the brick up as if to display it proudly.

No response.

"Give me something at least! A reason to come over there and hear your side of things. What can you offer me that he can't?"

Still no response. Instead, the boy whispered something Kael couldn't hear and opened his arms once again in open invitation for a hug. Kael almost laughed.

"Yeah, that's what I thought," he said, shaking his head defiantly.

"Nothing."

And as Kael placed the brick and turned back toward the boy in black, he failed to notice it multiply to become yet another tier of broken masonry, one that extended into the abysses on both sides and disappeared beyond what sight could see.

CHAPTER 26

Kael slept for fourteen hours straight before being woken up by Thackery smacking his face. Since it was Saturday with nothing better to do until six, he decided to train. At least it would help pass the time, he thought.

"Hey! I'm heading into the Canvas," Kael called from the top of the steps. "Is it fixed? Or am I going to end up coming out around Christmas this time?"

From the couch, Shen closed his eyes for a moment, mentally correcting the improper time dilation that had thrown them a week into the future. When he opened them again, his irises faded from their supernatural blue to a more mortal brown.

"It's fixed!" Shen called back. "But I switched it and made it so that hours in there will now only be minutes out here. You may notice some gravitational distortions. Just avoid them!"

"So much for passing the time," Kael muttered. But he could still train in the Canvas and spend the rest of the day trying to fix the Mustang. Shen never said he couldn't take it on his date if he happened to fix it himself.

The young King spent several hours climbing the Tower, then spent several more trying to lift the heaviest boulders in the Garden using the power of The Word. Which was far easier when they weren't being chucked at him like missiles.

The Tower spun faster on every floor past the eleventh one. But he continued up the next few tiers regardless. Whereas before, the challenge exhausted him, it now exhilarated him. Even though he was nowhere near the bull's head, his improvement was inspiring.

After getting a decent workout in, Kael retired from the separate dimension to try his hand at repairing the Mustang. However, try was all he did. After spending the dilated hours he saved in the Canvas trying to fuse the atomic elements of the car back together, he eventually just decided to give up and get ready for his date with Laney.

Once showered, Kael came back into his room to find a brand-new thin black hoodie and pair of blue jeans on his bed. No doubt Shen's doing. After throwing them on and looking in the mirror, it amazed him how the old man knew his style better than he did.

However, before he could analyze himself to make sure he looked good enough for a date, he heard the doorbell ring. Confused, Kael waited for Shen to answer the door, which he quickly realized was a mistake.

"Oh, hello, Laney!" Shen said from downstairs. "Please come in!"

Kael was at the top step just in time to see Laney step through the front door.

"Thank you, Mr. Shen," she replied kindly. "It's nice to see you again. How have you been?"

As Shen stepped aside, Kael finally got a good look at his date. She always looked beautiful, but she had clearly taken extra time to look even more so. Her golden hair fell in wavy curls beyond her shoulders, and whatever little makeup she did have on made her blue eyes shimmer. She was dressed simply in a white blouse, ripped jeans, and some jewelry, but she still looked stunning.

"I've been well, thank you," Shen said, bowing his head. "I must say, you are as beautiful as your mother."

The thought made Laney smile wider than Kael had ever seen. "Thank you." She blushed. "She was a big fan of yours."

"The feeling was mutual."

Kael made his presence known by starting down the steps. "What are you doing here?" he asked, smiling. "I thought I was going to pick you up?"

Laney looked up to meet her handsome date's eyes. "Yeah, but I thought it'd be easier if I drove. The carnival is on the outskirts of town, and it can be a little hard to find if you don't know where you're going," she explained. "Besides, I didn't think you had a car?"

"He doesn't," Shen interjected.

Kael glared. "Yet," he said with confidence before turning his attention back to Laney. "So, are you ready to go?"

"Yep!" she smiled. "Thank you again, Mr. Shen. Dad always says I look like Mom, but it's nice hearing it from someone else for a change. I really appreciate it."

"Please give your father my regards," Shen replied. "But Laney, would you mind if I had a word with Kael privately before you leave?"

Laney shook her head. "No, of course not," she said politely before turning back to Kael. "I'll be outside."

Kael nodded and waited for her to close the door. "Please tell me you're not about to give me the birds and the bees talk."

Shen ignored him and pulled his wallet out from his back pocket. Fingering through lines of twenty-dollar bills, he handed Kael ten of them.

"You pay for everything," he said, handing Kael his jacket to put on. When he did, Shen started adjusting the collar and hood in the back. "Tell her how beautiful she looks. Even if you aren't driving, open her door for her and every other door after that."

"You act like I've never been on a date before," Kael said, shrugging away Shen's grooming. As he stuffed the bills into his own beat-up wallet, he realized it was empty. He hadn't even thought about money and suddenly realized how grateful he was to have it.

"Every woman is different, Kael," Shen said. "Don't treat this like any other date. I've lived a long time and even before it had a name, I can tell you this: Chivalry is timeless."

Despite his attitude, Kael was grateful to Shen—for the clothes and especially for the cash. For once, he didn't feel like a homeless orphan. And that meant a lot. "Thanks, Gray," he said, combing his fingers through his hair one last time. "I'll see you later, okay?"

As Shen nodded, Kael opened and disappeared through the front door. He jogged down the porch steps to meet Laney on the grass.

"Ready to go?" she asked.

"Yeah," he replied. He paused for a second before adding, "You look amazing, by the way."

A genuine smile framed her response. "Thanks," she said, casting her eyes to the ground while trying not to blush. "You don't clean up so bad yourself."

The two made their way to Laney's car parked on the street, and after Kael opened the driver's door for her, he rounded the hood to sit in the passenger seat. Their first date had officially begun.

Back inside Shen's house, the old angel sat down on one of the recliners in his library of films. Thackery was standing in the cased opening of the foyer, peering at his master, who was looking older and sadder than he was used to.

When Shen noticed the cat's green eyes on him, he tilted his head in the direction of the front door. "Go," he said. And before he could blink, Thackery ran and phased through the large wooden door, leaving Shen to sink back into his chair with an irredeemable sigh.

CHAPTER 27

Laney drove through parts of Kearney Kael hadn't seen before. He hated to admit it, but the more he saw of the town, the more he grew to enjoy it. It had everything it needed without all the superfluous luxury it didn't. Having only ever lived in a city before, he could appreciate what Kearney had to offer.

Simplicity.

Which was something he desperately needed in his life.

As the houses and buildings of the town became lost behind them, Kael noticed that fall was fully in season. The sun was already starting to set, and the colder weather had begun to whither the plants and trees in the area. Laney was driving them toward the outskirts of town. No doubt to some random open field where the carnival had been set up.

"So you said you go to this every year?" Kael asked.

"Yeah, it's one of my favorite places," Laney said with a grin. "I'm actually really excited to show you. Mom used to take me when I was little."

Kael studied Laney for a moment, admiring her smile that put the sunset behind them to shame. "Excited looks good on you," he said.

After several more twists and turns down dirt roads that were sandwiched between rows of cornstalks, Kael finally saw the open field he'd been expecting with hundreds of cars parked in it. Beyond them were dazzling lights and multiple structures, all belonging to the largest carnival he had ever seen. As the orange sky began to settle into a dark blue, the lights of the festival became that much brighter.

"Here we are!" Laney said excitedly.

Kael stared at the illuminated sight in awe. Even from a distance, he could hear the screams and cheers of the people inside. Smiling faces were pouring in and out. There was a colossal circus tent toward the back and countless rows of booths and games leading up to it. There was even a massive Ferris wheel that painted the horizon with its well-lit structure. Everything was decorated for fall and Halloween, and everyone was running from their cars to the front gate. The entire spectacle looked like something out of a dream.

Noticing Kael's astonishment, Laney realized she was on a date with someone who had never been to a carnival before. Grabbing his hand in hers, she said, "Come on," and pulled Kael into a slight jog toward the front gate.

With the money Shen had given him, Kael paid to enter and was immediately overcome by the crowd inside. Had Laney not been holding his hand, he would've lost her. But once immersed in the chaos, everything became intensified. The smell of freshly buttered popcorn and cotton candy filled their nostrils. The flashing lights, the carnival sounds, their fingers interlaced around each other's—every sense served to heighten the experience.

Smiling, the two wasted no time. With Laney leading the way, they played every single game the carnival had to offer from the front gate to the Ferris wheel. The ring toss, balloon darts, hoop shot, ski ball, and water gun game all fell to either their combined teamwork or Laney's gifted physical prowess. Even the mallet strike didn't stand a chance against her unnatural strength, which still shocked Kael when she easily won it on her first swing…

"What?" she said, popping a handful of cotton candy into her mouth. "It's all about accuracy."

As they played more games, Kael eventually realized he was having fun—something he couldn't remember doing for a long time. Every action in his life had always been a premeditated move to achieve some goal. But not this. This was enjoyment for enjoyment's sake. And he realized just how much he needed it.

The two eventually came upon a booth that had a small crowd gathered around it. The object was to swing a ball suspended from a string and hit a bottle on its return stroke. A little girl and her father were playing, trying to win an oversized pink teddy bear, though they weren't having any luck.

"Just one more, Daddy?" the little girl asked. "I almost had it!"

"I'm all out of money, sweetheart," the father said. "It's rigged anyway. You can't win it."

Watching his potential crowd of customers begin to disperse due to the accusation, the patron of the game took offense and responded, "Hey, don't blame the game just because your talentless daughter can't win it. I'm sure there's someone good enough out there who can!"

"That one really is rigged," Laney said to Kael. "I hate ones like that. Carnivals are supposed to be fun, you know? Especially for kids."

Kael analyzed the game and the man running it. "Maybe it's time to teach him a lesson then," he said. "I'll play!"

Kael's declaration drew back the attention of the crowd. When the one running the game noticed this, he became even more excited. "Finally! A challenger brave enough to step up! That'll be one dollar, sir." As soon as Kael laid the bill on the counter, it disappeared into the man's sleeve. He grabbed the bottle and prepared to explain the rules of the game.

"As you can see, there's nothing abnormal about this bottle," he said, tossing it around to show it wasn't glued down or anything. He then placed it on the table. "All you have to do is take this ball and..." The patron swung the ball out in such a way that it hit and knocked over the bottle on its way back. "Easy, right? And certainly not rigged if I just did it myself! Now it's your turn."

As the patron reset the bottle, Kael noticed he put it in a slightly different spot than before. Both positions looked like the dead center of the table, but they weren't, though there was no way to prove it. Not that Kael had to. He released the ball. Everyone could see the arch was completely off. There was no way it could...

Hit.

The ball struck the bottle dead center and knocked it over, earning Kael applause from the crowd and a smile from Laney.

The surprise on the booth owner's face was apparent. "A lucky shot," he said, reaching under the table to present a small stuffed turtle to Kael.

"Hey!" the little girl from earlier cried out. "You said before if you won, you got the big one!"

"Oh, no, no, no, little girl," the swindler replied. "You have to win five in a row for the big one!"

Kael shrugged and put down a ten. "How about this then? If I get ten in a row, you give me the bear and my money back."

Laney eyed her date suspiciously. But the man smiled devilishly and made the bill disappear into his sleeve just like the one before it. "Deal!" he said, setting up the game.

Kael didn't blink. He swung the ball out ten times and hit the bottle on the way back all ten times. Even when the owner of the game tried to reposition it perfectly so that hitting it would be impossible, The Word took over and manipulated the laws of motion to make them null and void. By the end of it, Kael won ten stuffed turtles that he kept passing out to random kids around him and the one gigantic pink teddy bear that he handed to the little girl who had originally played.

The irate gamemaster muttered curses while closing down his booth.

"Thank you," the father said with a handshake.

Kael reciprocated and slipped the ten-dollar bill he'd won back into the man's hand. "Have a good time with your daughter."

Before the confused parent could react, Kael walked away and over to a clapping Laney. "That was really sweet," she said, smiling.

"You didn't think I'd forget about you, did you?" he replied, revealing from behind his back that he'd saved one of the stuffed turtles he won just for her.

"My hero," she said, squeezing the turtle close and grinning.

"So what's next?"

"Hmm," Laney pondered, looking around before realizing how close they were to one of her favorite things. "Come on." She grabbed Kael's hand and led him to it.

They stepped into the line at the bottom of the Ferris wheel, where Kael realized what his date had in mind. He stared up at the large metal wheel with injected eyes—his fear of heights still very much intact.

When it was finally their turn to get on, the two were ushered into the rocking white metal seat and instantly thrust backwards into the air. It wasn't until they were halfway up the back side of the wheel that Laney noticed Kael was gripping the metal bar in front of them as tightly as his fear was gripping him.

"What's wrong?" she asked.

"Nothing," he replied with as much casual pretense as he could manage. But Laney was too discerning for it.

"Are you scared of heights?"

Kael knew he couldn't hide it or deny it. "Just not the biggest fan," he replied. The wheel suddenly came to an abrupt stop and sent their seat swaying back and forth in the wind, forcing him to close his eyes and take a deep breath.

Laney felt bad for practically dragging him onto his worst fear. "You should've told me," she said sympathetically. "I wouldn't have made you get on."

"It's fine," Kael said. "Let's just change the subject. What about you? You got any irrational fears?"

"Snakes," she replied instantly. "I hate them."

As the Ferris wheel started back up, Laney gave her date a playful smile. She figured talking about her fear could make Kael forget about his—at least temporarily.

Kael cocked an eyebrow. "Why snakes?"

After a few seconds of contemplation, Laney began a story. "When we were eight, Mercury and I were playing on her property outside of town. She wanted to go back inside and play Barbie dolls, but I wanted to have a race."

"That sounds about right."

Laney grinned. "Anyway, I convinced her I would play dollhouse with her if she at least tried to beat me. And so we took off toward the edge of her farm. I was way ahead of her… knew I was going to win. Which is why I couldn't hear her screaming for me to stop. She was trying to warn me about her family's old well. By the time I realized what she was saying, I'd already fallen in."

Kael cocked his head, wondering what her story had to do with her fear.

Laney continued. "Next thing I know, I'm lying in a pit of snakes. And not just any snakes. Rattlesnakes." She shuddered as she thought about her next words. "I can still feel the vibrations of their tails against my skin."

Kael was confused. No eight-year-old could fall into a nest of venomous snakes and live to tell the tale. Unless… "What happened?"

"That's just it," she replied. "Nothing happened. They never bit me. They hissed and slithered all around me, but they never once bit me. When Mr. Grant pulled me out, he got bit on the wrist and had to go to the hospital. Later, he said it was a miracle I was alive. The only other thing I remember is Mom telling me not to tell anyone." Laney brushed the hair out of her face. "I never did until just now actually."

Kael wondered why Laney's mom would want to keep that a secret but decided he had already asked enough intrusive questions for one evening. This was supposed to be a fun night after all.

"Maybe those snakes just knew who they were dealing with," he said, winning a small smile from the blonde beauty.

As Laney peered off into the distance, Kael noticed that her earlier shudder had turned into a full-blown shiver—a combination of telling her story and the air becoming more frigid the higher they ascended. Kael took his jacket off and put it around her shoulders.

"Thanks," Laney said, pulling the jacket tightly around her arms and holding it close, realizing it smelled like him.

With one last lurch from the Ferris wheel, the two were finally on their way to the very top. Once they hit the zenith and their chair came to a gentle halt, Kael realized why this was Laney's favorite place to be.

The view was beyond incredible. With the sun having almost fully set and the darkness of night threatening the sky, the last painted colors of the horizon blurred to black. From his pinnacle position, and for just a moment, Kael could see everything.

Kearney.

The roads around it.

The empty fields stretching beyond before being swallowed up by the night.

And for just a moment, Kael wasn't so afraid anymore. When all he could see was darkness, he realized the only thing that lit up his world was sitting right next to him.

They both turned to stare into the other's eyes. Her azure blue melted into his dual colors. And as they remembered the night Laney kissed him on the cheek, they both leaned in closer, ready to finish what she had started then.

As their lips came just inches from each other, and they felt their breath hitting and mixing between them, the Ferris wheel suddenly started up again, sending them both flying forward and breaking the would-be kiss before it could connect.

Descending all the way back down to solid ground, the two began to laugh. They had to. It was either that or scream.

Instead of letting the interruption of what could've been a romantic first kiss ruin their night, Laney led Kael to play even more carnival games. And even though he lost all of them to her, he resisted the urge to use his powers, even though her humble bragging made it difficult.

The two strolled down the grassy dirt paths on their way to another booth when they were stopped by a familiar face.

"Mr. Cade?" Laney asked, noticing the handsome man in his thirties standing outside the carnival bathrooms holding a stick of pink cotton candy.

He spun around. "Oh, well if it isn't two of my favorite students," he said with a smile. "Are you two enjoying the carnival?"

"It's my first one," Kael replied, stealing a glance at Laney. "But it's definitely the best I've been to."

Laney smiled sheepishly before directing her attention back to their English teacher. "How about you, Mr. Cade? Are you here alone or...?"

As if on cue, the door to the women's bathroom flung open. Out stumbled a beautiful woman in a red dress with long auburn hair and amber eyes. Without her glasses, it took them both a moment to realize it was actually their science teacher Ms. Gilbert, whom they'd both only previously seen wearing pencil skirts with her hair tied in a bun.

"Sorry it took so long!" she said, not yet seeing the two adolescents while she was rummaging through her small purse. "There was a long line and—" She finally looked up. "Oh! Laney! Kael!" She was obviously flustered. "Umm… what brings you here?"

Kael gave his teacher a strange look. Laney was more gracious.

"Oh, you know, just showing Kael the carnival," she replied kindly. "It's my favorite place to be this time of year."

"Of course!" Ms. Gilbert said, seeing her excuse manifest itself. "Me too. That's what we're doing as well. When I remembered that Mr. Cade was new and had never been, I extended a professional invitation."

"Really?" Kael asked. "Looks like a date to me."

The science teacher immediately became red in the face and tried her best to articulate a response. "Of course not, Kael," she babbled, shaking her head while adjusting glasses that weren't actually there. "Really. We're professionals, and that would be highly unprofessional. It's just one colleague of the teaching profession introducing another colleague to the town as a sort of, umm…" She gulped.

"Professional courtesy?" Mr. Cade offered, amusedly noting her overuse of the word.

"Yes," Ms. Gilbert said. "Absolutely. That is all."

"Mhmm," Kael replied.

Laney grinned. "Well, then you have to take Mr. Cade to the circus," she said, offering to change the subject. "I think someone who enjoys Gatsby as much as he does will really enjoy it."

Finally regaining her composure, Ms. Gilbert smiled. "Of course, the circus is the best part of the whole carnival. We'll see you two there?"

It was obvious the awkward young teacher wanted to end the conversation. While Kael could have continued the torment, Laney, in her infinite mercy, decided to let her. She just nodded as they all said their goodbyes and went off in different directions.

"Well, that couldn't have been more awkward," Kael said.

"Really? I wonder why…" Laney teased, obviously blaming Kael. "I think our science teacher has a crush on our English teacher."

"Yeah, her and every other girl in the school."

"Not every girl."

Kael glanced at her skeptically. "You don't? Really? Have you ever looked into the guy's eyes? They're almost ultraviolet they're so blue." And that was coming from a guy who'd seen an angel's eyes.

"You sure you're not the one with the crush on him?"

"Very funny," Kael replied. "Seriously though…"

Laney shrugged. "Everyone's got blue eyes." She looked at Kael with hers. "I'm attracted to something a little more unique."

Before long, the two came across a small tent that Laney stopped and stared at. It had a large sign hanging above it that read: Madame Zatella – Fortuneteller of the Past, Present, and Future."

"You're kidding, right?" Kael asked with an arched eyebrow.

"What?" Laney replied. She took a step forward. "She's a friend. And maybe she can shed some light on what to do about our possessed football player problem."

"I didn't think Christians were supposed to like people like psychics and fortunetellers?"

Laney gave him a strange look. "Christians are supposed to love everyone, Kael," she said. "Besides, she's not that type of fortuneteller. There are prophets all throughout the Bible. Who's to say they aren't still around?"

Laney grinned and disappeared behind the dusty tent flap. Soon after, Kael reluctantly followed. The only things he liked less than religion were con artists. And he hated to waste his money on one, even if it wasn't really his money.

Once inside, Kael noticed a trio of college students, one guy and two girls, sitting in front of a small table that had a glowing crystal ball on it. Behind the table was an older olive-skinned woman chanting and waving her bony fingers over the ball in various patterns. The whole scene reminded Kael exactly why he didn't want to come into the tent in the first place.

Laney pulled him to the side so they could wait their turn, but Kael was already over it.

"Off to a great start," he whispered. He rolled his eyes when Laney shushed him.

Suddenly, Madame Zatella stopped chanting and opened her eyes. "He cheats on you," she said with a strong Romani accent, directing her statement to the girl on the boy's left side.

"What!?" the girl asked angrily.

"With her." A skeletal finger jabbed at the other girl. Their eyes became wide with shock as they both tried to explain it wasn't true. It didn't matter. The first girl stormed out of the tent faster than either her friend or boyfriend could stop her.

"Wait!" Madame Zatella cried out. "You forgot to pay me!" But as the three fled the tent, she slumped in her chair and sighed, muttering that she had to remember to get the payments up front.

Laney stepped out of the shadows with Kael behind her. The fortuneteller never lifted her head. "Laney Lessenger..." as if sensing the girl's presence before opening her eyes, causing Kael to roll his once again. "Laney, my dear! Welcome!"

"Hey, Zat," the blonde replied, walking around the table to hug her gypsy friend. Kael still found it hard to believe the two would even know each other, let alone be friends. The fortuneteller's lips were stained red with the color of wine, and she carefully moved a bottle under the table with her sandaled foot during her embrace with Laney.

"Sit! Sit!" Zatella said, moving back to her own seat. "And who's this handsome creature?"

"Shouldn't she already know?" Kael muttered, earning a swift elbow to the side from his date.

"Zat, meet Kael," Laney said. "He's a bit of a nonbeliever in the things he can't see. Kael, meet the world-famous Madame Zatella!"

The mystic made a grand gesture with her arms before extending her hand to grasp the young man's. When he reluctantly reciprocated, Zatella stared deeply into his heterochromatic eyes.

"I already like this one better than the quarterback, Laney," she said. "Much better eyes."

"Thanks?" Kael replied awkwardly. He let go of her hand and sat next to Laney in one of the cheap chairs across from the soothsayer.

"So, what brings you to see Madame Zatella?"

"Well, we were wondering if you could help us with a problem," Laney said, unsure of exactly how to word their particular dilemma. "What do you know about possession?"

Zatella narrowed her eyes. "Enough to know you shouldn't be messing with it. Why do you ask?"

"We think some kids at school may be possessed," Laney said. Kael was surprised by her candor. It wasn't something he was expecting her to broadcast so openly. "We want to stop it."

Instead of responding, Madame Zatella turned her gaze onto Kael. She stared at him like she was staring through him. Like she saw something he didn't. It made him intensely uncomfortable.

She grinned. "Laney, will you give this boy and me a moment?"

The young girl was confused by the sudden request. "Umm, sure," she replied. "I'll just wait outside, I guess."

As Laney got up to leave, Zatella maintained her keen focus on Kael. When they were alone, she didn't hesitate to start a new conversation. "Does she know?"

"Know what?" Kael asked, already prepared for whatever trick the old woman might use to convince him she was the real deal.

"Know what you are..."

Or maybe she was, he thought, quickly composing himself to process what she could be insinuating. "What do you mean?"

"I know you are a King," Zatella continued. "Knew it the second I saw your right eye…"

"How?"

"Only Kings have those eyes," she explained. "Though I will say, yours are different from most Kings I've met… Why do you keep it continually active? And in only one eye? That's a new one."

"What are you talking about?" Kael was confused. He wasn't using his powers at all at the moment.

Zatella looked through him again, like she was seeing something unseen. "Ah, never mind."

Kael didn't like the way she said that. Or the way she seemed to know more about him than he did. He got enough of that with Shen. "So you know about the Crown then?" he challenged.

"I know a lot of things," she replied, "except for why you aren't protecting the one you should be protecting… the Seventh Seal?"

Any doubt Kael had about Laney's friend had all but evaporated. She knew too many specifics to be guessing.

"Who are you?" Kael asked. "An angel? Because, lady, I don't think I can deal with any more angels in my life right now."

Zatella shook her head. "Not an angel. A Seer. Like your mother."

"You knew my mom?"

"Not personally," Zatella replied. "Just by reputation. But we're getting off topic. Now, tell me. Why do you refuse your destiny to protect Laney?"

"Because I'm not the one who should be protecting anyone," Kael answered. "And anyway, she doesn't need me; have you seen her?"

"And have you seen the forces of darkness she's up against?" Zatella asked before raising her hand. "Never mind. I already know you have."

Kael was annoyed. It was like talking to the female version of Shen. But where the angel had earned his respect, this fortuneteller hadn't. "Look, lady, I'm looking to master these powers, stop whatever's going on in this town, and then get on with my life. I never asked for any of this. I'm not a King."

"A King who doesn't want to be a King?" the Seer remarked as if Kael wasn't even in the room. "That's another new one…"

"Yeah, it's a real riot at all the Kings' conventions I attend, too."

Zatella paused, again staring deeply into the eyes of the young man before her. She was ominously more serious. "I see. You're used to being the wolf, aren't you? Taking what you want… traveling where you want… doing what you like…" As the words left her mouth, she shook her head in disappointment. "You're right, you're no King. And this world doesn't need any more wolves. It needs lions. Come see me again when you're ready to be one."

Before Kael could ask any more questions, Madame Zatella went back to chanting over her crystal ball, waiting for her next customer to enter. Kael stood up and headed for the exit but paused at the tent flap. He turned back. He wanted to say something, but he had no idea what. Realizing that, he exited with an irritated look on his face.

He already knew he wasn't a King.

CHAPTER 28

Kael walked out of the tent, still trying to process Madame Zatella's words of admonition. Laney was waiting for him with her arms crossed several feet away.

"What'd she say?" she asked.

Kael shook off the ominous words of the fortuneteller. "Nothing helpful," he replied. "She didn't know anything. We're on our own."

Laney furrowed her brow skeptically. She was sure Madame Zatella would have the answers they needed. She was about to turn to go back into the small tent to ask her when...

"Hey, didn't you want to go to the circus?" Kael asked to pull her attention back to him. He nodded to the giant tent in the distance. "It looks like it's about to start."

Calliope pipe and accordion music had suddenly started blaring, accompanied by massive searchlights that shot their intense yellow beams into the night sky. Every other light, sound, and event of the carnival suddenly became second fiddle to the show that was about to begin.

Laney nodded toward the spectacle. "Ms. Gilbert's right, you know. It really is the best part of the whole carnival."

"Then lead the way." Kael moved to the side, allowing Laney to take his hand and guide him down the long dirt path that led to the oversized circus tent. Once there, he finally got a look at the rapidly growing line that disappeared into the distance. "Guess you weren't kidding..."

Laney smirked and pulled Kael to the front of the line, drawing the attention of the person who was stopping people from entering—a gargantuan man with small eyes and a curled mustache. He practically beamed when he saw her.

"Laney!" he yelled, shoving his bucket of tickets to the much smaller man beside him and rushing over to greet her.

"Is there anyone here you don't know?" Kael whispered, right before the giant grabbed her in a bear hug and began shaking her from side to side.

"It's so good to see you again!"

"It's good to see you too, Christoph!" she laughed, trying and failing to hug the man back through his enthusiasm. After several seconds, he finally put her back down.

"Are you here for..." he began to ask, pausing long enough for Kael to register his thick Russian accent. "You are, aren't you? Perfect! The others will be so happy!"

Laney smiled wide. "Is the ringmaster inside?"

"Yes! Yes!" Christoph replied. "Here, follow me!"

The giant led them through the entrance of the tent, much to the grumbling annoyance of everyone in line. Kael shrugged at them with a cocky grin before continuing into the big top, unaware that someone farther back in the line was watching him...

After passing between two enormous sets of bleachers, Kael was finally greeted with the sight of a true circus. With the stands reposing on all sides, the center of the tent was a mix of dirt and sand surrounded by a large ring that encompassed several obstacles, presumably for the animals. High above lay suspended ropes and platforms that Kael could only assume was trapeze equipment.

However, in the middle of it all stood a dashing man dressed in a very colorful tailcoat and top hat. His eyes were slowly circling the arena, as if he was taking it all in for the very first time. A small smile made his pride in it all very clear.

"Uncle Leo!" Laney practically screamed. She rushed into the center of the ring to embrace the man in a leaping hug.

Uncle? Kael thought.

"Hey there, Sparrow!" Leo replied, returning the hug with a single spin around himself before setting her back down. "I'm so glad you made it!"

"I wouldn't miss it for the world," Laney said. "Though Dad wasn't too happy about it."

"When is my brother ever happy about anything?" he asked, finally taking notice of Kael and Christoph entering the ring. "Well, well, well, who'd you bring with you?"

As Kael stepped up, Laney stepped aside. "Uncle Leo, this is Kael Clark," she said. "Kael, this is my Uncle Leo. The greatest ringmaster of any circus today."

"Any circus ever," Leo corrected. He reached out to shake Kael's hand.

Hoping for a more normal encounter with someone Laney knew, Kael politely reciprocated the handshake. "It's nice to meet you."

The ringmaster pulled Kael closer until they were eye-to-eye. "Did you know tigers can eat up to a hundred pounds of meat per day and crush bones with over a thousand-pound bite force? We have three tigers here that love Laney probably more than their own lives. Tell me, Kael, how much do you weigh?"

So much for normal.

"Uncle Leo..." Laney said disapprovingly.

Releasing Kael's hand and taking a step back, Leo shrugged. "What? My brother's a cop. I'm just saying..." He turned an insidious glare back on Kael. "I know how to get rid of a body."

"Alright, well," Laney said, grabbing Kael's arm to lead him away. "Introduction over. We'll just see you after the show, okay?"

As Laney led Kael to the rapidly filling bleachers, Christoph turned to his boss, sighing and shaking his head.

"What?" Leo replied. "Don't look at me like that. Help Mario sell tickets."

Kael could tell Laney was mortified. And he wasn't about to let it go. "So," he teased. "Your uncle seems nice."

"He's just a little... overprotective."

"Can't wait to meet your dad then."

"Oh, he's worse," Laney replied. "He's got a gun."

"Pretty sure I'd prefer a gun to tigers," Kael said. He knew he could stop a gun from firing after all. Based on how hard it was to control one bear, he wasn't anxious to try it with three six-hundred-pound felines.

When they finally took their seats in the bleachers, the majority of the tent was already filled to capacity. Kael couldn't see Mr. Cade or Ms. Gilbert anywhere, but he did manage to spot Brody taking a seat on the other side of the arena. He was alone, which struck Kael as highly unusual. When he made eye contact, the quarterback turned away.

"So," Kael said, turning his attention back to Laney. He wanted to bring up the elephant in the room... in a room where there were literally about to be elephants in the room. "Your family runs a circus?"

Laney smiled at him. "Yep," she replied. "It's actually how my mom and dad met. She used to be one of the trapeze artists for my uncle."

"What, seriously?" Kael asked. "Your mom used to be a trapeze artist?"

Laney nodded. "She loved it. Said it was the closest she could come to actually flying."

A horrible realization came over Kael. "Wait, that's not how she..." he said before he could stop himself.

"Oh, no!" Laney answered. "She quit when she met my dad during one of the shows here in Kearney. He wanted a boring normal life. She wanted him. They had me, and the rest is history."

Kael shook his head in disbelief. Just when he thought he knew Laney Lessenger, there was something else that completely surprised him. If there was one thing she absolutely wasn't, it was boring. "So have you ever thought about stepping into her shoes?" he asked.

She grinned. "Once or twice…"

Suddenly, the lights in the tent went dark and a spotlight began circling the arena. When it finally stopped, it landed right on Leo, who, with all the talent of a great showman, captivated the audience with a boisterous introduction.

"Ladies and gents, welcome!" he called. "To the Circus S'more! My name is Leo Lessenger, the world's greatest ringmaster, and I will be your host for the evening! Tonight, your eyes and your ears will be teased, titillated, and tantalized, as you witness history in the making. We have for you a show that is beyond your wildest imagination, and an act that will leave you wondering if even you can soar amongst the sparrows! To start, please welcome someone very near and dear to my heart… born and raised right here in Kearney…"

Kael suddenly became aware of what was happening and couldn't hide his surprise.

"You know her! You love her! Please welcome the Sparrow herself, my beautiful niece, Miss Laney Lessenger!"

As thunderous applause filled the arena, Laney leapt from her seat and jogged into the ring to meet her uncle. She gave him a high five on her way past and began quickly climbing up the ladder connected to one of the posts holding up the tent. She reached the platform at the top in under a minute, but Kael was in too much of a shocked daze to join in the clapping. He couldn't believe what he was seeing.

"Now, Laney, remind our audience members," Leo said. "How long's it been since you've done what you're about to do?"

One of the trapeze artists put a microphone to Laney's mouth.

"Well, I'd say since last year when you asked me that same question, Uncle Leo," she replied, kicking off her shoes before being handed the trapeze bar.

"You hear that, folks? A whole year! Just goes to show that you never forget how to ride a bike or how to soar dozens of feet in the air suspended by nothing more than your teenage sarcasm!"

As the audience laughed, Laney prepared herself while her uncle explained in a hushed whisper just what his niece was about to do.

"Now remember, folks, Laney is attempting to leap from one bar to the next mid swing, make it to the other platform without dismounting, and then return back to her starting platform without any assistance. Against my wishes, she's chosen to do this in street clothes, because… get this… she's on a date." After waiting for the audience's laughter to subside, he continued. "Teenage girls, am I right? But hey, first one to bring me the guy's address after the show gets next year's ticket admission free!"

Kael leaned forward and flipped up his hood.

After a scowling look to her uncle for embarrassing her, Laney took a deep breath and nodded to the trapeze artist on the opposite platform to release the bar he'd been holding. Without a moment's hesitation, Laney swung out on her own bar to meet it in the middle. As the two bars came into close proximity, Kael and the crowd held their breath. The petite blonde let go of her bar and flipped to the next, grabbing hold of it easily while swinging to the other side. She turned and let the pendulum motion carry her back, flipping once again in a perfect somersault back to her original bar.

For a moment, it really did look like she was flying. More beautiful than the real-life angels Kael had seen before. And just as impressive.

When Laney dismounted and landed on the platform she started from, the crowd exploded into cheers and applause—Kael included.

"One more time, ladies and gentlemen!" Leo announced from below as Laney put on her shoes and climbed down the ladder. "Give it up for our Sparrow!"

As Laney waved to the crowd through their continuous applause, she made her way back over to Kael and took her seat, acting almost as if nothing had even happened.

"Once or twice?" Kael asked.

Laney grinned but kept her eyes focused on the ring. "I spent a few summers traveling with my uncle after Mom died. He thought I had in me what she did. I think Dad still holds it against him. Why? Too much for a first date?"

"Oh no, you'd be surprised by how many trapeze artists I've gone out with," Kael replied. "They're everywhere in Omaha."

Side-eyeing her date, Laney laughed as her uncle took back over the show, congratulating his niece one last time before continuing his usual routine. The next hour was filled with clowns, elephants, firebreathers, stilt walkers, acrobats, knife throwers, horseback jugglers, and even dancing monkeys. When Kael asked about the aforementioned tigers, Laney explained that her uncle was one of the first circuses to do away with the lion and tiger tamer acts. He never mistreated any of his animals but didn't want to normalize the abuse that was done with whips in other circuses. "Though he really does still own three tigers," she said with a smirk.

The finale of the show was a choreographed routine that had every performer return to the ring, including all the animals from the previous acts. The setup foretold of an extraordinary display. And no one was disappointed.

With an original pop rock song blasting from the speakers around them, the performers moved in perfect unison with their animal counterparts. Monkeys, horses, and elephants danced just as gracefully as the clowns who whirled around them. With trapeze artists above and everything else below, there wasn't a place in the tent Kael could look without seeing something astonishing. The entire spectacle looked more like a party than a show, and everyone agreed that it was well worth the year's wait to attend it again.

After the most thunderous applause of the night, the show was over. Leo gave his gratitude to the audience members, and they all funneled en masse out the three open exits. Once outside themselves, Kael and Laney waited for the massive crowd to disperse so they could see the performers one last time.

"Well, I have to say," a voice said from behind them, "that really was worthy of Fitzgerald's writing." It was Mr. Cade, accompanied by his professional courtesy of a date, Ms. Gilbert. "And you were just magnificent, Laney. I don't think I've seen any seventeen-year-old make anything like that look so effortless before."

"Thanks," Laney replied, blushing.

"Yes, Laney," Ms. Gilbert added. "As always, your uncle outdid himself again this year."

Back inside the big top tent, the circus hands were tearing down and loading everything into the trucks parked behind the gates of the carnival. However, a pair of dark eyes remained seated in the now empty bleachers. Dark eyes belonging to Coach Winters.

"Hey, buddy!" one of the workers called. "I'm glad you enjoyed the show and all, but we got a job to do here. Get a move on, will ya?"

The dark entity possessing Winters smiled. "You know, I'm amazed at how well-trained you have these creatures. But I wonder how well they listen when they're afraid?"

"What?" the worker asked, confused.

Suddenly, each animal began acting strangely one by one. The elephants were shaking their heads back and forth, the horses became restless, and the monkeys began jumping up and down, whooping and screeching as loudly as they could.

"They are just beasts, after all…" Legate stood and released from his hands creatures of darkness that began soaring around the tent, weaving in between and around the circus animals like wraiths.

None of the humans could see what was happening, but they weren't meant to. The animals could sense it. And with those senses came fear.

Without warning, one of the elephants reared up and almost came down on a clown beneath it, trampling his leg before taking off in a wild charge toward the tent's exit. It was the inciting incident that caused absolute pandemonium to occur.

The workers in the path of the elephant leapt to the side to avoid it, scrambling over top of each other to get out of the way. This caused the horses to take off in their own random directions, each searching for an exit to escape and knocking down anyone who got in their way. The other older elephant reared when one of the shadow demons came too close to his face, backing up on its hind legs into a pillar that supported half the big top. Crashing through it like it was a giant toothpick, the seven-ton beast landed and began its own charge to escape the tent, which had begun its imminent collapse.

As chaos ensued and everyone raced for an exit, Legate began whistling as he strolled out the back of the structure and lit up a cigarette. He'd been waiting for Brody Maxwell to make his move and steal the King's Arch Steel all night. With this as a distraction, he'd better follow through, he thought, tossing his flaming match back through the open tent flap.

Outside, Kael and Laney heard the commotion and watched in horror as half the big top began to fall. From it, horses sprinted in a dead run onto the grassy dirt paths of the carnival. They were confused and aimless and didn't know where to go, so they went wherever they could. Which happened to be through dozens of panicking, screaming people.

Among the bedlam, Mr. Cade and Ms. Gilbert were trying to help some of the carnival goers get to safety inside the game booths. However, one of the horses was racing directly toward them, and Kael knew they were too distracted to see it coming...

He didn't think. He just reacted.

"*Trip!*"

He projected his power farther than he ever had before. It worked. The horse tripped over its own feet and went crashing to the ground right in front of the two teachers. At the same time, though, Ms. Gilbert tripped and smacked her head against the counter of the booth, knocking her out cold.

Mr. Cade scooped her up to hand her to the people inside the booth, but the horse got back up and continued its charge—flying right past their English teacher and heading straight for Laney and Kael. The young King grabbed his stunned date and pulled her into his arms, just barely avoiding getting trampled.

"Thanks," Laney said.

"Don't mention it," Kael replied, looking around at all the chaos. "What's going on?"

"I don't know," Laney answered, her nerves shot with shock. "Something must have spooked the animals..." Before she could finish her thought, however, the half-erected circus tent suddenly caught ablaze. "Oh no, Uncle Leo!"

Laney wrenched herself from Kael's grip and took off running toward the towering inferno. Kael tried to stop her, but he was overcome by the familiar stinging in his right eye that told him something worse was coming. Just as the older, larger circus elephant exploded from the tent's side entrance to escape the fire, he saw the worse...

Surrounding the rampaging giant were a multitude of dark wraithlike creatures that Kael somehow knew only he could see. When one of them noticed his glowing eye, the others turned slowly, licking their dead black lips before soaring toward him at the speed of darkness.

Kael was set upon and attacked by the creatures in a flurry of shadowy strikes. Covering his face and closing his eyes, he was surprised when none of them reached him. Through tiny slits in his eyelids, he swore he saw shining white feathers of a being moving in flashes around him. Though he knew he had a literal guardian angel protecting him, one of the demons still managed to pierce the defense and claw at Kael's head, taking him to the ground with the attack.

As he struggled with the dark arms of the monster above him, Kael felt the radiating heat of the Arch Steel against his chest. Pulling it from his neck, he took the cross and shoved it into the demon's razor-sharp jaws, watching as it lit up white hot and obliterated the evil spirit like embers being cast out of a fire.

When he stood back up, he felt his eye return to normal as he clenched the Arch Steel in his hand. It still held so much power, even in a form that should've had none. However, Kael didn't have time to think about it. The elephant broke loose from the carnival hands trying to tie it down. The tusked beast charged toward him and used its trunk to cast the boy to the side like a ragdoll. Again, it was something that should've broken every bone in his body but didn't, thanks to his unseen supernatural protector.

Picking himself up off the dirt, he became instinctively aware that the warmth of the Arch Steel in his hand was gone, realizing that it must have been knocked away in the elephant's charge. Looking around, he spotted it lying in the grass just a few feet away.

Before he could move to grab it, though, Brody rushed past him and picked up the necklace so fast that Kael could barely tell who it was. The quarterback took off at top speed and disappeared into the fleeing crowd.

Kael had to decide whether to chase after him or go help Laney...

It wasn't a choice.

✝✝✝

Laney had leapt through the fire at the front of the tent like a cat, covering her eyes from the intense heat as she rolled through the flames. But as hot as it was leaping through fire, it was even hotter being surrounded by it in an enclosed space. With her eyes stinging, she desperately searched for her uncle.

The ringmaster was trying to save one of his horses that had gotten its leg caught on a loose chain attached to the bleachers. However, in its frantic state, he couldn't get anywhere near it. Every time he tried, the horse raised on him, threatening to crush him.

"Uncle Leo!" Laney yelled, rushing to his side.

"We have to get Sasha free!" he said, repressing the urge to yell at his niece for coming back inside the tent instead of staying safely outside. There just wasn't time. "You distract her while I try to untangle the chain!"

When Laney nodded and raised her arms to get the horse's attention, Leo didn't hesitate. He slid around the terrified animal and unraveled the chain from its hind leg in one fluid motion. The horse was already halfway to the exit when Leo and Laney heard the creaking precursor of metal giving way. Melted by the heat, the supports on the bleachers broke apart, sending the steel and aluminum crashing down with Leo underneath it.

Kael came up to the flaming entrance of the tent and just barely dodged the horse fleeing through it at full speed. It was moving so fast the rushing gust put out the cinders on its mane and created a brief break in the fire for Kael to leap through.

"Laney!" he cried out. A meteor of falling scaffolding missed his head by inches. "Laney!"

She never answered, but when he finally spotted her through the smoke, he realized why.

The small girl who barely weighed over a hundred pounds was lifting over a thousand with her bare hands, moving the hot metal that had fallen on her uncle to the side as she pulled him free. When the young man appeared beside her to help, he quickly realized he wasn't needed.

"Kael..." she said, wondering if he'd seen what she just did.

"Come on," Kael said. "We have to go."

But as they lifted Laney's unconscious uncle and moved toward the exit, the inferno suddenly intensified, roaring on all sides while completely blocking their only means of escape.

Kael knew he'd survive this like he survived everything else, but he wasn't the one he was worried about. He had to figure out a way to save Laney and her uncle. And there was only one way to do that...

He had to use the power of The Word.

Raising his hand toward the flame-drenched exit, he was about to speak and extinguish the blaze before them, revealing his secret and forcing him to tell Laney everything. But before he could, the flames suddenly extinguished themselves, creating a pathway just large enough for them to walk through.

Utterly confused but unwilling to question it, the two carried Leo through the scorched opening and far enough away from the conflagration to turn and watch the circus tent collapse completely, wondering how on earth they escaped.

Though it made no sense to them, it made perfect sense to the one watching them... who still needed them alive just a little longer to fulfill what he had planned.

CHAPTER 29

After stealing Kael's necklace, Brody Maxwell sprinted through the entire carnival before he finally managed to look down at his prize. He still couldn't tell what was so special about it, but he didn't really care. He was just happy he'd finally done what Coach Winters wanted. Now he'd help make his dreams come true, he thought.

However, rounding one of the last booths that would lead him to an exit, Brody found himself face-to-face with a hissing black cat with a white spot on its chest. Thackery changed his hiss to a low growl and swiped at the quarterback from the counter, startling him enough that he dropped the necklace and fell backward.

The cat-sith wasted no time. He leapt from his perch and hit the ground running like a panther, grabbing the Arch Steel in his mouth and rocketing toward the grassy field that served as the carnival's parking lot—where everyone had gathered in the aftermath of the chaos.

"You're lucky no one was killed, Leo!" Sam Lessenger yelled at his little brother, who was sitting on a stretcher next to one of the ambulances and nursing a horrible headache from smoke inhalation and his run-in with the bleachers. "Do you have any idea what could've happened!?"

Everyone that gathered outside the front gates were being treated by paramedics while the police and firefighters did their jobs inside the carnival grounds. The fire had been extinguished, but after the circus show from hell, the line of people awaiting medical attention was enormous.

"You think I don't know that, Sam?" Leo fired back. In his sheriff's uniform, his older brother looked even more intimidating than when they were kids. "The animals have never acted like that before. Never! But I feel bad enough about it, alright? So can we just skip this for now and find Tubs?"

Luckily, all the animals had been regathered and accounted for. All but one. The elephant that nearly trampled Kael was still on the loose. It had escaped through the front gate and crushed several cars in the parking lot on its way out—Laney's included.

"And to bring Laney back into this again without even asking me?" The sheriff was purposefully ignoring his brother's attempt to change the subject.

"She told me she asked you! And even if she didn't, who cares? She's almost eighteen, Sam! She can do what she wants!" Leo fell back and rubbed his aching head. "Boy, why Laurel chose a stick-in-the-mud like you I'll never understand..."

Not far away from the bickering brothers, Kael and Laney were leaning on the trunk of a stranger's car next to another ambulance, where Ms. Gilbert was being treated for a possible concussion.

"Are your dad and uncle always so—"

"Argumentative?" Laney finished. "This is nothing. You should've seen them on my sixteenth birthday. Do you know what happens when a sheriff and a circus master try to throw a surprise party together? It's not good."

"Well," Kael said, "I haven't met your dad yet. Maybe I should go over and..." Laney's immediate look of shock told him all he needed to know. "So that's why you wanted to pick me up. You never told him we were going out, did you?"

"Let's see, tell my dad I'm going on a date with the juvenile delinquent who led his officers on a high-speed chase or…" Laney mimed scales like she was weighing her options.

"Point taken," Kael said. "But aren't you worried your uncle's going to tell him? Or, you know, he'll just look over here?"

"He hates it, but he knows we're friends," she explained. "Nothing weird about us hanging out. And besides, Uncle Leo won't say anything. He loves knowing things Dad doesn't."

"Like how strong you are?" Kael asked, finally posing the question he'd been wanting to ask since the fire. "I saw you lift those bleachers. Not even sure I could've done that…" He could've, he thought, but only with the power of The White.

Laney shrugged. "Just adrenaline, I guess."

She prayed Kael wouldn't press her on it any further. He didn't. But his scrutinizing gaze told her he didn't buy it either.

Once Sheriff Lessenger was finished berating his brother, he gripped the walkie on his shoulder to call in their current crisis. "Dispatch, we have a 10-91. A loose…" He paused to stare down Leo. "…elephant. Please advise all officers in the area to be on alert."

It took a moment for the radio to beep off and on again before the woman at the station sent out the order. "All cars be advised. 10-91 in progress. Loose elephant. Shoot to kill."

Both brothers' eyes went wide. "Negative! Negative!" the sheriff commanded. "Belay that order. We're not killing an innocent animal just because my little brother's an idiot. Get the carfentanil ready."

"Thanks, Sam," Leo said, hopping off the stretcher to follow his brother to his cruiser.

"Don't thank me," he replied. "We need evidence for insurance that there was a real-life elephant causing property damage in Nebraska. Besides, I'm saving the ammunition to use on you later anyway."

As the two opened the doors to the sheriff's cruiser, Sam Lessenger called out to his daughter. "Laney, this is probably gonna take a while. Get a ride home, okay?" he said before noticing Kael beside her. "Not with him."

"Hey, the kid did help save my life, Sam..."

"Oh? Did he?" the sheriff replied sarcastically before turning his attention back to his daughter. "Then definitely not with him. Call Mercury."

After the two got into the police cruiser and took off, Laney jumped down from the trunk of the stranger's car and pulled out her phone. "I'm sure Merc will give you a ride home too," she said before walking away to make the call.

Kael leaned back on the trunk with his elbows and craned his neck back to look up at the stars. Before he could, though, he heard a thump next to him and turned his head. Thackery had jumped up on the trunk next to him, holding the Arch Steel by its chain in his mouth.

"Thack!" he said. "Where'd you come from? And how'd you get this? You know what, I don't even care." Kael took it and put it back around his neck. "You're awesome, cat. I owe you one."

Thackery nodded knowingly and accepted the scratching behind his ear from Kael as the appropriate compensation. From the ambulance to his right, Kael could hear Ms. Gilbert blabbering incoherently to the EMT checking her out. She kept testifying that Mr. Cade, who was sitting next to her, was the hottest man she'd ever seen in her life.

"Definitely concussed," Kael said to Thackery, who nodded in agreement.

"Alright," Mr. Cade laughed, stepping out of the back of the ambulance. "Just let the man do his job. I'll be right back."

The teacher walked over to Kael and pulled out his keys. "I need to go with Ms. Gilbert to the hospital," he said. "You want to give Laney a ride home and bring my car back to me on Monday?"

Kael was stunned. "You mean... the Lexus?" he asked in disbelief.

"Are you serious? What's the catch?"

"No catch," Mr. Cade replied. "Based on the hit Veronica took to the head, she probably won't be cleared until tomorrow evening to go home. A gentleman never leaves a woman in distress, so I won't need my car until Monday morning. Just don't wreck it. Deal?"

The keys landed in Kael's hand with the weight of an anvil. Grinning at his student's shock, Mr. Cade turned and walked back toward the ambulance. "Oh, and you better have the next few bars of your song done by then too!"

As the paramedics closed the ambulance doors and took off, Kael pondered why on earth his English teacher would trust him with the most expensive car in Kearney. Shrugging the why off completely, he decided that Tobias Cade was just that cool. There didn't need to be a why.

"So bad news," Laney said, walking back over. "I can't get ahold of Mercury. Should I try Lee?"

Kael turned, holding up the key fob with its signature L on the back. "No need," he said arrogantly. "We have a ride."

With Kael behind the wheel of the supercar, the drive back to Glenwood Park wasn't the straight shot it should've been. Every long stretch of highway surrounding the outskirts of Kearney was another excuse to hit a hundred miles per hour. And with a V10 engine that could go zero to sixty in three and a half seconds, that was Kael taking it easy.

Though neither Laney nor Thackery thought so.

When they pulled in front of their houses and opened the doors, the black cat bolted from the sports car like his tail was on fire. Laney was a little less phased but still had no desire to get back into another car with Kael anytime soon.

"Now I see why my dad didn't want me riding with you."

"I want this car," he said, ignoring her admonition. "You think Cade will notice if I just don't bring it back to school on Monday?"

"The way you drive, I'll be surprised if it makes it until Monday," Laney replied.

When the two crossed the street and Kael walked Laney up to her front door, she turned around to face him before looking down and shaking her head. "Well, this date didn't exactly go as planned, huh?"

"I don't know," Kael replied. "Seems pretty consistent for us. Besides, no one got too hurt. And I found out a few things I didn't know about Laney Lessenger."

"Things you liked?" Laney asked, brushing the hair out of her face.

Kael smiled in response.

"Well, you know," she said, "it's not midnight yet. Our date doesn't have to be..."

Her eyes focused on Kael's forehead.

"What is it?" he asked.

"You're bleeding..."

Kael felt the slightest trickle of something wet running down the side of his face and reached up to touch it with two of his fingers. When he brought his hand away to look, he saw two red spots on his fingertips. It must have been from when that demon attacked him, he thought. The cut must have been masked by his thick brown hair. "Hmm," he uttered, remembering there was a supernatural limit to what his guardian could protect him from.

"Come on," Laney said, turning to unlock her front door. "We'll get you cleaned up."

Stepping inside the Lessenger household, Kael noted how dissimilar it was to Shen's. It was mostly white with hardwood accents and metal furnishings, and upon entering the foyer, the stairs were on the right side instead of the left. Also, unlike the old man's house, there were large rooms on both sides of the front door instead of just one massive library of films to the right.

Laney quickly ran upstairs to grab a sterilizing agent and gauze pads while Kael tried to wait for her in the foyer area. However, etiquette was never his specialty. When curiosity got the better of him, he began to look around.

"Do you prefer peroxide or rubbing alcohol?" Laney yelled from the upstairs bathroom.

"Either's fine!" he called back. The cut wasn't that deep, and he was pretty sure it was already closing up again. It must have just temporarily broken loose on the way home.

Kael wandered down the hallway next to the stairs, looking at pictures on the wall of Laney and her father. They looked happy. There were also a few of Laney when she used to be a cheerleader, which he made a mental note to comment on when she got back downstairs. However, the thought was stricken from his mind when he reached the last picture on the wall…

It was of Laney and her mom. Only Kael had to stare at it for several seconds to even believe it, his face contorting into some unholy mixture of shock, confusion, and denial.

"It can't be," he muttered. "That's impossible…"

The woman in the picture was his mom.

CHAPTER 30

Once he realized that the impossible picture before him was real, Kael fled from Laney's house as quickly as he had entered it. He didn't even bother to shut the door behind him, just raced across the street like a man possessed. There was only one person who could explain this mystery to him. And Kael wasn't going to take any vague half-truths as answers this time.

Back in Laney's house, the young blonde came trotting down the stairs with medical supplies in hand only to find her front door swinging wide open to the cool night air.

"Kael?" she asked blankly. But the boy she called for had already crossed the street and was running up the stairs of Shen's front porch.

As he burst through the door, he called out with authority, "Gray!" and began moving with purpose through the kitchen to the library to the movie room to anywhere else he could be, almost angry he wasn't in any of his usual spots.

"Gray! Where are you!?"

After searching the entire house, Kael came to the unsatisfactory conclusion that he'd either stepped out completely or...

Rushing upstairs, Kael came to the door that would lead him into the Canvas.

"*Open.*"

He said the word, but unlike every day for the last several weeks, it wouldn't budge for him.

"*Open.*"

He said it again. Again, nothing. Not even a twisting of the locks. For his final attempt, he centered himself in The White and allowed his emotion to fuel his desire. This time, his command wouldn't become reality. In his head, it already was.

"*Open!*"

The large antique oaken jaws of the door burst free, breaking past the supernatural locks that held it in place. However, before Kael could step through the opening of his own volition, he was violently sucked through by what felt like a tornado.

As the door slammed shut behind and above him, it took Kael a moment to realize that he was in total freefall, plummeting through the clouds and sky with no control whatsoever. With his eyes adjusting to the embattled winds and vapors encompassing him, he realized that he was falling through a storm the likes of which he'd never seen before.

Clouds and lightning were above him… wind and rain all around him…. but below him lay the true danger. A harsh and unforgiving ocean with waves the size of cities.

Even though his landing zone was water, falling into it from his current height would feel like smacking into concrete. And have the same effects. Concentrating quickly, Kael once again empowered his body with The White, making it strong enough to survive the impact into the tumultuous waves. As he hit, he elongated his body like a knife to cut through the water.

Once underneath the storming seas, Kael realized he had less control in the water than he did in the air. He had to continue using The White to propel himself upward faster than he was being sucked down by the raging current below. When he surfaced, he took a breath. Just one. Before a monstrous wave slammed back onto him without mercy.

When he surfaced again, he wondered where Shen was and why he would turn the Canvas into such a dangerous landscape. But he didn't have time to think about it as another wave rose above him. This time much larger than the first. And it wasn't alone…

A colossal wooden ship was just beginning to breach the crest, ready to ride the surge all the way down. The only problem was the way down led right through Kael. And there was no way to stop it. No way to escape.

A bolt of lightning illuminated the sky behind the massive, ancient-looking boat. Kael saw a winged figure in the distance trying to carry something—someone—but struggling to do so against the maelstrom.

Even though the creature had two gray wings, Kael finally recognized it was Shen, though much younger-looking. Who he was carrying and why was still a mystery, but one that Kael didn't have time to solve at the moment. His survival demanded all his attention.

"Gray!" he yelled, but even he couldn't hear his own voice. The storm drowned out everything, even words. "Gray!" he tried again, but it was too late. The wooden ship had cleared the brink of the wave and was letting gravity carry it down its slope straight onto Kael's head.

Energizing himself with The White again, Kael survived the initial impact with the bow of the mighty vessel but was pushed underneath the water by the pressure of its passing. Caught in the slipstream, Kael was violently thrashed around below the sea until he lost focus and took an involuntary breath.

With the inhale came a rushing intake of saltwater into his lungs. The heavy foot of asphyxiation pressed against his chest, as he not only lost all his strength but was slowly being pushed lower and lower into the depths of the ocean. As he was sinking, the violent sounds that silenced him earlier now seemed far away.

"Gray..." he tried to utter, pushing out with his power through The Word...

Silence was his response.

Hear.

Darkness after it.

From high above, the angel who was trying to keep his passenger from the waves below suddenly felt a jolt of panic in his head. Then a voice. Snapping out of his present nightmare, the older one-winged Shen phased out of his dual-winged younger self and soared into the waters below, locating his target and latching on to him with perfect precision.

With a thought, the two were pocketed in an air bubble created by Shen's wing. The waters of the surrounding ocean began swirling aggressively all around them. The water itself formed an orb that eventually displaced dimensions and splashed back onto the blank white landscape of the Canvas.

Kael turned over on his side to violently cough up seawater as he came out of his near-death experience. Realizing he'd returned to his usual training ground, the drenched young man turned back to Shen with bloodshot eyes.

Shen looked even older somehow—aged and sad unlike anything Kael had seen in him before. He didn't like it.

"I'm sorry, Kael," Shen said, standing to turn away. "You weren't meant to see that."

"What do you mean? Where were we? What was that?"

Shen took several moments to respond, unsure if he even wanted to... if he even should. But his apprentice deserved the truth. The old angel had avoided it for too long already.

"We were in my mind's recreation of the Great Flood," he explained. "I relive it once a year on the anniversary of my greatest mistake."

Great Flood? Kael thought. Like Noah? But before he could ponder it further, he thought of Shen's second statement, and the implication of angels making mistakes. He remembered how sin darkened their wings until they became someone like Andriel and thought back on what he saw. The younger Shen's wings were already a light gray. What kind of mistake could have grayed them further?

"It looked like you were carrying someone," Kael said. "Who was he?"

Shen was still turned away, his eyes staring off into the white void while trying not to cry. "His name was Shi Hou," he finally said. "He was my son."

"Your son?" Kael was confused. "How's that possible? Can angels even have kids?"

"They can, but they shouldn't. It's forbidden. But that's how I fell from grace. I was a part of the Watchers who saw that the daughters of man were beautiful. Some of us fell into lust over them. I fooled myself into thinking I fell into love. I sinned, and we had a son together—a Nephilim son—half-angel and half-human."

"But I don't understand," Kael said, momentarily forgetting why he'd torn into the Canvas looking for Shen in the first place. "How could your son be your greatest mistake?"

The old angel took another moment, flexing and looking at his gray wing before turning his head to acknowledge Kael. "I never told you where demons come from, did I?"

The young man shook his head, prompting Shen to continue.

"Nephilim were never meant to exist. They are aberrations of the natural order. As the offspring between spiritual beings and ones of flesh, they hold great power. But long ago, they used that power along with fallen angels to subjugate humans, becoming their gods of old for a time. However, Nephilim lack what both humans and angels possess…"

"What?"

"A soul," Shen replied. "Souls are the conscience light that allow a being to know the moral law—the difference between right and wrong. Without it, light does not exist. Only darkness. While living, a Nephilim is driven by that darkness to perform evil, selfish acts. And once they die, that darkness becomes manifest as a new disembodied spiritual force. A demon."

Kael's head was spinning. But if Shen's son was a Nephilim and Nephilim were evil, then… "What happened to your son, Gray?"

Shen stared back into the distance, reliving in his memory what he tried to recreate in the Canvas.

"The storm was so fierce, driven by the unlimited power of my Father. He knew I was making a mistake, so He gave me chance after chance to correct it. But I was too stubborn. Lightning blasted Shi out of my arms so many times, and so many times I caught him, soaring higher and higher in an attempt to save him above the clouds. But it was no use. I realized I had only one choice…"

Kael listened with bated breath.

Shen reached over his left shoulder with his right hand, burning away the coat and shirt he was wearing to reveal the wrinkled back of an elderly Chinese man. However, juxtaposed with the gray wing on his right side was a long red scar that ran down his left shoulder blade. With the sight of it, Kael began to understand.

"An angel's wings are the source of their power and immortality," Shen explained, his voice unsteady and broken. "They connect us to The White in a way no other creature can imagine. Sacrificing one can even allow an angel to make what mortals might call a wish. Almost anything. Knowing I could not save Shi any other way, I used my Arch Steel to cut off my left wing. After wrapping him up in it, I wished him to be saved." Shen sank to his knees while telling his story, his gray wing collapsing under the weight of his regret. "And so he was."

The sadness in Shen's voice made Kael feel like he was drowning all over again. It poured from Shen like an unceasing cascade of gloom. But Kael struggled past it, needing to know the rest of Shen's story.

"But why's that a bad thing, Gray?" he asked with uncertainty, not knowing if he really wanted to know.

Shen struggled. "I thought saving my son's life would save his soul… give him the chance to prove he had one." He shook his head, almost in tears. "All it did was give him the opportunity to corrupt others… grant him the chance to end more lives." His audible sobs made something apparent that Kael didn't want to believe. "And he ended so many…" Tears erupted from the old man's eyes. "So many until…"

Kael couldn't help but reach out for his mentor. His friend. "Gray…"

"I was forced to take his…" As he said it, all of his self-control was gone. "I killed him… I killed my own son." Uncontrollable tears streamed through the aged cracks in his fingers, as Shen lost himself to his own agony. To him, it didn't matter what Shi had done. He was his father. His protector. He was supposed to guide him… guard him… love him… How could he be the one to end his life?

Kael couldn't comprehend the thought of it. To him, Shen wouldn't hurt a fly, let alone take his own son's life. It didn't seem possible.

However, as he rounded his kneeling angelic mentor, Kael could hear him murmuring, "I failed him… I failed him…" over and over again to the ground. And as the young King took a knee in front of him, he watched the weeping angel with sadder eyes than he'd ever had for anyone.

To be responsible for someone else's death was something he knew all too well.

Knowing no words could ever possibly be the right ones, Kael remained silent and let his actions speak for him. For the first time since his mom died, he reached out and took someone else by the shoulders into a hug. He was a boy back then looking for comfort. In this moment, he was a man looking to give it.

Shen's tears were momentarily frozen with surprise. He expected a lot of things out of Kael, but he never expected this. With his wing lying prone on the Canvas floor, Shen returned the hug with tenfold strength. As Shen let the pain of his loss wash over him, Kael realized two things...

Even angels could cry.

And even someone like him could ease the tears.

CHAPTER 31

Kael held Gray in his arms for several minutes before the old angel finally broke away and wiped his face free from tears. He was trying to regain his composure as best as he could, feeling just the slightest hint of embarrassment for breaking down so passionately in front of someone so much younger.

"If you broke past my barrier," Shen said, using one hand on his knee to help him stand, "it must be because you were unusually driven to speak with me. What about?"

Kael had almost forgotten the reason he sought Shen out in the first place. Even though the mystery was eating at him again, it somehow didn't seem important next to the death anniversary of his mentor's son.

"It can wait, Gray."

"No, I'm okay," the old angel replied. "I needed a moment. And that moment has passed. Tell me what you wanted to ask."

It wasn't so much of a question as it was an explanation. He needed to know why Laney's mom looked like his mom. Or worse, somehow was his mom. "I went inside Laney's house..."

Shen immediately understood. "And you saw a picture of her mother, correct?" When Kael's blank stare told him yes, he continued. "Then I believe it's time you knew the truth."

The way Shen said those words made Kael far more apprehensive than he already was. He didn't want to believe anything his mind had already conjured up.

Shen lifted his arm into the air and summoned the Canvas door high above them. When it opened on its own, Kael wasn't quite sure what he expected to see, but he didn't expect to see nothing. When the door closed on its own and evaporated, he looked back to Shen with a puzzled expression.

"I have released the barrier that was keeping your guardian from entering the Canvas," Shen said, his eyes once again fire blue. "It's alright," he continued, no longer addressing Kael but rather the large being standing behind him. "Show yourself."

As Kael slowly turned around, the first thing he caught sight of was one enormously large white wing. Whiter than anything he'd ever seen before. And as he stepped back, he saw the other one protruding majestically from the other side. But the man that stood between them was what truly caught his attention.

"What is this?" he asked, utterly confused by what he was seeing.

The angel standing before him looked like the perfect version of him. He was older and more muscular, with two shining green eyes instead of Kael's heterochromatic purple. But everything else from scalp to sole screamed Kael Clark.

"Every human conceived is born with a guardian angel," Shen explained, stepping up to join his shocked student. "And from their creation, all guardian angels look like perfect versions of the ones they are sworn to protect."

Kael stared deep into the malachite eyes of his guardian. It was like looking into a mirror that wiped away all the imperfections he didn't like. The angel was shirtless except for the white cape draping over his right shoulder and the Arch Steel hanging from his neck. It was in the pattern of a Welsh cross similar to his own, but still different. He also had on white pants and golden gauntlets and grieves, though all of it paled in comparison to the luminescence of his wings. Whiter than any star.

"Who are you?" Kael asked.

No response.

"His name is Ceartael," Shen replied, earning a nod from the guardian. "He cannot speak to you. Angels only gain their voices and move freely once their status as guardian has ended."

"How does that happen?"

"Either they choose not to protect anymore and become fallen angels, or the one they choose to protect dies and they ascend to be reborn as archangels."

"Why does anyone ever die if everyone has a guardian angel?" Kael asked. He was unable to keep the searing sardonicism out of his voice for his last comment. "Seems like a lot of them are slacking."

Shen frowned and held up his hand. The blankness of the Canvas changed to a daylit downtown where people were strolling along the sidewalks. "People have no idea what angels protect them from, Kael."

Suddenly, the scene shifted colors to show the unseen world Kael could usually only see with his King Sight. Everyone had an angel surrounding them, fighting off evil spirits that surrounded them far more. The odds were insurmountable.

Kael watched in horror as an infinite multitude of dark creatures stalked and attacked with razor-sharp claws and rows of pointed teeth. It was a scene of nightmares.

"Like angels, demons come in all shapes and sizes," Shen said. "Some are far more powerful than others. Guardian angels protect humans from the supernatural world while also protecting them from the material one. But darkness moves just as fast as light, and even an angel cannot be everywhere at once."

"Then God should be," Kael said. "If he's all-powerful, then why does he allow evil to exist?"

"The height of human arrogance is thinking that God cannot possibly have a reason for the things He allows."

"Then you tell me the reason."

Shen shook his head. "The height of an angel's arrogance would be pretending I could. My Father has a plan, Kael. And a purpose. For everyone. You decide whether you want to follow it, but you cannot lie on the tapestry and claim you see the whole design. You have to stand above it. And there's only one who does."

Instead of arguing further, Kael shifted his attention back to his guardian. He had protected him from so much over the years that he almost resented him for it. Even when Kael wanted to die, he couldn't. And the ones he wanted his guardian angel to protect always died because of it.

"You said every guardian angel looks just like their human?" he asked, a slow realization forming in his mind. When Shen nodded, he continued, "So then Laney's mom…"

"Was your mother's guardian angel. Yes."

Kael's face contorted into one of disgusted confusion. "So, what? Does that mean we're like related or something?"

"All human beings are related," Shen said before relenting to Kael's serious and worried expression. "But no, not in the way you are thinking. Spiritual beings like angels do not have DNA."

The seventeen-year-old mentally breathed a sigh of relief. That was something he desperately didn't want to think about. "But still," he said, "that would make Laney a Nephilim…" When Shen nodded, Kael became more confused. "That's crazy, Gray. The evil ones without souls who become demons after they die? Pretty sure Laney Lessenger's got the purest soul of anyone I've ever met. You know, except when you're arguing with her."

"There's a reason," the angel replied ominously.

Kael wasn't buying it. "And you said guardian angels always stay close to their humans. Mom and I lived in Lincoln. Laney was born here in Kearney. You're saying mom's guardian just up and abandoned her?"

Shen shook his head. "I told you your mother was a Seer," he said calmly. "A Seer's power is sight. The past. The unseen present. The future. Eventually, she saw a future she did not like, and even though she was forbidden to do so by the Circle of Prophets, she sought to change it. Maria found me nearly eighteen years ago to do so."

"Why? What'd she see?"

"She had just become pregnant with you, and the future she saw was of her own death. Beyond it, she saw a life of suffering for you. Having heard the myths of the gray-winged angel who saved his own son, she used her abilities to seek me out for help. When she found me, she learned the truth of what happened. Knowing she could never ask her guardian to do what I did, she became resigned to the fate she saw. However, Laurel loved your mother. She loved her so much that, without a word, she sacrificed one of her wings to grant you the powers of a King in her womb. If your mother had to die, at least you could live a life free from the suffering she foresaw."

"Yeah, well, it didn't work," Kael replied sullenly. Though it suddenly made sense why he only had one purple eye when other Kings had two. He was never meant to be a King in the first place. "Why didn't she just save my mom? I'd gladly give up all this for that."

"Death comes for all mankind, Kael. And when you change the future, it keeps changing. Saving your mom from cancer could have meant killing her from something else, solidifying the future she saw for you. Laurel knew that, and so did your mom. Their priority was you."

Kael remained silent. Everyone's priority had always been him. And everyone always ruined their own lives because of it.

"After Laurel made you a King," Shen continued, "Maria was so grateful that she renounced her as her guardian, giving her the freedom to leave and live her life. Laurel traveled for a time after that, meeting Leo Lessenger and joining his circus. And even though she tried her best not to, she fell in love with his brother right here in Kearney. She knew it was forbidden, she knew it meant falling, but she revealed her true self and married Sam Lessenger. That's when they moved in across the street."

"That still doesn't explain how Laney isn't some pure evil creature of darkness," Kael said. Though it did explain how she was so ridiculously strong and fast, he thought.

"From my warnings, Laurel knew what having a child by Sam meant. However, despite their best efforts, she still became pregnant with Laney. When she was born, Laurel held out hope that her daughter would be different from the other Nephilim. As she grew older, she realized that was not the case. And so, she made the ultimate sacrifice..."

Kael unconsciously leaned forward.

"Laurel cut off one wing to make in you the powers of a King," Shen said. "She cut off her other one to make in Laney the soul of a human."

Kael winced at the thought of what that meant, earning a pensive nod from the elderly angel. "What happens to an angel with no wings?" he asked.

"They become mortal," Shen answered. "Our wings are what connect us to The White. Without them, we are little more than human. And susceptible to all the same terrors."

Kael didn't have to ask how Laurel died. Cancer. Same as his mom. It had been the tragic coincidence that first connected him to Laney. Though he wasn't so sure it was coincidence anymore.

"Laurel's final act was relinquishing her Arch Steel to a young man in Lincoln." Shen waited for Kael to understand before pointing to the boy's chest. "That's what you wear now. Normally, a King's guardian angel protects them perfectly until they are ready for the Inheritance, an offering process that relinquishes their Arch Steel to the King they guard. Arch Steel is made from life, so when an angel relinquishes it, they lose theirs. Laurel died for you to protect her daughter, all the while allowing Ceartael to perfectly protect you."

Gripping his necklace, Kael allowed himself a moment to process all the information Shen was throwing at him.

"Does Laney know what she is?" he asked.

"She knows her mother was an angel," Shen answered. "And she knows she's something else. But that's not what you're asking, is it?"

Kael mentally cursed to himself. Laney obviously knew she was a Nephilim. But she couldn't possibly know she was the Seventh Seal. That was something Kael didn't know how to even begin to explain to her.

Upon summoning the door to leave the Canvas, Kael gave one last look to his guardian angel, who was still standing like a sentry staring at him. "He doesn't seem to like me very much," the teen remarked.

With his hand on the doorframe, Shen looked back as well, sensing the angel's thoughts. "You just make his life difficult," he said compassionately. "He loves you. Just wishes you wouldn't be so reckless."

Shen stepped into the hallway while Kael grinned at his angel. "No promises."

As Kael followed Shen, Ceartael faded back into invisible obscurity behind his King. Without mastering his powers, Kael knew it would be the last time he'd see him until he could fully control his King Sight.

Once Kael and Shen passed through the door, they made their way downstairs for a nightcap of tea. However, on their way to the kitchen, both heard a small knock at the front door.

"Who's that?" Kael asked, surprised. When Shen's irises went blue, he knew he was about to get an exact answer.

"Laney," the angel replied. "She looks concerned."

"I did bail on her," Kael admitted. "But that was at least an hour ago."

"Not out here. I changed the time dilation, remember? It's probably only been seconds since you left her."

"Great…" Kael said, unsure of what he would actually say to his date. Last time he saw her, he thought she was just an abnormally strong human Seal for the apocalypse. Now he knew she was a demi-angel Seal with a soul, and their moms were connected through supernatural circumstances. He probably wouldn't lead with that, he thought.

"Ask her if she wants some tea!" Shen called from the kitchen as Kael made his way to the door.

"Yeah," he murmured, "sure, Gray…"

When he opened the front door, Laney was standing a few steps back on the porch, nervously holding her elbows on the sleeves of his jacket. She did look concerned.

"What happened?" she asked immediately. "Are you okay?"

Kael had to remember it'd only been seconds for her. "Yeah," he replied, quickly stepping outside and shutting the door behind him. "Sorry. I, uh, just didn't realize how late it was. Had to check on Gray. Save him from…" He realized he was still a little wet from the ocean water. "… the bathtub." He winced when he realized how awkward that sounded.

Laney's face softened. "Oh no, that's okay," she replied. "I just got worried about you. How's your head?"

Kael reached up to finger through his damp hair where the cut had been, now all closed up due to a combination of saltwater and the time he'd spent in the Canvas. "It's fine." He smiled reassuringly.

"Good." Laney smiled back. There was an awkward silence between them for several seconds as she struggled for the words that would continue their conversation. She found herself not wanting to leave. Not wanting the night to be over… "Oh," she finally said. "I wanted to give you back your jacket."

She started to take it off when Kael stopped her. "Keep it," he said. "It's cold, and it looks better on you anyway. Just give it back whenever."

Laney smiled as her eyes darted down to the wood panels of the porch. "Thanks," she almost whispered. "So, I guess I'll see you Monday then?"

"Yeah," Kael replied. A thousand thoughts had been racing through his head since he opened the front door. All he wanted to do was tell her every single one of them. He knew things she didn't, and somehow that made him feel guilty. Still, he had no idea how she'd respond to him knowing. She kept her life a secret for a reason. What right did he have to expose it?

But when Laney turned to walk away, Kael realized he didn't care about any of that. Not the demons. Not the secrets. Not how crazy their lives had become since meeting each other.

At that moment, all he cared about was her.

Grabbing her by the hand, he quickly pulled her back into his arms and finished what he started on the Ferris wheel. With his left hand on the side of her face, he kissed her with all the pent-up passion he'd been holding back since the first day they met.

Surprised at first, Laney immediately let herself melt into Kael's kiss, throwing her arms over his shoulders and behind his neck. Her lips pressed hard against his for a single moment that blurred into oblivion—a moment she never wanted to end.

As they slowly broke the kiss and Laney backed just inches away from Kael, her blue eyes locked with his hypnotic purple and green. With the heat between them a supernova and her heart pounding like a meteor shower, it took every ounce of will Laney had to continue backing up. But reluctantly, she did, moving gracefully down the steps while only mouthing the word "goodnight" to Kael. Which he mouthed back with a smile.

When Kael reentered the house, he finally allowed himself to appreciate what just happened. It may not have been his first kiss, but it was his best. Nothing else felt the same.

Grinning from ear to ear, Kael walked through the house until he found Shen on his couch next to Thackery, about to watch a movie.

"I assume you did not ask her if she wanted tea," Shen teased, sensing Kael come up from behind him.

"She wasn't thirsty," the teenager replied, earning a skeptical look from Thackery.

"Mhmm." Shen grinned. "Ah, to be young and in love."

Kael stared at the back of his mentor's head. "Whatever, Gray," he said, strolling out of the film room.

"I do not suppose you would like to stay up and watch a movie with us?" Shen called over his shoulder. "No school tomorrow, and you deserve a day of rest every once in a while!"

No response. Shen pursed his lips and sighed with the expected disappointment. "I guess it's just you and me as always, Thackery," he said, smiling sadly.

Suddenly, Kael leapt over the back of the couch with a bag of M&Ms in one hand and his tea in the other, landing and sitting gracefully next to Shen. "Sorry, had to grab some snacks," he said, putting his tea on the coffee table in front of them. "So, what are we watching first?"

Surprised, the elderly angel's shock quickly became joy. Smiling so wide the wrinkles around his eyes tripled, Shen immediately grabbed the remote and hit play.

"I thought we would start with The Mark of Zorro. The original, not the Frank Langella remake. Then we could move to Indiana Jones. And then…"

Kael knew what it was like to be alone in his sadness. And he wasn't about to let the person who pulled him out of it be alone in his on the anniversary of his son's death.

He owed Shen too much for that.

CHAPTER 32

On an early November morning inside the Canvas, two steel swords could be heard echoing off each other throughout every corner of the white void. The only pauses from the metal clanging came in the form of monolithic boulders crashing against the ground like meteors falling from the sky. Ultimately, it all sounded like a symphony of natural disasters.

Dodging another telekinetically thrown obelisk, Kael rushed Shen with his carbon steel broadsword dragging the ground at his side. Clashing again in rapid succession, the two warriors moved around each other like dancers rather than fighters. They had been training together so much over the last few weeks that they had memorized each other's movements so perfectly that their sparring matches began to look more like choreography than combat.

Kael was fighting extra hard though. With him leaving on a field trip to the high school football championship later that day and a ski trip to the mountains after that, he realized this morning's match would be the last time for a week he'd have the chance to finally defeat his angelic sparring partner.

"Okay, dragons?" Kael asked, blocking another sword strike. Lately, he used their matches as a way to ask questions about many of Earth's great mysteries. After all, who better to ask than someone who lived through them all?

"Did you know the word 'dinosaur' wasn't created until 1842?" Shen replied, deflecting Kael's counterattacks effortlessly. "Before that, many cultures used other terms."

"Like dragon," Kael said, making sense of it in his mind. "So you're saying dinosaurs existed when man did?"

"Scientists get a lot wrong," Shen stated. "Until they get it right."

"So real dragons never existed then?"

Shen grinned. "Well, I never said that."

Kael attempted another flurry of attacks against Shen, who blocked and parried with all the grace and experience of someone who'd lived thousands of years. In all their training, Kael had never landed a single hit against his sparring partner—much to his chagrin. His only hope was to distract him with questions long enough to land one.

"What's the meaning of life?"

"To seek it."

"Why does evil exist?"

"It doesn't."

"Why do bad things happen to good people?"

"They don't."

"What is true happiness?"

"A choice."

"How do I understand infinity?"

"Start at zero."

"Do aliens exist?"

"Depends on your perspective."

"What is God?"

Shen paused and took a step back in confusion. "You never ask about God."

"Because I needed to distract you long enough for this!" Transforming his sword into magnesium, Kael raised it high and yelled.

"*Burn!*"

Igniting the atoms of his blade, it sparked to life with the same luminescence of a flash grenade. Hoping to blind Shen, Kael charged at him with an onslaught of attacks that seemed to rain down from every conceivable direction. Shen managed to block them but realized his focus was broken, his defenses were failing him, and his student was about to finally land his first hit on him ever. So he changed tactics.

As Kael's next sword strike fell, it crashed against the silver-white glow of Shen's blade, a blade that was no longer just steel. But true Arch Steel.

In one fluid motion, the angel maneuvered Kael's dimming broadsword around his own jian one and cut it in half just above the hilt. The young King watched in horror as his severed blade fell to the ground, and he was left defenseless against the angelic sword pointed at his chest.

"No, that's cheating!" he complained. "You cheated!"

"Is it cheating to use your own powers against your opponent?" Shen asked. "Besides, you should've known better than to use an attack of light against a creature of light."

Kael stared in disbelief at the fractured hilt still in his hand. "Well, I hope you're proud of yourself, Gray. You broke it."

"An angel's weapon cannot break. Any piece disconnected from it remains forever what it was when it was severed while the piece in your hand remains unchanged. Remember, Arch Steel is made from life itself. Think of the blade reforming, and it will reform."

Frowning, Kael did what he was told. He formed a mental picture of the broken sword in his hand returning to its original carbon steel state. Before he could blink, it looked good as new.

"Yeah, well," he grumbled. "You still used a cheap trick."

"You're one to talk trying to distract me," Shen said. "Do you ask these same theological questions to Laney as well?"

It was true that the two had spent the last few weeks of their dating life talking about her faith and his lack of it. Kael remained astounded by the irony of someone who shouldn't have possessed a soul trying to save his. Still, she knew the truth about her origins. She should've despised God but didn't. He wondered why.

"Well, at least she doesn't lie," he finally responded. "Like evil not existing? Seriously?"

"Does cold exist?" Shen asked. "Darkness?" The questions prompted Kael to pause. "There are no such things as cold and darkness, Kael. They're just the absence of heat and light. And evil is the absence of good. The absence of God."

"Fine, but bad things not happening to good people? They do, Gray, all the time."

"Only one time," Shen said, summoning the door to the Canvas. "And He volunteered."

As Kael followed Shen through the doorway, he took a moment to look back at his training ground. In a place where days meant minutes in the real world, he'd come so far in a relatively short amount of time. And yet when he looked at the three arenas painting the white landscape—the Tower, the Garden, the Heptagon—he realized...

Despite almost reaching the top...

Despite nearly stopping the stones...

Despite practically defeating Shen...

He hadn't mastered a single one of them. There was a pillar that always smacked him out of the way when he reached the bull's head. One of the rocks Shen chucked was always too heavy to stop. Even the car in Shen's garage remained in pieces despite his best efforts to repair it. Closing the door, Kael wondered silently how far he'd really come if his progress was still so shallow.

When he stepped into his bedroom, Kael was surprised to find the morning light already streaming through his window. He had woken up before dawn to train with Shen before school, but they must have spent longer than he thought inside the other dimension. He barely had time to shower, change clothes, and pack for the field trip before racing downstairs to eat some breakfast. However, as he stepped into the kitchen and dropped his backpack, what he found surprised him far more than how late it was.

"Surprise!" Shen cheered, holding a richly layered chocolate cake in his hands with candles on top. "Happy eighteenth birthday!" To his left, Thackery sat on the kitchen table with a cone-shaped party cap on his head and a noisemaker in his mouth, blowing it loudly.

Kael was shocked. He completely forgot it was November 20. Spending so much time in another dimension made time lose meaning in the real world. Not to mention it had been nine years since he'd celebrated his birthday.

"Gray," he said. "You didn't have to do this." He stepped forward to get a better look with a mischievous smile on his face. "Is that devil's food cake?"

"I wanted to make angel food cake," Shen replied. "But Thackery thought you would appreciate the irony of this more."

Kael grinned at the black feline, who closed his eyes and blew the noisemaker again in triumph. "Thanks, Thack."

"Well, go ahead and blow out your candles," Shen said. "Your present's actually in the mail, but it should be here when you return from your trip."

Kael blew out the candles, but as Shen cut a piece of cake for each of them, he realized he forgot to make a wish. He had one in mind too. A request for Shen.

Leaning against the countertop, Kael savored each flavorful bite of his triple chocolate cake before revealing something he'd been wrestling with for days. "So I think I'm going to tell Laney everything…"

Slowly eating his own cake, Shen didn't look surprised. "On your trip, you mean?"

"Yeah," Kael replied. "Laney and Lee have this plan to corner the football players in the mountains to free them from possession. She deserves to know what she's really getting into. Plus, I know everything about her. It's only fair that she knows everything about me too."

Shen nodded. "And have you changed your mind about committing your life to protecting the Seventh Seal?"

Kael sighed. That question had been easier to answer before he knew the Seventh Seal was Laney. Of course, he wanted to protect her. But was he really the right person to do it?

"I don't know, Gray," he said. "One thing at a time. Shouldn't my first priority be saving the town?"

"You think they're mutually exclusive?" Shen asked. Kael knew they weren't. Everything was connected; he just didn't know how. He still wasn't sure he wanted to know.

"What are you?" The abrupt question garnered a perplexed look from Kael, so Shen explained. "I told you your first night here that I had three questions to ask you. That's my third and final one. What are you?"

Kael remembered. And it didn't take him long to piece together what Shen was baiting him to say. "I'm not what you want me to be, Gray," he responded. "I wish I was, but I'm not."

"You're more than you know," Shen said sincerely, hoping for Kael to realize it.

He didn't, but he had something else preoccupying his mind. Something to ask for that he struggled to figure out how to say.

"Listen, I have a favor to ask," Kael said. "I never got why you didn't just take care of all the evil stuff in this town from the start, but I do now. I know it was to make me stronger. And it has. But if I'm being honest here..." For once in his life, Kael decided to put away his arrogance. "I'm terrified. I haven't mastered King Sight yet. I can't turn this thing into real Arch Steel." He looped his fingers through the chain of his necklace.

"I'm going into this fight blind and unarmed, and I don't think I can win. Lee thinks I'm some kind of superhero because I can't get hurt, but I'm not the one I'm worried about..."

Kael paused and took a breath. He realized he was rambling instead of just asking what he wanted. "Please... You can see the future, right? Then help me out just this once. Tell me what's going to happen."

"I can't."

"Can't or won't?" Kael asked, a little harsher than he intended. When Shen looked away, he continued more gently. "Come on, Gray, I've done everything you've asked. Everything. You talk about me protecting Laney. Well, this is me trying to do that. I'm not asking for you to do it all for me. I'm just asking for some help here... something... anything to give me an edge."

Shen looked into Kael's pleading eyes. There were so many things he wanted to tell him that he knew he never could. Never would.

"Time is both set and fluid, Kael," he said. "It's like a pond. Telling you the future would be like dropping a stone into the water. It would create ripples, altering what's on the surface and below. Telling you the future changes the future. And I'm not God. I can't see every possibility. I need a clear pond I can stare into."

Kael shook his head, letting out an angry sigh. "Well, a lot of good that does me," he said, pushing himself off the counter. "Whatever. It's not like I actually expected you to help me anyway. I'll do it alone like I always do." He picked his backpack up off the floor and headed for the front door. "Thanks for the cake. And for nothing."

Kael left without giving Shen the chance to respond. But the sad old angel did anyway, hoping Kael could feel it.

"You are never alone."

CHAPTER 33

Kael didn't tell Laney it was his birthday on the way to school. He didn't want her feeling guilty over it when he'd forgotten it himself. However, she could still tell something was wrong with him. When they got to school and she asked him, he shook it off as nothing. This would've worked on Lee but not so much with Laney, who just became that much more concerned about him.

"Seriously, what's wrong?" she asked.

"Nothing," Kael lied with a fake smile.

"Your one-word answers are never nothing," Laney replied. "Unless it's 'whatever,'" she imitated in the lowest octave she could manage. "That one has multiple meanings."

"Seriously," he chuckled. "I'm okay."

Before Laney could press further, Lee came running up to their lockers as excited as they'd ever seen him. "Yo, guys!" he practically yelled. "Who's ready to kick some major demon butt this weekend?"

Kael ducked his head. "You want to yell that a little louder? I don't think your ancestors heard you."

"Oh, yeah. Sorry," Lee replied, looking around sheepishly. "Just excited is all."

Over the last few weeks, the teenager had been coming over to Shen's every day to learn as much as possible about the supernatural world. And even though Laney was still in the dark about Kael's powers, she had been doing her own detective work to find out which students in the school were actually possessed—most of whom seemed to be on the football team.

Together, the two had come up with a plan to use the ski trip as an opportunity to isolate the players one by one and then use Kael's necklace to exorcize them completely. A plan only Kael had silent reservations about. He had seen things they hadn't. Fought with real demons up close, and, even with his guardian angel protecting him, still managed to get hurt. He didn't want to think what could happen to them.

They didn't know what they were truly up against.

"Hey, I promised Mercury I'd meet her before class," Laney said. "Something about the trip." She leaned up and kissed Kael on the cheek. "We'll talk about what's bothering you later."

As Laney walked away, Lee leaned against a locker and waited for her to be out of earshot. "So did you decide to tell her about you?"

"Yeah," Kael said. "I'm going to after the game."

"Good. She needs to know the big guns we're packing here before we take on Brody and his goons," Lee replied, fake punching at Kael's biceps.

"Yeah," he replied with uncertainty. "You sure this is the play we want to make? I have a bad feeling about it."

"Dude, you're a King," Lee said reassuringly. "You got this. Besides, it's your job. You know, besides finding the Seventh Seal…" Lee lingered on his last two words a little too long, cocking his head. For weeks, he'd been trying to convince Kael to reveal who it was.

"You're not the Seal, Lee," Kael said, grabbing the rest of his books from his locker. "It's a good thing too…" He smirked. "I'd probably just let them have you."

"That's messed up, man."

In English, they were reading Beowulf and had just finished the epic for homework the night before. Kael and Laney's discussions throughout the semester finally prompted the rest of the class to do their assigned readings so they could keep up. Even Brody was tired of listening to their debates without speaking up.

"So," Mr. Cade said, leaning against his desk with the poem in hand, "what'd you guys think of the ending?"

"I actually liked this one, Mr. Cade," Brody said from the back. "Beowulf's a total badass."

As the rest of the class chuckled, their teacher smiled at Brody. "Care to elaborate?"

"Well, I mean, he kills a beast of a monster, his ugly mom, and then slays a dragon when he's like a hundred. Doesn't get much more epic than that."

"I'm glad you enjoyed it, Brody." Mr. Cade stood to pace the front of the classroom. "It's actually my favorite story too. But can anyone tell me the themes they saw?"

Laney raised her hand. "Well, there's the obvious one of good versus evil," she said. "We're made to think that all three monsters are embodiments of darkness, especially considering Grendel is a descendant of Cain, but I don't know..."

"Here we go," Lee remarked, referring to Laney's inability to take anything at face value. Having learned her true origins, Kael finally understood why.

"I'm just saying," she continued. "Grendel acts out of isolation. Out of fear. We get the sense that he's been attacked by the people before and now only knows how to defend himself through retaliation. I felt sorry for him."

"Interesting points." Mr. Cade nodded. "And not completely unfounded since Grendel's mother and the dragon both act out of revenge for wrongs done against them as well." The teacher turned his attention to the young man sitting behind Laney. "Kael, you've been unusually quiet during all this. What stuck out to you from the story?"

"I don't know," the teenager replied laconically.

"Don't tell me this is the one story you didn't read?" Mr. Cade asked. "Come on, one big idea that caught your attention."

Kael wasn't in the mood for Socratic discussion but still thought about the question. There was only one answer that stuck out to him though.

"The difference between a good warrior and a good king," he said.

"Interesting," Mr. Cade encouraged. "Go on."

"Well, Beowulf's considered to be both. And I get why for the warrior part, but I wanted to see the fifty years we skipped that made him into a good king. How'd he do it? And then was he even a good king if he died and left his people kingless? I don't know, just seems like you can either be one or the other. Not both."

"Good point," Mr. Cade replied. "Maybe the two roles are irreconcilable?"

"Yeah…" Kael went back to his introspective stare. "Maybe."

After English, Kael moved through his next class in a fog. He thought about all the different ways he could tell Lee and Laney he wasn't on board with attacking the football players on their ski trip, but all of them sounded like he was just being a coward. Maybe he was.

Once his second block ended, he made his way to the music room for his final class of the day. The football championships were two and a half hours away in Omaha, so they were boarding the buses at noon. And after the game that evening, they'd be heading to the ski resort in Iowa for the weekend.

When he entered the music room, Kael saw Mr. Cade tidying some papers in the corner. He was still dressed in his usual dress clothes, which Kael didn't expect since he was chaperoning the game. Without turning, the teacher asked, "So, are you excited for the trip?"

Kael watched as his mentor smiled past him with a bundle of ungraded papers into his office. "If I say no, are you going to ask me why?"

"Not if you don't want me to."

Kael looked around the room, waiting for his teacher to return. When he did, Kael continued. "I don't know... Have you ever had people counting on you for something you weren't sure you could do?"

"What do you mean?"

"Like being the person they want you to be," Kael replied. "Not being sure if you can keep them safe while living up to their expectations."

Mr. Cade gave a thoughtful "Hmm" before glancing at Kael with a note of sympathy the young man hadn't seen in anyone except Shen and Laney. "Sometimes we just have to trust our friends."

"And what if they don't have all the facts?"

"Then they're just like the rest of us," the teacher replied. Kael's eyes fell, obviously disappointed by the answer. Mr. Cade moved over to the piano and began arranging the sheet music. After tapping a few keys, he looked at Kael.

"Earlier in class, you asked what made a good king," he said. "A good king trusts in his people. Beowulf never would've slayed the dragon if it wasn't for Wiglaf. And Wiglaf never would've survived if it wasn't for Beowulf. Sometimes being a good king means being a good friend. And following them into the battles they feel like they need to fight."

Kael let the words resonate. Maybe he did need to trust his friends more, he thought. Laney was far from helpless, and Lee probably knew more about the supernatural at this point than he did. And even if it was just a necklace, they did have the Arch Steel. If they could remove the demons, it could destroy them, he thought, remembering the one at the carnival that practically exploded under its power. Their plan could work.

"Thanks," Kael finally said.

"Thank me by finishing this song," Mr. Cade replied, offering the piano bench to his student. "I hear Requiem for a Prince in my sleep now."

Kael grinned, walked over to sit on the bench, and then let his fingers begin their dance across the keys. Their plan had to work.

CHAPTER 34

The bus ride from Kearney to Omaha took a little less than three hours. On the way, Kael convinced Laney that he really was alright, which was actually true thanks to his chat with Mr. Cade. Who needed Shen when he had someone who actually listened to him and gave useful advice?

As they approached the city, Kael stared pensively at the skyline, overcome with feelings of horrible nostalgia. There were places that held memories he'd rather not remember—ones he'd forget if he could. When they arrived at Burke Stadium, he was happy for the change of scenery.

The cheerleaders and football players were ushered off the buses first and headed straight for the locker rooms to change. The other students were allowed to take their seats in the stands, which were ice cold thanks to the Nebraskan winter settling into the area. It wasn't snowing, but the frigid air and overcast sky certainly threatened it.

"I think I'm going to get some snacks before the game starts," Laney said. She glanced over to Lee who was shivering despite his thick winter jacket. "And probably some hot chocolate," she added. "You guys want anything else?"

"You sit. I'll get it," Kael offered.

"No, it's okay," Laney said. "I'll just grab us some different stuff. I'll be right back."

A few minutes after Laney disappeared, the two teams and their cheer-leading squads took to the field to begin warming up.

"So," Lee said mischievously. "We don't know if The Word will work on the possessed, right? I think this might be a good opportunity to test your abilities. Maybe even use them to help the other team win?"

Kael side-eyed his friend, suddenly remembering his gambling addiction. "You want me… to use cosmic power that manipulates the fabric of reality… to win you a football game?" he asked. "Why'd you bet on the other team, Lee?"

"Dude, I wasn't betting on demons! That's gotta be like sacrilegious or something."

"Since when are you religious?" Kael asked.

"Since I met an angel in his living room," Lee replied. "I still don't understand how you aren't."

Kael shrugged, preferring not to have the same conversation he'd had with Shen and Laney over a thousand times now.

"Come on," Lee urged. "I'll split the profits with you."

Kael sighed and focused his eyes back on the field. "Whatever," he said. Reaching out, he thought about the words he wanted to impose upon the practicing players.

Trip.

Fall.

Miss.

Fumble.

But as he tried to will each of the actions into reality, all of them failed. Shen always said The Word was reliant on Kael's ability to understand what he was manipulating. He quickly realized he didn't understand the workings of spiritual beings. Of demons.

"It's not working," he said. "They must be immune."

Lee thought about it for a moment. "Or maybe it's because you don't believe enough?"

Kael gave him a disapproving look.

"What?" Lee asked. "I'm just saying what we're both thinking."

It wasn't long after Laney returned that the game started. And it wasn't long after that that it ended. Because of a mercy ruling from the referees, the game was called when Kearney High attained a massive seventy point advantage early in the second quarter. Against their supernatural opponents, the other team just didn't stand a chance. It was like watching professional players play against midget leaguers.

Though not the epic conclusion to the season most were expecting, it did mean the students got to start their ski trip early. The teachers had originally planned for the game to take three to four hours with just enough time to get to the lodge and check in before lights out. But since it was barely three o'clock and only a thirty-minute drive into Iowa, the students were given the option to do a few ski trails if they wanted.

"Let's enjoy the extra time we've got," Lee said. He leaned in closer to Kael and Laney to whisper, "We should scope the area anyway. We'll figure out a plan to exorcise the team tomorrow."

The resort itself was a mixture of huge wooden lodges and small cabin areas, all spaced out about halfway up a snow-covered mountain. Some of the lodges had large lounge areas with center fireplaces that many of the students flocked to upon arrival. Kael wanted to just chill in one of those, but he was overruled by his friends.

After changing out of their game attire, Laney and Mercury emerged from the main lodge with their skis wearing matching pink and yellow jackets and black ski pants. Conversely, Kael was dressed in his normal clothes with a rented snowboard in hand. He had never skied before and had no idea what he was doing, but he figured if he could fight angels, he could glide across ice crystals on a piece of fiberglass.

Lee was the one who surprised them all though. He was overly en-thusiastic to get started and raced to the ski lift with his own snowboard in hand. The three wondered why he looked so confident.

Once at the lift, he stood in the path of the coming chair and offered his hand out to Mercury, who winced at him instead of taking it. "I'll take the next one, thanks," she replied curtly, letting Lee get carried off before stepping forward to take her own chair.

As Kael watched his friends get whisked up the mountain, a brief mo-ment of panic seized him before Laney grabbed his hand. "It'll be okay," she said. "I promise."

He knew she was right. But he also knew it wasn't the fear of heights that gripped him as hard as he gripped the metal bar in front of him. It was the memory associated with it. Omaha just brought it all back to the surface.

Once they reached the top, both jumped off and glided over to where Lee and Mercury were standing at the edge of the slope. "Finally!" Lee exclaimed. "You guys ready? We probably only have time for one run, and I really wanted to get sta—."

"Guh, do you ever stop talking?" Mercury asked. "Why are you so excited to fall on your face anyway, Muramasa?"

"I'm actually not too bad," he said, smiling as an idea formed in his head. "But I'll tell you what, beautiful. You beat me down the hill and I won't say a word around you until after Christmas. But if I beat you, we spend an evening around the fire together. Deal?"

After waiting for a response that never came, Lee shrugged and jumped in one fluid motion onto the slope, shredding down the mountain like a pro.

The dark-haired girl turned to her friends. "Silence out of that kid for a month is too good of an opportunity to pass up." She pushed off, tucked, and shot down after Lee, determined to beat him down the hill.

Laney turned to Kael. "You okay?" she asked.

Kael nodded. With the sun setting in the distance and no one around them, he wondered if he should take the chance to explain everything he knew to Laney. They were alone. No one could interrupt them. But he still decided against it. "Go," he said instead. "I'll be right behind you."

When Laney saw the confidence in his eyes, she eventually nodded back and used her ski poles to propel herself off the edge. Kael watched as her petite frame bounded in a zigzag pattern down the hill. And with a little assistance from The White to empower his body and The Word to empower his snowboard, Kael followed after her just as skillfully.

✝✝✝

Halfway down the hill, Mercury lost sight of her target and stopped off the side by an embankment of trees to get her bearings. "Where did he even go?" she asked, adjusting her goggles to get a better view.

Just before she was about to continue on, she heard a light crying coming from the small forest beside her that sounded like a little girl.

"Hello?" she asked.

The cries intensified. Stepping out of her skis, the sable-haired girl planted them firmly in the snow and investigated the noises with trepidation.

"Hello? Is anyone there?" Now off the trail completely and in the woods, she saw a shadow standing behind one of the larger trees. "It's okay," she said. "You can come out."

When they did, Mercury saw that it wasn't a little girl at all.

"Coach Winters?" she asked. "What are you doing up here?"

But the older man didn't respond, only flashed an evil grin before summoning a manifestation of darkness from his hand. Darkness that attacked and infected Mercury with all the swiftness of the approaching night.

As the sun fell against the horizon, so too did Mercury's soul against the demon possessing her. Her eyes turned black with the shadows encompassing the mountain, and the evil spirit inside her leered at the one standing across from it.

Legate's plan was finally ready to be put into action.

CHAPTER 35

In the gathering gloom at the bottom of the slopes, Lee, Laney, and Kael watched intently as night began to fall. Every other student had descended the mountain and trudged their way through the snow to get into the lodge behind them, but the trio were still waiting for their friend to appear. It had only been minutes, but it felt like hours.

"I'm going to look for her," Laney said. Kael nodded.

"Wait!" Lee pointed. "There she is!"

Mercury skied down the mountain effortlessly and came to a skidding halt in front of her friends with a smirk on her face.

"Merc! Where were you? We were about to start a search party."

"Relax," Mercury said, taking off her goggles and toboggan to free her hair. "I just got a little lost, that's all. I'm fine."

Laney eyed her friend with suspicion. She was about to speak when Kael interrupted.

"We're just glad you're alright," he said. "Still, it'd be nice if I could start this trip without getting yelled at by Winters in the first hour. Personal records and all."

Kael and Laney led the way to the lodge while Mercury turned to the Japanese boy in front of her and smiled. "Guess you were right, Lee," she said. "You are pretty good."

But as she passed him to follow their two friends inside, the young man stood back with his eyebrows drawn in. Lee? he thought. Mercury only ever called him Muramasa.

The students were allowed to stay in the lodge for a few more hours after sundown. By midnight, though, most of them had trickled out and headed back to their cabins for sleep. Kael and Laney were two of the only ones left on the enormous wraparound couch when Mr. Cade appeared to usher a few straggling sophomores to bed. He was wearing a black turtleneck sweater and jeans. Glancing to each other in surprise, Kael and Laney realized it was the first time they'd seen their teacher in something other than a suit.

The two seniors were about to comply when Mr. Cade waved his hand. "You two are fine," he said. "I trust you. Just make sure you bring those two in when you go to bed." The teacher nodded to Lee and Mercury, who had been outside on the deck of the lodge looking out at the night snow for hours. "Preferably before they get frostbite."

"Will do, Mr. Cade," Laney said, tucking herself back under Kael's arm with her hot chocolate. When the teacher nodded and left, Kael's eyes were drawn to the large windowpanes that showed his two friends standing beyond them. He was surprised that Mercury was taking her bet with Lee so seriously.

"You know," Laney said, breaking his concentration. "You've still never told me why heights…"

Kael realized he must not have hidden his fear on the ski lift as well as he would've liked. "You don't want to know," he said soberly.

"You don't trust me?"

That wasn't it at all. With his arms wrapped around her and her head resting against his chest, throwing off faint wisps of her scent, he doubted there was anyone in the world he trusted more. He was just afraid of what she'd think of him after he told her…

"After my mom died, I bounced around in foster care for a couple years until I was adopted by this young couple in Omaha." Kael paused, mustering the strength to say what he needed to say. "They already had a little girl of their own. She was eight."

Laney sat up from her comfortable position to look Kael in the eyes, sensing a tremor in his voice.

"I wasn't always afraid of heights," he continued. "Mr. and Mrs. Leon lived on the top floor of these high-rise apartments that overlooked the city. They had a balcony they kept locked, but I used to pick it and climb over the railing to pretend I was flying."

Kael didn't reveal this was where his powers began to manifest. "One day, I found Lucy standing out there doing the same thing. I must have forgotten to lock the door back. She always used to mimic me. Do everything I did. I ran to her and grabbed her hand, but I scared her." The memory was as clear in his head as it had ever been. It chilled him to his very core. "I couldn't hold on..."

Laney's eyes were wide with a strange mixture of confusion and compassion.

"I watched her fall thirty stories," Kael said. "They couldn't keep me after that. I didn't blame them."

"Kael, I'm so sorry..."

"Laney, there's something else I have to tell you..."

✝✝✝

Outside the lodge windows, Lee leaned against the deck railing with Mercury beside him. They had barely spoken three words in three hours, but he wasn't about to jinx being alone with the girl of his dreams by talking to her.

"It's a nice night, isn't it, Lee?" she asked, staring blankly out onto the wintry landscape. The mixture of darkness and snow created contrasting regions of black and white. With the fire of the lodge as the only source of light behind them, it was hauntingly beautiful.

"Yeah, it is," Lee said, unsure of how to respond to a Mercury who wasn't insulting him.

"What's wrong?"

"Nothing," he replied. "You just… never call me Lee."

"Oh, you're right. I don't, do I?" she agreed, smiling at him. "Sorry about that."

"Are you okay?"

"Yep, just waiting."

"Waiting for what?"

"You'll see," Mercury said ominously. She stood straight and turned toward Lee while removing her winter jacket. "In the meantime…" She was only wearing a black tank top underneath. "Are you going to kiss me?"

Lee's eyes went wide with shock as he turned to stare at his crush. "Umm, what?"

"I know you want to," she said. "You should. Or I could do it for you if you want."

Without hesitation, Mercury took Lee's face into her hands and pulled him into a rough kiss that sent him into another world. It wasn't anything like he'd imagined it, but he didn't care. He was kissing Mercury Grant.

When she finally let him go, it took Lee several seconds to open his eyes. When he did, he realized Mercury had turned her head and was staring beyond the confines of the deck with a far more serious expression.

Lee followed her gaze to the snow to find that every single football player was marching from their cabins into the forest of trees leading around the mountain. They looked like zombies.

"Well," Mercury said, "it's time to go. You should get Kael and Laney. If you don't follow, they're going to kill me."

"What?" But before Lee could question her further, the raven-haired girl vaulted over the railing and landed on the snow some twenty feet below. Unaffected, she marched until filing right in behind her fellow zombies.

†††

"Laney, there's something else I have to tell you… I—"

"Guys!" Lee burst through the doors of the lodge. "Get out here!"

As he disappeared back onto the deck, Kael and Laney quickly made their way outside to join him, witnessing the mass exodus that was making their friend so frantic.

"What are they doing?" Laney asked. "Wait, is that Mercury?"

"I think she might be possessed," Lee said. "Ah, nasty, which means I just kissed a demon!"

"What? You and Mercury kissed!?"

"Can we focus please?" Kael said.

"Mercury said if we don't follow, they're gonna kill her," Lee explained, prompting a look of shock from Laney. "What should we do? Where do you think they're going?"

"Only one way to find out."

Before either of the boys could object, Laney jumped the railing and began chasing after the players into the forest. Lee followed after her only for Kael to reluctantly follow after him. He wanted a plan. They didn't have one.

After stealthily tailing the possessed high schoolers through the snow-drenched forest for miles, the three finally ducked behind some trees and watched as their targets ascended a small hill in the distance.

"I'm getting a bad feeling about this," Kael said. He pulled the Arch Steel from under his jacket and gripped it for warmth. "Like we're walking into a trap."

"Yeah," Laney replied. "But it's not like we have a choice."

"I just want to know why they're going so far from the lodge?" Lee asked, panting so heavily from the exertion that he needed his inhaler. "I mean what, is their secret headquarters out here or something?"

"What the hell's going on?"

The voice came from behind them. It spiked the trio's adrenaline so high they flipped around as if they were one body. The person they found surprised them.

"What?" Brody asked.

"They found us!" Lee cried. He reached over and yanked Kael's Arch Steel from his neck and held the cross up to Brody. "The power of Christ compels you!"

"Lee…" Kael tried.

"The power of Christ compels you!"

"Lee!" he said more forcefully. "He's not possessed."

"How do you know!?"

Kael grabbed the Arch Steel back from his friend and pushed the cross up against Brody's cheek. Nothing. "He grabbed this at the carnival and ran with it. If he was possessed, he wouldn't have been able to do that."

"Get that out of my face, Clark!" Brody said, smacking Kael's hand away before turning his attention back to Lee. "Wait, you thought I was possessed? By what? Like demons?"

"Well, yeah!" Lee exclaimed. "You're the one hanging out with them. And how else do you explain trying to steal Kael's necklace? Or getting so much stronger all of a sudden?"

"I took steroids, you moron," Brody replied. "And I only took the necklace because Coach told me to. Almost lost my spot on the team when he found out I lost it. But are you guys serious? Demons?"

Kael didn't have time for a recap. "Listen, Brody, did you overhear anything? Do you know what they're doing?"

"No! I followed Drew and Frankie out here when they left our cabin. They said something about finally breaking the seal or whatever, and then they bolted."

Kael froze. So did they know who the Seal was? he wondered. And if they did, was this their plan all along?

"Well, I'm not waiting here," Laney said, watching as the last player disappeared over the top of the hill. "Whatever's going on and whatever's up there is going to be sorry they kidnapped my best friend."

Laney sprinted from the trees up the snowy hill with the boys following close behind her. When the four reached the top, instead of following the players, they continued farther up a side hill to get a better vantage point.

From the cover of more trees, they saw a large snowfield that ascended with the forest to an old abandoned mental institution in the distance. Behind the building was a cliff that dropped vertically off the mountainside. However, the bleak landscape didn't compare to what occupied it. The group they'd been following had only comprised about thirty-four football players. The group they found numbered dozens more, all facing sideways from the friends' viewpoint, standing at attention like rows of cavalry.

"Is that Mr. Dampé?" Laney asked.

It was. And Kael noticed several other citizens he'd seen around Kearney as well, including the biker who attacked him when he first arrived in town. Some of them looked like they'd been standing in the snow for days. Most of them actually.

"What are they doing?" Brody asked, quieted by the sight of Coach Winters walking around the crowd to climb a large rock with Frankie and Drew behind him.

"There's Mercury." Laney pointed, spotting her friend in the back of the crowd.

"Laney, wait!" But before Kael could stop her, she bounded down the snowy embankment to fall in with the stragglers standing in the back.

Coach Winters had ascended the stone and lifted both arms to greet his followers. "Brothers!" he shouted. "Tonight's the night you've been waiting for! The night when we finally kill the King and take his Arch Steel!"

As the crowd roared, Laney approached her friend and grabbed her on the back of the shoulder. "Merc... Merc, it's me. Turn around."

Kael, Lee, and Brody rounded the field to come up behind Laney as Winters continued his speech. "The treble six year of the Seal rapidly approaches! After disposing of the King, we will deliver what was promised to Choshek and receive our reward!"

"Laney," Kael said through the cheers. "We have to go. Now."

"Luckily..." Winters smiled, staring beyond his followers to the small band of teenagers in the back. "They've come to us."

In one uniform motion, the massive group turned as a single entity, the snow beneath their feet crunching down like the jaws of a beast. Their eyes all black as one too.

Mercury's evil grin made Laney take a step back in shock.

"I think you were right about this being a trap," Lee muttered.

"Ah, the King finally graces us with his presence!" Legate bowed sardonically. "It's nice we can finally drop the ridiculous pretenses and talk like men, don't you think?" When Kael remained silent in his staring, the demon shrugged. "Or maybe not."

"Coach?" Brody asked. "What's going on? What's wrong with you?"

"Please stop referring to me by that frivolous title, boy. I'd prefer you use my real name. You can call me Legate."

"So why bring us all the way out here, Legate?" Kael asked, stepping forward. "If you wanted me alone, all you had to do was ask."

"Oh, that wit... Can't say I'll miss it. But I didn't want the witnesses. And besides, you know you're not the only one I wanted..."

"You know who the Seal is?" Kael's question earned a puzzled look from Laney, who began to realize the suspicions she had about her boy-friend were correct.

"Oh, yes," Legate replied devilishly. "Don't you?"

"What's he talking about, Kael?" Laney asked. He wished he could've explained it to her earlier. Now he had to show without the tell.

He pulled the Arch Steel from his neck and transformed it into magnesium.

"We can't fight them here," Kael said over his shoulder before turning his attention back to the possessed army in front of him. "Get ready to cover your eyes and run for that hospital."

Shen said Kael should've known not to try what he was about to against a creature of light. He was hoping it would work better against creatures of darkness. At least as a bluff…

"Do you guys know what happens when a demon's exposed to holy light?" Kael asked, analyzing the perplexed faces of the possessed before him. "They burn. Run!"

As his friends sprinted away, Kael shot his arm into the air and trans-formed the magnesium cross in his hand into a magnesium sword.

Ignite.

And with the thought came the result. The blade exploded in the darkness of night with such ferocious luminosity that the army shrank back shrieking. Using their fear of his angelic weapon against them, Kael took off after his friends.

CHAPTER 36

Kael's blinding distraction affected the supernatural creatures until they realized it had no effect on them. The light was natural, not holy. They'd been tricked.

"You fools!" Legate yelled at his minions. "After them! Do not harm the Seal and bring the Arch Steel back to me! Do whatever you like to the others."

The demons erupted in pursuit up the hill, running and leaping like wild animals. Kael and the others burst through the double doors of the hospital in a panic. They shut and held them closed as body after body slammed against them. Thinking quickly, Lee grabbed a nearby metal pole and shoved it through the door handles, pulling up on it as best he could to make a brace.

Several moments of banging were succeeded by several more of abrupt silence. The group listened intently through the eerie quiet of the mental institution until they eventually heard the sound of glass shattering on the upper floors.

"Awesome," Lee said.

"What the hell was that light outside?" Brody asked.

"Magnesium oxide." Kael began checking various paths they could take from the entrance.

"And what was that sword you were holding? If you have a sword, why don't we start using it to hack our way out of here?"

"Because we're not gonna kill innocent people," Kael shot back. "They're possessed. They're not in control."

"But then—"

"Shut up, Brody!" Laney and Lee yelled in unison. Lee turned his attention to Kael. "So what's the plan?"

"Kael, how did you do that outside?" Laney asked, ignoring her friend's question in favor of her own. "And why did Coach Winters call you a King?"

"That's what I was about to tell you in the lodge. Cards on the table, Laney, I'm different. And I know you are too. I wish we had time to talk about it, but we don't. You're just going to have to trust me."

"Just tell me this then," she said. "Am I this Seal they're talking about?"

Kael hesitated, then nodded, finally admitting the truth. "I promise I'll explain everything later, but right now, we've got to move." He waved toward one of the three empty hallways. "This way. Come on."

Laney had never seen Kael so focused. She didn't know why, but it made her feel safe. She trusted it, like someone telling her everything was going to be okay.

The four sprinted down the dilapidated hallways of the hospital, trying to find a room they could hide in. The building must've been under construction when it was shut down because most of the rooms were missing doors, and there were tools and workbenches everywhere. Kael mentally assessed everything, checking for what could be useful and what wasn't. He grabbed two old handheld radios and threw them to Lee.

However, it wasn't long before their first demon found them... the fat biker from the jail cell.

Kael gripped the Arch Steel cross in his fist with the top part sticking through the gap between his middle and index fingers—like someone preparing to punch with their keys. It was an idea he'd come up with after realizing he wouldn't have access to a weapon of true Arch Steel.

The possessed attacker charged the group like a rabid boar, but Kael countered him with a punch across the face that flashed white as it struck. The supernatural blow knocked the man out cold on the tile floor.

Kael was about to attempt their theory of an exorcism using the Arch Steel when someone dove at him from behind. However, the attack missed him completely. His guardian angel at work. Instead, Laney grabbed and threw the new assailant against the wall hard enough that it cracked the plaster. Kael then used the same tactic as before to knock him out.

Before they could take a breath, five more possessed rounded the far end of the hallway. Kael was about to attack them when Laney charged ahead. She leapt from the wall to punch one down, elbow another in the face, and kick a third so hard in the chest they soared backward. The other two football players tried to grab her by the arms, but she used her Nephilim strength to pull them into each other, then a sweep takedown to put them both on the floor.

"Whoa…" Lee and Brody said simultaneously.

Kael smirked, but before they could celebrate, a new horde of possessed spilled into the hallway—this time too many to fight.

The group sprinted off again, but as they did, one of the players picked up a hammer and threw it with supernatural strength at the back of Brody's head. Kael turned just in time to see it.

"*Stop.*"

The tool halted in midair six inches behind Brody's skull, who swiveled his head to see just how close he'd come to death. Kael let the hammer fall behind them as they continued running, rounding several more corners before finally finding a room that still had a door. Which was locked.

"*Open.*"

The friends listened as it clicked and led them into the hospital's kitchen. Closing and locking the door behind them, they waited to hear their pursuers race past the door without checking it.

Everyone breathed a sigh of relief.

Everyone except Brody, who was groaning. "This can't be real. This isn't happening. This is just a dream. This is—"

"You know you saying crap like that isn't helpful, right?" Lee said, about to continue his chastisement until he noticed Kael searching the back of the room. "What are you looking for?"

"There's an exit back here," he said. "It leads outside. You guys can escape and—"

"And what?" Laney interjected. "You're not coming? Not happening."

"Yeah, dude, whatever," Lee added. "We're not leaving you."

"I'm actually totally okay with leaving you." Brody waved and power walked toward the back door.

"Good luck if they find you out there alone!" Lee said.

The quarterback skidded to a halt, rethought his position, and turned back slowly.

"Listen, I have this." Kael held up the Arch Steel by its chain. "You guys don't. I can't fight them and protect you at the same time."

"Who said anything about protecting us?" Laney asked. "If you haven't noticed, I can take care of myself just fine."

Lee nodded. "Not to mention there are like a hundred of them out there. You can't fight them all yourself anyway."

Kael knew he couldn't. Even with Ceartael protecting him, he knew he'd be overwhelmed. Just like at the carnival.

Laney locked eyes with him. "I get why you're worried," she said. "But you don't have to do everything alone. We can do this if we do it together."

Kael remembered Mr. Cade's advice to trust his friends. He wasn't doing that. Maybe he should be. "Do you guys even have a plan?"

"Well," Lee said, "Mr. Shen said the Arch Steel will exorcize any demon. A full exorcism leaves a nasty mark, but the burn scar should protect them from getting possessed again."

"What? Are we going to exorcize each person one by one?" Kael asked.

"Well, I kind of had an idea for that too..." Lee said hesitantly. "This building's old, but not pre-sprinkler system old. I noticed them on the way in. What if we use the Arch Steel to make a little holy water?"

Kael arched an eyebrow. "Did Gray tell you that would work?"

"Not exactly. It's just a guess."

"It's worth a try," Laney said. "But if we're going to do it, we should test it on a small group of them first."

"That's gonna be hard," Kael said. "They've probably grouped together again by now, and they're after the Arch Steel. They'll go wherever it does."

Lee pondered that. "Not necessarily. Mr. Shen said demons are drawn to fear above everything else. They're like addicts for it. All we need is someone to be scared enough to draw them away..."

The trio's eyes slowly turned to Brody, who had been pacing nervously in the corner the entire conversation. He stopped when he felt their gazes upon him.

"What? No! I'm not being the bait! That's suicide!"

Their eyes weren't sympathetic.

✝✝✝

After finding a map of the building on the wall, the group had Brody stand in the hallway just outside the kitchen door. His job was to lead most of the possessed away from them long enough to test Lee's theory and then guide them to the largest room in the hospital—the cafeteria.

"Brody?" Laney asked over the radio in his hand. "Can you hear me?"

"I hate you guys," the quarterback replied, jumping at every echo in the empty hallway.

"Listen, you just need to let them chase you for a few minutes. We'll meet you in the cafeteria after that."

Brody could hear a struggle for the walkie-talkie on the other end before Lee added, "Better hope those steroids are still kicking."

Laney grabbed the radio back. "You remember where it is, right?"

"Yeah, yeah..."

The cafeteria was on the back side of the hospital. Depending on which end of the hallway the possessed attacked him from, it would either be really easy to get to or... not so easy.

Behind the closed door of the kitchen, Laney turned to Kael. "So a King, huh?"

He shook his head. "That's what Gray calls it."

Laney smiled. "I kind of like it. It suits you."

Kael still didn't agree with that but smiled regardless. It didn't suit him half as much as being half-angel suited her, he thought.

In the hallway, Brody was becoming truly afraid. His head kept snapping back and forth from one end of the hall to the other, waiting for something to appear. Nothing did for a long time, and somehow, that was far more terrifying.

However, while his heart raced waiting for something to happen, it stopped cold when something finally did. From the darkness of the hallway in front of him, Brody heard far-off screeches and pounding. Pounding that grew louder and louder... closer and closer...

Suddenly, the shadows poured forth dozens of twisting bodies, all charging at Brody like savage beasts. With his eyes wide, his body moved on instinct alone, sprinting in the opposite direction as fast as his legs would carry him.

When Kael and Laney heard most of the chaos pass beyond the door, they quickly swung it open and yelled so that some of the demons would notice them. Mercury was the first to turn around, twisting her head slowly with several of the possessed. Then several more… more than they wanted.

After darting back into the kitchen, the trio waited as Mercury and a dozen others charged into the room. Six of them attacked Laney, trapping her against the wall. Six others tackled Kael before he could activate the sprinklers.

Mercury went for Lee, leaping at him like a feral cat and pinning him to the floor.

"Ah, this is not the way I imagined it in my dreams!" Lee yelled, struggling with the vicious black-eyed vixen on top of him.

Seeing Laney start to overpower the demons with her superior strength and realizing Ceartael was protecting him from the swipes of his own attackers, Kael turned his head to his friend. "Lee!" he called out. And threw his necklace to him.

Lee caught it and immediately stuck it against Mercury's arm, reversing their positions as he rolled on top of her. Keeping the cross firmly pressed against her bare skin, he watched as the metal lit white hot and the demon inside her screamed in agony. Wisps of black smoke poured off her before the dark creature inside finally rose from her body, as if being pulled out by the Arch Steel.

When the ugly shadow was completely separated, Lee realized he could still see it so long as it was connected to the Arch Steel. He pushed and pinned it to the side of Mercury. The cross in his hands glowed brighter and brighter until its white light formed cracks all over the demon's spirit. Soon after, it exploded into ashes.

"Muramasa…?" Mercury asked groggily.

"It's okay," Lee said, helping her up. "I've got you."

However, though Kael's six attackers were being stopped by his guardian, he was still struggling with their weight and ferocity. "That's really touching, guys, but…!"

"Oh, right!" Lee rushed to the corner and yanked the rusted lever to activate the sprinklers in the kitchen. It took them a moment, but when they finally came on, they quickly flooded the room with water.

Lee threw the Arch Steel back to Kael, who caught it in midair and smacked the wet floor with its power. Instantly, all twelve of the possessed were seized by white lightning arcing from the water. They fell to the soaked floor shaking and smoking violently as the spirits inside them were lifted from their vessels. A moment later, they were destroyed.

As the sprinklers kicked off and Kael rose to his feet, he saw that all their former attackers were unconscious. "Guess that answers that question," he said and turned to Lee. "Good job. Now stay with Mercury. I got the rest."

Laney chased Kael toward the cafeteria, both hoping Brody had succeeded in leading the horde there. When they arrived, they saw that he had climbed a stack of tables and was desperately kicking off the demons trying to reach him—Frankie and Drew included.

Kael scanned the room for a lever to the sprinklers. There wasn't one visible. To his left were stairs that dropped midlevel and large windows that made up an entire wall, peering out onto the snowy back gardens of the hospital, but everything else was obscured by cloth tarps, chairs, and tables.

Deciding not to waste time searching, he transformed his necklace into a rod of pure metal potassium and peeled off a piece of it like butter. Shen said whatever broke off Arch Steel stayed the element it broke off as, which he was counting on.

He climbed atop the nearest salad bar and stuck the potassium against a sprinkler head. The demons finally noticed him and attacked, but Laney intercepted them so Kael could concentrate.

Potassium ignites when dropped into water due to the loss of an electron. Understanding this, he could make it happen with a word.

"Soak."

Manipulating the water molecules in the air to clump together around the potassium, Kael made the malleable metal burst into flames, which triggered the sprinklers' activation. Kael dropped his necklace onto the floor and watched as all the possessed were seized with the same holy power that purified their fellow fiends in the kitchen.

A few more ran in from the other side of the cafeteria, but the second they touched the wet floor, they were assaulted by white lightning as well. Frankie and Drew took the longest to fall, but even they succumbed to the Arch Steel's exorcizing power. Eventually, the whole cafeteria was full of black smoke as all the demons inside the citizens of Kearney disintegrated and dispersed under the shower of divine water.

After the sprinklers died off and silence reigned, Brody jumped down from his perch as Lee and Mercury entered the room. They were all staring at the dozens of unconscious people.

"That's it?" Lee asked. "We did it?"

But as they were about to celebrate, Kael got the uniquely bad feeling that they were being watched. Glancing out the frosted windows that made up the back wall of the cafeteria, he saw why…

On the edge of the cliff that jutted out from the mountainside behind the institution stood Legate. He raised his arms in open invitation for the group to come outside. Without hesitating, Kael picked up his Arch Steel and descended the stairs to do just that—Laney, Lee, Mercury, and Brody following closely behind him.

Once outside, the group was battered by a frigid blast of air that howled as it chilled. They looked up to see the clouds swallow the moon and become dark with the threat of a storm…

Legate clapped, grinning from ear to ear. "Congratulations! It's been over a thousand years since a human being bested nearly a hundred of my kind at once. I must say, I'm impressed."

Kael nodded. "Yeah, I probably would be too if I just lost all my minions to a bunch of teenagers."

Legate's grin soured. "A King defeats some pawns and suddenly thinks he's the strongest piece on the board?"

"What? Are you saying that's you? You know that makes you the queen, right?"

"Foolish child," Legate hissed. "You have no idea what I am…"

Kael gripped the Arch Steel in his fist. "Then why don't you come over here and show me?"

"Gladly."

Lifting his palms, Legate seized Kael's friends by their necks with an unseen force and raised them into the air, pulling them to float helplessly behind him—just shy of the cliffside.

Without hesitating, Kael transformed his necklace into the carbon steel broadsword he'd spent so many hours training with Shen. Empowering himself with The White, he rushed Legate with all the speed of the wind wailing around them.

With one hand, Legate shot out the same invisible force that appeared to miss Kael completely. Ceartael. But with the other, he struck with a back hand that simultaneously blocked the young man's sword and sent him skidding back through the snow.

As he tried to stand, Kael realized he had several broken ribs from the single strike alone. Before he knew it, he was assaulted once again by dozens of invisible strikes from every direction at once. Sinking to one knee, he planted his sword to keep from falling completely.

"Hmm, as I thought," Legate said. "Just a frail little boy who can't activate his King Sight or his Arch Steel. Killing you is almost too pathetic." The demon shrugged and sighed. "But rules are rules. I'll tell you what though—you give the Arch Steel up willingly, and I'll at least let your friends go. All but the Seal, of course. She's coming with me."

Kael looked up at Laney. She wasn't used to being so powerless, but her eyes pleaded with Kael to take the deal. That wasn't an option though.

Rising to his feet, the young man pulled his sword from the snow. "I've killed a hundred demons today. What's one more?"

Legate shook his head, raising his hand to the sky to summon his invisible forces above Kael's head. "You're not fighting just any demon, boy. You're fighting an archdemon. And you're about a thousand years too early to do so..."

The dropping of Legate's hand was like the dropping of a curtain.

All Kael saw next was black.

CHAPTER 37

"Kael…" a voice said from the darkness. "Kael…"

When Kael woke up, he found himself lying on a plane of pure blackness. As his eyes adjusted to it, he looked around to find an ethereal brick wall next to him and artifacts of his past scattered all around. But at the center of the darkness sat an eighteen-year-old boy who looked just like him.

A boy in black.

"I know this place…" Kael said while standing.

"Well, of course you do," the boy replied. "You've been here many times. Though you haven't visited for a long while now. I was beginning to think you'd forgotten about me."

Unlike any time before, the boy was wearing an expensive black suit with a crimson tie. He was sitting on a large throne of ebony and black velvet and encircling him was the silhouette of a naked girl—someone he thought he recognized.

"Who are you?"

"Think about it, Kael. You already know."

Suddenly, memories came flooding back to him. He remembered all the times he'd met with the boy. All the times he'd been there and gotten exactly what he wanted from him.

"You're me..." Kael said, suddenly recalling all the times Thackery had brought him there over the last few months. "And this is the Soulscape."

"Bravo."

"But why am I here?" Kael looked around. The place had changed since the last memory he had relived. The wall behind him was even higher—unclimbable—and there were immeasurably more items surrounding him and the boy in black.

Pickpocketed bills, stolen cars, broken and unmoving bodies of the people he'd hurt... Even the girl dancing seductively around the boy on the black throne was someone he knew—the only relationship he'd ever had before Laney...

All fragments of his past. All deadly reminders of his mistakes.

He didn't know what to call them. So he called them nothing and ignored them all.

"Answer the question," he said. "Why am I here right now? I was fighting Legate before..." His eyes went wide. "Laney!"

"Oh yes, you lost that fight." The boy in black stared into the obsidian ring adorning his finger. After several seconds, he turned his attention back to Kael. "Or at least you're about to lose. We are in the space between heartbeats. You'll die when the next beat comes. And then your friends in the one that would've come after that."

"How do I save them?"

"You can't."

"There has to be a way," Kael said frantically, remembering all the times the boy had given him exactly what he desired. "What do you want? Another brick on the wall? Give it to me."

As Kael extended his hand, he locked eyes with the boy who looked just like him. He knew in that moment he was dancing with something he didn't understand, but he didn't care. He wasn't going to let his friends die.

"Hmm, no." The boy shook his head. "I appreciate your enthusiasm, Kael, but that's not good enough this time. There are enough bricks on the wall. So many you can barely even see the boy on the other side through the missing pieces. If we're going to make a deal, I want something a little more... valuable."

"What?"

The boy crossed his legs on his throne. "You want the power to save your friends, right? Well, only King Sight and the Arch Steel can do that. I can give you both, but both rely on the power of your soul. That's what I'll need..."

"You want my soul?"

"Just to empower it," he replied. "I'll hold it, but it'll still belong to you. I promise."

The way he said the final two words made Kael uneasy. He thought for a moment before remembering the spirit wall behind him... and who was on the other side.

Turning to it, he peered through one of the few open spaces at eye level to find the boy in white standing in the blank void that reminded him of the Canvas. He was so much younger than Kael remembered, though he hadn't changed at all since his first memory of the Soulscape. Unlike the boy in black who aged as Kael did, the boy in white was still forever nine years old. And staring at him with the same sad eyes.

"What do you have to offer me?" Kael asked through the hole.

No response. Same as always.

"Come on!" he demanded. "Give me something! A reason not to do this!"

Behind him, the boy in black interlaced his fingers while resting his elbows on the arms of the throne. "You know he won't help you, Kael. He looks at you the same way he's always looked at me. With judgment."

Kael peered back through the missing space in the wall, thinking he saw the boy in white mutter something inaudibly. He didn't have time to make sense of it. Shen failed him. The boy in white failed him. He was tired of waiting around for the ones he should've been able to count on.

"You promise I'll have the power to save them?" Kael asked the boy in black without turning back around. That was the only thing that mattered. Not his life. Not his soul. Only theirs.

He wasn't going to lose anyone else.

"Kael... would I ever lie to you?"

He locked eyes with his darker self. "It's all you've ever done."

The boy in black sat up in his throne and extended his hand, smiling. "But do we have a deal?"

Kael marched from the wall to the boy in black and grasped his hand in his own.

"Yeah. Deal."

And then he woke up.

CHAPTER 38

As Legate's forces plunged toward their fallen target, a dark light exploded from Kael that engulfed the area in an unnatural twilight. Alternating waves of black and white energy poured from the rising King, vaporizing the wraithlike demons above him before condensing to enshroud only him. The black energy consumed the white until there was nothing left but a silhouette of Kael standing tall in the energy of darkness.

And a single purple eye shining through it.

The energy faded and returned the snowy cliffside to its normal color, but Kael realized he could see everything. The demons fighting Ceartael high above him. The demons holding his friends above Legate. Even the demons pinning down two other guardians who looked just like Lee and Brody.

The unseen had become seen. And he realized something else too.

The sword in his hand wasn't the dull metal hue of carbon steel anymore. It was the brilliant silver-white of true Arch Steel.

"That's impossible," Legate said as Ceartael slayed the demons he was fighting above. "How'd you master the Arch Steel so quickly?"

"You're the chess buff," Kael replied. His guardian landed like a meteor behind him, disappearing for a moment until his white wings spread to overshadow all. "Sometimes you make sacrifices to win the game."

Kael didn't hesitate. Empowering himself with The White, he dashed forward faster than he ever had before. Even faster than the wind could keep up.

Legate extended his hands and summoned more demons to soar for Kael and his guardian. However, their black fangs and claws never reached anything but the glimmering blades of their opponents' Arch Steel.

As he cut through his first demon, Kael suddenly realized what power was. True power. One slash was all it took to fell the evil creature attacking him. And one slash again for another. And another… Each slice from the angelic blade increased his confidence and disintegrated theirs, along with their dark forms.

One by one, dozens of demons fell to Kael and Ceartael's combined attacks. With the King Sight to see the terrors surrounding him and the Arch Steel to vanquish them, Kael realized his enemies had no way to hurt him anymore.

"Free."

He spoke The Word over his blade and launched it like a discus with his intentions in mind. The sword spun perfectly through the demons holding his friends, then returned to his hand.

Now only Legate remained. He took a single step back in shock as the four freed teenagers rushed past him to join their friend.

Laney and Lee looked at Kael like he was a hero. Brody and Mercury like he was a monster.

He wasn't sure which it was.

"Any more pawns?" Kael asked. "Or is that check?"

Legate recomposed himself and began to laugh. "You think you've won this game, little King? I haven't even begun to play!"

Kael gripped the warm handle of the silver-white broadsword in his hand and prepared for anything. But as he readied his weapon, a change came over Legate. With his eyes black as coal, he lifted his arms and gave a sick smile.

The wind that had been whistling around them picked up to cyclonic speed, transforming into a windstorm so ferocious it threatened to throw everyone off the side of the mountain.

"Kael!" Laney yelled, trying desperately to hold on to the others but unable to keep her footing.

Plunging his sword into the snow, Kael reached back with his free hand to call upon the power of The Word.

"*Push*."

An invisible wave cascaded from his palm into the four friends behind him. It threw them back against the gale to the exterior walls of the institution where they grabbed on to whatever they could for stability.

Kael turned back to Legate, who redirected the wind to become a freezing one-directional blast against the King. With the Arch Steel cutting through the ground beneath him like butter, Kael was slowly being pushed back. However, realizing his opponent was still on the edge of the cliff, he had an idea.

He transformed the angelic blade into a stone sword that stopped him from being pushed back and reached out toward Legate with an open palm.

"*Shatter!*"

The archdemon flinched at first, but then laughed over the raging tempest. "You have no idea what you're doing, do you, boy? You should know better than to try and manipulate something you don't understand!"

"Who said I was aiming for you?"

The sound of rock shattering beneath them was barely heard through the sound of the storm. But as a large crack appeared between Kael and Legate, the sound grew in its intensity. The archdemon quickly realized what his opponent's true target had been...

"No!" he yelled as the edge of the cliffside cracked off and collapsed, shearing down a mountainside hundreds of feet in the air. As it tumbled and broke into countless pieces, the demon and his haunting screams became lost in the rain of cold rock.

Once the echo ceased, the storm did as well, and the wind returned to normal. Kael sighed with the breeze but kept his eyes focused on the new edge of the cliff. He'd watched enough horror movies with Shen in the last month to know not to turn his back.

Lee tackled Kael from behind. "Dude! That was awesome!" he squealed. "You were totally boss."

Kael pulled his sword from the ground and turned to meet the eyes of his friends. He only noticed his King Sight was still active when he saw the guardian angels of Lee and Brody standing behind them—perfect winged versions of both.

"I guess freak eyes was the right nickname for you, huh?" Brody said, staring absentmindedly at Kael's unnaturally bright purple eye.

Realizing he could deactivate the King Sight at will, Kael did so and returned the sword in his hand to its necklace form to put back around his neck. "Are you guys okay?"

"I don't know what just happened, but if someone doesn't explain to me right now what's going on…"

"What do you remember, Merc?"

"The last thing I remember was skiing down the mountain. Next thing I know, I'm waking up with Muramasa on top of me. Everything in between just feels like a nightmare. Actually, the waking up part too. Definitely a nightmare."

"Hey…" Lee said.

The formerly possessed who had been knocked out in the cafeteria began stumbling through the rear doorways as if in a daze.

"What happened?"

"Where are we?"

But before Kael and his friends could even think of an explanation, the group heard an all-too-familiar voice call from the side of the hospital.

"Kael! Laney!" It was Mr. Cade, who rushed over to them with a concerned look on his face. "Is everyone alright?"

Brody opened his mouth, but Lee beat him to the punch. "It was Coach Winters!" he said. "He led us out here! I think he was starting some kind of cult or something and—"

"Brody! Aaron! Mercury!"

When Lee stopped to listen to the other voices coming from the front of the hospital, Mr. Cade explained, "We started a search party to look for you. They're right behind me." The teacher raised his voice to address the confused group still pouring out of the cafeteria. "Alright, everyone!" he shouted. "Please make your way around the creepy mental institution to get back to the lodge! We'll sort everything out there!"

Obediently, the large group began marching around the side of the hospital to meet with the teachers and students calling their names out front.

"Lee, Brody, Mercury," Mr. Cade said. "Go with them."

As the three teenagers moved to follow the crowd around the side of the building, Mr. Cade turned back to Kael and Laney. "Is that really what happened?"

The two exchanged a glance. "You heard Lee, Mr. Cade," Laney said. "We're lucky to be alive." She grabbed Kael's hand and pulled him toward the rest of the group while Mr. Cade's eyes fell back on the broken edge of the cliff.

✝✝✝

At the bottom of the mountain, buried under tons of snow and rock, the mangled and broken body of Coach Winters twitched once. Then again.

And kept on until Legate dragged himself from the carnage of the avalanche, twisting and snapping his arms, legs, scapula, and spine firmly back into place.

Standing straight, Legate pressed exposed bones back into the confines of his fleshy vestment and popped his broken neck back into an upright position. After analyzing the other bloody wounds his vessel had sustained, he stared up at the mountain he had fallen from and let out a low, insidious growl.

He took a deep breath, closed his eyes, and concentrated.

"Come to me, brothers…"

As he began to trudge through the thick snow at the bottom of the cliff, a single shadow flew from the sky into Legate's chest, causing the body to spasm as it accepted its new intruder. When another shadow did the same thing from a different direction, a small black crack appeared on the face of the man they were possessing.

The more demons that came…

The more cracks appeared…

Until the skin of Coach Winters looked more like a dark maze than flesh.

CHAPTER 39

When the group returned to the lodge around two in the morning, the ones suffering from hypothermia and frostbite were examined by paramedics. Due to the victims' gaps in memory and lost time, the teachers were advised to send any affected townspeople and students in buses to the hospitals in Omaha and then return to pick everyone else up in the morning.

Obviously, the ski trip was cancelled.

At dawn, when the buses returned, the teachers gave everyone explicit orders to pack their things and begin boarding. An hour later, the lodge was filled with every student who refused to go to the hospital, all smiling as if nothing had even happened. Even Brody, who was catching Frankie, Drew, and Aaron up on the last few weeks of their lives, was laughing with them.

Lee found Mercury rearranging her bag on one of the center tables and decided to seize the moment. "So, beautiful," he said, "how much do you remember about that kiss you gave me last night?"

"Me? Kiss you? Dream on, Muramasa."

"I mean, yeah, you were possessed at the time, but—"

"Possessed?" Mercury asked. "Just how many horror movies did you and Kael watch last night?"

Lee laughed awkwardly before he realized the girl was being serious. "Come on, you don't at least remember the hospital?"

Mercury shrugged. "All I remember is staying up late with Laney talking about boys," she said, finally getting her bag zipped. But before Lee could respond, she leaned in close to his ear. "And if you tell anyone anything different, especially about our lips even being in the same vicinity, I'll make sure you don't remember anything either…" She grinned and patted him on the cheek.

"Scary girl…" Lee said, watching her walk away.

On the other side of the lodge, Kael leaned against a wooden pillar with his arms crossed. He wasn't sure how to rationalize the normalcy he saw before him with the insanity from last night. He was happy to see it, even though something in the back of his mind kept bothering him.

"What's wrong?" Laney asked, coming up beside him with her packed bag.

"Nothing." Kael was still staring at the crowd. "Just a bad feeling."

"I don't like your bad feelings," she replied. "They're usually right. But hey, we won, didn't we? Even with all the lies between us."

Kael looked at Laney, who looked down. He could tell she almost regretted saying the last part, even if it was exactly how she felt.

"I'm sorry," Kael said. "I'm sorry I didn't tell you about me. There were so many times I wanted to. So many times I should have. It's just…"

Laney shook her head. "I don't even know why I'm upset. It's not like I told you everything about me either. Dad's kept so much from me over the years that I must have gotten pretty good at it too. Let's just make a promise, okay? No more secrets."

"I promise," Kael said. "I'll tell you everything on the way home."

Laney nodded. "Okay, so now stop beating yourself up. Just look at everyone. You saved them."

Kael's eyes drifted back to the crowd as he thought about the ones who weren't there. About the ones who were fighting frostbite in the hospital. About Coach Winters... "Not all of them," he said.

"You're only human, Kael." Laney caressed his face with her hand to pull his stare back to her. "Even a King can't save everyone."

Then he shouldn't be called a King, he thought.

Still laughing with his teammates, Brody paused and looked over to Kael and Laney. After saying he'd catch up with his friends on the bus, he walked over to the couple and stood awkwardly.

"So the boys are back to normal," he said, scratching his head. "They don't seem to remember much either. Just flashes here and there. I told them Coach drugged them, which I think they bought with the whole steroids thing. Plus, I guess it's kind of true."

Kael and Laney nodded, unsure of what to say.

"Anyway, Clark... I mean Kael... Thanks. I don't understand any of this, but I know you didn't have to do what you did. You could've run, but you didn't. And you saved me when I probably wouldn't have saved you." Brody hesitated, trying to think of the right words. "Anyway, I guess what I'm trying to say is sorry for all the crap I've given you this year." He offered a handshake. "We cool?"

Kael eyed the gesture for a moment before Laney nudged him in the side. "Yeah," he said, accepting the handshake. "We're good."

Brody nodded and smiled before rejoining his group. "Well, that was unexpected," Laney said. "I guess one good thing came out of all this."

Kael smirked before noticing Ms. Gilbert and the other teachers quieting the room. "Alright, everyone!" she announced. "We're leaving! Text your parents and let them know we'll be stopping in Omaha first, but we'll be home around four!"

In the thirty minutes it took to get to Omaha, the weather shifted from snow to sun within the same mile. Seeing the clear winter sky made Kael feel more at ease, but the bus still lacked the privacy he needed to tell Laney everything she wanted to know.

Once they were in the city, the students were dropped off on the restaurant-laden streets across from Heartland of America Park and allowed to eat wherever. Mr. Cade stayed behind to chaperone while the other teachers took one of the buses to pick up the rest of the students still at the hospital.

Sitting in a sparsely populated café, Kael finally explained everything he knew to Laney about the prophecy of the Seven Seals.

"So my mom was your mom's guardian angel?" she asked. She was twelve when she manifested her strength and her dad told her the truth about her half-angel origins. At seventeen, she thought she was prepared for anything else life could throw at her. She was wrong.

"I know. I thought it was weird too."

"And I'm a target for demons and these people called Judges because I'm this... Seventh Seal? The one that stops the end of the world from happening?"

Kael nodded.

"That must be why my dad wants to take me away from Kearney before my eighteenth birthday," Laney said. "He must know all this too."

Kael sighed. "I don't know everything, but Legate seemed pretty obsessed with getting his hands on you before you turned eighteen."

"Yeah." Laney took a sip of her tea, processing everything Kael had revealed to her. It would've been hard to believe had she not already believed in the unbelievable. Really, only one thing surprised her. "So Mr. Shen's an angel too?"

Kael arched an eyebrow. "That's your question? You're taking this way better than I did."

Laney smiled from behind her cup. "That's because I know everything's going to be okay. You're the King who's supposed to protect the Seventh Seal, right? Well, I've seen you in action. I'm not worried."

Kael smiled but wasn't sure he meant to. But before he could say anything, a bird struck the large window next to their table. When they looked outside, they noticed the wind had picked up, moving so chaotically it blew loose trash around the street in small whirlwinds and violently swayed the streetlights to the point of almost falling.

Kael and Laney exited the café to find dark gray storm clouds hanging oppressively low in the sky. After they grouped up with other students on the sidewalk, Lee was the first to comment on the strange meteorological phenomenon that was sending people running for cover.

"It's still November, right?" he yelled over the wind. "Why's the air so hot all of a sudden?"

"We should get back to the bus!" Mercury said. "Has anyone seen Mr. Cade?"

The bus was parked less than a mile away, but peering down the far end of the street, Kael almost couldn't believe his eyes. With the windstorm raging around him, there was a man slowly approaching them in the middle of the road. A man they all recognized.

Coach Winters.

He was limping, as if every step took an exorbitant amount of effort, but he was also pulsating with some kind of palpable, malevolent energy. Stepping into the street, Kael activated his King Sight to see that his skin had black cracks all over it, shining with a sort of antilight, as if his body couldn't contain all the power being stored inside it.

"Coach Winters?" one of the students asked.

Kael knew better. "Legate."

"No longer Legate…" The voice wasn't one entity but thousands speaking in fractured unison. All with a dark, low growl that told of their inhumanity.

"I am Legion," they said, their numbers finally coming together in chaotic harmony.

"For we are many…"

Without warning, the body that used to belong to Coach Winters exploded into a pillar of darkness that reached far into the sky above. Thousands upon thousands of demonic spirits erupted from it, some breaking free from their brethren to terrorize the city, others rising higher until they became lost in the clouds above.

The windstorm became hurricane force in its intensity, forcing the students behind Kael to shield their eyes as he alone witnessed the horror of what Legion's army could accomplish. From the black sky, a dozen tornadoes descended onto several points of the city at once, throwing cars and shredding buildings apart as they touched down.

Pandemonium ensued as Omaha's populace shifted from perplexity to panic. The activation of the city's outdoor warning sirens caused mass hysteria. Some rushed for cover while others scrambled to evacuate, but one thing drove every action.

Fear. And the demons loved every second of it.

"Kael! What's happening?" Lee's hand fell on his friend's shoulder. His question made Kael remember that normal people couldn't see the supernatural element behind all this. To them, it was just an unprecedented natural disaster.

Before he could respond, dozens of quadrupedal demons leapt from the pool of shadows that used to be Coach Winters. While most of them ran in different directions to wreak havoc, six of them sensed the fear in the students behind Kael and charged.

Ripping the cross from his neck, Kael transformed it into a true Arch Steel blade and slashed through three of the creatures in an instant. The other three had already been dealt with by Ceartael before he could react. All of them disintegrated into black smoke with the stench of sulfur filling the air.

"What were those!?" Mercury asked, having seen a flash of the demons' true forms the moment they were bifurcated by Kael's blade. When Kael turned, he had to ignore the shocked faces of his classmates who were either staring at his glowing purple eye or holy metal sword. Neither of which he had time to explain.

"Laney, you have to get everyone out of here. These things are going to tear this city to the ground."

"What about you?" she asked. "What are you going to do?"

"I'll try and buy you guys some time. They should still want the Arch Steel. I'm going to give it to them."

"Kael…"

"I'll be okay. Trust me."

Laney did. More than anything. This wasn't like him asking her to leave him behind in the hospital. That was a suicide mission. This was different. This was his mission.

Instead of arguing, she leaned up and kissed Kael on the cheek. "For luck," she said with a smile. "You'll get the real one when you meet us back at the bus."

Kael returned the smile. After Laney stepped back, the students behind her nodded at him. Seeing most of their guardian angels standing guard behind them made him feel better about leaving them. They weren't alone.

"Dude, you better stay alive," Lee said. "You know how long it took to find a best friend?"

Kael grinned. "I will. I promise."

Lee nodded and hurried after Laney, who led the students away through the stormy streets. Kael searched the surrounding buildings for a fire escape. When he found one, he empowered himself with The White and made the climb to the top of the small brick building within seconds. He felt stronger than ever.

But the higher vantage point only gave him a better look at the chaos and devastation engulfing Omaha. Steered by thousands of dark entities, the twelve tornadoes had already carved a path of destruction so great it even reached the outskirts of the city.

Any demons that weren't inside the twisters were soaring around like phantoms in an attempt to harm the people still evacuating. Guardian angels were doing their best to fight off the hordes, but even if one angel was worth a hundred demons, for every hundred there were a hundred more.

With the city in ruin, the storm siren blaring, and demons covering every inch of the sky and streets, it truly did look like hell on earth.

Kael raised his sword into the air. Shen said that true Arch Steel was every element at once. Hoping that was true, he looked at the silver-white of his upraised steel and thought of the word that would turn his weapon into a beacon.

"*Shine.*"

The blade beamed with the whiteness of every star in the galaxy and cast off such an intense light that it consumed the entire city block. Unlike the natural light he'd used before, this light shined with a supernatural strength that burned the flying demons it came into contact with.

However, when the monsters realized this, they grouped together in a tight wave to charge through the light. Their cindering spirits came hurling at Kael with enough speed that he was forced to cease the emanation from his sword and hack through them alongside Ceartael.

After slicing down a dozen flying wraiths, Kael paused as every demon in downtown Omaha took notice of him and began crawling up, landing on, or soaring around the buildings around him. The landbound ones licked their razor-sharp teeth with long black tongues while the airborne levitated menacingly on all sides. They all looked similar but still distinctly unique. Like one might describe humans.

At least their attention was focused on him, Kael thought.

He readied his Arch Steel in a defensive posture next to his guardian and waited for the demons to make the first move. They lunged without hesitation.

Kael slashed through the first few without issue but was quickly over-whelmed by their sheer numbers. Even with Ceartael defending him, hundreds of dark bodies broke through and pushed Kael off the side of the building, rocketing him to the street below. Had he not enhanced his body's durability with The White just before impact, he surely would've died.

Ceartael flew and fought through the mass of darkness smothering his human. Freed, Kael stood and rooted himself in The White. He was battling not only against the demons but the dark winds that accompanied them. After empowering his body with speed, his arms acted instinctually, slashing through and disintegrating demon after demon with the Arch Steel broadsword in his hands.

He was being swarmed on all sides, but he fought back.

He nearly lost limbs to gnashing teeth and serrated claws, but he fought back.

It was only when one of the twelve twisters rounded the block on the corner that he realized he had no idea the real force he was fighting back against...

†††

On his couch in Kearney, in the room where he enjoyed his movies, Shen picked up the remote and paused the film he and Thackery had been watching.

"It's time, Thackery." Shen scratched the black cat behind his ear. "We'll have to finish this one another day."

Thackery meowed loudly and rubbed his head against the hand of his owner.

Shen smiled. "Thank you, old friend. You too."

Standing, Shen closed his eyes and focused. He extended his single gray wing to the wall and glowed with silver light before vanishing from the room in a flash.

Thackery curled up next to the spot where the man who'd been his only friend for last few centuries normally sat.

He meowed pitifully. And waited for his return.

†††

With wind and demons overwhelming him, and the twister spawning both threatening to consume him, Kael looked to Ceartael.

The two shared a moment of resignation that told Kael even his guardian couldn't save him this time. A natural tornado wouldn't have been a problem. But one swirling with thousands of demons was too much for the lowest choir of angel to handle.

However, as they struggled against the demons surrounding them, they heard a shout of thunder high in the clouds above. With silver light parting the shadows, a beam shot down from the sky directly into the center of the twister.

It exploded with holy power, dispelling the funnel completely and dissolving the demons inside it with holy flame. Everything stopped. Even the darkness. Silence took hold as they all watched to see what arose from the cracked pavement.

With azure eyes, Shenriel stood and spread his gray wing to full extension, looking just as young and powerful as he had when he fought Andriel and Parael.

"Go ahead," he said with a grin. "Make my day."

The demons that had been attacking Kael and Ceartael shifted all their attention to the new threat before them. Snarling, they completely ignored their original targets and charged Shenriel with all the strength their numbers afforded them. But Shen retaliated with more than their strength. More than an angel's strength…

He fought with the strength of an archangel.

Transforming the Chinese cross on his neck into his customary jian sword of Arch Steel, Shen moved with all the finesse of a true swordsman. He dodged and struck, dancing around the shadowy creatures like they were children. Which they might as well have been.

Every lunge from a demon was met with a precise stab from the archangel. He flipped over them, spinning his wing underneath to bat several away while slashing through several more with sweeping strikes. He was an artist. This was his canvas. And he painted the streets with his opponents' ashes.

As hundreds turned to dozens and dozens to single digits, eventually, all that was left was a solitary spirit unable to hide its own fear against the Gray-Winged Angel.

Turning away, it fled into the air until Shen reached out his hand.

"Burn."

The demon combusted and evaporated into black smoke before making it past the first building.

After watching the entire scene unfold, Kael turned back to Shen, a mixture of relief and fear covering his face. "What happened to not changing the future you saw?"

"This is the future I saw."

Kael nodded, understanding what he couldn't yesterday. "Well then, that's one evil tornado down. Only eleven to go." Suddenly, however, his expression became somber with regret. "Gray… I'm sorry for what I said yesterday. I was—"

"I know." Shen smiled. "Mistakes live in the past. But the present requires focus."

There was something about having his mentor by his side that made

Kael feel safe. Something other than just him defeating a thousand demons single-handedly. Something warm.

"What do you need me to do?"

"Protect Laney." Shen looked up. "I will draw the ones in the air. You and Ceartael handle the ones on the ground."

The split wasn't even. Not even close. Ninety percent of the demons were airborne. Shen was only asking him to take ten percent of the load.

But before Kael could argue, the archangel flapped his gray wing once and took to the skies, becoming a force of nature against the forces of darkness.

Kael brought his gaze back down to the street where more demons crawled like spiders around the edges of the buildings surrounding him. Bringing his sword to bear, he charged them with Ceartael by his side. It was a straight shot to Laney and the others. A mile-long straight shot filled with spiteful spirits.

✝✝✝

Unaware of the invisible war raging around them, the students running behind Laney fought their own battle against the wind as they finally spotted the bus parked diagonally across the width of the street. Debris pelted them as they raced for it, but it wasn't until a car's hubcap sailed from the sky that any serious injury occurred. The shredded aluminum gashed the top of Brody's leg, cutting so fast and deep there wasn't even blood. At least not at first. When the pain finally registered, the quarterback cried out and crumpled to the ground.

Laney moved to help him into the arms of the others, ushering them onto the empty bus before peering back down the street where they'd left Kael. Even with her eagle-perfect eyesight, she couldn't see him.

"Laney!" The girl turned to see Mr. Cade running from one of the side streets. "I've been looking everywhere for you guys! Where's Kael?"

"We got... separated," she replied, unsure how to tell her English teacher that his favorite student was battling real-life demons.

Looking back and forth between the bus windows and the wrecked street, the teacher undid his tie and took off his jacket. "Use the tie as a tourniquet to stop Brody's bleeding. The jacket to keep him from going into shock. I'll get Kael."

But as the teacher took off down the street, Laney reached out to yell over the wind. "Wait, Mr. Cade! I can help!"

"No!" he shouted back. "You stay with the others! Protect them! I'll be back!"

As Mr. Cade disappeared, Laney boarded the bus and began tending to Brody's injury. Once she had applied the tourniquet, she let the others take over as she stood and looked out one of the windows. She felt useless. And she hated it.

†††

High above the city, Shenriel wasted no time soaring for one of the twisters ravaging its landscape. Igniting in his hand a star of angel fire, he hurled it into the funnel's center mass and watched as it became an inferno of holy power, scorching the air and all the demons within.

With another tornado gone, the faceless phantasms scouring the city took notice and flew after the archangel. Even with the odds a million to one, Shenriel almost felt sorry for the ones attacking him.

Every dark lunge was effortlessly dodged. Every shadowy swipe met with either the end of the archangel's blade or a blast of his heavenly flame. If possible, he was even more graceful in the air than he was on the ground. He was at home there, and even the demons knew they were trespassing in his domain.

However, after lighting another tornado ablaze and consuming count-less more spirits, Shenriel felt the first fringes of something he hadn't felt in a long time. Fatigue. Though he knew he couldn't let it take him before he took back the city.

On the ground below, Kael and Ceartael swept the streets clear of every demon attacking them, moving in concert with one another to produce a near flawless tempo of strikes and counters. To Kael, it almost felt like playing the piano. His less graceful strokes took the role of falling flat and sharp while Ceartael's superior ones were the natural keys that made their teamwork effective. Together, they produced a beautiful chord of ruin for their enemies.

After cleaving through the last demon before him, Kael looked sky-ward. His King Sight allowed him to see everything perfectly, zooming in like a telescope and focusing on details no normal human could see. An ability he regretted in that moment. After all, watching Shenriel burn away thousands of demons at a time made his own efforts seem meaning-less by comparison.

When his eyes returned to the street, he spotted a nine-year-old girl cowering on the sidewalk ahead of him. The dilapidated and wind-torn bricks of the building beside her were already in the process of falling when Kael empowered his legs for speed. He was above her in an instant, covering her, and Ceartael was above him, covering them both.

"You're safe now," Kael said as the debris above scattered off his guard-ian's canopy of wings. But before she could respond, Kael heard a familiar voice behind him.

"Cabbagepatch?"

When he turned, he found a slack-jawed Graves staring in utter disbe-lief at what he just saw. With an Arch Steel sword in hand and a glowing purple eye, Kael wasn't sure what to say.

"Graves... I..."

"I always knew there was something special about you, kid," he said. His shocked expression had melted into one of pride. Suddenly, Kael wished he had more time to explain everything to him. He didn't need to though. Graves already knew there were things beyond this world he could never understand.

"Can you get her somewhere safe for me?" Kael asked, indicating the little girl now clutching his pants leg.

"Of course," Graves said, stepping forward to take the little girl up in his arms. "You know it figures I would retire, and the world would end the next day."

The cranky old man's voice made Kael grin. "I'll try to make sure it doesn't so you can still get that vacation you've been looking forward to."

Graves grinned back and stole one last glance at the boy who had become a man before his very eyes. "Come on, little one," he said to the girl in his arms. "Let's find your mom."

But as they took off down the street, the nine-year-old looked back at the one who saved her… and Kael thought he saw a flash of purple in her eyes.

Was that…?

Thunder broke into Kael's thoughts, forcing him to look to the sky again. Beyond Shen and his battle with the hordes of darkness, he noticed a shift.

Parts of the leaden-hued storm clouds became blacker than night, swirling and mixing around until an unholy face appeared in their gaseous bodies. The evil countenance reminded Kael of something, but he couldn't quite put his finger on it.

Suddenly, the face swelled with the sky, producing tendrils of darkness around a bubble of billowing shadows. With the unholy becoming the abominable, the accretion of clouds finally cracked open like an egg, dropping nothing at first…

And then hell itself.

Countless more demons rained from the fractured sky, engulfing it in further darkness. Some swarmed Shenriel while others joined together to recreate the twisters the archangel had destroyed—bringing their number back to twelve. But as nightmarish as the spectacle was, it didn't compare to what fell after the wraiths.

Plummeting to the ground like a meteor was a black behemoth larger than any demon Kael had seen. It had bull-like horns and a muscular humanoid shape. Black holes for eyes and a body far sturdier than the mist-like transience of its minions.

Cratering the earth with a shockwave, it eventually rose to stand taller than any of the buildings surrounding it. At least a mile away, it looked directly at Kael, and Kael looked back… suddenly recognizing the terrible creature for everything it was…

The face he saw in the sky.

The entity possessing Coach Winters.

The archdemon who called himself… Legate.

"Bring me the Arch Steel, puny King!" he roared. "Or watch this city die!"

Raising his massive arms, a thirteenth tornado manifested around the dark beast. One that made the others look like dust devils. As the funnel extended to meet the clouds, it consumed the buildings around it and absorbed thousands of demons above it, who all began encircling its exterior like sentries protecting a castle. But as the storm of shadows moved forward, Kael's King Sight magnified to see what was in its path…

The bus.

Laney and the others had been inexplicably trapped on it. The vehicle wouldn't start, and even her Nephilim strength couldn't pry the doors open. All they could do was helplessly peer out one side of their yellow coffin as the massive tornado came for them.

In the sky, Shenriel continued fighting off the demonic wave of reinforcements, but he was unable to counter their new numbers. His superior skill could even the odds against slightly stronger foes like Andriel and Parael. But against an army he needed power. Power he feared he didn't have anymore.

Disintegrating another hundred with a repulse of angel fire, he briefly lamented the shell of his former self he had become. But he didn't have time for it. His enemy was relentless. And he was exhausted. Breaking through his defenses, they scratched, chewed, and bled him of the red ichor that made up his immortal being.

Time slowed as Kael's King Sight drank in the horrified faces of the students on the bus. When they disappeared, his vision zoomed back out to see that they had been devoured by the colossal tornado tearing the city apart. Lifted into the vortex, the bus became obscured by wind, demons, and debris.

Fear gripped Kael.

Then resolve.

Until finally, an idea.

Slicing down two more demons on the street, Kael turned around to look for a car. He didn't care what kind, but after spotting one, he realized just how low his expectations had been...

2024 Shelby Mustang GT500 Convertible—magnetic gray and miraculously untouched by the storm. The irony of the car's model wasn't lost on Kael.

Kael marched over to it and placed his hand on the hood, projecting the words that would wake it from its slumber and unlock it for his use. As the car roared to life, Kael slung himself into the driver's seat and threw it into gear.

He gunned the engine and rocketed down the street at a hundred miles per hour. It would only take seconds to reach the tornado, so he analyzed everything ahead of him with his King Sight. And he could see it all. The path ahead and the dangers surrounding it.

High above, Shenriel blasted off his attackers again just in time to witness Kael driving the Mustang straight for the base of Legate's tornado. But seeing the demons riding the wind of its exterior, howling like banshees for the one racing toward them, the archangel knew...

"He's not going to make it."

Kael uncoupled the two latches underneath the visors to put down the convertible top. But before he could hit the button, the top was gone, ripped off by the increasing power of the wind.

He didn't know if Ceartael could protect him from every single demon surrounding Legate, but he had to try. Laney and the others would die if he didn't.

Nearing the monstrous funnel, Kael's King Sight illuminated a tow truck with its ramp down a few hundred feet away. As he pushed the pedal to the floor and redlined, he positioned the car in front of the ramp.

"*Drive.*"

Pouring the word into the car, it took on a mind of its own as he climbed onto the center console and crouched, holding on to the headrests for support. Wind whipped his hair and garbage pummeled the car, but all he had to do was wait...

Shenriel was swarmed once again by the armies of Legate, who smothered him in their darkness and brought him falling him to the streets below. But he couldn't hold back anymore. Exploding with angel fire, Shen blasted his attackers away and soared for the clouds.

He wasn't going to let this city down. Or Kael.

Pulling his fist close to his chest, Shen closed his eyes to concentrate. Demons licked at his heels, but they couldn't catch him. They'd never catch him. His hand began glowing with unnatural golden light. Soon, it encompassed his whole arm. Then his entire body.

Kael accelerated forward.

Shen accelerated upward.

Kael felt the rush of his own adrenaline.

Shen felt the warmth of a light that didn't belong to him at all.

When Kael hit the ramp, Shen hit the clouds. And let loose all the power he'd been charging.

Light exploded in a million different rays from the archangel's body, burning up the storm clouds over the city and sending out surges of golden power that tracked down and shot through every last demon.

With their dark presence gone, the other twelve tornadoes dissipated from the sky downward, leaving only the thirteenth and largest controlled by Legate.

The Mustang Kael was riding soared from the ramp into the air, ripping itself apart from the sheer force of wind. Using the car as a platform, Kael leapt from it with sword in hand, ready to cut through the demons forming a barrier around the twister. However, Shen's blast of light intervened, incinerating every last one of them while also striking Ceartael beside him.

But not to injure.

To empower.

As Kael passed through the funnel, Ceartael felt strength like he never had before. Glowing, he moved like a spherical beam of light around his human, guarding him not just from debris but the very wind itself. He didn't know what was happening to him but wondered if this was the power that awaited him as an archangel...

When Kael landed against the roof of a building rotating around the tornado, he saw the bus spinning high above him. Not questioning how he wasn't being affected by the wind, he empowered his legs and leapt for the next destroyed building. And the next. Until, spotting a steel beam above him, he grabbed the bottom flange and pulled himself onto it.

It was then that he realized... he had done this before. Every step. Every pattern. Every rotation. All of it.

This wasn't a tornado. It was the Tower.

Letting The White control his movements, he lunged from one piece of cityscape to the next. Every car was another spirit block. Every sequence the same one he had completed hundreds of times before.

And with Ceartael protecting him from the dangers of being inside an actual tornado, he was able to complete them all again.

Bounding from a side wall, Kael ran along several broken pieces of pavement until he reached a gap. A leap. Closing his eyes, he jumped, springing from a small windshield to an array that led to him rolling on top of the school bus—somehow still untouched by the storm.

His friends were inside. Kael wanted to check on them, but he couldn't stop. He had to put an end to the cause of their danger.

The bull's head from his training.

Legate now.

Kael sprinted along the length of the bus before leaping off. The terrified students within listened with confusion as his footfalls rang loudly throughout their metal cage. Peering through one of the side windows, Lee pointed.

"Laney! Look!"

Kael inhumanly ascended the circling debris, finally spotting the massive black body of the archdemon floating at the epicenter of the tornado. He was relishing in the chaos and destruction of his work.

Grabbing loose rebar, Kael pulled himself up onto another chunk of concrete. He leapt again. Bounded again. Climbed until he was at eye level with the dark beast, spinning around it to the point of nausea.

But the path was clear. What he'd always failed before became clear. And he wouldn't fail again. He couldn't.

As platforms of shattered city spun at supersonic speed before him, his feet moved even quicker to intercept them. Ceartael was a barrier of light around the bullet that was Kael. A bullet aimed directly for Legate's head.

From the final platform Kael leapt and drew his sword back with both hands, aimed to plunge directly between Legate's eyes. Seeing his attacker coming, the archdemon swung out his shadowy arm to stop him.

The pillar.

But unlike in the Canvas, Kael had his guardian. Ceartael flung Kael even higher, taking the dark fist for him full force, disappearing through the edge of the tornado with the blow.

Legate readied another attack, but it was too late. Kael was already coming down between the demon's horns, the Arch Steel poised to plunge directly through his head without mercy.

"Checkmate," he said. And it was. With his sword entering between the eyes of the archdemon, Kael landed on its snout and twisted the blade to finish the job. The holy power of his angelic steel began glowing brighter than it ever had before.

Legate roared as his body cracked apart with white light from head to hoof. When he exploded, the shockwave sent Kael soaring outside the tornado so fast he almost didn't have time to register a reaction. Charging himself with The White, he righted himself in midair and stuck his sword out to catch the pavement below. When it did, it slowed his backward propulsion just enough for him to land in a skid and step forward, leaving the planted sword behind him.

He knew what was coming next...

Without its maker, the massive tornado vanished into wisps of wind and darkness. But that still left everything it had picked up in its wake.

As pieces of the city fell like meteors back to the earth, Kael spotted the yellow bus being flung from its own position high in the sky. Almost in slow motion, it spun out of its wind trap and nosedived in a parabolic curve toward Kael on the street below.

Kael had both hands ready. And all his faith. He knew the fundamental forces needed to halt such a heavy object from descending to the pavement. He just needed to trust in himself and believe what he was about to say would actually work.

"*Stop!*"

The bus was a few dozen feet away from crushing him when The Word took hold. It did stop, hovered in suspended animation above the street, its headlights and silver grill staring Kael down with harmful intent.

The shocked eyes of every teenager on the bus stared at Kael through the windshield as he lowered them from the air to the ground. Except for Lee and Laney, no one could believe what they were seeing. Their frozen faces were jolted, though, when the tires touched the pavement, bouncing the bus slightly to the left so that the doors faced Kael. Relief and the realization of their safety replaced all confusion.

Kael sighed and smiled, making direct eye contact with Laney. He did it. He actually did it.

Though something wasn't right... She wasn't smiling anymore. She was screaming. Silently screaming. No sound. At least not to Kael.

Metal filled the young man's mouth. The taste of metal. Blood. Though he didn't realize what it was until it was pouring off the corners of his jaw.

As his hearing returned and Laney's screams finally reached him, Kael heard the faint sound of a whisper on the back of his ear.

"It took a long time to get this away from you..."

He knew that voice.

"Longer to make sure it could reach you..."

It was his friend. His teacher.

Tobias Cade...

Kael's eyes fell to the silver-white blade protruding from his chest, coated crimson with the color of his blood. As he went to touch it, he fell to his knees and coughed up even more of the life that was rapidly leaving his body.

It had pierced his heart.

Cade pulled the sword from Kael's back and cleared it of blood with a swipe to his right. He was already strolling past the young man when Kael fell face-first to the ground. Struggling to breathe, he peered up from the red-stained concrete.

Laney burst from the bus doors, running for Kael faster than she'd ever run in her life. It didn't matter.

"*Sleep.*"

Cade put his palm on her forehead as she rushed past, knocking her out mid-step before catching her limp body over his shoulder in a spin.

Lee, Mercury, and the others attempted to race off the bus to help their friends when Cade held his sword hand up to them from the side. He extended his index and pinky fingers while the others gripped the stolen sword.

"*Lock.*"

The doors slammed shut and were bound with the same supernatural force that had kept them from being opened before. Cade had done that too. Protected them inside the twister. All for this moment.

"Sorry, Kael." His head swiveled back to the dying teenager. "But a deal's a deal. Even when it's with the devil."

As Cade turned away with Laney still over his shoulder, Kael tried to move. Tried to even breathe. But his next breath wouldn't come. He willed it, but his body wasn't his to command anymore.

Death superseded him. The silence and the slowness of death. Stillness followed. Darkness after that...

Lee and Mercury finally forced the bus doors open and raced to their fallen friend. But by the time they reached him, he was already gone.

Kael Clark was dead.

†††

Far across the city, still reeling from the blow Legate dealt to him, Ceartael stood and looked at his hands. They were glowing. So was his Arch Steel on the ground in front of him. Suddenly, he understood what that meant.

"Kael…"

And then he disappeared. Light beamed from the earth into the sky— disappearing from the sky to somewhere else entirely.

CHAPTER 40

Kael awoke slowly in the darkness. Blackness all around him. The stench of death around it.

To his left, ethereal bricks were steadily materializing and fitting themselves into the open spaces on the wall beside him. He didn't need to look to his right to know where he was.

The Soulscape.

Again.

"I must say…" The boy in black tapped his fingers on his throne of the same color. "That was even sooner than expected."

"What happened?" Kael asked, rising from his prone position to see the same replications of his past mistakes littered around the black throne.

"You died."

"What?"

Kael turned his head to look closely at the wall behind him. Bricks kept appearing and filling in the open gaps that had been there since the wall began.

"Or rather, you were killed." The boy said it with such a callous ease that it jarred Kael. "That Tobias Cade never disappoints."

"Cade…" Kael remembered the blade through his chest. "Why?"

"He works for me, of course. Came to me some time ago to save his wife and daughter. Made a similar deal you did. Their lives for his service. It's worked out quite well for me since then."

Kael's eyebrows came together in confusion. But the boy in black was him... his darkness. How could he have...?

"Who are you?"

The diseased smile on the boy's lips made Kael's stomach turn. The menacing evil written legibly upon his face was one Kael knew he couldn't replicate. But there it was.

His face. Someone else's evil.

"Send me back," Kael said, purple and green eyes locking with the same pair across the darkness. He remembered Laney. Knew he had to save her. "I just need a little more time."

Still smiling, almost laughing, the boy nodded to the wall behind him. "Time's up."

Looking back at the last few bricks filling their positions, Kael continued more desperately. "There has to be something. Just name your price. Whatever you want. I'll do anything..."

"Well..." The boy's expression changed, watching as Kael's turned to one of hope. He enjoyed crushing it. "Just kidding." The sickening smile returned. "You already gave up your soul. There isn't anything more delicious than that."

In that instant, Kael knew the boy was just toying with him. Prolonging a conversation that was going nowhere. And he didn't have time for it.

Spinning around, Kael started for the nearly completed wall of pulsating ethereal bricks. He could just barely see the boy in white through one of the open spaces. He was blurred, but he was there. His last hope...

However, as Kael took a step, a chain shot from the hood of one of the cars he'd stolen years ago and wrapped itself around his wrist. When he tried to fight it, another shot from a different car and bound his other arm.

"It's futile, Kael," the boy in black taunted from behind. "He can't save you now."

Kael empowered himself with The White, giving his body the strength to pull against the horsepower of the vehicles behind him. When he started to make headway toward the wall, one of the kids he'd viciously attacked as a child latched onto his leg—pulling it down to one knee.

"No one can save you from me."

Forcing himself to stand, Kael moved until an older teenager grabbed his other ankle and pulled it back as well. He ignored him and pressed forward...

"Why fight what you deserve?"

The naked girl circling the throne sauntered from her position to embrace Kael seductively from behind, weighing him down by the chest.

"Did you think there wouldn't be consequences?"

Kael lurched forward...

"There are always consequences."

Jewelry he'd stolen linked together and lashed around his neck like a whip.

Lies he'd told spewed from his mouth like oil.

Chains from every theft. Shackles from every injury. Weights upon weights until...

"It's time to pay for them."

He wasn't moving anymore.

Every mistake he'd made. Everyone he'd hurt. Everything he'd ever done dragged him down into the black plane, drowning him in darkness that suddenly felt more like sand than solid ground.

With his eyes and throat burning, his mind reeling, Kael could just barely make out the boy in white through the final remaining space in the wall.

"Please..." he begged between heartbeats. "...help."

Before the last brick could be fully fitted into place, the wall exploded in an instant, scattering the bricks into the black plane and reopening the path to the white.

Shining with the light of a thousand suns stepped through a man Kael didn't recognize. Clothed in white that flowed off him like fire and eyes of lightning that silenced the shadows, he stepped from one dimension into the next like a radiant lion.

Every step made the darkness tremble. Every step made the specters binding Kael shrink back in fear. As the wall behind the man crumbled into oblivion, so too did the light settle around him. White hair and eyes became gentler shades of brown as his transcendent presence became far more human in appearance. But he looked nothing like the boy in white. Nothing like Kael.

Drawing near, he reached out...

Kael closed his eyes, not knowing what to expect. His fears were silenced by warm hands touching the chains around his wrists and neck. They were instantly broken upon the man's touch, disintegrating back to their points of origin.

When Kael opened his eyes, his unknown savior helped him up, smiled, and put a hand on his shoulder. With a reassuring wink, he passed by him to address the boy in black.

"No... No!" the doppelganger cried, finally standing from his throne. "You can't do this. You're too late. The boy already traded his soul."

"You know as well as I that it isn't his to trade," the man in white said clearly. Every word somehow felt familiar to Kael. As if power filled every syllable.

"He's mine. That's the deal. Those are the rules."

"You speak to me of rules?"

The boy in black hesitated, becoming far more desperate than Kael had ever seen him.

"He renounced you!"

"*And then cried out to me.*"

"He doesn't believe."

"*And yet I am here.*"

"He gave up your love for my power!"

"*Love is power.*" These last words were spoken with such authority that there came no retort. Only silence, until the man in white uplifted a single palm. "*Enough of the mask. Reveal yourself.*"

With the command, the visage of the boy in black broke apart. What once looked like Kael became an ashen creature of inhuman features. Hooding himself with a dark robe, the figure concealed the ugliness of his appearance. Kael saw claws and horns, but what drew his attention the most were the glowing red eyes of the evil entity before him…

"This isn't over, Son of Man," he hissed. "He'll fall again. They always fall again."

"*And I'll chase him down again,*" the stranger replied. "*All of them. Every time.*" The man in white twisted his upraised hand while staring down his adversary. "*Now… flee.*"

And with the word, it was so. The dark presence vanished deep into the shadows, leaving behind only the empty throne and the mistakes of Kael's past around it.

The man in white turned back to Kael, who stared at him in disbelief. He could do nothing against the boy in black or the things that tried to drag him into the darkness. But this man… this man dealt with all of them in seconds. Effortlessly.

"Are you… the boy in white?"

"*Yes and no,*" the man said. "*His spirit connects you to me. When you called out, I found you. And I've been searching for a long time, Kael.*"

"Who are you?"

"*Who do you say that I am?*"

Somehow, Kael knew the answer before he asked the question. Even though he never once believed it, the truth was staring him in the face.

The King of Kings.

He didn't say it, but the man smiled as if he did.

"What happened to the boy in black?" Kael asked.

"*I sent him away.*" The man looked around the plane of darkness. "*But he'll be back eventually. He stalks this place like a wolf. A ravenous beast ready to consume lost souls.*"

"Why did he change form like that? What is he really?"

His eyes met Kael's reassuringly. "*A great liar.*"

Kael noticed the entities cowering behind the cars and throne—desperate to stay away from the one who had shown so much power over them already.

"They almost took me somewhere... empty. If you hadn't come, I..." Kael's voice was quivering. He looked down to see his hands were shaking, recalling the icy darkness of their fatal embrace.

"*Sin,*" the King of Kings explained, noticing Kael's unease. "*Your sin.*"

The young man winced at the remark. They were bad choices, sure. Mistakes, definitely. But sin...?

"*You don't like that word,*" the King of Kings said. "*You're not meant to.*"

Kael's eyes fell downcast. "People don't like it because it makes them feel judged."

"*Judged? Or responsible?*"

Kael stared into the man's sympathetic gaze. He knew the truth, but his insecurities became desperate to change the subject. "If you really are who I think you are, why would you come to help me?"

"*Because you asked me to.*"

"I know, but why?"

"*Because I love you.*"

Kael felt a vise around his heart. His throat constricted. "How?" he asked harshly at first, then softer. "How could you love me? I've given you every reason in the world not to."

"*Exactly.*"

Kael shook his head in disbelief. "No, you don't understand," he pressed. "The boy in black was right. I've never believed in you. I've hurt the ones who do. I've mocked you. I've hated you..." He paused on his last word, barely able to believe what he was about to say. "I think I still hate you..."

The expression from the man before him wasn't one Kael expected. It wasn't one of anger. Or wrath. Or retaliation. But patience. Peace. Understanding.

"*How you feel about me doesn't change how I feel about you. I'm going to love you if you love me. And I'm going to love you if you hate me. There's nothing you can ever do to change that. It's my choice. And no one's ever going to make me choose otherwise.*"

Before he could respond, Kael's attention was arrested by a shuffling sound behind the vehicles in the darkness. Peering from car to car, he found the one making the noise. The one he chose to ignore for the longest time. The person he'd failed the most...

Lucy.

She approached them, her tiny body bloody from the fall of her death. All Kael's self-control disappeared. He fell to his knees and grabbed her by the arms, looking desperately into the eyes of his little sister. Dead eyes. Dead expression. His fault.

He knew it wasn't really her. Just the memory of his failure. But still...

"Why did you let this happen?" he sobbed, pushing his head into her small stomach. "She didn't deserve this. She loved you."

"*And I love her.*"

"Then why didn't you save her!?"

"*Kael,*" he replied, his heart breaking for the young man at his feet.

"*I did.*"

Kael was defeated with those words. He knew what they meant, but his anger always kept him from believing them. But he was tired of being angry. He was just tired period.

"What do you want from me?" he asked.

"*You already know.*"

It couldn't be that easy, he thought. Nothing was that easy.

"How?" he asked. "How can you forgive me after everything I've done?" His eyes scanned his sins in the darkness. "Forgive me for all this?" He finally returned them to Lucy. "For her?"

"*Ask.*"

Kael closed his eyes in resignation. He couldn't reconcile what he'd done with what the man before him was offering. It didn't make any sense. He didn't deserve it.

But he took a deep breath anyway, thinking of every wrong he'd ever committed. Like hooks in his heart, they weighed him down with unseen stones. He couldn't carry them all. Couldn't even count them all.

Not alone.

"Please..." he said at last. "...forgive me..."

Without hesitation, all things in the dark plane began disintegrating. Thefts. Injuries. Lies. Even the black throne. All turned to ash that was carried off as far as the east is from the west.

Still on his knees, Kael's eyes snapped to the King of Kings, who shifted his own gaze back to Lucy. When Kael looked at her, his eyes widened with shock. She was no longer the same walking corpse he had been holding in his arms. She was healed. No bruises. No blood. Completely restored.

The girl hugged him without a word. In that hug, all the weights on Kael were lifted. All the pain gone. In that hug, he was just as restored as she was. Made new.

"Thank you," Kael uttered, still relishing in the embrace of his little sister. When he finally released her and stood, the King of Kings was walking back toward the white plane.

"Wait, will you send me back?"

He turned around before reaching the edge of darkness. "*I don't have to. It isn't your time. You have those who love you more than your enemies hate you.*"

Relief washed over Kael like rushing waters. He could still save Laney. Save everyone. He was ready.

Kael finally saw the man for who he really was. Pure light in a space of pure darkness. He didn't belong in this place. And Kael was ashamed for bringing him into it.

"I'm sorry I made you come here."

The King of Kings smiled. "*There's nowhere I won't go to find you, Kael.*" He extended a hand. "*Now follow me. Because you don't belong here either.*"

Lucy grabbed Kael's hand in her own, beckoning him to take a step. He did. Then another. And another until he reached his savior. The three of them walked together until they crossed the gray line that separated light and darkness.

And with his first step into the white... white became the last thing he saw.

CHAPTER 41

Kael's eyes shot open as he violently sucked in air for a single breath. It felt like the first he had ever taken. Barely making out the blue sky above him, he realized he was back in his own body, lying on the ground of his ruined city with something heavy covering him.

When he went to remove it, it faded into feathers in his hands. Gray feathers. Too many gray feathers. An entire wing's worth...

No...

"Kael," Lee said a few feet away from him.

When his sight finally returned, Kael looked to where Lee and Mercury were standing. They were hovering over someone.

"No..." he repeated, this time aloud, scrambling on hands and feet to reach them, collapsing to his knees when he did. "No, no, no, no..."

Shen.

The archangel was red with blood. Covered in cuts, bruises, and lacerations. Injuries sustained from his battle with Legion's army. Injuries that wouldn't have mattered to him if not for the one thing that made them matter—a severed piece of bone extending from his right shoulder blade.

What was missing confirmed to Kael what he'd been covered with.

What Shen had done.

"He tried to heal you," Mercury said softly. "But... you were already gone. So, he..."

"It's good to have you back..." the old man said weakly, grinning through the blood trickling from the corners of his mouth. "...Superman."

Kael's face twisted into a sad smile. "That's Spider-Man 2, Gray, remember? We watched it a couple days ago and..." He choked on his own words. The happy memories that came with them were too much to bear. But he didn't have time for them. He had to fight through his sadness in favor of resolve.

"Just hang on," Kael said, placing his hands on his mentor's chest and summoning all the power of The Word.

"*Heal.*"

He concentrated harder than he ever had before. Nothing.

"*Heal.*"

He said it again, picturing the wounds closing, the body repairing itself. Nothing still.

"*Heal!*"

He yelled it, forgetting about the how and just begging for it to work... Nothing at all.

"It's okay," Shen said, reaching up to stop Kael from trying. The boy's face tightened in response. He didn't know how to fix an angel. He didn't know how to fix anything at all.

"Why, Gray?" he asked, his voice an octave higher than it should've been, choking back the tears welling up in his eyes.

"Because you're worth the trade." Shen continued smiling despite the sadness of those around him. Kael could hear the stifled sobs of Lee and Mercury above his own. "I failed one son already... I refuse to fail another."

Any defense Kael thought he had came crashing down. Tears burst forth. Nine years' worth. They cascaded down his cheeks onto the body of his friend. His father.

"Don't die, Gray..." Kael pleaded. "Please don't die." His voice was trembling. "Don't leave me."

Shen shook his head. "You're strong enough now."

"No, I'm not! There's still so much training left. And what about Thackery? And our movie nights? And..." Kael was sucking in breaths too fast to catch them. "I can't, Gray..." His eyes were clenched shut. "I can't do this. I can't! Not alone. Not again..."

Shen reached for his chest and pulled the Chinese cross from his neck. He put it into Kael's hand and closed his fingers into a fist. "You can. And you are never alone." White light emanated through the cracks of their hands as Shen relinquished his Arch Steel to him.

"Gray..."

"I love you, Kael," the archangel said. "Thank you for reminding me what that means. And why it's worth fighting for."

Before Kael could respond, Shen's entire body faded into gray feathers between his fingertips, forcing the young man to the pavement with only a handful of plumes beneath his palms.

He stayed there a moment, head drawn down as the wind picked up the rest of the feathers and carried them high into the air.

When he finally opened his eyes, the last of his tears spilled to the ground. Their uselessness had been replaced by something far more equipped to serve him.

When he stood, his eyes blazed with determination. Gripping Shen's Arch Steel tightly in his fist, he marched in the direction he felt Laney. Felt the Seventh Seal.

"Where are you going?" Lee asked.

Kael didn't bother turning back around. "To kill our English teacher."

CHAPTER 42

With Laney still unconscious over his shoulder, Tobias Cade kicked open the doors of a large cathedral, shutting and locking them back with a twist of his wrist. The interior sanctuary was just as beautiful as any Gothic architecture he'd seen. Tall columns extended high to surround the beautiful murals painted on the ceiling, bathed in the light of several golden chandeliers suspended down the center aisle. Rows of elegant wooden pews lined the left and right sides of the nave leading up to the chancel steps. But raised behind them was Cade's target.

A large marble altar.

Whistling up the stairs, Cade faced the entrance of the sanctuary and deposited his burden onto the slab of stone. The storm had evacuated the city for him, so he had nothing to worry about except finishing the task he'd been given.

To eliminate the Seventh Seal before she came of age.

Not wasting any time, he spun the Arch Steel into a dagger that he gripped and lifted high above his captive's chest.

"Nothing personal, Laney," he said. "But it's better this way. Though if it makes you feel any better, I will miss our conversations in class."

As Cade came down with the dagger, Laney's eyes shot open, and she caught his wrist with her right hand. Moving quickly, she used all her strength to pull him into a headbutt that dislocated his jaw and forced him to recoil a few steps.

Holding his jaw in one hand, he extended the other that was still holding the dagger.

"*Paralyze.*"

Frozen in place halfway off the altar, Laney tried desperately to move her legs but couldn't. Meanwhile, Cade turned his attention on the injury she'd caused him.

"*Heal.*"

There was an audible pop as the bone and tendons mended themselves back together under his power. Stroking his jaw while chuckling, Cade stepped over to Laney and pushed her paralyzed frame back onto the smooth stone.

"Well, aren't you dangerous."

"Let me go and I'll show you just how dangerous I can be." Her voice was seething with fury. She wanted nothing more than to break every bone in his body.

"Yeah, I don't think so," he replied. "Still upset about Kael, I see."

Laney averted her eyes to the ceiling, clenching her teeth too tightly to bear. She refused to show weakness, even though the thought of what had happened made her feel utterly weak. "Why are you doing this?"

"Kael was a necessary sacrifice," Cade said, flipping the dagger around in his hands. "And so are you..."

"Are you one of the Judges?"

Cade laughed. "No, not nearly as fanatical as that bunch. Call this self-preservation."

Laney's eyes narrowed in confusion. "Self-preservation?"

Cade tilted his head, staring at the helplessly bound girl in a mix of awe and pity. She knew she was a Nephilim and the Seventh Seal. Yet...

"You really don't know, do you?"

"Know what?"

Before Cade could answer, the sanctuary doors blasted open, slamming into the walls so hard they fell off their hinges. Blocking the exterior sunlight stood a silhouette of the boy Cade had killed. Kael. Back from the dead.

Laney couldn't believe her eyes.

"Wow…" Cade said, raising his arms to the side in astonishment. "The old man actually decided to go through with it, huh? Man, I gotta tell you… good. I wasn't sure I could take an archangel."

Kael ignored him and made eye contact with Laney. "Are you okay?" She couldn't even nod due to Cade's paralysis, but her eyes told the truth. Even shocked as they were.

"So, Kael," the man above her continued. "You gotta tell me. What was it like? I've never seen an angel die before. Was it all fireworks and light-shows, or was it more subtle? I imagine for someone like Shenriel, it was—"

"Don't talk about him," Kael seethed, transforming Shen's Arch Steel into a broadsword, albeit with a more eastern design around the handle. "Actually, don't talk period. No speeches. No offers. No bad guy mono-logues. Just get down here, so I can kill you."

Cade grinned devilishly. "Now, why would I do that?" he asked, bran-dishing the Arch Steel dagger in his hand directly over Laney's heart. "When I can just do this…"

Cade's hand shot down fast, but Kael spoke faster.

"*Protect!*"

With an outstretched arm, the young King created a barrier around Laney's body that deflected Cade's knife to the side, slicing through the altar like it wasn't even there. Confused for a moment, Cade tapped the blade against the invisible shield Kael had erected.

Created out of pure emotion, it was impenetrable. At least for the moment.

"Think very hard about your decision, Kael," he said. He strolled around the altar and down the steps. "You really want to do this?" His dagger reformed into a rapier with various elaborate handguards around the hilt.

"Shut up," Kael replied. "And fight."

Cade chuckled and saluted with a flourish of his blade before dropping into a standard fencing stance, one arm behind his back. "As you like it."

His blue eyes ignited purple. Kael's indigo glowed in response. With King Sight and the power of The White fueling their bodies, they rushed each other with unimaginable speed.

Striking in hard, left to right, Kael realized he'd never seen Arch Steel clash with Arch Steel before. Sparks of light flickered from their blades every time they so much as grazed each other.

Cade did not meet Kael's larger sword with brute force. Instead, he utilized the slightest movements of his wrist, stabbing his blade under Kael's and lifting in circles to deflect every blow to the side.

Kael wasn't used to fighting someone like this. Shen was a dancer. He evaded and countered. But Cade was a musician. He knew the right notes to hit at just the right time to produce a prelude in his favor. And smirked the entire time he was doing it.

Kael found his footing, redoubled his efforts, and spun with strikes so fast he must have seemed like lightning. More fluid though. He'd bounce off Cade's blade only to turn and come around for another strike on the other side. The White redlined his speed. But there was something else empowering his movements.

Anger.

Cade's defensive posture was perfect. Footwork perfect. Distinguished by years of experience Kael didn't possess. Still, he trained with an archangel. That had to count for something.

As another one of Kael's wide-sweeping attacks flew off the mark, his opponent traded defense for offense. In a reversal, Cade pressed ahead, thrusting his blade toward Kael's chest—the tear in his shirt acting as the target for the tip of the rapier.

It was Kael's turn to parry, but his opponent moved back and forth like a metronome. Perfectly rhythmic. Perfectly balanced. Avoiding blocks before they ever had the chance to connect. Realizing he was on his back-foot, being pressed toward the entrance, Kael improvised.

"*Slide.*"

One of the pews to his right screeched along the floor between him and Cade, creating a barrier and momentary break in the action.

"Hmm," Cade sneered. "And here I was thinking this was going to be an old-fashioned swordfight."

"Yeah, well, what can I say?" Kael reached up, concentrating on the first thing he noticed when he entered the building. "I fight dirty."

"*Fall.*"

He weakened the chain of the chandelier directly above his opponent, causing it to break loose and plummet toward the ground. Cade had already jumped back to avoid it, but as its metal frame crashed ineffectually to the floor, Kael made another fall. And another. Forcing Cade to leap back again and again until he spun gracefully back on the steps of the altar. No more chandeliers to avoid.

Peering over the obstacle-laden path between them, the teacher's confident smile returned. "Whew, almost had me there, Kael."

The boy on the other side of the nave used his power to slide the pew out of his way. "It was you, wasn't it?" he asked, weaving around the broken chandeliers to make his way back to the front of the sanctuary. "Every time things just seemed to work out for us... It was you."

Cade shrugged.

"Why bother if you were just going to kill us?"

"I needed everything to play out here in Omaha. To get the Arch Steel and get rid of your angel friends."

Kael bit back his rage. "How'd you know what would happen?"

"You're not the only one who knows some Seers," Cade said. He stepped down from his perch to begin rounding his opponent. Kael followed suit, and the two formed a circle of animosity. "They don't usually play nice, but they believe in this particular mission."

"What mission? Some traitor King looking to break bad? A little cliché, don't you think?"

"Oh, I'm no King. Not anymore."

"Whatever." Kael raised his sword diagonally across his chest. "Like I care what you call yourself."

Cade grinned. "You know, you could join me, Kael. An orphan with a bad attitude and worse temper? You're practically made to be the devil's lapdog. And I could always use a partner..."

Kael's eyes were sinisterly serious. "What'd I tell you about talking so much?"

"The offer's a mercy, Kael. I suggest you take it." When it was obvious his student wasn't wavering from his position, the fencer sighed and dropped back into his ready stance. "Fine then. One last lesson. Show me what you got."

Kael didn't hesitate. He sprang forward in a flurry of attacks from every conceivable direction. He was a whirlwind of motion, losing himself to The White and becoming the Arch Steel in his hands. With his energy amped to eleven, he burned between speed and power at an inconceivable rate.

But he was attacking a wall.

Every swing. Every slash. Every cut, thrust, chop, and stab... Cade defeated all of them with subtle dodges and parries. Barely expending any energy. While Kael ate through all of his.

"Did I ever tell you why Beowulf is my favorite book?" Cade asked, cutting another strike to the ground.

"I couldn't care less," Kael replied, lunging forward through the parry to hamper Cade's movement, locking their blades between them for a brief reprieve.

"Because it's one of the only stories where the hero dies fighting the dragon," he explained. "Even with his best friend helping him, he still falls. I love the realism of that. See, people envy kings, but kings always let you down. A dragon never does. It's true to what it is. Power. And I realized a long time ago I didn't want the disappointment of being a King. No… I much prefer being the Dragon."

Kael locked purple eyes with his opponent. "You know the dragon dies in the end too, right?"

Cade leaned in with his own evil grin. "Yeah, but unlike Beowulf… I don't see Wiglaf anywhere."

He cut free from Kael's deadlock with a single slash and waited. When the boy returned full steam, the teacher parried and riposted, scoring a light mark on the boy's left arm before feinting backward. Kael felt the blood running off his elbow before he felt the cut. With his adrenaline surging, he barely felt anything at all.

"Come on, Kael, where's that spirit you showed earlier?"

The youth shifted his broadsword from hand to hand for a better grip, refusing to let his anger get the better of him. He exploded fiercely with his Arch Steel flashing all about. Cade's own blade became a barrier of silver-white around him, blocking every blow until an opening in Kael's offensive presented itself. Cade landed a well-timed side kick to the boy's chin and sent him staggering backward. The stale stench of dirt from Cade's dress shoes filled Kael's nostrils as he recovered.

"Maybe I was wrong. Maybe I could've taken the archangel," Cade said. "Especially if this is all his training's worth."

That did it.

Roaring, Kael charged again with blinding speed. Blinding savagery.

Cleaving from side to side… raining down and rising up with vicious strikes… He became an orchestra all his own. Every beat with the sole intent of taking his opponent's life.

But Cade spun, twisted, and redirected every one of Kael's attacks, playing them in perfect concert with his own.

He wasn't just a musician. He was the maestro. This was his stage. And his rapier was the instrument of his opponent's destruction.

Kael deflected an attack, repositioned his sword by his face, and lunged forward with his own stabbing maneuver. Cade spun his sword along his back as he spun around Kael, switching their positions around only to come on faster than before.

Kael barely turned in time to meet the first thrust.

Cade redoubled and thrust again. And again. Still, he increased his speed. Quarter notes became eighth notes became sixteenths. Eventually, his sword was moving so fast that it wrapped around Kael's like a serpent. And with a flick of his wrist, the serpent took hold and lifted the boy's weapon from his hands.

As Shen's Arch Steel flew haplessly through the air, it returned to its original cross pendant state and landed underneath one of the shattered chandeliers. Cade didn't let Kael chase after it. He finished his performance with a quick slash across the left cheek that sent his former pupil spinning to the ground.

The duel was over.

"I'll admit it," Cade said, brandishing his blade over Kael's hunched and panting form. "You're naturally more gifted than most Kings I have to fight. But giftedness is a bad substitute for experience." He brought the rapier in a parabolic arc over his head, using his free hand to lock on to the same spot on Kael's back he'd stabbed through before. "Now, let's see if we can't make that first death of yours a little more permanent…"

Time slowed. The Arch Steel cut gradually through the air behind him, aimed directly for his heart. Kael turned his head to Laney. His eyes pleaded with hers to forgive him. He wasn't strong enough. He hated that he wasn't strong enough.

As he looked down, ready to accept his fate, he thought of all the ones he'd failed to save. His mom, Lucy, Ceartael, Shen... and now Laney. But in the fractions between defeat and death, as he wrestled with shame and failure, a single gray feather fell from the interior lining of his jacket. He stared as it floated to the ground. And an all-too familiar voice floated with it...

What do you love?

Kael knew. Looking back at Laney, it was the only thing he knew...

Her.

What are you afraid of?

It used to be so much. Maybe it still was. But in that very moment...

Nothing.

What are you?

He never wanted to say it. But all he could do now was believe...

A King.

Time resumed. Confusion became clarity. He no longer wanted to kill Tobias Cade. He wanted to save him.

As Cade's blade came down at the speed of death, Kael turned at a speed beyond it. He missed the sword by mere millimeters as he formed one of his own in his right hand. But Shen's Arch Steel was too far away. This was something else. Something more. Something Shen had mentioned a lifetime ago...

The Sword of the Spirit.

It was a blade of translucent white energy that looked like a Roman gladius sticking out of Kael's hand. One that had already pierced into Cade's heart, shocking him into utter stillness. Only there was no wound.

A sword that doesn't cut everything.

After pushing himself up with his other arm, Kael gripped the radiant sword in both hands and began tearing it out of Cade's side. There was resistance. But Kael willed it to move with all his heart until it began ripping something out of Cade's body like a ghost. Not a demon, but something just as dark.

With one final cry, Kael tore his sword through Cade's side in a spin that threw the specter of darkness onto the hallowed ground of the church, destroying it in ashless flames. When Kael turned back to look at Cade, the man took several steps back in utter confusion. Soundless tears began streaming down his face. A face stained and contorted by anguish and guilt. Dropping his rapier, both hands went to his head in madness as he fought with his own horrified heart.

Screams turned to cries turned to sobs as Tobias Cade collapsed to his knees, struggling to understand what was happening to him.

"H-h-how did you summon that sword!?" His insanity was evident. "You shouldn't be able to do that. You're not that powerful!"

"You're right," Kael replied. He reached down and retrieved the Celtic cross Cade had stolen from him. "I'm not."

As Kael moved to grab Shen's Arch Steel from the chandelier, Cade continued.

"You don't know what you're doing," he said, his hands trembling so violently that he wouldn't have been able to continue fighting even if he wanted to. "What she is... the plans they have for her... Choshek, the Judges, every fallen angel on this planet will be gunning for you. You're not protecting just any Seal..."

With the Sword of the Spirit in one hand and two Arch Steel crosses in the other, Kael was on the chancel steps when he stopped.

"Then I would get as far away from us as possible if I were you." When he heard no sound of movement, Kael half-turned his head back to his fallen opponent. "The offer's a mercy, Cade. I suggest you take it."

Freed from her paralysis, Laney was already rising from the altar when Kael reached her. She threw her arms around him and buried herself into his shoulder. The spirit sword in his hand disappeared as he hugged her back as tightly as he could.

Peering over the altar, they noticed Tobias Cade was already gone.

"What was that?" Laney asked. "What'd you do to him?"

"I'm not sure…" Kael stared at his now empty hand before looking back up. "But I think I restored him. It was like I could feel the stone around his heart. When I tore it out, everything else just came crashing down with it."

Laney looked at Kael like she had never looked at him before. There was something different about him. Behind his eyes. Something strong. It made her smile until she thought of what Cade said.

"What did he mean?" she asked. "When he said I'm not just any Seal?"

"I don't know." Kael had already tied Shen's Chinese cross around his neck. He put the Celtic one around hers. "But I'm not going to let anything happen to you, Laney. I promise."

All it took was him saying it for her to believe it. As she wrapped her arms around the back of his neck, her eyes became lost in his. And as he pulled her in close by the waist, his lips finally found hers.

Outside, Lee and Mercury ran up to the cathedral with a bat and steel pipe they'd found on the street. They were ready for a battle to save their friends. However, when they reached the open doors of the sanctuary, they realized how little saving their friends needed.

Watching Kael and Laney kiss passionately at the altar, Mercury smiled to see her best friend safe. Taking the romantic cue, Lee looked over to his raven-haired princess.

"Not a chance, Muramasa."

Lee nodded awkwardly. "No, right, of course. Stupid."

CHAPTER 43

The news was calling the supernatural weather phenomena the Omaha Tornado Complex. Of course, no one but Kael, Laney, Lee, and Mercury knew what really happened. After finding the other students in the aftermath, the four were surprised to learn no one but Brody remembered anything about what they had seen. A last gift from Shen, Kael surmised.

After returning to Kearney, the four teenagers drove back to Glenwood Park. Pulling in, the street felt emptier than usual, completely devoid of life. The winter air and dark sky didn't help the feeling.

"So what now?" Lee asked, shutting his car door as everyone gathered on the street in front of Shen's house.

"I don't know," Kael replied. "Cade said others will be coming for Laney. Something happens on her eighteenth birthday that'll draw them. I don't think we can stay here."

"What do you mean you can't stay here?" Mercury asked. "This is your home!"

Kael knew that. For the first time in a long time, he had someplace to call home. He didn't want to leave. But he also refused to put Laney in any more danger.

"Hey, umm… guys?" Lee said nervously, his eyes laser-focused on the end of the street. When they followed his stare, they saw what had him so scared.

Standing alone at the end of the road was a tall man in a black suit and tie with slicked back hair, sunglasses, and a large overcoat. As the man approached them, Kael stepped forward cautiously, putting himself between the unknown figure and his friends.

When he was within speaking distance, the stranger stopped.

"Mr. Clark?"

Kael narrowed his eyes at being called by name.

"Is your name Kael Clark?"

"Yeah…"

"I've got something for you…"

The young King gripped the Arch Steel cross hanging from his neck as the stranger began walking forward.

"From Gregory Shen."

At the mention of his mentor's name, Kael's serious expression fell apart. The mysterious man pulled a large old leather attaché from his coat and offered it to Kael.

"Who are you?" Kael asked, unraveling the leather straps binding the envelope to reveal a Bible, a journal, and a cache of other documents.

"You can call me Agent K. I'm from the Bank," he said. "We deal exclusively with the affairs of the supernatural. Mr. Shen was very explicit that I be here at exactly this time and say exactly what I said. He told me it reminded him of some movie."

Of course it did.

Kael's attention turned to the contents in his hand. There was a letter sticking out from the pages of the journal that he felt drawn to read first. He unfolded and held the letter over the leather envelope.

Dear Kael,

Do you remember the end of Back to the Future II when the clerk from Western Union delivers the letter to Marty after Doc's disappearance? Wonderful scene. I hope this played out just like that. Unfortunately, I won't be there to see it. Still, please tell Agent K thank you for me. (His title is actually Agent 9, but how could I resist having him call himself Agent K from Men in Black? Double reference. Very proud of myself).

Anyway, I can't tell you what happens next because I don't know. I haven't been able to see anything beyond my own death for many years now. All I know is what I believe. That you won and are standing there now with Laney, Lee, and Miss Grant reading this over your shoulder. Other than that, all that's important is what I've already told you. My death for your life was worth it. You're worth it. And I'd do it all over again.

Enclosed you will find your own copy of the Bible and my journal. Study both. You've just learned to wield the Sword of the Spirit. My hope is that you'll soon learn to put on the full Armor of God and be prepared for what's to come... Laney will need you to be. Protect her. She's more valuable than you know.

Please tell Lee I will miss our conversations. He's been a wonderful friend to you. And a good student. I only ask that he check in on Thackery every once in a while, to keep him company. He'd never admit it, but even a cat-sith can get lonely sometimes. It would make me happy to know that he still has a friend. And Lee, since I suspect you're probably reading this too, you're going to do great things. I haven't seen it, but I don't need to see the future to know it's true.

Lastly, Kael, the birthday present I mentioned would be arriving upon your return. I have instructed the Bank to make you the sole beneficiary of my entire estate. My only request is that you leave the house and my movies to Thackery. He knows what to do with them. And I know you'll know what to do with the rest.

I love you, Kael. You were the best son I ever could have asked for. Thank you for reminding me what it is to be a father.

Your friendly neighborhood angel man,

Gregory Shen

Kael smiled to keep from crying. He'd already done enough of that, and he knew Shen wouldn't want him to anymore. As he refolded the letter and put it back behind the cover of the journal, Agent 9 took one step closer.

"May I?"

Kael handed back the contents of the leather envelope. The man sifted through them in a sedulous manner until he had a series of papers on top of the stack.

"This is what you've inherited," he said.

"Whoa…" Mercury said over his shoulder.

"That cannot be a real number…" Lee added.

Kael's shocked eyes met the stoic expression of Agent 9. "You sure that's right?"

The man nodded professionally. "Interest. When you deal with creatures who live thousands of years, you occasionally deal with wealth that can break the world's economy." He clicked open an odd-looking pen. "Please sign at the bottom."

When Kael went to take the pen, Agent 9 moved too fast for him to react and pricked the edge of his finger with it, allowing a single drop of blood to spill onto the page.

"Hey!"

"Thank you for your cooperation." The agent tore off the page, folded it, and put it into the interior pocket of his overcoat. "Will you be requiring any further assistance today?"

Kael's eyes narrowed as he sucked the blood from his finger. "No thanks."

The agent nodded. "The Bank appreciates your time and discretion. Directions for how to contact us are enclosed. Have a nice day." Making his way around the group of teenagers, he began walking toward the opposite end of the street, then disappeared around the corner without another word.

Lee was about to comment when the group heard sirens coming from a police car behind them. Sheriff Lessenger screeched to a stop in front of them and practically sprinted from his car to embrace his daughter.

"I was so worried," he said, refusing to let her go. "Tornadoes have been touching down all over the state. When I heard about Omaha, I—"

"I'm okay, Dad," she said, hugging back tightly. "Thanks to Kael."

Releasing his daughter, the sheriff looked to the boy standing next to them. Only he didn't look like a boy anymore. In his war-torn clothing, with cuts and bruises littered all over his body, he looked more like a man.

"Dad, I know everything..." Laney was struggling with what she knew she had to say. "They came for me. To kill me. If Kael hadn't been there, I would've..."

Sheriff Lessenger stared compassionately at his daughter. "And now you have to go with him, don't you?" he asked before taking a deep breath. "Your mother always told me this day would come. That I wouldn't be able to protect you anymore. That another would have to take my place."

He looked to Kael, who nodded back respectfully. "I just wish I could've hidden you away a little longer... forever even."

"I know," Laney said quietly. "But you've been the best dad any girl could ask for. And I wouldn't trade everything you've done for me for anything. I love you, Daddy."

She rushed him for another hug. He reciprocated with tears in his eyes. "I love you too, Lanebug."

When they finally separated, the sheriff noticed Mercury standing behind him, sniffling with glossy eyes of her own. Stepping aside, he let go of his daughter so she could comfort her best friend.

"But what about prom?" Merc asked meekly. "And graduation? And college? Who's going to walk me through the front doors on the first day?"

Laney smiled, tears pooling in her ocean blue eyes as she took the hands of her best friend. "I'm going to write you every day," she said. Then she took off the rose gold cross necklace her mom had given her and put it around Mercury's neck, prompting a confused look.

"I have a new one," Laney said. "So I want you to have this one. No matter how far apart we are, whenever you're scared or lonely, I want you to look down and remember I'm here, Merc. Always."

Mercury couldn't contain herself any longer. Crying, she lunged forward and grabbed Laney in a weeping hug. Laney returned it while breaking down herself. Saying goodbye had become too much for even her Nephilim strength to bear.

"You'll protect her, won't you?" Sam asked Kael as he watched the two girls crying. "Give your life for her?"

"As many times as it takes," Kael replied, knowing the sheriff had no way of knowing he already had.

"This is crap, man," Lee said off to the side. "I finally make a friend, and he has to leave town…"

"I'd ask you to come with us," Kael replied, "but there's no way I'd do that to your family. Or to my best friend."

Lee raised an eyebrow. "Best?"

Kael smirked. Clasping hands, the two brought each other in for a hug while patting the other's back. "Thanks, man," Kael said. "For everything."

"Yeah, you would've been pretty lost without me," Lee replied, grinning. "Just pay me back by staying alive."

Kael nodded.

Sam Lessenger hugged his daughter one last time, then walked back to his cruiser before he had a chance to change his mind. "Come on, you two," he said to Lee and Mercury. "There's still a tornado watch for the area, and it's not safe for you to be on the road. I'll take you home."

Kael and Laney exchanged last-minute goodbyes with their friends, who climbed into the back of the police car. When it pulled away, they watched it disappear around the edge of the neighborhood before they made their way up to Shen's closed garage door.

After throwing it open, both teenagers stared at the mangled remains of Shen's 1967 Shelby Mustang. Laney looked at Kael with a confused expression as he stared resolutely at the black heap of shredded metal before him.

He'd grown so much since the last time he saw it. He knew he could do now what he could never do then. Believe.

"Repair."

With an extended hand, The Word carried power into the broken parts. All of them lifted, stretched, and reformed into their designated spaces, making the garage sound more like a factory in its tiny space. Tires repaired themselves. Upholstery stitched itself back together. Even the glass and the paint shards fused perfectly back to their original forms.

Finally, the shattered vintage car stood whole once again.

"Wow... beats my Camry," Laney said. "Are you ready?"

She seemed unsure. Kael was even more so. "Yeah," he said. "Just one more thing."

As she got into the passenger side, Kael walked out of the garage to the front porch. The thin black frame of Thackery was already sitting there, waiting for him.

Bounding from the top step, he purred and rubbed against Kael's shins, who knelt to pet him behind the ear. Caressing the cat from head to tail, he choked on what he was going to say. "I'm so sorry, Thack..." He stood and pulled out the gray feather that had fallen from his jacket during his battle with Cade. "I failed him... He's gone."

Thackery dropped his head for a moment. Kael thought it was to grieve until the cat's fangs sunk into his ankle and brought him to one knee. "Ouch, Thack! What are you—"

The black cat swatted him on the forehead to stop him from talking before placing his paw on his chest. Over Shen's cross. Over his heart. Staring into the emerald eyes of the wizardly feline, Kael began to understand.

As Thackery nodded and disappeared back into the house, Kael stood and analyzed the gray feather that saved him against Cade. Until that moment, he never fully understood the complexity of a single feather before. Damaged as it was from everything that occurred, from quill to vane, each part still served its own unique purpose.

And that was when Kael realized it.

Pressing on it, everything joined back together as one, fusing so perfectly that the once-fractured feather became whole again. Barbs were split. Some were even missing. But they still joined. Healed. Restored.

Kael lay the completed feather on the porch. "Thank you, Gray," he said while staring at it. "Thank you for everything."

He walked back to the open garage and fell into the driver's seat of the Mustang, not realizing his eyes were red with the threat of tears.

"Are you okay?" Laney asked.

"Yeah." Kael nodded.

"How are we going to do this?"

Kael stared at the road in front of him and smiled. "Together."

Pulling out of the garage, the black Mustang disappeared down the street that brought Kael to Kearney in the first place.

Back then, it had been to escape a life. Now, it was to start one.

ABOUT THE AUTHOR

Justin Hart Crary is an author of YA Christian fantasy and supernatural fiction. Born and raised in West Virginia, he developed a passion for his faith as well as "all things nerd" at a young age. After traveling the country, he returned to his home state to teach and earn his M.A. in English.

In response to a lack of contemporary Christian literature appealing to young adults, one of Justin's goals is to create fast-paced, interesting narratives that demonstrate how stories within the genre can be more than what people have come to expect. He seeks to tell tales with a unique, action-oriented writing style designed to resonate with today's readers. And give them something different.

When he's not writing or teaching his incredible students, Justin enjoys training in martial arts, ministering to his community, and spending time with his beautiful wife.

You can connect with him on Facebook, Instagram, and Twitter @ justinhartcrary or by visiting his website below. He'd love to hear from you!

www.justinhartcrary.com

Made in the USA
Coppell, TX
07 March 2022